Dear Reader,

It's that time of year again. You might assume I mean Christmas and New Year's, and while that's true, I'm also referring to my two-in-one Christmas book. As you may know, I generally have two Christmas volumes published within a short period. The first is an original hardcover; this year's book, *A Cedar Cove Christmas,* focuses on my fictional town in the Pacific Northwest. The second is usually the paperback version of the hardcover from the year before, plus an added-value story from my backlist. For 2008 my publisher and I broke with tradition. (We're trying to keep everyone on their toes!) *Small Town Christmas* contains two of my backlist titles reissued in a special edition just for you.

With the trade paperback publication of the HEART OF TEXAS series we felt my readers would enjoy the follow-up story, *Return to Promise,* with its Christmas theme and setting. The second book in *Small Town Christmas* is *Mail-Order Bride,* an early traditional romance I wrote more than twenty years ago for Silhouette Books. It's a light romantic comedy that's sure to bring a smile, and that's my goal. I want to leave you, my readers, with a festive, happy feeling during the craziness that surrounds the holidays.

All that said, I invite you to curl up next to the fireplace with your choice of Christmas cheer and enjoy. Have a wonderful Christmas!

Debbie Macomber

P.S. I always enjoy hearing from readers, so please log on to DebbieMacomber.com and leave a message in my Guest Book. Or write me at P.O. Box 1458, Port Orchard, WA 98366.

DEBBIE MACOMBER

Small Town Christmas

MIRA®

MIRA®

ISBN-13: 978-0-7783-2595-6
ISBN-10:   0-7783-2595-4

SMALL TOWN CHRISTMAS

Copyright © 2008 by MIRA Books.

The publisher acknowledges the copyright holder of the individual works as follows:

RETURN TO PROMISE
Copyright © 2000 by Debbie Macomber.

MAIL-ORDER BRIDE
Copyright © 1987 by Debbie Macomber.

www.MIRABooks.com

Printed in U.S.A.

CONTENTS

RETURN TO PROMISE

To
Ruthanne Devlin, Bookseller Extraordinaire,
for blessing my life with your friendship

One

Cal Patterson knew his wife would be furious. Competing in the annual Labor Day rodeo, however, was worth Jane's wrath—although little else was.

Bull riding had always enticed him, even more than bronc riding or roping or any of the other competitions. It was the thrill that got to him, the danger of riding a fifteen-hundred-pound bull, of staying on for eight seconds and sometimes longer. He craved the illusion that for those brief moments he was in control. Cal didn't do it for the trophy—if he was fortunate enough to take top prize—or to hear his name broadcast across the rodeo grounds. He was drawn by the challenge, pitting his will against the bull's savage strength, and yes, the risk. Jane would never understand that; she'd been raised a city girl and trained as a doctor, and she disapproved of what she called *unnecessary* risk. In her opinion, bull riding fell squarely into that category. He'd tried to explain his feelings about it, but clearly he'd failed. Jane still objected fervently whenever he mentioned his desire to enter rodeo competitions. Okay, okay, so he'd busted a rib a few years back and spent several pain-filled weeks recuperating. Jane had been angry with him then, too. She'd gotten over it, though, and she would again—but not without inducing a certain amount of guilt first.

He watched her out of the corner of his eye as she ushered their three-year-old son, Paul, into the bleachers. Cal dutifully followed behind, carrying eighteen-month-old Mary Ann, who was sound asleep in his arms. As soon as his family was settled, he'd be joining the other competitors near the arena. A few minutes later, Jane would open the program and see his name. Once she did, all hell would break loose. He sighed heavily. His brother and sister-in-law would be arriving shortly, and if he was lucky, that'd buy him a couple of minutes.

"Glen and Ellie are meeting us here, aren't they?" Jane asked, her voice lowered so as not to disturb the baby. His daughter rested her head of soft blond curls against his shoulder, thumb in her mouth. She looked peaceful, downright angelic—quite a contrast to her usual energetic behavior.

"They'll be here soon," Cal answered, handing Mary Ann to Jane.

With two children demanding her time and attention, plus the ranch house and everything else, Jane had cut back her hours at the medical clinic to one weekend a month. Cal knew she missed practicing medicine on a more frequent basis, but she never complained. He considered himself a lucky man to have married a woman so committed to family. When the kids were in school, she'd return to full-time practice, but for now, Paul and Mary Ann were the focus of her life.

Just then, Jane reached for the schedule of rodeo events and Cal tensed, anticipating her reaction.

"Cal Patterson, you *didn't!*" Her voice rose to something resembling a shriek as she turned and glared at him.

"Cal?" She waited, apparently hoping for an explanation.

However, he had nothing to say that he hadn't already said dozens of times. It wouldn't do any good to trot out his rationalizations yet again; one look told him she wouldn't be easily appeased. His only option was to throw himself on her good graces and pray she'd forgive him quickly.

"You signed up for the *bull ride?*"

"Honey, now listen—"

"Are you *crazy?* You got hurt before! What makes you think you won't get hurt this time, too?"

"If you'd give me a chance to—"

Jane stood, cradling Mary Ann against her. Paul stared up at his parents with a puzzled frown.

"Where are you going?" he asked, hoping he could mollify her without causing a scene.

"I refuse to watch."

"But, darling…"

She scowled at him. "Don't you darling me!"

Cal stood, too, and was given a reprieve when Glen and Ellie arrived, making their way down the long row of seats. His brother paused, glancing from one to the other, and seemed to realize what was happening. "I take it Jane found out?"

"You knew?" Jane asked coldly.

Ellie shook her head. "Not me! I just heard about it myself."

"Looks like Jane's leaving me," Cal joked, trying to inject some humor into the situation. His wife was over-reacting. There wasn't a single reason she should walk out now, especially when she knew how excited their three-year-old son was about seeing his first rodeo.

"That's exactly what you deserve," she muttered, bending to pick up her purse and the diaper bag while holding Mary Ann tightly against her shoulder.

"Mommy?"

"Get your things," she told Paul. "We're going home."

Paul's lower lip started to quiver, and Cal could tell that his son was struggling not to cry. "I want to see the rodeo."

"Jane, let's talk about this," Cal murmured.

Paul looked expectantly from his father to his mother, and Jane hesitated.

"Honey, please," Cal said, hoping to talk her into forgiveness—or at least acceptance. True, he'd kept the fact that he'd signed up for bull riding a secret, but only because he'd been intent on delaying a fight. *This* fight.

"I don't want Paul to see you injured," she said.

"Have a little faith, would you?"

His wife frowned, her anger simmering.

"I rode bulls for years without a problem. Tell her, Glen," he said, nodding at his brother.

"Hey," Glen said, raising both hands in a gesture of surrender. "You're on your own with this one, big brother."

"I don't blame you for being mad," Ellie said, siding with Jane. "I'd be furious, too."

Women tended to stick together, but despite Ellie's support, Cal could see that Jane was weakening.

"Let Paul stay for the rodeo, okay?" he cajoled. "He's been looking forward to it all week. If you don't want him to see me compete, I understand. Just leave when the bull riding starts. I'll meet you at the chili cook-off when I'm done."

"Please, Mommy? I want to see the rodeo," Paul said again, eyes huge with longing. The boy pleaded his case far more eloquently than *he* could, and Cal wasn't fool enough to add anything more.

Jane nodded reluctantly, and with a scowl in his direction, she sat down. Cal vowed he'd make it up to her later.

"I'll be fine," he assured her, wanting Jane to know he loved and appreciated her. He slid his arm around her shoulders, hugging her close. But all the while, his heart thundered with excitement at the thought of getting on the back of that bull. He couldn't keep his gaze from wandering to the chute.

Jane might have been born and raised in the big city, but she was more than a little bit country now. Still, she'd probably never approve of certain rodeo events. Cal recognized her fears, and as a result, rarely competed anymore—hadn't in five years. But he expected Jane to recognize the impulses that drove him, too.

Compromise. Wasn't that what kept a marriage intact?

* * *

Jane had no intention of forgetting Cal's deceit, but now wasn't the time or place to have it out with her husband. He knew how she felt about his competing in the rodeo. She'd made her views completely clear, even before they were married.

Still, she'd acquiesced and held her tongue. She glanced at Cal's brother and sister-in-law and envied them. Their kids were with a baby-sitter, since they planned to attend the dance later that evening. Jane would've preferred to stay, too, but when she'd mentioned it to Cal, he'd balked. Dancing wasn't his favorite activity and he'd protested and complained until she dropped it.

Then he'd pulled *this* stunt. Men!

Partway through the rodeo, Paul fell asleep, leaning against her side. Cal had already left to wait down by the arena with the other amateur riders. As the time approached for him to compete, she considered leaving, but then decided to stay. Her stomach would be in knots whether she was there watching him or not. Out of sight wasn't going to put her risk-taking husband out of mind, and with Paul asleep, there was no reason to go now.

"Are you worried?" Ellie asked, casting her a sympathetic look.

She nodded. "Of course, I don't know what Cal was thinking."

"Who said he was thinking at all?" Ellie teased.

"Yeah—it's the testosterone," Jane muttered, wondering what her husband found so appealing about riding such dangerous beasts. Her nerves were shattered, and that wasn't going to change. Not until she knew he was safe.

"I was hoping you and Cal would come to the dance."

Ellie was obviously disappointed, but no more than Jane herself. She would've loved an evening out. Had she pressed the issue, Cal would eventually have given in, but it hadn't seemed worth the arguments and the guilt. Besides, getting a sitter would've been difficult, since nearly everyone in Promise attended the annual Labor Day rodeo—and Ellie had managed to snag the services of Emma Bishop, one of the few teenagers available for baby-sitting.

"Cal didn't want to leave the kids," she explained. There'd be other dances, other opportunities, Jane reassured herself.

"He's up next," Glen said.

"Go, Cal!" Ellie squealed. Despite her sister-in-law's effort to sound sympathetic, Jane could tell she was excited.

When Cal's name was announced, Jane didn't want to look but couldn't stop herself. Cal was inside the pen, sitting astride the bull, one end of a rope wrapped around the saddle horn and the other around his hand. She held her sleeping child more tightly and bit her lower lip hard enough to draw blood. Suddenly the gate flew open and fifteen hundred pounds of angry bull charged into the arena.

Almost immediately, Glen and Ellie were on their feet, shouting. Jane remained seated, her arms around her children. "What's happening?" she asked Ellie in a tight, urgent voice.

"Cal's doing great!" she exclaimed. Jane could barely hear her over the noise of the crowd. Ellie clapped wildly when the buzzer went. "He stayed on!" she crowed. "So far, he's ahead!"

Jane nodded. How he'd managed to last all those seconds, she had no idea.

"Whew. Glad that's over." Ellie sank down next to Jane.

"My brother's got a real flair for this," Glen said to no one in particular. "He could've gone on the circuit if…" He let the rest fade.

"If he wasn't married," Jane said, completing his thought. Actually Glen's assessment wasn't really accurate. Her husband was a long-established rancher before she'd come on the scene. He'd competed in rodeos since he was in his teens, but if he'd been inter-ested in turning professional, he would have done so when he was much younger. She had nothing to do with that decision.

"Glen," Ellie said, squeezing her husband's arm, "who's that woman over there?" Ellie was staring at a brunette standing near the fence.

"What woman?" Glen asked.

"The one talking to Cal."

Jane glanced over, and even from this distance she could see that the other woman was lovely. Tall and slender, she looked like a model from the pages of a Western-wear catalog in her tight jeans, red cowboy boots and brightly checked shirt. It was more than just her appearance, though. Jane noticed the confidence with which she held herself, the flirtatious way she flipped back her long brown hair. This was a woman who knew she looked good—especially to men.

"She seems familiar," Ellie said, nudging Glen. "Don't you think?"

"She does," he agreed, "but I can't place her."

"Apparently she's got a lot to say to Cal," Ellie added, then glanced apologetically toward Jane as though she regretted mentioning it.

Jane couldn't help being curious. The woman wasn't anyone she recognized. She wasn't the jealous type, but she found herself wondering how this Rodeo Princess knew her husband. It was clear that the woman was speaking animatedly to Cal, gesturing freely; for his part, Cal seemed more interested in what was happening with the rodeo than in listening to her.

Jane supposed she should be pleased by his lack of interest in another woman, and indeed she was. Then, as if aware of her scrutiny, her husband turned toward the bleachers and surveyed the crowd. His face broke into a wide grin when he caught her eye, and he waved. Earlier she'd been annoyed with him— in fact, she still was—but she'd never been able to resist one of Cal's smiles. She waved in return and blew him a kiss.

An hour later, after Cal had been awarded the trophy for the amateur bull-riding competition, they decided to leave. With Mary Ann in the stroller and Paul walking between them, they made one last circuit of the grounds before heading toward the parking lot. They passed the chili cook-off tent, where the winner's name was posted; for the first time in recent memory, it wasn't Nell Grant. But then, Jane understood that Nell had declined to enter this year.

It was near dusk and lights from the carnival rides sparkled, delighting both Paul and Mary Ann. Cal's arm was around Jane's shoulder as they skirted the area set aside for the dance. The fiddle players were entertaining the audience while the rest of the musicians set up their equipment. People had gathered around, tapping their feet in anticipation.

The lively music had Jane swaying to the beat. "I wish we were staying," she murmured, swallowing her disappointment.

"We'd better get home," Cal said, swinging his trophy at his side. "I didn't want to say anything before, but I'm about as sore as a man can get."

"Your rib?" she asked.

He grimaced, obviously in pain. "Are you going to lecture me?"

"I should," she told him. "But I won't. You knew the risks."

He leaned forward and kissed her cheek. "You're right. I did."

What really bothered her was that he'd known—and participated, anyway. He was fully aware that he could've been badly injured, or worse. And for what? She simply didn't understand why a man would do anything so foolish when he had so much to lose.

"I'm ready to go home," he said. "How about you?"

Jane nodded, but glanced longingly over her shoulder at the dance floor. Maybe next year.

The phone rang, shattering the night silence. Cal bolted upright and looked at the glowing digital numbers of the clock radio, then snatched the receiver from its cradle without bothering to check call display. It went without saying that anyone phoning at 3:23 a.m. was calling with bad news.

"Pattersons'," he barked gruffly.

"Cal? It's Stephanie."

Jane's mother. Something was very wrong; he could hear it in her voice. "What's happened?"

"It's…it's Harry," she stammered.

Jane awoke and leaned across the bed to turn on the bedside lamp. "Who is it?" she asked.

He raised one hand to defer her question. "Where are you?"

"At the hospital," Stephanie said, and rattled off the name of a medical facility in Southern California. "Harry's fallen—he got up the way he sometimes does in the middle of the night and…and he slipped."

"Is he all right?"

"No," his mother-in-law answered, her voice trembling. She took a moment to compose herself. "That's why I'm calling. His hip's broken—and it's a very bad break. He's sedated and scheduled for surgery first thing in the morning, but…but the doctors told me it's going to be weeks before he's back on his feet."

"Cal?" Jane was watching him, frowning, her hair disheveled, her face marked by sleep.

"It's your mother," he said, placing his hand over the mouthpiece.

"Is this about my dad?"

Cal nodded.

"Let me talk to her," Jane demanded, instantly alert.

"Stephanie, you'd better talk to Jane yourself," he said, and handed his wife the phone.

Cal was pretty much able to follow the conversation from that point. With her medical background, Jane was the best person to talk to in circumstances like this. She asked a number of questions concerning medication and tests that had been done, explained the kind of orthopedic surgery her dad would undergo and reassured her mother. She spoke with such confidence that Cal felt his own sense of foreboding diminish. And then she hesitated.

"I'll need to talk to Cal about that," she told her mother, voice dropping as though he wasn't supposed to hear.

"Talk to me about what?" he asked after she'd replaced the receiver.

Jane paused for a moment, then took a deep breath.

"Mom wants me and the kids to fly home."

"For how long?" The question was purely selfish; still, he needed to know. Being separated would be a hardship on all of them. He understood the situation and was willing to do whatever he could, but he didn't like the thought of being apart for any length of time.

"I don't know. A couple of weeks, maybe longer."

"Two *weeks?*" He hated the telltale irritation in his voice, but it was too late to take back the words.

Jane said nothing. Then, as though struck by some brilliant idea, she scrambled onto her knees and a slow smile spread across her face.

"Come with us," she said.

"To California? Now?" That was out of the question, but he hated to refuse his wife—especially after what he'd done at the rodeo. "Honey, I can't. Glen and I are getting ready for the bull sale this week. I'm sorry, but this just isn't a good time for me to be away."

"Glen could handle the sale."

What she said was true, but the prospect of spending two weeks at his in-laws' held little appeal. Cal got along with Jane's mother and he liked her father well enough, but Harry had a few annoying mannerisms. Plus, the two of them tended to become embroiled in ridiculous arguments that served no real purpose and usually went nowhere. Cal suspected it was more a matter of competing for Jane's attention. Jane was Harry's only daughter and he doted on her. Cal figured he'd be doing Harry a favor by staying away. Besides, what would he do with himself in a place like Los Angeles?

"Don't be so quick to say no," she said. "We could make this a family vacation. We always talk about going somewhere and it never happens." She knew he found it hard to leave the ranch for longer than a few days, but still…

"A vacation? I don't think so, not with your father laid up and your mother as worried as she is. Besides, Stephanie doesn't want *me* there."

"That's not true."

"It's not me she needs, it's you. Having the kids around will boost your father's spirits, and your mother's too. I'd just be in the way."

Jane's disappointment was obvious. "You're sure?"

He nodded. "You go. A visit with you and the kids will be the best thing for your parents, and you'll have a chance to connect with your friends, too. It'll do everyone good."

Still Jane showed reluctance. "You're *sure* you don't mind me being gone that long?"

"I'll hate it," he admitted, and reached for the lamp to turn off the light. Then he drew his wife into his arms.

Jane released a deep sigh. "I'm going to hate it, too."

Cal closed his eyes, already experiencing a sense of loss, and Jane and the children hadn't even left yet.

The next morning was hectic. The minute she got up, Jane arranged the flight to California and threw clothes, toiletries, toys and baby supplies into several suitcases. No sooner had she finished than Cal piled them all into the car, and drove his family to San Antonio. Paul was excited about riding in an airplane, and even Mary Ann seemed to realize there was adventure ahead.

As always, San Antonio International Airport was bustling with activity. Cal quickly ushered Jane and the kids to the airline's check-in counter, where they received their boarding passes.

Kneeling down to meet his son at eye level, Cal put both hands on Paul's shoulders. "You be good for Mommy, understand?"

His three-year-old nodded solemnly, then threw his small arms around Cal's neck, hugging him fiercely.

"I'm counting on you to be as much help to your grandma and grandpa as you can," Cal added. He felt a wrenching in his stomach. This would be the first time he'd been apart from his children.

"I will," Paul promised.

Cal noted that his son's "blankey" was tucked inside his backpack, but said nothing. The blanket was badly worn. It'd been a gift from Jane's friend Annie Porter, and a point of contention between him and Jane. Cal didn't like the idea of the boy dragging it around, and Jane felt that Paul would give it up when he was ready.

Cal stood and scooped Mary Ann into his arms. His daughter squirmed, eager to break free and explore this wonderful new place.

"I'll phone often," Jane said when he'd kissed her.

"We'll talk every day."

Saying goodbye to his family was even more difficult than Cal had expected.

"I'm going to miss you," he murmured.

"Two weeks will go quickly."

"Right," Cal agreed, but at the moment those weeks loomed before him in all their emptiness.

Juggling two bags and clutching both children, Jane moved toward the security area. Cal left then, waving to the kids as he did. The feeling of emptiness stayed with him, and he knew he'd let his wife down. He should have gone with her; it was what she'd wanted, what she'd asked of him, but he'd refused. He shook his head miserably. This wasn't the first time he'd disappointed Jane.

As he made his way to the parking garage, Cal couldn't shake his reaction to seeing his wife leave. He didn't want to go to California, and yet he regretted not being on that plane with his family.

"You heard about Jane, didn't you?" Dovie Hennessey asked her husband. Frank had just come home from the golf course, where he'd played eighteen holes with Phil Patterson, Cal's father.

Frank, who'd retired three years earlier from his position as sheriff, nodded and walked straight to the refrigerator. "According to Phil, Cal drove Jane and the kids to the airport yesterday morning."

"I give him a week."

Frank turned around, a pitcher of iced tea in his hand. "A week before what?"

"Before Cal comes into town."

"Why?"

Exasperated, Dovie rolled her eyes. "Company. He's going to rattle around that house like a lost soul."

"Cal? No way!" Frank argued, pouring himself a glass of tea. "You seem to forget he was a confirmed bachelor before he met Jane. I was as surprised as anyone when he decided to marry her. Don't get me wrong. I think it was the smartest thing he ever did...."

"But?" Dovie said.

"Cal isn't any stranger to living alone," Frank continued, sitting down at the kitchen table with his tea and the newspaper. "He did it for years. Now, I know he loves Jane and the kids, but my guess is he's looking forward to two weeks of peace and quiet."

Dovie couldn't help herself. *Peace and quiet?* Frank made it sound as though Cal would welcome a vacation from his own family. Hands on her hips, she glared at her husband. "Frank Hennessey, what a rotten thing to say."

He glanced up from his paper, a puzzled expression on his face. "What was so terrible about that?"

"Jane and the children are *not* a nuisance in Cal's life," she said in a firm voice. "Don't you realize that?"

"Now, Dovie—"

"Furthermore, you seem to be implying that he's going to *enjoy* having them gone."

"I said no such thing," Frank insisted. "Cal's going to miss Jane—of course he is. The children, too. What I was *trying* to say is that spending a couple of weeks without his wife might not be all that bad." Flustered and avoiding her eyes, Frank rubbed his face. "That didn't come out right, either."

Dovie suppressed a smile. She knew what he meant, but she liked giving him a hard time once in a while— partly because he made it so easy. He'd remained a bachelor for the first sixty years of his life. Like Cal, he'd grown accustomed to his own company. He and Dovie had been involved for more than ten years, but Frank had resisted marriage until Pastor Wade McMillen had offered a solution. They became husband and wife but kept their own residences. In the beginning, that had worked beautifully, but as time passed, Frank ended up spending more and more nights with her, until it seemed wasteful to maintain two homes. Since he'd retired, Dovie, who owned an antique store, had reduced her hours. They were traveling frequently now, and with Frank taking a role in local politics and becoming active in the senior citizens' center, why, there just weren't enough hours in a day.

Patting her husband's arm as she passed, Dovie said, "I thought I'd make Cal one of my chicken pot pies and we could take it out to him later this week."

Frank nodded, apparently eager to leave the subject behind. "Good idea." Picking up his paper, he claimed the recliner and stretched out his legs. Almost immediately, Buttons, the black miniature poodle they'd recently acquired, leaped into Frank's lap and circled a couple of times before settling into a comfortable position.

"Nap time?" Dovie asked with a grin.

"Golf tires me out," Frank said.

Dovie laughed. "I meant the dog."

"I guess we're both tired...."

"You promised to drive me to the grocery store," she reminded him, although she was perfectly capable of making the trip on her own. It was the small things they did together that she enjoyed most. The ordinary domestic chores that were part of any marriage.

"In a while," Frank said sleepily, lowering the newspaper to the floor.

True to his word, an hour later Frank sought her out, obviously ready to tackle a trip to the supermarket. Once they got there, he found a convenient parking spot, accompanied her inside and grabbed a cart. Dovie marched toward the produce aisle, with Frank close behind.

"Do you have any idea what Cal would enjoy with his chicken pot pie?" she asked.

"I know what *I'd* enjoy," Frank teased and playfully swatted her backside.

"Frank Hennessey," Dovie protested, but not too loudly, since that would only encourage him. She didn't really mind, though. Frank was openly affectionate, unlike her first husband. Marvin had loved her, she'd never doubted that, but he'd displayed his feelings in less overt ways.

"Who's that?" Frank asked, his attention on a tall brunette who stood by the oranges, examining them closely.

It took Dovie a moment to remember. "Why, that's Nicole Nelson."

"Nicole Nelson," Frank repeated slowly, as though testing the name. "She's from Promise?"

"She lived here a few years back," Dovie said, taking a plastic bag and choosing the freshest-looking bunch of celery.

"She seems familiar. How do I know her?" Frank asked, speaking into her ear.

Which told Dovie that Nicole had never crossed the law. Frank had perfect recall of everyone he'd encountered in his work as sheriff.

"She was a teller at the bank."

"When?"

"Oh, my." Dovie had to think about that one. "Quite

a few years ago now…nine, maybe ten. She and Jennifer Healy were roommates."

"Healy. Healy. Why do I know that name."

Dovie whirled around, sighing loudly. "Frank, don't tell me you've forgotten Jennifer Healy!"

He stared back at her, his expression blank.

"She's the one who dumped Cal two days before their wedding. It nearly destroyed the poor boy. I still remember how upset Mary was, having to call everyone and tell them the wedding had been canceled." She shook her head. "Nicole was supposed to be Jennifer's maid of honor."

Frank's gaze followed the other woman as she pushed her cart toward the vegetables. "When Jennifer left town, did Nicole go with her?"

Dovie didn't know, but it seemed to her the two girls had moved at about the same time.

"Cal was pretty broken up when Jennifer dumped him," Frank said. "Good thing she left Promise. Wonder why this one came back…"

"Mary was worried sick about Cal," Dovie murmured, missing her dearest friend more than ever. Cal's mother had died almost three years ago, and not a day passed that Dovie didn't think of her.

"I know it was painful when it happened, but Jennifer's leaving was probably a lucky break for Cal."

Dovie agreed with him. "I'm sure Jane thinks so, too."

Frank generally didn't pay much attention to other women—unless they were potential or probable felons. His noticing Nicole was unusual enough, but it was the intensity of his focus that perturbed her.

She studied Nicole. Dovie had to admit that the years had been kind to Jennifer's friend. Nicole had been lovely before, but immature. Time had seasoned her beauty and given her an air of casual sophistication. Even the way she dressed had changed. Her hair, too.

Dovie saw that her husband wasn't the only man with his eye on this woman; half the men in the store had noticed her—and Nicole was well aware of it.

"I'll admit she looks attractive," Dovie said with a certain reluctance.

When Frank turned back to her, he was frowning. "What is it?" she asked.

"What she looks like to me," he said, ushering her down the aisle, "is trouble."

Two

Cal had lived in this ranch house his entire life, and the place had never seemed as big or as empty as it did now. Jane hadn't been gone a week but he couldn't stand the silence, wandering aimlessly from room to room. Exhausted from a day that had started before dawn, he'd come home and once again experienced a sharp pang of loneliness.

Normally when Cal got back to the house, Paul rushed outside to greet him. The little boy always launched himself off the porch steps into his father's arms as if he'd waited for this moment all day. Later, after Cal had showered and Jane got dinner on the table, he spent time with his daughter. As young as Mary Ann was, she had a dynamic personality and persuasive powers to match. Cal knew she was going to be a beauty when she grew up—and he'd be warding off the boys. Mary Ann was like her mother in her loveliness, her energy…and her stubborn nature.

Cal's life had changed forever the day he married

Jane. Marriage wasn't just the smartest move of his life, it was the most comfortable. Being temporarily on his own made him appreciate what he had. He'd gotten used to a great many things, most of which he hadn't stopped to consider for quite a while: shared passion, the companionship of the woman he loved, a family that gave him a sense of purpose and belonging. In addition, Jane ran their household with efficiency and competence, and he'd grown used to the work she did for her family—meals, laundry, cleaning. He sighed. To say he missed Jane and the kids was an understatement.

He showered, changed clothes and dragged himself into the kitchen. His lunch had been skimpy and his stomach felt hollow, but he wasn't in the mood to cook. Had there been time before she left, Jane would have filled the freezer with precooked dinners he could pop into the microwave. When they heard he was a temporary bachelor, Frank and Dovie had dropped off a meal, but that was long gone. The cupboards were full, the refrigerator, too, but nothing seemed simple or appealing. Because he didn't want to bother with anything more complicated, he reached for a bag of microwave popcorn. That would take the edge off his hunger, he decided. Maybe later he'd feel like putting together a proper meal.

The scent of popped corn enticed him, but just as he was about to start eating it, the phone rang. Cal grabbed the receiver, thinking it might be Jane.

"Pattersons'," he said eagerly.

"Cal, it's Annie."

Annie. Cal couldn't squelch the letdown feeling that came over him. Annie Porter was his wife's best friend and a woman he liked very much. She'd moved to Promise a few years back and had quickly become part of the community. The town had needed a bookstore and Annie had needed Promise. It wasn't long before she'd married the local vet. Cal suddenly remembered that Jane had asked him to phone Annie. He'd forgotten.

"I just heard about Jane's dad. What happened? Dovie was in and said Jane went to stay with her parents—she assumed I knew. I wish someone had told me."

"That's my fault," Cal said. "I'm sorry, Annie. On the way to the airport, Jane asked me to call…." He let his words drift off.

"What happened?" Annie asked again, clearly upset. Cal knew she was close to Jane's parents and considered them a second family.

Cal told her everything he could and apologized a second time for not contacting her earlier. He hoped Annie would see that the slight hadn't been intentional; the fact was, he hated making phone calls. Always had.

"I can't imagine why Jane hasn't called me herself," she said in a worried voice.

Cal had figured she would, too, which only went to show how hectic Jane's days must be with her parents and the children.

"Jane will be home in a week," Cal said, trying to sound hopeful and reassuring—although a week seemed like an eternity. He pushed the thought from his mind and forced himself to focus on their reunion.

"Why don't you give her a call?" he suggested, knowing Annie was going to want more details. "I'm sure she'd love to hear from you."

"I'll do that."

"Great… Well, it's been good talking to you," he said, anxious to get off the phone.

"Before we hang up, I want to ask you about Nicole Nelson."

"Who?" Cal had no idea who she was talking about.

"You don't know Nicole? She came into the book-store this afternoon and applied for a job. She put you and the bank down as references."

"Nicole Nelson." The name sounded vaguely familiar.

"I saw you talking to her at the rodeo," Annie said, obviously surprised that he didn't remember the other woman.

"Oh, yeah—her," he said, finally recalling the incident. Then he realized how he knew Nicole. She'd been a good friend of Jennifer's. In fact, they'd been roommates when he and Jennifer were engaged. "She put my name down as a job reference?" He found that hard to believe.

"She said she's known you for quite a while," Annie added.

"Really?" To be fair, Cal's problem hadn't been with Nicole but with Jennifer, who'd played him for a fool. He'd been too blinded by his first encounter with love to recognize the kind of woman she was.

"Nicole said if I had any questions I should ask you."

"It's been years since I saw her—other than at the

rodeo last week." He did remember talking to her briefly. She'd said something about how good it was to be back in Promise, how nice to see him, that sort of thing. At the time Cal had been distracted. He'd been more interested in watching the rodeo and cheering on his friends than in having a conversation with a woman he'd had trouble recognizing. Besides, Jane was upset with him, and appeasing her had been paramount. He'd barely noticed Nicole.

"Did she list any other personal references?" he asked.

"No, I told her you and the bank were the only ones I needed," Annie said. "So can you vouch for her?"

"I guess so. It's just that I haven't seen her in a long time. We—"

"You went out with her?"

Leave it to Annie to ask a question like that. "No, with her best friend. We almost got married." No need to go into details. Jennifer had taught him one of the most valuable lessons of his life. The worth of that experience could be measured in the pain and embarrassment that resulted when she'd callously canceled the wedding. He could've lived with her breaking their engagement—but why did she have to wait until they were practically at the altar?

"I talked with Janice over at Promise First National about her job history," Annie said, interrupting his thoughts. "She doesn't have anything negative to say about Nicole, but if you're uncomfortable giving her a recommendation…"

"Oh, I'm sure Nicole will do a great job for you."

The length of Annie's hesitation told him he hadn't been very convincing.

"Nicole's fine, really," he said. He didn't actually remember that much about her. She always seemed to be there whenever he picked up Jennifer, but he couldn't say he *knew* her. Years ago she'd been a sweet kid, but that was the extent of his recollection. He certainly couldn't dredge up anything that would prevent her from selling books. He'd never heard that she was dishonest or rude to customers, and those were things that would definitely have stuck in his mind. It was difficult enough to attract good employees; Cal didn't want to be responsible for Annie's turning someone down simply because he had negative feelings about that person's friends.

"I was thinking of hiring her for the bookstore."

"Do it," Cal said.

"She seems friendly and helpful."

"Yeah, she is," Cal said, and glanced longingly at the popcorn.

"Thanks, Cal, I appreciate the input."

"No problem." He didn't know what it was about women and the telephone. Even Jane, who had a sensible approach to everything and hated wasting time, could spend hours chatting with her friends. He sighed. Thinking about his wife produced a powerful yearning. Nothing seemed right without her.

"I'll call Jane tomorrow," Annie was saying.

"Good plan." He checked his watch, wondering how much longer this would take.

"Thanks again."

"Give Nicole my best," he said, thinking this was how to signal that he was ready to get off the phone.

"I will," Annie promised. "Bye, now."

Ah, success. Cal replaced the receiver, then frowned as he attempted to picture Nicole Nelson. Brown hair— or blond? He hadn't paid much attention to her at the rodeo. And he couldn't imagine what would bring her back to Promise. Not that she needed to justify the move, at least to him. His one hope was that Annie wouldn't regret hiring her.

Mary Ann's squeal of delight woke Jane from a deep sleep. She rolled over and looked bleary-eyed at the clock radio and gasped. Ten o'clock. She hadn't slept this late since she was in high school. Tossing back the covers, she grabbed her robe and headed out of the bedroom, yawning as she went.

"Mom!" she called.

"In here, sweetheart," her mother said from the kitchen.

Jane found the children and her mother busily playing on the tile floor. Mary Ann toddled gleefully, chasing a beach ball, intent on getting to it before her brother. Because he loved his little sister, Paul was letting her reach it first, then clapping and encouraging her to throw it to him.

"You should've woken me up," Jane said.

"Why? The children are fine."

"But, Mom, I'm supposed to be here to help you," she protested. The last week had been difficult. Taking Paul and Mary Ann away from home and the comfort of their normal routines had made both children irritable. The first night, Mary Ann hadn't slept more than a few hours, then whined all the next day. Paul had grown quiet and refused to talk to either grandparent. The children had required several days to adjust to the time change, and with the stress of her father's condition, Jane was completely exhausted.

"You needed the sleep," her mother said.

Jane couldn't argue with that. "But I didn't come all this way to spend the whole morning in bed."

"Stop fussing. Paul, Mary Ann and I are having a wonderful visit. If you intend to spoil it, then I suggest you go back to bed."

"Mother!"

"I'm the only grandma they have. Now, why don't you let us play and get yourself some breakfast?"

"But—"

"You heard me." Stephanie crawled over to the lower cupboards, then held on to the counter, using that as leverage to get up off the floor. "I'm not as limber as I once was," she joked.

"Oh, Mom…" Watching her, Jane felt guilty. She gathered Mary Ann into her arms, although the child immediately wanted to get down. Paul frowned up at her, disgruntled by the interruption.

"I called your father, and he's resting comfortably," her mother informed her. "He wants us to take the day for ourselves."

"Dad said that?" He'd been demanding and impatient ever since Jane had arrived.

"He did indeed, and I intend to take him up on his offer. I promised the kids lunch at McDonald's."

"Dad *must* be feeling better."

"He is," her mother said. "By the way, Annie phoned earlier."

"Annie?" Jane echoed. "Is everything all right at home?"

"Everything's just fine. She wanted to know how your father's doing. Apparently no one told her—"

"I asked Cal to tell her. I meant to phone her myself, but…you know how crazy it's been this week."

"I explained it all, so don't you worry. She'd already talked to Cal, who apologized profusely for not phoning her. She sounds well and has some news herself."

Jane paused, waiting, although she had her suspicions.

"Annie's pregnant again. She says they're all thrilled—Annie, Lucas and the children. She's reducing her hours at work, hiring extra help. It was great to chat with her."

"A baby. That's wonderful." Annie was such a good mother, patient and intuitive. And such a good friend. Her move to Texas had been a real blessing to Jane.

Thinking about Promise made Jane's heart hunger for home. A smile came as she recalled how out of place she'd once felt in the small Texas town. She'd accepted a job in the medical clinic soon after she'd qualified. It wasn't where she'd wanted to settle, and she'd only taken the assignment so she could pay off a portion of her huge college loans. The first few months had been dreadful—until she'd become friends with Dovie, who'd introduced her to Ellie.

This was networking at its finest. Soon afterward, Ellie and Glen had arranged Jane's first date with Cal. What a disaster that had been! Cal wasn't the least bit interested in a blind date. Things had changed, however, when Cal and his brother and Ellie had started to teach her how to act like a real Texan. When she'd decided to take riding lessons, Cal had volunteered to be her teacher.

Jane had never meant to fall in love with him. But they were a good match, bringing out the best in each other, and they'd both realized that. Because of Cal, she was a better person, even a better physician, and he reminded her often how her love had enriched his life. They were married within a year of meeting.

After the children were born, Jane felt it necessary to make her career less of a priority, but she didn't begrudge a moment of this new experience. In fact, she enjoyed being a full-time wife and mother—for a while—and managed to keep up her medical skills with a few weekend shifts.

Annie, too, had found love and happiness in their small town. The news of her latest pregnancy pleased Jane.

"Have you connected with Julie and Megan yet?" her mother asked.

Along with Annie, Julie and Megan had been Jane's best friends all through high school. Julie was married and lived ten minutes away. Megan was a divorced single mother. Jane hadn't seen either woman in three years—make that four. How quickly time got away from her.

"Not yet," Jane told her.

"I want you to have lunch with your friends while you're home."

"Mom, that isn't necessary. I'm not here to be entertained."

"I don't want you to argue with me, either."

Jane grinned, tempted to follow her mother's suggestion. Why not? She'd love to see her friends. "I'll try to set something up with Julie and Megan this week."

"Good." Her mother gently stroked Jane's cheek. "You're so pale and exhausted."

The comment brought tears to her eyes. *She* wasn't the one suffering pain and trauma, like her father, who'd broken his hip, or her mother who'd had to deal with the paramedics, the hospital, the surgeon and all the stress.

"I came here to help *you*," Jane reiterated.

"You have, don't you see?" Her mother hugged Paul. "It's time with my precious grandbabies that's helping me cope with all this. I don't see nearly enough of them. Having the grandkids with me is such a treat, and I fully intend to take advantage of it."

Jane went to take a shower, looking forward to visiting with her friends. She missed Cal and Promise, but it was good to be in California, too.

The metallic whine of the can opener made Cal grit his teeth. This was the third night in a row that he'd eaten soup and crackers for dinner. The one night he'd fried himself a steak, he'd overcooked it. A few years back he'd been a pretty decent cook, but his skills had gotten rusty since his marriage. He dumped the ready-to-heat soup into the pan and stared at it, finding it utterly unappetizing.

Naturally he could always invite himself to his brother's house for dinner. Glen and Ellie would gladly set an extra plate at their table. He'd do that when he got desperate, but he wasn't, at least not yet. For that matter, he could call his father. Phil would appreciate the company, but by the time Cal was finished with his chores on the ranch, dinner had already been served at the retirement home.

Come to think of it, he was in the mood for Mexican food, and no place was better than Promise's own Mexican Lindo. His mouth had begun to water at the mere thought of his favorite enchiladas, dripping with melted cheese. He could practically taste them. Needing no other incentive, he set the pan of soup inside the refrigerator and grabbed his hat.

If he hurried, he'd be back in time for Jane's phone call. Her spirits had seemed better these past few days. Her father was improving, and today she'd met a couple of high-school friends for lunch.

Soon Harry would be released from the rehab center, and once his father-in-law was home, Jane and the children would return to Texas. Cal sincerely wished Jane's father a speedy recovery—and his good wishes weren't entirely selfish, either. He liked Harry Dickinson, despite their long-winded arguments and despite his father-in-law's reservations about Jane's choice in a husband. He'd never actually said anything, but Cal knew. It was impossible not to. Still, Harry's attitude had gotten friendlier, especially after the children were born.

Promise was bustling when Cal drove up Main Street. All the activity surprised him, although it shouldn't have. It was a Thursday night, after all, and there'd been strong economic growth in the past few years. New businesses abounded, an area on the outskirts of town had been made into a golf course, and the city park had added a swimming pool and tennis courts. Ellie's feed store had been remodeled, but it remained the friendly place it'd always been. She'd kept the wooden rockers out front and his own father was among the retired men who met there to talk politics or play a game of chess. The tall white steeple of the church showed prominently in the distance. Cal reflected that it'd been a long time since he'd attended services. Life just seemed to get in the way. Too bad, because he genuinely enjoyed Wade McMillen's sermons.

The familiar tantalizing aroma of Texas barbecue from the Chili Pepper teased his nostrils, and for a moment Cal hesitated. He could go for a thick barbecue sandwich just as easily as his favorite enchiladas, but in the end he stuck with his original decision.

When he walked into the stucco-walled restaurant, he was immediately led to a booth. He'd barely had time to remove his hat before the waitress brought him a bowl of corn chips and a dish of extra-hot salsa. His mouth was full when Nicole Nelson stepped into the room, eyed him boldly and smiled. After only the slightest pause, she approached his table.

"Hello, Cal." Her voice was low and throaty.

Cal quickly swallowed the chip, almost choking as

he did. The attractive woman standing there wasn't the kid he'd known all those years ago. Her jeans fit her like a second skin, and unless he missed his guess, her blouse was one of those designer numbers that cost more than he took to the bank in an average month. If her tastes ran to expensive clothes like that, Cal couldn't imagine how she was going to live on what Annie Porter could afford to pay her.

"Nicole," he managed. "Uh, hi. How're you doing?"

"Great, thanks." She peered over her shoulder as though expecting to meet someone. "Do you have a couple of minutes?"

"Uh…sure." He glanced around, grateful no one was watching.

Before he realized what she intended, Nicole slid into the booth opposite him. Her smile was bright enough to make him blink.

"I can't *tell* you how wonderful it is to see you again," she said.

"You, too," he muttered, although he wasn't sure he would've recognized her if he'd passed her in the street.

"I guess you're surprised I'm back in Promise."

"A little," he said. "What brings you to town?" He already knew she'd made the move without having a job lined up.

She reached for a chip, then shrugged. "A number of things. The year I lived in Promise was one of the best of my life. I really did grow to love this town. Jennifer and I got transferred here around the same time, but she never felt the way I did about it."

"Jennifer," he said aloud. "Are you still in touch with her?"

"Oh, sure. We've been friends for a lot of years."

"How is she?"

"Good," Nicole told him, offering no details.

"Did she ever marry?" He was a fool for asking, but he wanted to know.

Nicole dipped the chip in his salsa and laughed lightly. "She's been married—and divorced—twice."

"Twice?" Cal could believe it. "Someone told me she was living with a computer salesman in Houston." He'd heard that from Glen, who'd heard it from Ellie, who'd heard it from Janice at the bank.

"She married him first, but they've been divorced longer than they were ever married."

"I'm sorry to hear that." He wasn't really, but it seemed like something he should say.

"Then she met Mick. He was from Australia."

"Oh," he said. "Australia, huh?"

"Jennifer thought Mick was pretty hot," Nicole continued. "They had a whirlwind courtship, got married in Vegas and divorced a year later."

"I'll bet she was upset about that," Cal said, mainly because he didn't know how else to comment.

"With Jennifer it's hard to tell," Nicole said.

The waitress approached the table and Nicole declined a menu, but asked for a margarita. "Actually I'm meeting someone later, but I saw you and thought this was a good opportunity to catch up on old times."

"Great." Not that they'd *had* any "old times." Then, because he wasn't sure she knew he was married, he added, "I could use the company. My wife and kids are in California with her family for the next week or so."

"Oh…"

He might've been wrong, but Cal thought he detected a note of disappointment in her voice. Surely she'd known he was married; surely Annie had told her. But then again, maybe not.

"My boy's three and my daughter's eighteen months."

"Congratulations."

"Thanks," Cal said, feeling a bit self-conscious about dragging Jane and the kids into this conversation. But it was the right thing to do—and it wouldn't hurt his ego if the information got back to Jennifer, either.

Nicole helped herself to another chip. "The last time Jennifer and I spoke, she said something that might interest you." Nicole loaded the chip with salsa and took a discreet nibble. Looking up, she widened her eyes. "Jen said she's always wondered what would've happened if she'd stayed in Promise and you two *had* gotten married."

Cal laughed. He knew the answer, even if Nicole and Jennifer didn't. "I would've been husband number one. Eventually she would have moved on." In retrospect, it was easy to see Jennifer's faults and appreciate anew the fact that they weren't married.

"I don't agree," Nicole said, shaking her head. "I think it might've been a different story if she'd stayed with you."

The waitress brought her drink and Nicole smiled. She

took a sip, sliding her tongue along the salty edge of the glass. "Jennifer's my best friend," she went on, "but when it comes to men she's not very smart. Take you, for example. I couldn't *believe* it when she told me she was calling off the wedding. Turns out I was right, too."

Cal enjoyed hearing it, but wanted to know her reasoning. "Why's that?"

"Well, it's obvious. You were the only man strong enough to deal with her personality. I think the world of Jennifer, don't get me wrong, but she likes things her own way and that includes relationships. She was an idiot to break it off with you."

"Actually it was fortunate for both of us that she did."

"Fortunate for you, you mean," Nicole said with a deep sigh. "Like I said, Jennifer was a fool." After another sip, she leaned toward him, her tone confiding. "I doubt she'd admit it, but ever since she left Promise, Jennifer's been looking for a man just like you."

"You think so?" Her remark was a boost to his ego and superficial though that was, Cal couldn't restrain a smile.

The waitress returned with his order, and Nicole drank more of her margarita, then said, "I'll leave now and let you have your dinner."

She started to slip out of the booth, but Cal stopped her. "There's no need to rush off." He wasn't in any hurry and the truth was, he liked hearing what she had to say about Jennifer. If he missed Jane's call, he could always phone her back.

Nicole smiled. "I wanted to thank you, too," she murmured.

"For what?" He cut into an enchilada with his fork and glanced up.

"For giving me a recommendation at Tumbleweed Books."

"Hey," he said, grinning at her. "No problem."

"Annie called me this morning and said I have the job."

"I'm glad it worked out."

"Me, too. I've always loved books and I look forward to working with Annie."

He should probably mention that the bookstore owner was Jane's best friend, and would have, but he was too busy chewing and swallowing—and after that, it was too late.

Nicole checked her watch. "I'd better be going. Like I said, I'm meeting a…friend. If you don't mind, I'd like to buy your dinner."

Her words took him by surprise. He wondered what had prompted the offer.

"As a thank-you for the job reference," she explained.

"It was nothing—I was happy to do it. I'll get my own meal. But let me pay for your drink."

She agreed, they chatted a few more minutes, and then Nicole left. She hadn't said whom she was meeting, and although he was mildly curious, Cal didn't ask.

He sauntered out of the restaurant not long after Nicole. He'd been dragging when he arrived, but with his belly full and his spirits high, he felt almost cheerful as he walked toward his truck. He supposed he was sorry about Jennifer's marital troubles—but not *very* sorry.

As it happened, Cal did miss Jane's phone call, but

was quick to reach her once he got home. In her message she'd sounded disappointed, anxious, emotionally drained.

"Where were you?" she asked curtly when he returned her call.

Cal cleared his throat. "I drove into town for dinner. Is everything okay?"

"Mexican Lindo, right?" she asked, answering one question and avoiding the other.

"Right."

"Did you eat alone?"

"Of course." There was Nicole Nelson, but she hadn't eaten with him, not exactly. He'd bought her a drink, that was all. But he didn't want to go into a lengthy explanation that could only lead to misunderstandings. Perhaps it was wrong not to say something about her being there, but he didn't want to waste these precious minutes answering irrelevant questions. Jane might feel slighted or suspicious, although she had no reason. At any rate, Annie would probably mention that she'd hired Nicole on his recommendation, but he could deal with that later. Right now, he wanted to know why she was upset.

"Tell me what's wrong," Cal urged softly, dismissing the thought of Nicole as easily as if he'd never seen her. Their twenty minutes together had been trivial, essentially meaningless. Not a man-woman thing at all but a pandering to his ego. Jane was his wife, the person who mattered to him.

"Dad didn't have a good day," Jane said after a moment. "He's in a lot of pain and he's cranky with me and Mom. A few tests came back and, well, it's too early to say, but I didn't like what I saw."

"He'll be home soon?"

"I don't know—I'd thought, no, I'd hoped..." She let the rest fade.

"Don't worry about it, sweetheart. Take as long as you need. I'll manage." That offer wasn't easy to make, but Cal could see she needed his support. These weeks apart were as hard on her as they were on him. This was the only way he could help.

"You *want* me to stay longer?" Jane demanded.

"No," he returned emphatically. "I thought I was being noble and wonderful."

The tension eased with her laugh. "You seem to be getting along far too well without me."

"That isn't true! I miss you something fierce."

"I miss you, too," Jane said with a deep sigh.

"How did lunch with your friends go?" he asked, thinking it might be a good idea to change the subject.

"All right," she said with no real enthusiasm.

"You didn't enjoy yourself?"

Jane didn't answer immediately. "Not really. We used to be close, but that seems so long ago now. We've grown apart. Julie's into this beauty-pageant thing for her daughter, and it was all she talked about. Every weekend she travels from one state to another, following the pageants."

"Does her daughter like it?"

"I don't know. It's certainly not something I'd ever impose on *my* daughter." She sighed again. "I don't mean to sound judgmental, but we have so little in common anymore."

"What about Megan?"

"She came with her twelve-year-old daughter. She's terribly bitter about her divorce. She dragged her husband's name into the conversation at every opportunity, calling him 'that jerk I was married to.'"

"In front of her kid?" Cal was shocked that any mother could be so insensitive.

"Repeatedly," Jane murmured. "I have to admit I felt depressed after seeing them." She paused, then took a deep breath. "I wonder what they thought of me."

"That concerns you?" Cal asked, thinking she was being ridiculous if it did.

"Not at all," Jane told him. "Today was a vivid reminder that my home's not in California anymore. It's in Promise with you."

Three

"I hate to trouble you," Nicole said to Annie. She sat in front of the computer in the bookstore office, feeling flustered and annoyed with herself. "But I can't seem to find this title under the author's name."

"Here, let me show you how it works," Annie said, sitting down next to Nicole.

Nicole was grateful for Annie Porter's patience. Working in a bookstore was a whole new experience for her. She was tired of banking, tired of working in a field dominated by women but managed by men. Her last job had left her with a bitter taste—not least because she'd had an ill-advised affair with her boss—and she was eager to move on to something completely new. Thus far, she liked the bookstore and the challenge of learning new systems and skills.

Annie carefully reviewed the instructions again. It took Nicole a couple of tries to get it right. "This shouldn't be so difficult," she mumbled. "I mean, I've worked with lots of computer programs before."

"You're doing great," Annie said.

"I hope so."

"Hey, I can already see you're going to be an asset to the business," Annie said cheerfully, taking the packing slip out of a shipment of books. "Since you came on board, we've increased our business among young single men by two hundred percent."

Nicole laughed and wished that was true. She'd dated a handful of times since her return to Promise, but no one interested her as much as Cal Patterson. And he was married, she reminded herself. Married, married, married.

She should've known he wouldn't stay single long. She'd always found Cal attractive, even when he was engaged to Jennifer. However, the reason she'd given him for moving back to Promise was the truth. She had fallen in love with the town. She'd never found anywhere else that felt as comfortable. During her brief stint with the Promise bank, she'd made friends within the community. She loved the down-home feel of the feed store and the delights of Dovie's Antiques. The bowling alley had been a blast, with the midnight Rock-and-Bowl every Saturday night.

Jennifer Healy had never appreciated the town or the people. Her ex-roommate had once joked that Promise was like Mayberry RFD, the setting of that 60s TV show. Her comment had angered Nicole. These people were sincere, pleasant and kind. *She* preferred life in a town where people cared about each other, even if Jen didn't.

Only it wasn't just the town that had brought her back. She'd also returned because of Cal Patterson.

Almost ten years ago, she'd been infatuated with him, but since he was engaged to her best friend, she couldn't very well do anything about it. When Jennifer had dumped Cal, that would've been the perfect time to stick around and comfort him. Instead, she'd waited— and then she'd been transferred again, to a different branch in another town. Shortly after she'd left Promise, she'd had her first affair, and since then had drifted from one dead-end relationship to another. That was all about to change. This time she intended to claim the prize— Cal Patterson.

At the Mexican restaurant the other night, Nicole had told Cal that Jennifer compared every man she met to him, the one she'd deserted. Nicole hadn't a clue if that was the case or not. *She* was the one who'd done the comparing. In all these years she hadn't been able to get Cal Patterson out of her mind.

So he was married. She'd suspected as much when she made the decision to return to Promise, but dating a married man wasn't exactly unfamiliar to her. She would have preferred if he was single, although his being married wasn't a deterrent. It made things more…interesting. More of a challenge. Most of the time the married man ended up staying with his wife, and Nicole was the one who got hurt. This was something she knew far too well, but she'd also discovered that there were ways of undermining a marriage without having to do much of anything. And when a marriage was shaken, opportunities might present themselves….

"Nicole?"

Nicole realized Annie was staring at her. "Sorry, I got lost in my thoughts."

"It's time for a break." Annie led the way into the back room. Once inside, she reached for the coffeepot and gestured toward one of two overstuffed chairs. "Sit down and relax. If Louise needs any help, she can call us."

Nicole didn't have to be asked twice. She'd been waiting for a chance to learn more about Cal, and she couldn't think of a better source than Annie Porter.

Annie handed her a coffee in a ceramic mug, and Nicole added a teaspoon of sugar, letting it slowly dissolve as she stirred. "How do you know Cal?" she asked, deciding this was the best place to start.

"His wife. You haven't met Jane, have you?"

Nicole shook her head. "Not yet," she said as though she was eager to make the other woman's acquaintance.

"We've been friends nearly our entire lives. Jane's the reason I moved to Promise."

Nicole took a cookie and nibbled daintily. "Cal said he has two children."

"Yes."

The perfect little family, a boy and a girl. Except that wifey seemed to be staying away far too long. If the marriage was as wonderful as everyone suggested, she would've expected Cal's wife to be home by now.

"This separation has been hard on them," Annie was saying.

"They're separated?" Nicole asked, trying to sound sympathetic.

She was forced to squelch a surge of hope when

Annie explained, "Oh, no! Not that way. Just by distance. Jane's father has been ill."

"Yes, Cal mentioned that she was in California with her family." Nicole nodded earnestly. "She's a doctor, right?" She'd picked up that information without much difficulty at all. The people of Promise loved their Dr. Jane.

"A very capable one," Annie replied. "And the fact that she's with her parents seems to reassure them both."

"Oh, I'm sure she's a big help."

"I talked to her mom the other day, who's *so* glad she's there. I talked to Jane, too—I wanted to tell her about the baby and find out about her dad. She's looking forward to getting home."

"I know I'd want to be with my husband," Nicole said, thinking if she was married to Cal, she wouldn't be foolish enough to leave him for a day, let alone weeks at a time.

"The problem is, her father's not doing well," Annie said, then sipped her coffee. She, too, reached for a cookie.

"That's too bad."

Annie sighed. "I'm not sure how soon Jane will be able to come home." She shook her head. "Cal seems at loose ends without his family."

"Poor guy probably doesn't know what to do with himself." Nicole would love to show him, but she'd wait for the right moment.

"Do you like children?" Annie asked her.

"Very much. I hope to have a family one day." Nicole knew her employer was pregnant, so she said what she figured Annie would want to hear. In reality, she herself didn't plan to have children. Nicole was well aware that, unlike Annie, she wouldn't make a good mother. If she was lucky enough to find a man who suited her, she'd make damn sure he didn't have any time on his hands to think about kids—or to be lured away by another woman.

"I understand you're seeing Brian Longstreet," Annie murmured.

"We had dinner the other night." The night she'd run into Cal. It was to Brian's disadvantage that she'd met him directly afterward, when Cal was all she could think about.

"Do you like him?"

Nicole shrugged. "Brian's okay."

"A little on the dull side?"

"A little." She'd already decided not to date the manager of the grocery store again. He was engaging enough and not unattractive, but he lacked the *presence* she was looking for. The strength of character. His biggest fault, Nicole readily admitted, was that he wasn't Cal Patterson.

"What about Lane Moser?"

Nicole had dated him the first week she'd returned. She'd known him from her days at the bank. "Too old," she muttered. She didn't mind a few years' difference, but Lane was eighteen years her senior and divorced. "I'm picky," she joked.

"You have a right to be."

"I never seem to fall for the guys who happen to be available. I don't know what my problem is," Nicole said, and even as she spoke she recognized this for a bald-faced lie. Her problem was easily defined. She fell for married men because of the challenge, the chase, the contest. Single guys stumbled all over themselves to make an impression, whereas with married men, *she* was the one who had to lure them, had to work to attract their attention.

Over the years she'd gotten smart, and this time it wouldn't be the wife who won. It would be her.

"Don't give up," Annie said, breaking into her thoughts.

"Give up?"

"On finding the right man. He's out there. I was divorced when I met Lucas and I had no intention of ever marrying again. It's too easy to let negative experiences sour your perspective. Don't let that happen to you."

"I won't," Nicole promised, and struggled to hide a smile. "I'm sure there's someone out there for me— only he doesn't know it yet." But Cal would find out soon enough.

"We'd better get back," Annie said, glancing at her watch.

Nicole set aside her mug and stood. Cal had been on his own for nearly two weeks now, if her calculations were correct. A man could get lonely after that much time without a woman.

He hadn't let her pay for his meal at the Mexican restaurant. Maybe she could come up with another way to demonstrate just how grateful she was for the job reference he'd provided.

"How long's Jane going to be away?" Glen asked Cal as they drove along the fence line. The bed of the pickup was filled with posts and wire and tools; they'd been examining their fencing, and doing necessary repairs all afternoon.

Cal didn't want to think about his wife or about their strained telephone conversations of the last few nights. Yesterday he'd hung up depressed and anxious when Jane told him she wouldn't be home as soon as she'd hoped. Apparently Harry Dickinson's broken hip had triggered a number of other medical concerns. Just when it seemed his hip was healing nicely, the doctors had discovered a spot on his lung, and in the weeks since, the spot had grown. All at once, the big *C* loomed over Jane's father. *Cancer.*

"I don't know when she'll be back," Cal muttered, preferring not to discuss the subject with his brother. Cal blamed himself for their uncomfortable conversations. He'd tried to be helpful, reassuring, but hadn't been able to prevent his disappointment from surfacing. He'd expected her home any day, and now it seemed she was going to be delayed yet again.

"Are you thinking of flying to California yourself?" his brother asked.

"No." Cal's response was flat.

"Why not?"

"I don't see that it'd do any good." He believed that her parents had become emotionally dependent on her, as though it was within Jane's power to take their problems away. She loved her parents and he knew she felt torn between their needs and his. And here he was, putting more pressure on her....

He didn't mean to add to her troubles, but he had.

"Do you think I'm an irrational jerk?"

"Yes," Glen said bluntly, "so what's your point?"

That made Cal smile. Leave it to his younger brother to say what he needed to hear. "You'd be a lot more sympathetic if it was *your* wife."

"Probably," Glen agreed.

Normally Cal kept his affairs to himself, but he wasn't sure about the current situation. After Jane had hung up, he'd battled the urge to call her back, settle matters. They hadn't fought, not really, but they were dissatisfied with each other. Cal understood how Jane felt, understood her intense desire to support her parents, guide them through this difficult time. But she wasn't an only child—she had a brother living nearby—and even if she had been, her uncle was a doctor, too. The Dickinsons didn't need to rely so heavily on Jane, in Cal's opinion—and he'd made that opinion all too clear.

"What would you do?" he asked his brother.

Glen met his look and shrugged. "Getting tired of your own cooking, are you?"

"It's more than that." Cal had hoped Jane would force her brother to take on some of the responsibility.

She hadn't.

Cal and Glen reached the top of the ridge that overlooked the ranch house. "Whose car is that?" Glen asked.

"Where?"

"Parked by the barn."

Cal squinted and shook his head. "Don't have a clue."

"We'd better find out, don't you think?"

Cal steered the pickup toward the house. As they neared the property, Cal recognized Nicole Nelson lounging on his porch. Her *again?* He groaned inwardly. Their meeting at the Mexican Lindo had been innocent enough, but he didn't want her mentioning it to his brother. Glen was sure to say something to Ellie, and his sister-in-law would inevitably have a few questions and would probably discuss it with Dovie, and… God only knew where this would all end.

"It's Nicole Nelson," Cal said in a low voice.

"The girl from the rodeo?"

"You met her before," he told his brother.

"I did?" Glen sounded doubtful. "When? She doesn't look like someone I'd forget that easily."

"It was a few years ago," Cal said as they approached the house. "She was Jennifer Healy's roommate. She looked different then. Younger."

He parked the truck, then climbed out of the cab.

"Hi," Nicole called, stepping down off the porch. "I was afraid I'd missed you."

"Hi," Cal returned gruffly, wanting her to know he was uncomfortable with her showing up at the ranch like this. "You remember my brother, Glen, don't you?"

"Hello, Glen."

Nicole sparkled with flirtatious warmth and friendliness, and it was hard not to react.

"Nicole." Glen touched the rim of his hat. "Good to see you again."

"I brought you dinner," Nicole told Cal as she strolled casually back to her car. She seemed relaxed and nonchalant. The way she acted, anyone might assume she made a habit of stopping by unannounced.

Glen glanced at him and raised his eyebrows. He didn't need to say a word; Cal knew exactly what he was thinking.

"After everything you've done for me, it was the least I could do," Nicole said. "I really am grateful."

"For what?" Glen looked sharply at Cal, then Nicole.

Nicole opened the passenger door and straightened. "Cal was kind enough to give me a job recommendation for Tumbleweed Books."

"Annie phoned and asked if I knew her," Cal muttered under his breath, minimizing his role.

"I hope you like taco casserole," Nicole said, holding a glass dish with both hands. "I figured something Mexican would be a good bet, since you seem to enjoy it."

"How'd she know *that?*" Glen asked, glaring at his brother.

"We met at the Mexican Lindo a few nights ago," Cal supplied, figuring the news was better coming from him than Nicole.

"You did, did you?" Glen said, his eyes filled with meaning.

"I tried to buy his dinner," Nicole explained, "but Cal wouldn't let me."

Cal suspected his brother had misread the situation. "We didn't have dinner together if that's what you're thinking," he snapped. He was furious with Glen, as well as Nicole, for putting him in such an awkward position.

Holding the casserole, Nicole headed toward the house.

"I can take it from here," Cal said.

"Oh, it's no problem. I'll put it in the oven for you and get everything started so all you need to do is serve yourself."

She made it sound so reasonable. Unsure how to stop her, Cal stood in the doorway, arms loose at his sides. Dammit, he felt like a fool.

"There's plenty if Glen would like to stay for dinner," Nicole added, smiling at Cal's brother over her shoulder.

"No, thanks," Glen said pointedly, "I've got a wife and family to go home to."

"That's why I'm here," Nicole said, her expression sympathetic. "Cal's wife and children are away, so he has to fend for himself."

"I don't need anyone cooking meals for me," Cal said, wanting to set her straight. This hadn't been his idea. Bad enough that Nicole had brought him dinner; even worse that she'd arrived when his brother was there to witness it.

"Of course you don't," Nicole murmured. "This is just my way of thanking you for welcoming me home to Promise."

"Are you actually going to let her do this?" Glen asked, following him onto the porch.

Cal hung back. "Dovie brought me dinner recently," he said, defending himself. "Savannah, too."

"That's a little different, don't you think?"

"No!" he said. "Nicole's just doing something thoughtful, the same as Dovie and Savannah."

"Yeah, right."

"I'm not going to stand out here and argue with you," Cal muttered, especially since he agreed with his brother and this entire setup made him uncomfortable. If she'd asked his preference, Cal would have told Nicole to forget it. He was perfectly capable of preparing his own meals, even if he had little interest in doing so. He missed Jane's dinners—but it was more than the food.

Cal was lonely. He'd lived by himself for several years and now he'd learned, somewhat to his dismay, that he no longer liked it. At first it'd been the little things he'd missed most—conversation over dinner, saying good-night to his children, sitting quietly with Jane in the evenings. Lately, though, it was *everything*.

"I'll be leaving," Glen said coldly, letting Cal know once again that he didn't approve of Nicole's being there.

"I'll give you a call later," Cal shouted as Glen got into his truck.

"What for?"

His brother could be mighty dense at times. "Never mind," Cal said, and stepped into the house.

Nicole was in the kitchen, bustling about, making herself at home. He found he resented that. "I've got the oven preheating to 350 degrees," she said, facing him.

He stood stiffly in the doorway, anxious to send her on her way.

"As soon as the oven's ready, bake the casserole for thirty minutes."

"Great. Thanks."

"Oh, I nearly forgot."

She hurried toward him and it took Cal an instant to

realize she wanted out the door. He moved aside, but not quickly enough to avoid having her brush against him. The scent of her perfume reminded him of something Jane might wear. Roses, he guessed. Cal experienced a pang of longing. Not for Nicole, but for his wife. It wasn't right that another woman should walk into their home like this. *Jane* should be here, not Nicole—or anyone else.

"I left the sour cream and salsa in the car," Nicole said breathlessly when she returned. She placed both containers on the table, checked the oven and set the glass dish inside. "Okay." She rubbed her palms together. "I think that's everything."

Cal remained standing by the door, wanting nothing so much as to see her go.

She pointed to the oven. "Thirty minutes. Do you need me to write that down?"

He shook his head and didn't offer her an excuse to linger.

"I'll stay if you like and put together a salad."

He shook his head. "I'll be fine."

She smiled sweetly. "In that case, enjoy."

This time when she left, Cal knew to stand several feet away to avoid any physical contact. He watched her walk back to her car, aware of an overwhelming sense of relief.

Life at the retirement residence suited Phil Patterson. He had his own small apartment and didn't need to worry about cooking, since the monthly fee included three meals a day. He could choose to eat alone in his room or sit in the dining room if he wanted company. Adjusting to life without Mary hadn't been easy— wasn't easy now—but he kept active and that helped. So did staying in touch with friends. Particularly Frank Hennessey. Gordon Pawling, too. The three men played golf every week.

Frank's wife, Dovie, and Mary had been close for many years, and in some ways Mary's death from Alzheimer's had been as hard on Dovie as it was on Phil. At the end, when Mary no longer recognized either of them, Phil had sat and wept with his wife's dear friend. He hadn't allowed himself to break down in front of his sons, but felt no such compunction when he was around Dovie. She'd cried with him, and their shared grief had meant more than any words she might have said.

Frank and Dovie had Phil to dinner at least once a month, usually on the first Monday. He found it a bit odd that Frank had issued an invitation that afternoon when they'd finished playing cards at the seniors' center.

"It's the middle of the month," Phil pointed out. "I was over at your place just two weeks ago."

"Do you want to come for dinner or not?" Frank said.

Only a fool would turn down one of Dovie's dinners. That woman could cook unlike anyone he knew. Even Mary, who was no slouch when it came to preparing a good meal, had envied Dovie's talent.

"I'll be there," Phil promised, and promptly at five-thirty, he arrived at Frank and Dovie's, a bouquet of autumn flowers in his hand.

"You didn't need to do that," Dovie said when she greeted him, lightly kissing his cheek.

As he entered the house, Phil caught a whiff of something delicious—a blend of delightful aromas. He smelled bread fresh from the oven and a cake of some sort, plus the spicy scent of one of her Cajun specialties.

Frank and Phil settled down in the living room and a few minutes later Dovie brought them an appetizer plate full of luscious little things. A man sure didn't eat this well at the retirement center, he thought. Good thing, too, or he'd be joining the women at their weekly weight-loss group.

Phil helped himself to a shrimp, dipping it in a spicy sauce. Frank opened a bottle of red wine and brought them each a glass.

They chatted amiably for a while, but Phil knew there was something on Dovie's mind. He had an inkling of what it was, too, and decided to break the ice and make it easier for his friends.

"It's times like this that I miss Mary the most," he murmured, choosing a brie-and-mushroom concoction next.

"You mean for social get-togethers and such?" Frank asked.

"Well, yes, those, too," Phil said. "The dinners with friends and all the things we'd planned to do…"

Dovie and Frank waited.

"I wish Mary was here to talk to Cal."

His friends exchanged a glance, and Phil realized he'd been right. They'd heard about Cal and Nicole Nelson.

"You know?" Frank asked.

Phil nodded. It wasn't as though he could *avoid* hearing. Promise, for all its prosperity and growth, remained a small town. The news that Nicole Nelson had delivered dinner to Cal had spread faster than last winter's flu bug. He didn't like it, but he wasn't about to discuss it with Cal, either. Mary could have had a gentle word with their son, and Cal wouldn't have taken offense. But Phil wasn't especially adroit at that kind of conversation. He knew Cal wouldn't appreciate the advice, nor did Phil think it was necessary. His son loved Jane, and that was all there was to it. Cal would never do anything to jeopardize his marriage.

"Apparently Nicole brought him dinner—supposedly to thank Cal for some help he recently gave her," Dovie said, her face pinched with disapproval.

"If you ask me, that young woman's trying to stir up trouble," Frank added.

"Maybe so," Phil agreed, but he knew his oldest son almost as well as he knew himself. Cal hadn't sought out this other woman; she was the one who'd come chasing after him. His son would handle the situation.

"No one's suggesting they're romantically involved," Frank said hastily.

"They aren't," Phil insisted, although he wished again that Mary could speak to Cal, warn him about the perceptions of others. That sort of conversation had been her specialty.

"Do you see Nicole Nelson as a troublemaker?" Phil directed the question to Dovie.

"I don't know… I don't *think* she is, but I do wish she'd shown a bit more discretion. She's still young—it's understandable."

Phil heard the reluctance in her response and noticed the way she eyed Frank, as though she expected him to leap in and express his opinion.

"Annie seems to like her," Dovie went on, "but with this new pregnancy, she's spending less and less time at the bookstore. Really, I hate to say anything…."

"I tell you, the woman's a homewrecker," Frank announced stiffly.

"Now, Frank." Dovie placed her hand on her husband's knee and shook her head.

"Dovie, give me some credit. I was in law enforcement for over thirty years. I recognized that hungry look of hers the minute I saw her."

Phil frowned, now starting to feel worried. "You think Nicole Nelson has her sights set on Cal?"

"I do," Frank stated firmly.

"What an unkind thing to say." Still, he sensed that Dovie was beginning to doubt her own assessment of Nicole.

"The minute I saw her, I said to Dovie, 'That woman's trouble,'" Frank told him.

"He did," Dovie confirmed, sighing.

"Mark my words."

"Frank, please," she said. "You're talking as though Cal wasn't a happily married man. We both know he isn't the type to get involved with another woman. He's a good husband and father."

"Yes," Frank agreed.

"How did you hear about her bringing dinner out to Cal?" Phil asked. It worried him that this troublemaker was apparently dropping Cal's name into every conversation, stirring up speculation. Glen was the one who'd mentioned it to Phil—casually, but Phil wasn't fooled. This was his youngest son's way of letting him know he sensed trouble. Phil had weighed his options and decided his advice wasn't necessary. But it seemed that plenty of others had heard about Nicole's little trip to the ranch. Not from Glen and not from Ellie, which meant Nicole herself had been spreading the news. She had to be incredibly naive or just plain stupid or… Phil didn't want to think about what else would be going on in the woman's head. He didn't know her well enough to even guess. Whatever the reason for her actions, if Jane heard about this, there could be problems.

"Glen told Ellie," Dovie said, "and she was the one who told me. Not in any gossipy way, mind you, but because she's concerned. She asked what I knew about Nicole."

"Do you think anyone will tell Jane?"

Dovie immediately rejected that idea. "Not unless it's Nicole Nelson herself. To do so would be cruel and malicious. I can't think of a single person in Promise who'd purposely hurt Jane. This town loves Dr. Texas." Dr. Texas was what Jane had affectionately been called during her first few years at the clinic.

"The person in danger of getting hurt here is Cal," Frank said gruffly. "Man needs his head examined."

Phil had to grin at that. Frank could be right; perhaps it *was* time to step in, before things got out of hand. "Mary always was better at talking to the boys," he muttered. "But I suppose I could have a word with him…."

"You want me to do it?" Frank offered.

"Frank!" Dovie snapped.

"*Someone* has to warn him he's playing with fire," Frank blurted.

Phil shook his head. "Listen, if anyone says anything, it'll be me."

"You'll do it, won't you?" Frank pressed.

Reluctantly Phil nodded. He would, but he wasn't sure when. Sometimes a situation righted itself without anyone interfering. This might be one of those cases.

He sincerely hoped so.

Four

Jane stood at the foot of her father's hospital bed, reading his medical chart. Dr. Roth had allowed her to review his notes as a professional courtesy. She frowned as she studied them, then flipped through the test results, liking what they had to say even less.

"Janey? Is it that bad?" her father asked. She'd assumed he was asleep; his question took her by surprise.

Jane quickly set the chart aside. "Sorry if I woke you," she murmured.

He waved off her remark.

"It's bad news, isn't it?" he asked again. "You can tell me, Jane."

His persistence told her how worried he was. "Hmm. It says here you've been making a pest of yourself," she said, instead of answering his question.

He wore a sheepish grin. "How's a man supposed to get any rest around here with people constantly waking him up for one thing or another? If I'd known how much blood they were going to take or how often, I swear I'd make them pay me." He paused. "Do you have any idea what they charge for all this—all these X-rays and CAT scans and tests?"

"Don't worry about that, Dad. You have health insurance." However, she was well aware that his real concern wasn't the expense but the other problems that had been discovered as a result of his broken hip.

"I want to know what's going on," he said, growing agitated.

"Dad." Jane placed one hand on his shoulder.

He reached for her fingers and squeezed them hard. For a long moment he said nothing. "Cal wants you home, doesn't he?"

She hesitated, not knowing what to say. Cal had become restive and even a bit demanding; he hadn't hidden his disappointment when she'd told him she couldn't return to Promise yet. Their last few conversations had been tense and had left Jane feeling impatient with her husband—and guilty for reacting that way.

"Your mother and I have come to rely on you far too much," her father murmured.

"It's all right," Jane said, uncomfortably aware that Cal had said essentially the same thing. "I'm not just your daughter, I'm a physician. It's only natural that you'd want me here. What's far more important is for you and Mom not to worry."

Her father sighed and closed his eyes. "This isn't fair to you."

"Dad," she said again, more emphatically. "It's all

right, really. Cal understands." He might not like it, but he did understand.

"How much time do I have?" he shocked her by asking next. He was looking straight at her. "No one else will tell me the truth. You're the only one I can trust."

Her fingers curled around his and she met his look. "There are very effective treatments—"

"How much time?" he repeated, more loudly.

Jane shook her head.

"You won't tell me?" He sounded hurt, as if she'd somehow betrayed him.

"How do you expect me to answer a question like that?" she demanded. "Do I have a crystal ball or a direct line to God? For all we know, you could outlive me."

His smile was fleeting. "Okay, give me a ballpark figure."

Jane was uncomfortable doing even that. "Dad, you aren't listening to what I'm saying. You're only at the beginning stages of treatment."

"Apparently my heart isn't in great shape, either."

What he said was true, but the main concern right now was treating the cancer. He'd already had his first session of chemotherapy, and Jane hoped there'd be an immediate improvement. "Your heart is fine."

"Yeah, sure."

"Dad!"

He made an effort to smile. "It's a hard thing to face one's failing health—one's mortality."

When she nodded, he said quietly, "I worry about your mother without me."

Jane was worried about her mother, too, but she wasn't about to add to her father's burden. "Mom will do just fine."

Her father sighed and looked away. "You've made me very proud, Jane. I don't think I've ever told you that."

A lump formed in her throat and she couldn't speak.

"If anything happens to me, I want you to be there for your mother."

"Dad, please, of course I'll help Mom, but don't talk like that. Yes, you've got some medical problems, but they're all treatable. You trust me, don't you?"

He closed his eyes and nodded. "Love you, Janey."

"Love you, too, Dad." On impulse, she leaned forward and kissed his forehead.

"Tell your mother to take the kids to the beach again," he insisted. "Better yet, make that Disneyland."

"She wants to spend the time with you."

"Tell her not to visit me today. I need the rest." He opened his eyes and gave her an outrageous wink. "Now get out of here so I can sleep."

"Yes, Daddy," she said, reaching for her purse.

She might be a grown woman with children of her own, but the sick fragile man in that bed would always be the father she loved.

"Mommy, beach?" Paul asked as he walked into the kitchen a couple of mornings later, dragging his beloved blanket behind him. He automatically opened the cupboard door under the counter and checked out the selection of high-sugar breakfast cereals. Her mother had spoiled the children and it was going to take work to undo that once they got home.

Home. Jane felt so torn between her childhood home and her life in Promise, between her parents and her husband. She no longer belonged in California. Texas was in her blood now and she missed it— missed the ranch, her friends…and most of all, she missed Cal.

"Can we go to the beach?" Paul asked again, hugging the box of sugar-frosted cereal to his chest as he carried it to the table.

"Ah…" Her father's doctor was running another set of tests that afternoon.

"Go ahead," her mother urged, entering the kitchen, already dressed for the day. "Nothing's going to happen at the hospital until later."

"But, Mom…" Jane's sole reason for being in California was to help her parents. If she was going to be here, she wanted to feel she was making some contribution to her father's recovery. Since their conversation two days ago, he'd tried to rely on her less, insisting she spend more time with her children. But the fewer demands her father made on her, the more her mother seemed to cling. Any talk of returning to Texas was met with immediate resistance.

"I'll stay with your dad this morning while you go to the beach," her mother said. "Then we can meet at the hospital, and I'll take the children home for their naps."

Jane agreed and Paul gave a shout of glee. Mary Ann, who was sitting in the high chair, clapped her hands, although she couldn't possibly have known what her brother was celebrating.

"Mom, once we get the test results, I really need to think about going home. I'm needed back in Promise."

Stephanie Dickinson's smile faded. "I know you are," she said with a sigh. "It's been so wonderful having you here…."

"Yes, but—"

"I can't tell you how much my grandkids have helped me cope."

"I'm sure that's true." Her mother made it difficult to press the issue. Whenever Jane brought up the subject of leaving, Stephanie found an even stronger reason for her to remain "a few extra days." Jane had already spent far more time away than she'd intended.

"We'll find out about Dad's test results this afternoon, and if things look okay, I'm booking a flight home."

Her mother lifted Mary Ann from the high chair and held her close. "Don't worry, honey," she said tearfully. "Your father and I will be fine."

"Mother. Are you trying to make me feel guilty?"

Stephanie blinked as if she'd never heard anything more preposterous. "Why would you have any reason to feel guilty?" she asked.

Why, indeed. "I miss my life in Texas, Mom— anyway, Derek's here," she said, mentioning her younger brother, who to this point had left everything in Jane's hands. Five years younger, Derek was involved in his own life. He worked in the movie industry as an assistant casting director and had a different girlfriend every time Jane saw him. Derek came for brief visits, but it was clear that the emotional aspects of dealing with their parents' situation were beyond him.

"Of course you need to get back," her mother stated calmly as she reached for a bowl and set it on the table for Paul, along with a carton of milk.

The child opened the cereal box and filled his bowl, smiling proudly at accomplishing this feat by himself. Afraid of what would happen if he attempted to pour his own milk, Jane did it for him.

"I want you to brush your teeth as soon as you're finished your breakfast," she told him. Taking Mary Ann with her, she left the kitchen to get ready for a morning at the beach.

Just as she'd hoped, the tests that afternoon showed some improvement. Jane was thrilled for more reasons than the obvious. Without discussing it, she called the airline and booked a flight home, then informed her parents as matter-of-factly as possible.

Stephanie Dickinson went out that evening for a meeting with her church women's group—the first social event she'd attended since Harry's accident. A good sign, in her daughter's opinion. Jane welcomed the opportunity to pack her bags and prepare for their return. Paul moped around the bedroom while she waited for a phone call from Cal. She'd promised her son he could speak to his father, but wondered if that had been wise. Paul was already tired and cranky, and since Cal was attending a Cattlemen's Association meeting, he wouldn't be back until late.

"I want to go to the beach again," he said, pouting.

"We will soon," Jane promised. "Aren't you excited about seeing Daddy?"

Paul's lower lip quivered as he nodded. "Can Daddy go to the beach with us?"

"He will one day."

That seemed to appease her son, and Jane got him settled with crayons and a Disney coloring book.

When the phone finally rang, she leaped for it, expecting to hear her husband's voice. Eager to hear it.

"Hello," she said. "Cal?"

"It's me." He sounded reserved, as if he wasn't sure what kind of reception he'd get.

"Hello, you," she said warmly.

"You're coming home?"

"Tomorrow."

"Oh, honey, you don't know what good news that is!"

"I do know. I'll give you the details in a minute. Talk to Paul first, would you?"

"Paul's still up? It's after nine, your time."

"It's been a long day. I took the kids to the beach this morning, and then this afternoon I was at the hospital with my dad when we got the test results." She took a deep breath. "Anyway, I'll explain later. Here's Paul."

She handed her son the receiver and stepped back while he chatted with his father. The boy described their hours at the beach, then gave her the receiver again. "Daddy says he wants to talk to you now."

"All right," she said. "Give me a kiss good-night and go to bed, okay? We have to get up early tomorrow."

Paul stood on tiptoe and she bent down to receive a loud kiss. Not arguing, the boy trotted down the hallway to the bedroom he shared with Mary Ann. Jane waited long enough to make sure he went in.

"I've got the flight information, if you're ready to write it down," she said.

"Yup—pen in hand," Cal told her happily. Hearing the elation in his voice was just the balm she needed.

She read off the flight number and time of arrival, then felt obliged to add, "I know things have been strained between us lately and—"

"I'm sorry, Jane," he said simply. "It's my fault."

"I was about to apologize to you," she said, loving him, anticipating their reunion.

"It's just that I miss you so much."

"I've missed you, too." Jane sighed and closed her eyes. They spoke on the phone nearly every night, but lately their conversations had been tainted by the frustration they both felt with their predicament. She'd wanted sympathy and understanding; he'd been looking for the same. They tended to keep their phone calls brief.

"I have a sneaking suspicion your mother's been spoiling the kids."

"She sees them so seldom…" Jane started to offer an excuse, then decided they could deal with the subject of their children's routines later.

"Your dad's tests—how were they?" Cal asked.

"Well, put it this way. His doctors are cautiously optimistic. So Dad's feeling a lot more positive."

"Your mother, too?"

"Yes." Despite Stephanie's emotional dependence on her, Jane admired the courage her mother had shown in the past few weeks. Seeing her husband in the hospital, learning that he'd been diagnosed with cancer, was a terrifying experience. At least, the situation seemed more hopeful now.

"I'll be at the airport waiting for you," Cal promised. "Oh, honey, I can't tell you how good it's going to be to have you back."

"I imagine you're starved for a home-cooked meal," Jane teased.

"It isn't your cooking I miss as much as just having my wife at home," Cal said.

"So you're eating well, are you?"

"I'm eating." From the evasive way he said it, she knew that most of his dinners consisted of something thrown quickly together.

"I'll see you tomorrow," Jane whispered. "At five o'clock."

"Tomorrow at five," Cal echoed, "and that's none too soon."

Jane couldn't agree more.

Cal was in a good mood. By noon, he'd called it quits for the day; ten minutes later he was in the shower. He shaved, slapped on the aftershave Jane liked and donned a crisp clean shirt. He was ready to leave for San Antonio to pick up his family. His steps lightened as he passed the bedroom, and he realized he'd be sharing the bed with his wife that very night. He hesitated at the sight of the disheveled and twisted sheets. Jane had some kind of obsession with changing the bed linens every week. She'd been away almost three weeks now and he hadn't made the bed even once. She'd probably appreciate clean sheets.

He stripped the bed and piled the dirty sheets on top of the washer. The laundry-room floor was littered with numerous pairs of mud-caked jeans and everything else he'd dirtied in the time she'd been away. No need to run a load, he figured; Jane liked things done her own way. He'd never known that a woman could be so particular about laundry.

The kitchen wasn't in terrific shape, either, and Cal regretted not using the dishwasher more often. Until that very moment, he hadn't given the matter of house-cleaning a second thought. He hurriedly straightened the kitchen and wiped the countertops. Housework had never been his forte, and Jane was a real stickler about order and cleanliness. When he'd lived with his brother, they'd divided the tasks; Cal did most of the cooking and Glen was in charge of the dishes. During the weeks his wife was away, Cal hadn't done much of either.

Still, he hadn't been totally remiss. He'd washed Savannah's and Dovie's dishes. Nicole Nelson's, too. He grabbed his good beige Stetson and started to leave yet again, but changed his mind.

He didn't have a thing to feel guilty about—but if Jane learned that Nicole had brought him a casserole, she'd be upset, particularly since he'd never mentioned it. That might look bad. He hadn't *meant* to keep it from her, but they'd been sidetracked by other concerns, and then they'd had their little spat. He'd decided just to let it go.

All Cal wanted was his wife and family home. That didn't strike him as unreasonable—especially when he heard about the way she seemed to be spending her days. How necessary was it to take the kids to Disneyland? Okay, once, maybe, but they'd gone three or four times. He'd lost count of their trips to the beach. This wasn't supposed to be a vacation. He immediately felt guilty about his lack of generosity. She'd had a lot of responsibility and he shouldn't begrudge her these excursions. Besides, she'd had to entertain the kids *somehow.*

Collecting the clean casserole dishes, Cal stuck them in the backseat of his car. He'd return them now, rather than risk having Jane find the dish that belonged to Nicole Nelson.

His first stop was at the home of Savannah and Laredo Smith. After a few minutes of searching, he found his neighbor in one of her rose gardens, winterizing the plants. They'd grown up next door to each other, and Savannah's brother, Grady Weston, had been Cal's closest friend his entire life.

Savannah, who'd been piling compost around the base of a rosebush, straightened when he pulled into the yard. She'd already started toward him by the time he climbed out of the car.

"Well, hello, Cal," she said, giving him a friendly hug.

"Thought I'd bring back your dish. I want you to know how much I appreciated the meal."

Savannah pressed her forearm against her moist brow. "I was glad to do it. I take it Jane'll be home soon?"

"This afternoon." He glanced at his watch and saw that he still had plenty of time.

"That's wonderful! How's her father doing?"

"Better," he said. He didn't want to go into all the complexities and details right now; he'd leave that for Jane.

"I should go," he told her. "I've got a couple of other stops to make before I head to the airport."

"Give Jane my best," Savannah said. "Ask her to call me when she's got a minute."

Cal nodded and set off again. His next stop was Dovie and Frank Hennessey's place. Besides a chicken pot pie, Dovie had baked him dessert—an apple pie. It was the best meal he'd eaten the whole time Jane was in California. Dovie had a special recipe she used for her crust that apparently included buttermilk. She'd passed it on to Jane, but despite several attempts, his wife's pie crust didn't compare with Dovie Hennessey's. But then, no one's did.

Frank answered the door and gave him a smile of welcome. "Hey, Cal! Good to see you." He held open the back door and Cal stepped inside.

"You, too, Frank." Cal passed him the ceramic pie plate and casserole dish. "I'm on my way to the airport to pick up Jane and the kids."

"So that's why you're wearing a grin as wide as the Rio Grande."

"Wider," Cal said. "Can't wait to have 'em back."

"Did Phil catch up with you?" Frank asked.

"Dad's looking for me?"

Frank nodded. "Last I heard."

"I guess I should find out what he wants," Cal said. He had enough time, since it was just after two and Jane's flight wasn't due until five. Even if it took him a couple of hours hours to drive to the airport, he calculated, he should get there before the plane landed. Still, he'd have to keep their visit brief.

Frank nodded again; he seemed about to say something else, then apparently changed his mind.

"What?" Cal asked, standing on the porch.

Frank shook his head. "Nothing. This is a matter for you and your dad."

Cal frowned. He had to admit he was curious. If his father had something to talk over with him, Cal wondered why he hadn't just phoned. From Frank and Dovie's house, Cal drove down Elm Street to the seniors' residence. He found his father involved in a quiet game of chess with Bob Miller, a retired newspaperman.

"Hello, Cal," Phil murmured, raising his eyes from the board.

"Frank Hennessey said you wanted to see me," Cal said abruptly. "Hi, Bob," he added. He hadn't intended any rudeness, but this was all making him a bit nervous.

Phil stared at him. "Frank said that, did he?"

"I brought back Dovie's dishes, and Frank answered the door. If you want to talk to me, Dad, all you need to do is call."

"I know, I know." Phil stood and smiled apologetically at Bob. "I'll be back in a few minutes."

Bob was studying the arrangement of chess pieces. "Take all the time you need," he said without looking up.

Phil surveyed the lounge, but there was no privacy to be had there. Cal checked his watch again, thinking he should preface their conversation with the news that he was on his way to the airport. Before he had a chance to explain why he was in town—and why he couldn't stay long—his father shocked him by saying, "I want to know what's going on between you and Nicole Nelson."

"Nicole Nelson?" Cal echoed.

Phil peered over his shoulder. "Perhaps the best place to have this discussion is my apartment."

"There's nothing to discuss," Cal said, his jaw tightening.

Phil ignored him and marched toward the elevator. "You take back her dinner dishes yet?" he pried. "Or have you advanced to sharing candlelit meals?"

Cal nearly swallowed his tongue. His father knew Nicole had brought him dinner. How? Glen wasn't one to waste time on idle gossip. Nor was Ellie. He didn't like to think it was common knowledge or that the town was feasting on this tasty tidbit.

His father's apartment consisted of a small living area with his own television and a few bookcases. His mother's old piano took up one corner. Double glass doors led to the bedroom and an adjoining bath. Although he didn't play the piano, Phil hadn't sold it when Cal's mother died. Instead, he used the old upright to display family photographs.

He walked over to a photo of Cal with Jane and the

two children, taken shortly after Mary Ann's birth. "You have a good-looking family, son."

Cal knew his father was using this conversation to lead into whatever nonsense was on his mind. Hard as it was, he kept his mouth shut.

"It'd be a shame to risk your marriage over a woman like Nicole Nelson."

"Dad, I'm *not* risking my marriage! There's nothing to this rumor. The whole thing's been blown out of proportion. Who told you she'd been out to the ranch?"

"Does it matter?" Phil challenged.

"Is this something folks are talking about?" That was Cal's biggest fear. He didn't want Jane returning to Promise and being subjected to a torrent of malicious gossip.

"I heard the two of you were seen together at the Mexican Lindo, too."

"Dad!" Cal cried, yanking off his hat to ram his fingers through his hair. "It wasn't *like* that. I was eating alone and Nicole happened to be there at the same time."

"She sat with you, didn't she?"

"For a while. She was meeting someone else."

Phil's frown darkened. "She didn't eat with you, but you bought her a drink, right?"

Reluctantly Cal nodded. He'd done nothing wrong; surely his father could see that.

"People saw you and Nicole in the Mexican Lindo. These things get around. Everyone in town knows she brought you a meal, but it wasn't Glen or Ellie who told them."

"Then who did?" Even as he asked the question, the answer dawned on Cal. He sank onto the sofa that had once stood in the library of his parents' bed-and-break-fast. "Nicole," he breathed, hardly able to believe she'd do something like that.

Phil nodded. "Must be. Frank thinks she's looking to make trouble." He paused, frowning slightly. "Dovie doesn't seem to agree. She thinks we're not being fair to Nicole."

"What do *you* think?" Cal asked his father. None of this made any sense to him.

Phil shrugged. "I don't know Nicole, but I don't like what I've heard. Be careful, son. You don't want to lose what's most important over nothing. Use your common sense."

"I didn't seek her out, if that's what you're thinking," Cal said angrily.

"Did I say you had?"

This entire situation was out of control. If he'd known that recommending Nicole for a job at the bookstore would lead to this, he wouldn't have said a word. It didn't help any that Jane's best friend, Annie Porter, owned Tumbleweed Books, although he assumed Annie would show some discretion. He could trust her to believe him—but even if she didn't, Annie would never say or do anything to hurt Jane.

"You plan on seeing Nicole again?"

"I didn't plan on seeing her the first time," Cal shot back. "I don't have any reason to see her."

"Good. Keep it that way."

Cal didn't need his father telling him something so obvious. Not until he reached the car did he remember the casserole dish. With his father's warning still ringing in his ears, he decided that returning it to Nicole could wait. When he had a chance, he'd tuck the dish in the cab of his pickup and drop it off at the bookstore. Besides, he no longer had the time. Because of this un-expected delay with his father, he'd have to hurry if he wanted to get to the airport before five.

Despite the likelihood that he'd now be facing rush-hour traffic, he had to smile.

His wife and family were coming home.

Exhausted, Jane stepped off the plane, balancing Mary Ann on her hip. The baby had fussed the entire flight, and Jane was pretty sure she had an ear infection. Her skin was flushed and she was running a fever and tugging persistently at her ear.

With Mary Ann crying during most of the flight, Paul hadn't taken his nap and whined for the last hour, wanting to know when he'd see his daddy again. Jane's own nerves were at the breaking point and she pitied her fellow passengers, although fortunately the plane had been half-empty.

"Where's Daddy?" Paul said as they exited the jetway.

"He'll be here," Jane assured her son. "He'll meet us at the entrance." The diaper bag slipped off her shoulder and tangled with her purse strap, weighing down her arm.

"I don't see Daddy," Paul cried, more loudly this time.

"Just wait, okay?"

"I don't want to wait," Paul complained. He crossed his arms defiantly. "I'm *tired* of waiting. I want my daddy."

"Paul, please, I need you to be my helper."

Mary Ann started to cry, tugging at her ear again. Jane did what she could to comfort her daughter, but it was clear the child was in pain. She had Children's Tylenol with her, but it was packed in the luggage. The checked luggage, of course.

She made her way to the baggage area; she'd get their suitcases, then she could at least take out the medication for Mary Ann.

With the help of a friendly porter, she collected the bags and brought them over to the terminal entrance, looking around for her husband. No Cal anywhere. She opened the smaller bag to get the Tylenol. She found it just as she heard her name announced over the broadcast system.

"That must be your father," she told Paul.

"I want my daddy!" the boy shrieked again.

Jane wanted Cal, too—and when she saw him she intended to let him know she was not pleased. She located a house phone, dragged over her bags and, kids in tow, breathlessly picked up the receiver.

She was put through to Cal.

"Where the hell are you?" he snapped.

"Where the hell are *you?*" She was tempted to remind him that she had two suitcases and two children to worry about, plus assorted other bags. The only items he had to carry were his wallet and car keys. She'd appreciate a little help!

"I'm waiting for you at the entrance," he told her a little more calmly.

"So am I," she said, her voice puzzled.

"You aren't at Terminal 1."

"No, I'm at 2! That's where I'm supposed to be." She tried to restrain her frustration. "How on earth could you get that wrong?"

"Stay right there and I'll meet you," Cal promised, sounding anxious.

Ten minutes later Paul gave a loud cry. "Daddy! Daddy!"

There he was. Cal strolled toward them, a wide grin on his face as Paul raced in his direction. He looked wonderful, Jane had to admit. Tanned and relaxed, tall and lean. At the moment all she felt was exhausted. He reached down and scooped Paul into his arms, lifting him high. The boy wrapped his arms around Cal's neck and hugged him fiercely.

"Welcome home," Cal said. Still holding Paul, he pulled her and the baby into his arms and embraced them.

"What happened?" Jane asked. "Where were you?"

"Kiss me first," he said, lowering his head to hers. The kiss was long and potent, and it told Jane in no uncertain terms how happy he was to have her back.

"I'm so glad to be home," she whispered.

"I'm glad you are, too." He put his son back on the floor and Paul gripped his hand tightly. "I'm sorry about the mixup." Cal shook his head. "I gave myself plenty of time, but I stopped off to see my dad and got a later start than I wanted. And then traffic was bad. And *then*

I obviously wasn't thinking straight and I went to the wrong terminal."

Jane sighed. Knowing she was going to have her hands full, he might've been a bit more thoughtful.

The hour and a half ride into Promise didn't go smoothly, either. Keyed up and refusing to sleep, Paul was on his worst behavior. Mary Ann's medication took almost an hour to kick in, and until then, she cried and whimpered incessantly. Jane's nerves were stretched to the limit. Cal tried to distract both children with his own renditions of country classics, but he had little success.

When he pulled into the driveway, Jane gazed at the house with a sense of homecoming that nearly brought tears to her eyes. It'd been an emotional day from the first. Her mother had broken down when she dropped Jane and the kids off at LAX; seeing their grandmother weep, both children had begun to cry, too. Then the flight and Mary Ann's fever and her difficulties at the airport. Instead of the loving reunion she'd longed for with Cal, there'd been one more disappointment.

"You and the kids go inside, and I'll get the luggage," Cal told her.

"All right." Jane unfastened her now-sleeping daughter from the car seat and held her against one shoulder.

Paul followed. "How come Daddy's going to his truck?" he asked.

Jane glanced over her shoulder. "I don't know." He seemed to be carrying something, but she couldn't see what and, frankly, she didn't care.

What Jane expected when she walked into the house

was the same sense of welcome and familiar comfort. Instead, she walked into the kitchen—and found chaos. Dishes were stacked in the sink and three weeks' worth of mail was piled on the kitchen table. The garbage can was overflowing. Jane groaned and headed down the hallway. Dirty clothes littered the floor in front of the washer and dryer.

Attempting to take a positive view of the situation, Jane guessed this proved how much Cal needed her, how much she'd been missed.

She managed to keep her cool until she reached their bedroom. The bed was torn apart, the bedspread and blankets scattered across the floor, and that was her undoing. She proceeded to their daughter's room and gently set Mary Ann in her crib; fortunately she didn't wake up. Jane returned to the kitchen and met Cal just as he was walking in the back door with the last of her bags.

Hands on her hips, she glared at him. "You couldn't make the bed?"

"Ah…" He looked a bit sheepish. "I thought you'd want clean sheets."

"I do, but after three hours on a plane dealing with the kids, I didn't want to have to change them myself."

"Mommy! I'm hungry."

Jane had completely forgotten about dinner.

"The house is, uh, kind of a mess, isn't it?" Cal said guiltily. "I'm sorry, honey, my standards aren't as high as yours."

Rather than get involved in an argument, Jane went

to the linen closet for a clean set of sheets. "Could you fix Paul a sandwich?" she asked.

"Sure."

"I want tuna fish and pickles," Paul said.

"I suppose your mother let him eat anytime he wanted," Cal grumbled.

Stephanie had, but that was beside the point. "Let's not get into this now," she said.

"Fine."

By the time Jane finished unpacking, sorting through the mail and separating laundry, it was nearly midnight. Cal helped her make the bed. He glanced repeatedly in her direction, looking apologetic.

"I'm sorry, honey," he said again.

Jane didn't want to argue, but this homecoming had fallen far short of what she'd hoped. At least Mary Ann was sleeping soundly. But without a nap, Paul had been out of sorts. Cal had put him down and returned a few minutes later complaining that his son had turned into a spoiled brat.

Jane had had enough. "Don't even start," she warned him.

He raised both hands. "All right, all right."

They barely spoke afterward.

At last Cal undressed and slipped between the fresh sheets. "You ready for bed?"

Exhausted, Jane merely nodded; she didn't have the energy to speak.

He held out his arms, urging her to join him, and one look told her what he had in mind.

Jane hesitated. "I hope you're not thinking what I suspect you're thinking."

"Honey," he pleaded, "it's been nearly three weeks since we made love."

Jane sagged onto the side of the bed. "Not tonight."

Cal looked crestfallen. "Okay, I guess I asked for that. You're upset about the house being a mess, aren't you?"

"I'm not punishing you, if that's what you're saying." Couldn't he see she was nearly asleep on her feet?

"Sure, whatever," he muttered. Jerking the covers past his shoulder, he rolled over and presented her with a view of his back.

"Oh, Cal, stop it," she said, tempted to shake him. He was acting like a spoiled little boy—like their own son when he didn't get what he wanted. At this point, though, Jane didn't care. She undressed and turned off the light. Tired as she was, she assumed she'd be asleep the instant her head hit the pillow.

She wasn't.

Instead, she lay awake in the dark, wondering how their reunion could possibly have gone so wrong.

Five

To say that Jane's kitchen cupboards were bare would be an understatement. One of her first chores the next morning was to buy groceries. Cal kept Paul with him for the day, instead of taking him to pre-school, and Jane buckled Mary Ann into her car seat and drove to town.

She was grateful to be home, grateful to wake up with her husband at her side and grateful that the unpleasantness of the night before seemed to be forgotten. With the washer and dryer humming and the children well rested, the day looked brighter all the way around. Even Mary Ann seemed to be feeling better, and a quick check of her ears revealed no infection.

Although she had a whole list of things to do, Jane took time to go and see Ellie. Later, when she'd finished with her errands, she planned to make a quick run over to Annie's.

"You look…" Ellie paused as she met Jane outside Frasier Feed.

"Exhausted," Jane filled in for her. "I'm telling you, Ellie, this time away was no vacation."

"I know," Ellie said, steering her toward the old-fashioned rockers positioned in front. "I remember what it was like. With my dad sick and my mother frantic, it was all I could do to keep myself sane."

Jane wished Cal understood how trying and difficult these weeks had been for her. He *should* know, seeing that his own mother had been so terribly ill, but then, Phil had protected his sons from the truth for far too long.

"I'm glad you're home." Ellie sank into one of the rockers.

"Me, too." Jane sat down beside her friend, balancing Mary Ann on her knee. She loved sitting right here with Ellie, looking out at the town park and at the street; she'd missed their chats. She could smell mesquite smoke from the Chili Pepper. California cuisine had nothing on good old Texas barbecue, she decided, her mouth watering at the thought of ribs dripping with tangy sauce. A bowl of Nell Grant's famous chili wouldn't go amiss, either.

"Everything will be better now," Ellie said.

Jane stared at her friend. "Better? How do you mean?"

Ellie's gaze instantly shot elsewhere. "Oh, nothing... I was thinking out loud. I'm just pleased you're back."

Jane was a little puzzled but let Ellie's odd remark slide. They talked about friends and family and planned a lunch date, then Jane left to get her groceries.

Buy-Right Foods had built a new supermarket on the outskirts of town, and it boasted one of the finest

produce and seafood selections in the area. The day it
opened, everyone in the county had shown up for the big
event—not to mention the music, the clowns who
painted kids' faces and, not least, the generous assortment of free samples. There hadn't been a parking space
in the lot, which had occasioned plenty of complaints.
People didn't understand that this kind of congestion
was a way of life in California. Jane had forgotten what
it was like to wait through two cycles at a traffic light
just to make a left-turn lane. A traffic jam in Promise
usually meant two cars at a stop sign.

Grabbing a cart at the Buy-Right, she fastened Mary
Ann into the seat and headed down the first aisle.
Everyone who saw Jane seemed to stop and chat, welcome
her home. At this rate, it'd take all day to get everything
on her list. Actually she didn't mind. If Cal had shown half
the enthusiasm her friends and neighbors did, the unpleasantness the night before might have been averted.

"Jane Dickinson—I mean, Patterson! Aren't you a
sight for sore eyes."

Jane recognized the voice immediately. Tammy Lee
Kollenborn. The woman was a known flirt and troublemaker. Jane tended to avoid her, remembering the grief
Tammy had caused Dovie several years earlier. After a
ten-year relationship, Dovie had wanted to get married
and Frank hadn't. Then, for some ridiculous reason,
Frank had asked Tammy Lee out. The night had been a
disaster, and shortly afterward Frank had proposed to
Dovie—although not before Tammy Lee had managed
to upset Dovie with her lies and insinuations.

"Hello, Tammy Lee."

The older woman's gold heels made flip-flop sounds as she pushed her cart alongside Jane's. "My, your little one sure is a cutie-pie." She peered at Mary Ann through her rhinestone-rimmed glasses. "I swear I'd die for lashes that long," she said, winking up at Jane.

Trying to guess Tammy Lee's age was a fruitless effort. She dressed in a style Jane privately called "Texas trash" and wore enough costume jewelry to qualify her for a weight-lifting award.

"From what I hear, it's a good thing you got home when you did," Tammy Lee said.

Jane frowned. "Why?"

Tammy Lee lowered her voice. "You mean to say no one's mentioned what's been going on with Cal and that other woman while you were away?"

Jane pinched her lips. If she was smart, she'd make a convenient excuse and leave without giving Tammy the pleasure of spreading her lies. They *had* to be lies. After five years of marriage, Jane knew her husband, and Cal was not the type of man to cheat on his wife.

"Her name's Nicole Nelson. Pretty little thing. Younger than you by, oh, six or seven years." Tammy Lee studied her critically. "Having children ages a woman. My first husband wanted kids, but I knew the minute I got pregnant I'd eat my way through the whole pregnancy. So I refused."

"Yes, well…listen, Tammy Lee, I've got a lot to do."

"I saw Cal with her myself."

"I really do need to be going—"

"They were having dinner together at the Mexican Lindo."

"Cal and Nicole Nelson?" Jane refused to believe it.

"They were *whispering*. This is a small town, Jane, and people notice these things. Like I said, I'm surprised no one's mentioned it. I probably shouldn't, either, but my fourth husband cheated on me and I would've given anything for someone to tell me sooner. You've heard the saying? The wife is always the last to know."

"I'm sure there's a very logical reason Cal was with Nicole," Jane insisted, not allowing herself to feel jealous. Even if she was, she wouldn't have said anything in front of Tammy Lee.

"When my dear friend finally broke down and told me about Mark seeing another woman, I said the very same thing," Tammy Lee went on. "Wives are simply too trusting. We assume our husbands would never betray us like that."

"I really have a lot to do," Jane said again.

"Now, you listen to me, Jane. Later on, I want you to remember that I'm here for you. I know what you're feeling."

Jane was sure that couldn't be true.

"If you need someone to talk to, come to me. Like I said, I've been down this road myself. If you need a good attorney, I can recommend one in San Antonio. When she's finished with Cal Patterson, he won't have a dime."

"Tammy Lee, I don't have time for this," Jane said, and forcefully pushed her cart forward.

"Call me, you hear?" Tammy Lee gently patted

Jane's shoulder. Jane found it a patronizing gesture and had to grit her teeth.

By the time she'd finished paying for her groceries, she was furious. No one needed to tell her who Nicole Nelson was; Jane had no trouble figuring it out. The other woman had approached Cal the afternoon of the rodeo. Jane had sat in the grandstand with her two children while that woman flirted outrageously with her husband.

For now, Jane was willing to give Cal the benefit of the doubt. But as she loaded the groceries into the car, she remembered Ellie's strange comment about everything being "better" now. So *that* was what her sister-in-law had meant.

The one person she trusted to talk this out with was Dovie. Jane hurried to her friend's antique store, although she couldn't stay long.

Dovie greeted her with a hug. The store looked wonderful, thanks to Dovie's gift for display. Her assortment of antiques, jewelry, dried flowers, silk scarves and more was presented in appealing and imaginative ways.

They chatted a few minutes while Dovie inquired about Jane's parents.

"I ran into Tammy Lee Kollenborn at the grocery store," Jane announced suddenly, watching for Dovie's reaction. It didn't take her long to see one. "So it's true?"

"Now, Jane—"

"Cal's been seeing Nicole Nelson?"

"I wouldn't say that."

"According to Tammy Lee, they were together at the Mexican Lindo. Is that right?"

Hands clenched in front of her, Dovie hesitated, then nodded.

Jane couldn't believe her ears. She felt as though her legs were about to collapse out from under her.

"I'm sure there's a perfectly logical reason," Dovie murmured, and Jane realized she'd said the very same words herself not ten minutes earlier.

"If that's the case, then why didn't Cal mention it?" she demanded, although she didn't expect an answer from Dovie.

The older woman shrugged uncomfortably. "You'll have to ask him."

"Oh, I intend to," Jane muttered as she headed out the door. She'd visit Annie another day. Right now, she was more interested in hearing what Cal had to say for himself.

When she pulled off the highway and hurtled down the long drive to the ranch house, the first thing she noticed was that the screen door was open. Cal and Paul walked out to the back porch to greet her. She saw that her husband's expression was slightly embarrassed, as if he knew he'd done something wrong.

"Don't be mad," he said when she stepped out of the car, "but Paul and I had a small accident."

"What kind of accident?" she asked.

"We decided to make lunch for you and…well, let me just say that I think we can save the pan." A smile started to quiver at the corners of his mouth. "Come on, honey, it's only a pan. I'm sure the smoke will wash off the walls."

"Tell me about Nicole Nelson," Jane said point-blank.

The amusement vanished from his eyes. He stiffened. "What's there to say?"

"Plenty, from what I hear."

"Come on, Jane! You know me better than that."

"Do I?" She glared at him.

"Jane, you're being ridiculous."

"Did you or did you not have dinner with Nicole Nelson?"

Cal didn't answer.

"It's a simple question," she said, growing impatient.

"Yeah, but the answer's complicated."

"I'll bet it is!" Jane was angrier than she'd been in years. If they'd had a wonderful reunion, she might have found the whole matter forgettable. Instead, he hadn't even bothered to show up on time or at the right terminal. The house was a mess and all he could think about was getting her in the sack. She shifted Mary Ann on her hip, grabbed a bag full of groceries and stomped into the house.

"Jane!"

She stood in the doorway. "I have all the answers I need."

"Fine!" Cal shouted, angry now.

"Daddy, Daddy!" Paul cried, covering his ears. "Mommy's mad."

"Is this what you want our son to see?" Cal yelled after her.

"That's just perfect," Jane yelled back. "You're running around town with another woman, you don't offer a word of explanation and then you blame *me* because our son sees us fighting." Hurt, angry and outraged, she stormed into the bedroom.

* * *

It was obvious to Glen that things weren't going well between his brother and Jane. He saw evidence of the trouble in their marriage every morning when he drove to work at the Lonesome Coyote Ranch.

He and Cal were partners, had worked together for years, and if anyone knew that Cal could be unreasonable, it was Glen. More importantly, though, Glen was well aware that his older brother loved his wife and kids.

By late October the demands of raising cattle had peaked for the season, since the greater part of their herd had been sold off. Not that the hours Cal kept gave any indication of that. Most mornings when Glen arrived, Cal had already left the house.

"Are you going to talk about it?" Glen asked him one afternoon. Cal hadn't said more than two words to him all day. They sat side by side in the truck, driving back to the house.

"No," Cal barked.

"This has to do with Jane, right?" Glen asked.

Cal purposely hit a pothole, which made Glen bounce so high in his seat that his head hit the truck roof, squashing the crown of his Stetson.

"Dammit, Cal, there was no call for that," Glen complained, repairing his hat.

"Sorry," Cal returned, but his tone said he was anything but.

"If you can't talk to me, then who can you talk to?" Glen asked. It bothered him that his only brother refused to even acknowledge, let alone discuss, his problems. Over the years Glen had spilled his guts any number of times. More than once Cal had steered him away from trouble. Glen hoped to do him the same favor.

"If I *wanted* to talk, you mean," Cal said.

"In other words, you'd prefer to keep it all to yourself."

"Yup."

"Okay, then, if that's what you want."

They drove for several minutes in tense silence. Finally Glen couldn't stand it anymore. "This is your wife—your *family*. Doesn't that matter to you? What's going on?" He could feel his patience with Cal fading.

Cal grumbled something he couldn't hear. Then he said in a grudging voice, "Jane paid a visit to Tumbleweed Books the other day."

His brother didn't have to explain further. Nicole Nelson worked at the bookstore, and although Jane was a good friend of Annie Porter's, Glen suspected she hadn't casually dropped by to see her.

"She talk to Nicole?"

Cal spoke through clenched teeth. "I don't like my wife checking up on me."

Glen mulled this over and wondered if Cal had explained the situation. "Jane knows you didn't take Nicole to dinner, doesn't she?"

"Yes!" he shouted. "I *told* her what happened. The next thing I know, she's all bent out of shape, slamming pots and pans around the kitchen like I did something terrible."

"Make it up to her," Glen advised. If his brother hadn't learned that lesson by now, it was high time he did.

"I didn't do anything wrong," Cal snapped. "If she doesn't believe me, then…"

"Cal, get real! Do what you've got to do, man. You aren't the only one, you know. Ellie gets a bee in her bonnet every now and then. Darned if I know what I did, but after a while I don't care. I want things settled. I want peace in the valley. Learn from me—apologize and be done with it."

Cal frowned, shaking his head. "I'm not you."

"Pride can make a man pretty miserable," Glen said. "It's…it's like sitting on a barbed-wire fence naked." He nodded, pleased with his analogy.

Cal shook his head again, and Glen doubted his brother had really heard him. Changing the subject, Glen tried another approach. "How's Jane's father?"

"All right, I guess. She talks to her mother nearly every day."

The ranch house came into view. Glen recalled a time not so long ago when they'd reached this same spot and had seen Nicole Nelson's vehicle parked down below. A thought occurred to him, a rather unpleasant one.

"Are you still in love with Jane?" Glen asked.

Cal hit the brakes with enough force to throw them both forward. If not for the restraint of the seat belts, they might have hit their heads on the windshield.

"What kind of question is that?" Cal roared.

"Do you still love Jane?" Glen yelled right back.

"Of course I do!"

Glen relaxed.

"What I want is a wife who trusts me," Cal said. "I

haven't so much as looked at another woman since the day we met, and she damn well knows it."

"Maybe she doesn't."

"Well, she should" was his brother's response.

To Glen's way of thinking, there was plenty a wife should know and often didn't. He figured it was the man's job to set things straight and to make sure his wife had no doubt whatsoever about his feelings.

In the days that followed it was clear that the situation between Jane and Cal hadn't improved. Feeling helpless, Glen decided to seek his father's advice. He found Phil at the bowling alley Friday afternoon, when the senior league was just finishing up. It didn't take much to talk Phil into coffee and a piece of pie. The bowling alley café served the best breakfast in town and was a popular place to eat.

As they slid into the booth, the waitress automatically brought over the coffeepot.

"We'll each have a slice of pecan pie, Denise," Phil told her.

"Coming right up," she said, filling the thick white mugs with an expert hand. "How you doin', Phil? Glen?"

"Good," Glen answered for both of them.

No more than a minute later they were both served generous slices of pie. "Enjoy," she said cheerily.

Phil reached for his fork. "No problem there."

Glen wasn't as quick to grab his own fork. He had a lot on his mind.

"You want to talk to me about something?" Phil asked, busy doctoring his coffee.

Glen left his own coffee black and raised the mug, sipping carefully.

"I didn't think you were willing to buy me a slice of pecan pie for nothing."

Glen chuckled. Of the two sons, he shared his father's temperament. Their mother had been a take-charge kind of woman and Cal got that from her, but she'd never held her hurts close to the chest, the way Cal did.

"I take it you're worried about your brother." Phil picked up his fork again and cut into his pie.

"Yeah." Glen stared down at his favorite dessert and realized he didn't have much of an appetite. "What should I say to him?"

"Listen." Phil leaned forward to rest his elbows on the table. "When your mother was alive and we had the bed-and-breakfast, she was constantly trying new recipes."

Glen couldn't understand what his mother's cooking had to do with the current situation, but he knew better than to ask. Phil would get around to explaining sooner or later.

"No matter what time of day it was, she'd sit down and eat some of whatever new dish she'd just made. When I asked her why, she said it was important to try a little of it herself before she served it to anyone else."

"Okay," Glen said, still wondering about the connection between his mother's culinary experiments and Cal and Jane.

"Advice is like that. Take some yourself before you hand it to others."

"I haven't given Cal any advice." Not for lack of trying, however. Cal simply wasn't in the mood to listen.

"I realize that. The advice is going to come from me, and I'm giving it to you—free of charge."

Glen laughed, shaking his head.

"Let Cal and Jane settle this themselves."

"But, Dad…"

Phil waved his fork at him. "Every couple has problems at one time or another. You and Ellie will probably go through a difficult patch yourselves, and when you do, you won't appreciate other people sticking their noses in your business."

"Do you think Cal and Jane are going to be okay?"

"Of course they are. Cal loves Jane. He won't do anything to jeopardize his family. Now eat your pie, or I just might help myself to a second slice."

Glen picked up his fork. His father knew what he was talking about; Cal did love Jane, and whatever was wrong would eventually right itself.

Jane noticed a change in Cal the moment he came into the house. They'd been ignoring each other all week. The tension was taking its toll, not only on her but on the children.

Cal paused in the middle of the kitchen, where she was busy putting together Halloween costumes for the children. As usual the church was holding a combined harvest and Halloween party.

Jane didn't leave her place at the kitchen table, nor did she speak to Cal. Instead, she waited for him to make the first move, which he did. He walked over to the stove and poured himself a cup of coffee, then approached the table.

"What are you doing?" he asked in a friendly voice.

"Making Mary Ann a costume for the church party." She gestured at a piece of white fabric printed with spots. "She's going as a dalmatian," Jane said.

Cal grinned. "One of the hundred and one?" They'd recently watched the Disney animated feature on DVD.

Jane nodded and held up a black plastic dog nose, complete with elastic tie.

"What about Paul?"

"He's going as a pirate."

Cal cradled his mug in both hands. "Do you mind if I sit here?"

"Please."

He pulled out the chair and set his coffee on the table. For at least a minute, he didn't say another word. When he finally spoke, his voice was low, deliberate. "This whole thing about Nicole Nelson is totally out of control. If you need reassurances, then I'll give them to you. I swear to you not a thing happened."

Jane said nothing. It'd taken him nearly two weeks to tell her what she already knew. His unwillingness to do so earlier had hurt her deeply. In her heart she knew she could trust her husband, but his pride and stubbornness had shut her out.

This situation with Nicole was regrettable. Not wanting to put Annie in the middle—it was awkward with Nicole working at Tumbleweed Books—Jane had asked general questions about the other woman. Annie had told her she liked Nicole. After their talk, Jane was convinced that the encounter between Nicole and Cal, whatever it was, had been completely innocent.

Because they lived in a small town, the story had spread quickly and the truth had gotten stretched out of all proportion; Jane understood that. What troubled her most was Cal's attitude. Instead of answering her questions or reiterating his love, he'd acted as if *she'd* somehow wronged him. Well, she hadn't been out there generating gossip! Still, Jane felt a sense of relief that their quarrel was ending.

She caught her husband staring at her intently.

"Can we put this behind us?" Cal asked.

Jane smiled. "I think it's time, don't you?"

Cal's shoulders relaxed, and he nodded. Seconds later, Jane was in her husband's arms and he was kissing her with familiar passion. "I'm crazy about you, Jane," he whispered, weaving his fingers into her thick hair.

"I don't like it when we fight," she confessed, clinging to him.

"You think I do?" he asked. "Especially over something as stupid as this."

"Oh, Cal," she breathed as he bent to kiss her again.

"Want to put the kids to bed early tonight?"

She nodded eagerly and brought her mouth to his. "Right after dinner."

Afterward, Jane felt worlds better about everything. They'd both been at fault and they both swore it wouldn't happen again.

For the next few days Cal was loving and attentive, and so was Jane, but it didn't take them long to slip back into the old patterns. The first time she became aware of it was the night of the church party.

Amy McMillen, the pastor's wife, had asked Jane to arrive early to assist her in setting up. She'd assumed Cal would be driving her into town. Instead, he announced that he intended to stay home and catch up on paperwork. Jane made sure Cal knew she wanted him to attend the function with her, that she needed his help. Supervising both children, plus assisting with the games, would be virtually impossible otherwise. But she decided not to complain; she'd done so much of that in the past couple of months.

When it came time for her to leave, Cal walked her and the children out to the car. Once she'd buckled the kids into their seats, she started the engine, but Cal stopped her.

"You've got a headlight out."

"I do? Oh, no…"

"I don't want you driving into town with only one headlight."

Jane glanced at her watch.

"Take the truck," he said. "I'll change the car seats."

"But—"

"Sweetheart, please, it'll just take a minute." Fortunately his truck had a large four-door cab with ample space for both seats.

"What's this?" Jane asked. In front, on the passenger side, was a cardboard box with a glass casserole dish.

Cal took one look at it and his eyes rushed to meet hers. "A dish," he muttered.

"Of course it's a dish. *Whose* dish?"

He shrugged as if it was no big deal. "I don't know if I mentioned it, but Dovie and Savannah brought me meals while you were away," he said, wrapping the safety belt around Mary Ann's car seat and snapping it in place.

"You mean to say half the town was feeding you and you still managed to nearly destroy my kitchen?"

Cal chuckled.

"I meant to return the dish." He kissed Jane and closed the passenger door. "I'll see to that headlight first thing tomorrow morning," he promised, and opened the door on the driver's side.

Jane climbed in behind the wheel. Normally she didn't like driving Cal's vehicle, which was high off the ground and had a stick shift. She agreed, however, that in the interests of safety, it was the better choice.

The church was aglow when Jane drove up. Pastor Wade McMillen stood outside, welcoming early arrivals, and when he saw Jane, he walked over and helped her extract Mary Ann from her seat.

"Glad to have you back, Jane," he said. "I hope everything went well with your father."

"He's doing fine," she said, although that wasn't entirely true. She was in daily communication with her mother. It seemed her father wasn't responding to the chemotherapy anymore and grew weaker with every treatment. Her mother was at a loss. Several times she'd broken into tears and asked Jane to talk Cal into letting her and the children come back for a visit over Christmas. Knowing how Cal would feel, she hadn't broached the subject yet.

"Would you like me to carry in that box for you?" Wade asked.

"Please." Both Dovie and Savannah would be at the church party, and there was no reason to keep the casserole dish in the truck.

"I'll put it in the kitchen," Wade told her, leading the way.

Paul saw the display of pumpkins and dried cornstalks in the large meeting room and shouted with delight. Although it was early, the place was hopping with children running in every direction.

Jane followed the pastor into the kitchen, and sure enough, found Dovie there.

"I understand this is yours," Jane said when Wade set the box down on the counter.

Dovie shook her head.

"Didn't you send dinner out to Cal?"

"I did, but he already returned the dishes."

"It must belong to Savannah, then," she said absently.

Not until much later in the evening did Jane see Savannah and learn otherwise. "Well, for heaven's sake," she muttered to Ellie as they were busy with the cleanup. "I don't want to drag this dish back home. Do you know who it belongs to?"

Ellie went suspiciously quiet.

"Ellie?" Jane asked, not understanding at first.

"Ask Cal," her sister-in-law said.

"Cal?" Jane repeated and then it hit her. She knew

exactly who owned that casserole dish. And asking Cal was what she intended to do. Clearly more had gone on while she was away than he'd admitted. How dared he do this to her!

Glen carried the box containing the dish back to the truck for her. Tired from the party, both Paul and Mary Ann fell asleep long before she turned off the highway onto the dirt road that led to the house.

No sooner had she parked the truck than the back door opened and Cal stepped out. Although it was difficult to contain herself, she waited until the children were in bed before she brought up the subject of the unclaimed dish.

"I ran into Dovie and Savannah," she said casually as they walked into the living room, where the television was on. Apparently her husband didn't have as much paperwork as he'd suggested.

"Oh? How was the party?"

Jane ignored the question. "Neither one of them owns that casserole dish."

Jane watched as Cal's shoulders tensed.

"Tell me, Cal, who does own it?"

Not answering, Cal strode to the far side of the room.

"Don't tell me you've forgotten," Jane said.

He shook his head.

A sick feeling was beginning to build in the pit of her stomach. "Cal?"

"Sweetheart, listen—"

"All I want is a name," she interrupted, folding her arms and letting her actions tell him she was in no mood to be cajoled.

Cal started to say something, then stopped.

"You don't need to worry," Jane said without emotion. "I figured it out. That dish belongs to Nicole Nelson."

Six

Cal couldn't believe this was happening. Okay, so his wife had cause to be upset. He should've mentioned that Nicole Nelson had brought him a meal. The only reason he hadn't was that he'd been hoping to avoid yet another argument. He knew how much their disagreements distressed her, and she'd been through so much lately. He was just trying to protect her!

Without a word to him, Jane had gone to bed. Cal gave her a few minutes to cool down before he ventured into the bedroom. The lights were off, but he knew she wasn't asleep.

"Jane," he said, sitting on the edge of the bed. She had her back to him and was so far over on her side it was a wonder she hadn't tumbled out. "Can we talk about this?" he asked, willing to take his punishment and be done with it.

"No."

"You're right, I should've told you Nicole came to the ranch, but I swear she wasn't here more than ten minutes. If that. She brought over the casserole and that was it."

Jane flopped over onto her back. "Are you sure, or is there something *else* you're conveniently forgetting?"

Cal could live without the sarcasm, but let it drop. "I thought we'd decided to put this behind us." He could always hope tonight's installment of their ongoing argument would be quickly settled. The constant tension between them had worn his patience thin.

Jane suddenly bolted upright in bed. She reached for the lamp beside her bed and flipped the switch, casting a warm light about the room. "You have a very bad habit of keeping things from me."

That was unfair! Cal took a deep calming breath before responding. "It's true I didn't tell you Nicole fixed me dinner, but—"

"You didn't so much as mention her name!"

"Okay…but when was I supposed to do that? You were in California, remember?"

"We talked on the phone nearly every night," Jane said, crossing her arms. "Now that I think about it, you kept the conversations short and sweet, didn't you? Was there a reason for that?"

Again, Cal resented the implication, but again he swallowed his annoyance and said, "You know I'm not much of a conversationalist." Chatting on the phone had always felt awkward to him. That certainly wasn't news to Jane.

"What else haven't you told me about Nicole Nelson? How many other times have you two met without my knowing? When she brought you dinner, did she make a point of joining you? Did you *accidentally* bump into each other in town?"

"No," he answered from between gritted teeth.

"You're sure?"

"You make it sound like I'm having an affair with her! I've done nothing wrong, not a damn thing!"

"Tell me why I should believe you, seeing how you habitually conceal things from me."

"You think I purposely hid the truth?" Their marriage was in sad shape if she made such assumptions. Jane was his partner in life; he'd shared every aspect of his business, his home and his ranch with her, fathered two children with her. It came as a shock that she didn't trust him.

"What about the rodeo?" she asked. "You signed up for the bull-riding competition and you deliberately didn't tell me."

"I knew you didn't want me participating in the rodeo and—"

"What I don't know won't hurt me, right?"

She had a way of twisting his words into knots no cowhand could untangle, himself included. "Okay, fine, you win. I'm a rotten husband. That's what you want to hear, isn't it?"

Her eyes flared and she shook her head. "What I want to hear is the truth."

"I tell you the truth!" he shouted, losing his temper.

"But not until you're backed into a corner."

"I've been as honest with you as I know how." Cal tried again, but he'd reached his limit. Glen had advised him to say what he had to say, do what he had to do—whatever it took to make up with Jane. He'd attempted that once already, but it hadn't been enough. Not only wasn't she satisfied, now she was looking to collect a piece of his soul along with that pound of flesh.

"Why didn't you attend the church party with me and the kids?" she asked.

He frowned. Jane knew the answer to that as well as he did. "I told you. I had paperwork to do."

"How long did it take you?"

Cal ran a hand down his face. "Is there a reason you're asking?"

"A very good one," she informed him coolly. "I'm trying to find out if you slipped away to be with Nicole."

Cal couldn't have been more staggered if his wife had pulled out a gun and shot him. He jumped off the bed and stood there staring, dumbstruck that Jane would actually suggest such a thing.

"I noticed you had the television on," she continued. "So you finished with all that paperwork earlier than you expected. Did you stop to think about me coping with the children alone? Or did you just want an evening to yourself—while I managed the children, the party and everything else on my own."

"Would you listen to yourself?" he muttered.

"I *am* listening," she shouted. "You sent me off to California with the kids, then you're seen around town with another woman. If *that* isn't enough, you lie and mislead me into thinking I'm overreacting. All at once everything's beginning to add up, and frankly I don't like the total. You're interested in having an affair with her, aren't you, Cal? That's what I see."

Cal had no intention of commenting on anything so ludicrous.

"What's the matter? Am I too close to the truth?"

Shaking his head, Cal looked down at her, unable to hide his disgust. "Until this moment I've never regretted marrying you." He headed out the door, letting it slam behind him.

Almost immediately the bedroom door flew open again. "You think *I* don't have regrets about marrying *you?*" Jane railed. "You're not alone in that department, Cal Patterson." Once again the door slammed with such force that he was sure he'd have to nail the molding back in place.

Not knowing where to go or what else to say, Cal stood in the middle of the darkened living room. In five years of marriage he and Jane had disagreed before, but never like this. He glanced toward their bedroom and knew there'd be hell to pay if he tried to sleep there.

Cal sat in his recliner, raised the footrest and covered himself with the afghan he'd grabbed from the back of the sofa.

Everything would be better in the morning, he told himself.

Cal had left the house by the time Jane got up. It was what she'd expected. What she *wanted,* she told herself. Luckily the children had been asleep and hadn't heard them fighting. She removed her robe from the back of the door and slipped it on. Sick at heart, she felt as though she hadn't slept all night.

The coffee was already made when she wandered into the kitchen. She was just pouring herself a cup when Paul appeared, dragging his favorite blanket.

"Where's Daddy?" he asked, rubbing his eyes.

"He's with Uncle Glen." Jane crouched down to give her son a hug.

Paul pulled away and met her look, his dark eyes sad. "Is Daddy mad at you?"

"No, darling, Daddy and Mommy love each other very much." She was certain Cal felt as sorry about the argument as she did. She reached for her son and hugged him again.

Their fight had solved nothing. They'd both said things that should never have been said. The sudden tears that rushed into Jane's eyes were unexpected, and she didn't immediately realize she was crying. The children *had* heard their argument. At least Paul must have, otherwise he wouldn't be asking these questions.

"Mommy?" Paul touched his fingers to her face, noticed her tears, then broke away and raced into the other room. He returned a moment later with a box of tissues, which made Jane weep all the more. How could her beautiful son be so thoughtful and sweet, and his father so insensitive, so unreasonable?

After making breakfast for Paul and Mary Ann and getting them dressed, Jane loaded the stroller and diaper bag into the car and prepared to drive her son to preschool. The truck was parked where she'd left it the night before. Apparently Cal had gone out on Fury, his favorite gelding. He often rode when he needed time to think.

Peering into the truck, Jane saw that the casserole dish was still there. She looked at it for a moment, then took it out and placed it in the car. While Paul was in his preschool class, she'd personally return it to Nicole Nelson. And when she did, Jane planned to let her know how happily married Cal Patterson was.

After dropping Paul off, Jane drove to Tumbleweed Books. Cal had indeed replaced her headlight, just as he'd promised, and for some reason that almost made her cry again.

"Hello," Nicole Nelson called out when Jane walked into the bookstore. Jane recognized her right away. The previous time she'd seen the other woman had been at the rodeo, and that was from a distance. On closer inspection, she had to admit that Nicole was beautiful. Jane, by contrast, felt dowdy and unkempt. She wished she'd made more of an effort with her hair and makeup, especially since she'd decided to meet Nicole face-to-face.

"Is there anything I can help you find?" Nicole asked, glancing at Mary Ann in her stroller.

"Is Annie available?" Jane asked, making a sudden decision that when she did confront Nicole, she'd do it looking her best.

"I'm sorry, Annie had a doctor's appointment this morning. I'd be delighted to assist you if I can."

So polite and helpful. So insincere. Jane didn't even know Nicole Nelson, and already she disliked her.

"That's all right. I'll come back another time." Feeling foolish, Jane was eager to leave.

"I don't think we've met," Nicole said. "I'm Annie's new sales assistant, Nicole Nelson."

Jane had no option but to introduce herself. She straightened and looked directly at Nicole. "I'm Jane Patterson."

"Cal's wife," Nicole said, not missing a beat. A knowing smile appeared on her face as she boldly met Jane's eye.

Standing no more than two feet apart, Jane and Nicole stared hard at each other. In that moment Jane knew the awful truth. Nicole Nelson wanted her husband. Wanted him enough to destroy Jane and ruin her marriage. Wanted him enough to deny his children their father. Cal was a challenge to her, a prize to be won, no matter what the cost.

"I believe I have something of yours," Jane said.

Nicole's smile became a bit cocky. "I believe you do."

"Luckily I brought the casserole dish with me," Jane returned just as pointedly. She bent down, retrieved it from the stroller and handed it to Nicole.

"Did Cal happen to mention if he liked my taco casserole?" Nicole asked, following Jane to the front of the bookstore.

"Oh," Jane murmured, ever so sweetly, "he said it was much too spicy for him."

"I don't think so," Nicole said, opening one of the doors. "I think Cal might just find he prefers a bit of spice compared to the bland taste he's used to."

Fuming, Jane pushed Mary Ann's stroller out the door and discovered, when she reached the car, that her hands were trembling. This was even worse than she'd thought it would be. Because now she had reason to wonder if her husband had fallen willingly into the other woman's schemes.

Jane had a knot in her stomach for the rest of the day. She was sliding a roast into the oven as Cal walked into the house at four-thirty—early for him. He paused when he saw her, then lowered his head and walked past, ignoring her.

"I...think we should talk," she said, closing the oven, then leaning weakly against it. She set the pot holders aside and forced herself to straighten.

"Now?" Cal asked, as though any discussion with her was an unpleasant prospect.

"Paul...heard us last night," she said. She glanced into the other room, where their son was watching a children's nature program. Mary Ann sat next to him, tugging at her shoes and socks.

"It's not surprising he heard us," Cal said evenly. "You nearly tore the door off the hinges when you slammed it."

Cal had slammed the door first, but now didn't seem to be the time to point that out. "He had his blankey this morning."

"I thought you threw that thing away," Cal said, making it sound like an accusation.

"He...found it. Obviously he felt he needed it."

Cal's eyes narrowed, and she knew he'd seen through her explanation.

"That isn't important. What *is* important, at least to me," she said, pressing her hand to her heart, "is that we not argue in front of the children."

"So you're saying we can go into the barn and shout at each other all we want? Should we arrange for a baby-sitter first?"

Jane reached behind her to grab hold of the oven door. The day had been bad enough, and she wanted only to repair the damage that had been done to their relationship. This ongoing dissatisfaction with each other seemed to be getting worse; Jane knew it had to stop.

"I don't think I slept five minutes last night," she whispered.

Cal said nothing.

"I...I don't know what's going on between you and Nicole Nelson, but—"

Cal started to walk away from her.

"Cal!" she cried, stopping him.

"Nothing, Jane. There's nothing going on between me and Nicole Nelson. I don't know how many times I have to say it, and frankly, I'm getting tired of it."

Jane swallowed hard but tried to remain outwardly calm. "She wants you."

Cal's response was a short disbelieving laugh. "That's crazy."

Jane shook her head. There'd been no mistaking what she'd read in the other woman's expression. Nicole had decided to pursue Cal and was determined to do whatever she could to get him. Jane had to give her credit. Nicole wasn't overtly trying to seduce him. That would have gotten her nowhere with Cal, and somehow she knew it. Instead, Nicole had attacked the foundation of their marriage. She must be pleased with her victory. At this point Jane and Cal were barely talking.

"Just a minute," Cal said, frowning darkly. "Did you purposely seek out Nicole?"

Jane's shoulders heaved as she expelled a deep sigh. "This is the first time I've met her."

"Where?"

"I went by the bookstore after I dropped Paul off at preschool."

"To see Annie?"

"No," she admitted reluctantly. "I thought since I was in town, I'd return the casserole dish."

Jane watched as Cal's gaze widened and his jaw went white with the effort to restrain his anger.

"That was wrong?" she blurted.

"Yes, dammit!"

"You wanted to bring it back yourself, is that it?"

He slapped the table so hard that the saltshaker toppled onto its side. "You went in search of Nicole Nelson. Did you ever stop to think that might embarrass me?"

Stunned, she felt her mouth open. "You're afraid I might have embarrassed *you?* That's rich." Despite herself, Jane's control began to slip. "How dare you say such a thing?" she cried. "What about everything you've done to embarrass *me?* I'm the one who's been humiliated here. While I'm away dealing with a family crisis, my husband's seen with another woman. And everyone's talking about it."

"I'd hoped you'd be above listening to malicious gossip."

"Oh, Cal, how can you say that? I was thrust right into the middle of it, and you know what? I didn't enjoy the experience."

He shook his head, still frowning. "You had no business confronting Nicole."

"No business?" she echoed, outraged. "How can you be so callous about my feelings? Don't you see what she's doing? Don't you understand? She wants you, Cal, and she didn't hide the fact, either. Are you going to let her destroy us? Are you?"

"This isn't about Nicole!" he shouted. "It's about trust and commitment."

"*Are* you committed to me?" she asked.

The look on his face was cold, uncompromising. "If you have to ask, that says everything."

"It does, doesn't it?" Jane felt shaky, almost light-headed. "I never thought it would come to this," she said, swallowing the pain. "Not with us..." She felt disillusioned and broken. Sinking into a chair, she buried her face in her hands.

"Jane." Cal stood on the other side of the table.

She glanced up.

"Neither of us got much sleep last night."

"I don't think—"

The phone rang, and Cal sighed irritably as he walked over and snatched up the receiver. His voice sharp, he said, "Hello," then he went still and his face instantly sobered. His gaze shot to her.

"She's here," he said. "Yes, yes, I understand."

Jane didn't know what to make of this. "Cal?" she said getting to her feet. The call seemed to be for her. As she approached, she heard her husband say he'd tell her. *Tell her what?*

Slowly Cal replaced the receiver. He put his hands on her shoulders and his eyes searched hers. "That was your uncle Ken," he said quietly.

"Uncle Ken? Why didn't he talk to me?" Jane demanded, and then intuition took over and she knew without asking. "What's wrong with my dad?"

Cal looked away for a moment. "Your father suffered a massive heart attack this afternoon."

A chill raced through her, a chill of foreboding and fear. The numbness she felt was replaced by a sense of purpose. She thought of the cardiac specialists she knew in Southern California, doctors her family should contact. Surely her uncle Ken had already reached someone. He was an experienced physician; he'd know what to do, who to call.

"What did he say?"

"Jane—"

"You should've let me talk to him."

"Jane." His hands gripped her shoulders as he tried to get her attention. "It's too late. Your father's gone."

She froze. Gone? Her father was dead? No! It couldn't be true. Not her father, not her daddy. Her knees buckled and she was immediately overwhelmed by deep heart-wrenching sobs.

"Honey, I'm so sorry." Cal pulled her into his arms and held her as she sobbed.

Jane had never experienced pain at this level. She could barely think, barely function. Cal helped her make the necessary arrangements. First they planned to leave the children with Glen and Ellie; later Jane decided she wanted them with her. While Cal booked the flights, she packed suitcases for him and the kids. Only when he started to carry the luggage out to the car did she realize she hadn't included anything for herself. The thought of having to choose a dress to wear at her own father's funeral nearly undid her. Unable to make a decision, she ended up stuffing every decent thing she owned into a suitcase.

"We can leave as soon as Glen and Ellie get here," Cal said, coming into the house for her bag.

"The roast," she said, remembering it was still in the oven.

"Don't worry about it. Glen and Ellie are on their way. They'll take care of everything—they'll look after the place until we're back."

"Paul and Mary Ann?" The deep pain refused to go away, and she was incapable of thinking or acting without being directed by someone else.

"They're fine, honey. I'll get them dressed and ready to go."

She looked at her husband, and to her surprise felt nothing. Only a few minutes earlier she'd been convinced she was about to lose him to another woman. Right now, it didn't matter. Right now, she couldn't dredge up a single shred of feeling for Cal. Everything, even the love she felt for her husband, had been overshadowed by the grief she felt at her father's death.

* * *

Cal did whatever he could to help Jane, her younger brother and her mother with the funeral arrangements. Jane was in a stupor most of the first day. Her mother was in even worse shape. The day of the funeral Stephanie Dickinson had to be given a sedative.

Paul was too young to remember Cal's mother, and Cal doubted Mary Ann would recall much of Grandpa Dickinson, either. All the children knew was that something had happened that made their mother and grandmother cry. They didn't understand what Cal meant when he explained that their grandfather had died.

The funeral was well attended, as was the reception that followed. Cal was glad to see that there'd been flowers from quite a few people in Promise—including, of course, Annie. Harry Dickinson had been liked and respected. Cal admired the way Jane stepped in and handled the social formalities. Her mother just couldn't do it, and her brother, Derek, seemed trapped in his own private pain.

Later, after everyone had left, he found his wife sitting in the darkened kitchen. Cal sat at the table beside her, but when he reached for her, she stiffened. Not wanting to upset her, he removed his hand from her arm.

"You must be exhausted," he said. "When's the last time you ate?"

"I just buried my father, Cal. I don't feel like eating."

"Honey—"

"I need a few minutes alone, please."

Cal nodded, then stood up and walked out of the room.

The house was dark, the children asleep, but the thought of going to bed held no appeal. Sedated, his mother-in-law was in her room and his wife sat in the shadows.

The day he'd buried his own mother had been the worst of his life. Jane had been by his side, his anchor. He didn't know how he could have survived without her. Yet now, with her father's death, she'd sent him away, asked for time alone. It felt like a rejection of him and his love, and that hurt.

Everyone handled grief differently, he reminded himself. People don't know how they'll react until it happens to them, he reasoned. Sitting on the edge of the bed, he mulled over the events of the past few days. They were a blur in his mind.

His arms ached to hold Jane. He loved his wife, loved his children. Their marriage had been going through a rough time, but everything would work out; he was sure of it. Cal waited for Jane to come to bed, and when she didn't, he must have fallen asleep. He awoke around two in the morning and discovered he was alone. Still in his clothes, he got up and went in search of his wife.

She was sitting where he'd left her. "Jane?" he whispered, not wanting to startle her.

"What time is it?" she asked.

"It's ten after two. Come to bed."

She responded with a shake of her head. "No. I can't."

"You've haven't slept in days."

"I know how long it's been," she snapped, showing the first bit of life since that phone call with the terrible news.

"Honey, please! This is crazy, sitting out here like

this. You haven't changed your clothes. This has been a hard day for you...."

She looked away, and in the room's faint light, he saw tears glistening on her face.

"I want to help you," he said urgently.

"Do you, Cal? Do you really?"

Her question shocked him. "You're my wife! Of course I do."

She started to sob then, and Cal was actually glad to see it. She needed to acknowledge her grief, to somehow express it. Other than when she'd first received the news, Jane had remained dry-eyed and strong. Her mother and brother were emotional wrecks, and her uncle Ken had been badly shaken. It was Jane who'd held them all together, Jane who'd made the decisions and arrangements, Jane who'd seen to the guests and reassured family and friends. It was time for her to let go, time to grieve.

"Go ahead and cry, Jane. It'll do you good." He handed her a clean handkerchief.

She clutched it to her face and sobbed more loudly.

"May I hold you?"

"No. Just leave me alone."

Cal crouched in front of her. "I'm afraid I can't do that. I want to help you," he said again. "Let me do that, all right?"

She shook her head.

"At least come to bed," he pleaded. She didn't resist when he clasped her by the forearms and drew her to her feet. Her legs must have gone numb from sitting there so long because she leaned heavily against him as he led her into the bedroom.

While she undressed, Cal turned back the covers.

She seemed to have trouble unfastening the large buttons of her tailored jacket. Brushing her hands aside, Cal unbuttoned it and helped take it off. When she was naked, he pulled the nightgown over her head, then brought her arms through the sleeves. He lowered her onto the bed and covered her with the blankets.

She went to sleep immediately—or that was what he thought.

As soon as he climbed into bed himself and switched off the light, she spoke. "Cal, I'm not going back."

"Back? Where?"

"To Promise," she told him.

This made no sense. "Not going back to Promise?" he repeated.

"No."

"Why not?" he asked, his voice louder than he'd intended. He stretched out one arm to turn on the lamp again.

"I can't deal with all the stress in our marriage. Not after this."

"But, Jane, we'll settle everything…."

"She wants you."

At first he didn't understand that Jane was talking about Nicole Nelson. Even when he did, it took him a while to control the anger and frustration. "Are you saying she can have me?" he asked, figuring a light approach might work better.

"She's determined, you know—except you *don't* know. You don't believe me."

"Jane, please, think about what you're saying."

"I have thought about it. It's all I've thought about for days. You're more worried about me embarrassing you than what that woman's doing to us. I don't have the strength or the will to fight for you. Not after today."

Patience had never been his strong suit, but Cal knew he had to give her some time and distance, not force her to resume their normal life too quickly. "Let's talk about it later. Tomorrow morning."

"I won't feel any differently about this in the morning. I've already spoken to Uncle Ken."

For years her uncle had wanted Jane to join his medical practice and had been bitterly disappointed when she'd chosen to stay in Texas, instead. "You're going to work for your uncle?"

"Temporarily."

Jane had arranged all this behind his back? Unable to hide his anger now, Cal tossed aside the sheet and vaulted out of bed. "You might've said something to me first! What the hell were you thinking?"

"Thinking?" she repeated. "I'm thinking about a man who lied to me and misled me."

"I never lied to you," he declared. "Not once."

"It was a lie of omission. You thought that what I didn't know wouldn't hurt me, right? Well, guess what, Cal? It does hurt. I don't want to be in a marriage where my husband's more concerned about being embarrassed than he is about the gossip and ridicule he subjects me to."

He couldn't believe they were having this conversation. "You're not being logical."

"Oh, yes, I am."

Cal strode to one end of the bedroom and stood there, not knowing what to do.

"You'll notice that even now, even when you know how I feel, you haven't once asked me to reconsider. Not once have you said you love me."

"You haven't exactly been proclaiming your love for me, either."

His words appeared to hit their mark, and she grew noticeably paler.

"Do you want me to leave right now?" he asked.

"I...I..." She floundered.

"No need to put it off," he said, letting his anger talk for him.

"You're right."

Cal jerked his suitcase out of the closet and crammed into it whatever clothes he could find. That didn't take long, although he gave Jane ample opportunity to talk him out of leaving, to say she hadn't really meant it.

Apparently she did.

Cal went into the bedroom where the children slept and kissed his daughter's soft cheek. He rested his hand on his son's shoulder, then abruptly turned away. A heaviness settled over his heart, and before he could surrender to regret, he walked away.

Seven

"I know how hard this is on you," Jane's mother said. It was two weeks since the funeral. Two weeks since Jane had separated from her husband. Stephanie busied herself about the kitchen and avoided eye contact. "But, Jane, are you sure you did the right thing?" She pressed her lips together and concentrated on cleaning up the breakfast dishes. "Ken's delighted that you're going to work with him, and the children are adjusting well, but…"

"I'm getting my own apartment."

"I won't hear of it," her mother insisted. "If you're going through with this, I want you to stay here. I don't want you dealing with a move on top of everything else."

"Mother, it's very sweet of you, but you need your space, too."

"No…" Tears filled her eyes. "I don't want to live alone— I don't think I can. I never have, you know. Not in my entire life and…well, I realize I'm leaning on you, but I need you so desperately."

"Mother, I understand."

"It's not just that. I'm so worried about you and Cal."

"I know," Jane whispered. She tried not to think of him, or of the situation between them. There'd been no contact whatsoever. Cal had left in anger, and at the time she'd wanted him out of her life.

"Did you make an appointment with an attorney?" her mother asked.

Jane shook her head. It was just one more thing she'd delayed doing. One more thing she couldn't make a decision about. Most days she could barely get out of bed and see to the needs of her children. Uncle Ken was eager to have her join his practice. He'd already discussed financial arrangements and suggested a date for her to start—the first Monday in the new year. Jane had listened carefully to his plans; however, she'd felt numb and disoriented. This wasn't what she wanted, but everything had been set in motion and she didn't know how to stop it. Yet she had to support herself and the children. So far she hadn't needed money, but she would soon. Cal would send support if she asked for it. She lacked the courage to call him, though. She hated the idea of their first conversation being about money.

"You haven't heard from Cal, have you?" Her mother broke into her thoughts.

"No." His silence wasn't something Jane could ignore. She'd envisioned her husband coming back for her, proclaiming his love and vowing never to allow any woman to stand between him and his family. Ignoring Jane was bad enough, but the fact that he hadn't seen fit to contact the children made everything so much worse. It was as though he'd wiped his family from his mind.

Two months ago Jane assumed she had a near-perfect marriage. Now she was separated and living with her mother. Still, she believed that, if not for the death of her father, she'd be back in Texas right now. Eventually they would've worked out this discord; they would have rediscovered their love. Instead, in her pain and grief over the loss of her father, she'd sent Cal away.

She reminded herself that she hadn't needed to ask him twice. He'd been just as eager to escape.

Nicole Nelson had won.

At any other time in her life Jane would have fought for her husband, but now she had neither the strength nor the emotional energy to do so. From all appearances, Cal had made his choice—and it wasn't her or the children.

"We should talk about Thanksgiving," her mother said. "It's next week...."

"Thanksgiving?" Jane hadn't realized the holiday was so close.

"Ken and Jean asked us all to dinner. What do you think?"

Jane had noticed that her mother was having a hard time making decisions, too. "Sounds nice," she said, not wanting to plan that far ahead. Even a week was too much. She couldn't bear to think about the holidays, especially Christmas.

The doorbell chimed and Jane answered it, grateful for the interruption. Facing the future, making plans—

it was just too difficult. A deliveryman stood with a box and a form for her to sign. Not until Jane closed the door did she see the label addressed to Paul in Cal's distinctive handwriting.

She carried the package into the bedroom, where her son sat doing a jigsaw puzzle. He glanced up when she entered the room.

"It's from Daddy," she said, setting the box on the carpet.

Paul tore into the package with gusto and let out a squeal when he found his favorite blanket. He bunched it up and hugged it to his chest, grinning hugely. Jane looked inside the box and saw a short letter. She read it aloud.

Dear Paul,
I thought you might want to have your old friend with you. Give your little sister a hug from me.
Love,
Daddy

Jane swallowed around the lump in her throat. Cal's message in that letter was loud and clear. He'd asked Paul to hug Mary Ann, but not her.

Jane was on her own.

The post office fell silent when Cal stepped into the building. The Moorhouse sisters, Edwina and Lily, stood at the counter, visiting with Caroline Weston, who was the wife of his best friend, as well as the local postmistress. Caroline had taken a leave of absence from her duties for the past few years, but had recently returned to her position.

When the three women saw Cal, the two retired schoolteachers pinched their lips together and stiffly drew themselves up.

"Good day, ladies," Cal said, touching the brim of his hat.

"Cal Patterson," Edwina said briskly. "I only wish you were in the fifth grade again so I could box your ears."

"How're you doing, Cal?" Caroline asked in a friendlier tone.

He didn't answer because anyone looking at him ought to be able to tell. He was miserable and getting more so every day. By now he'd fully expected his wife to come to her senses and return home. He missed her and he missed his kids. He barely ate, hadn't slept an entire night since he got back and was in a foul mood most of the time.

Inserting the key in his postal box, he opened the small door. He was about to collect his mail when he heard Caroline's voice from the post-office side of the box. "Cal?"

He reached for the stack of envelopes and flyers, then peered through. Sure enough, Caroline was looking straight at him.

"I just wanted to tell you how sorry Grady and I are."

He nodded, rather than comment.

"Is there anything we can do?"

"Not a thing," he said curtly, wanting Caroline and everyone else, including the Moorhouse sisters, to know that his problems with Jane were his business…and hers. No one else's.

"Cal, listen—"

"I don't mean to be rude, but I'm in a hurry." Not waiting for her reply, Cal locked his postal box and left the building.

When he'd first returned from California, people had naturally assumed that Jane had stayed on with the children to help Mrs. Dickinson. Apparently news of the separation had leaked out after Annie called Jane at her mother's home. From that point on, word had spread faster than a flash flood. What began as simple fact became embellished with each retelling. Family and friends knew more about what was happening—or supposedly happening—in his life than he did, Cal thought sardonically.

Only yesterday Glen had asked him about the letter from Paul. Cal hadn't heard one word from his wife or children, but then he hadn't collected his mail, either. When Cal asked how Glen knew about this letter, his brother briskly informed him that he'd heard from Ellie. Apparently Ellie had heard it from Dovie, and Dovie just happened to be in the post office when Caroline was sorting mail. That was life in a small town.

As soon as he stepped out of the post office, Cal quickly shuffled through the envelopes and found the letter addressed to him in Jane's familiar writing. The return address showed Paul's name.

Cal tore into the envelope with an eagerness he couldn't hide.

Dear Daddy,
Thank you for my blankey. I sleep better with it.
Mary Ann likes it, too, and I sometimes share with
her. Grandma still misses Grandpa. We're spending Thanksgiving with Uncle Ken and Aunt Jean.
                                          Love,
                                          Paul

Cal read the letter a second time, certain he was
missing something. Surely there was a hidden message
there from Jane, a subtle hint to let him know what she
was thinking. Perhaps the mention of Thanksgiving was
her way of telling him that she was proceeding with her
life as a single woman. Her way of informing him that
she was managing perfectly well without a husband.

Thanksgiving? Cal had to stop and think about the
date. It'd been nearly three weeks since he'd last talked
to Jane. Three weeks since he'd hugged his children.
Three weeks that he'd been walking around in a haze
of wounded pride and frustrated anger.

Not wanting to linger in town, Cal returned to the
ranch. He looked at the calendar and was stunned to see
that he'd nearly missed the holiday. Not that eating a big
turkey dinner would've made any difference to him.
Without his wife and children, the day would be just like
all the rest, empty and silent.

Thanksgiving Day Cal awoke with a sick feeling in
the pit of his stomach. Glen had tried to talk him into
joining his family. Ellie's mother and aunt were flying in

from Chicago for the holiday weekend, he'd said, but Cal was more than welcome. Cal declined without regrets.

He thought he might avoid Thanksgiving activities altogether, but should have known better. Around noon his father arrived. As soon as he saw the truck heading toward the house, Cal stepped onto the back porch to wait for him.

"What are you doing here, Dad?" he demanded, making sure his father understood that he didn't appreciate the intrusion.

"It's Thanksgiving."

"I know what day it is," Cal snapped.

"I thought I'd let you buy me dinner," Phil said blithely.

"I thought they served a big fancy meal at the retirement residence."

"They do, but I'd rather eat with you."

Cal would never admit it, but despite his avowals, he wanted the company.

"Where am I taking you?" he asked, coming down the concrete steps to meet Phil.

"Brewster."

Cal tipped back his hat to get a better look at his father. "Why?"

"The Rocky Creek Inn," Phil said. "From what I hear, they cook a dinner fit to rival even Dovie's."

"It's one of the priciest restaurants in the area," Cal muttered, remembering how his father had announced Cal would be footing the bill.

Phil laughed. "Hey, I'm retired. I can't afford a place as nice as the Rocky Creek Inn. Besides, I have something to tell you."

"Tell me here," Cal said, wondering if his father had news about Jane and the children. If so, he wanted it right now.

Phil shook his head. "Later."

They decided to leave for Brewster after Cal changed clothes and shaved. His father made himself at home while he waited and Cal was grateful he didn't mention the condition of the house. When he returned wearing a clean, if wrinkled, shirt and brand-new Wranglers, Phil was reading Paul's letter, which lay on the kitchen table, along with three weeks' worth of unopened mail. He paused, expecting his father to lay into him about leaving his family behind in California, and was relieved when Phil didn't. No censure was necessary; Cal had called himself every kind of fool for what he'd done.

The drive into Brewster took almost two hours and was fairly relaxing. They discussed a range of topics, everything from politics to sports, but avoided anything to do with Jane and the kids. A couple of times Cal could have led naturally into the subject of his wife, but didn't. No need to ruin the day with a litany of his woes.

The Rocky Creek Inn had a reputation for excellent food and equally good service. They ended up waiting thirty minutes for a table, but considering it was a holiday and they had no reservation, they felt that wasn't bad.

Both men ordered the traditional Thanksgiving feast and a glass of wine. Cal waited until the waiter had poured his chardonnay before he spoke. "You had something you wanted to tell me?" He'd bet the ranch that whatever it was involved the situation with Jane. But he didn't mind. After three frustrating weeks, he hoped Phil had some news.

"Do you remember when I had my heart attack?"

Cal wasn't likely to forget. He'd nearly lost his father. "Of course."

"What you probably don't know is that your mother and I nearly split up afterward."

"You and Mom?" Cal couldn't hide his shock. As far as he knew, his parents' marriage had been rock-solid from the day of their wedding until they'd lowered his mother into the ground.

"I was still in the hospital recovering from the surgery and your mother, God bless her, waltzed into my room and casually said she'd put earnest money down on the old Howe place."

Cal reached for his wineglass in an effort to stifle a grin. He remembered the day vividly. The doctors had talked to the family following open-heart surgery and suggested Phil think about reducing his hours at the ranch. Shortly after that, his parents decided to open a bed-and-breakfast in town. It was then that Cal and his brother had taken over the operation of the Lonesome Coyote Ranch.

"Your mother didn't even *ask* me about buying that monstrosity," his father told him. "I was on my death bed—"

"You were in the hospital," Cal corrected.

"All right, all right, but you get the picture. Next thing I know, Mary comes in and tells me, *tells* me, mind you, that I've retired and the two of us are moving to town and starting a bed-and-breakfast."

Cal nearly burst out laughing, although he was well aware of what his mother had done and why. Getting Phil to cut back his hours would have been impossible, and Mary had realized that retirement would be a difficult adjustment for a man who'd worked cattle all his life. Phil wasn't capable of spending his days lazing around, so she'd taken matters into her own hands.

"I didn't appreciate what your mother did, manipulating me like that," Phil continued. "She knew I never would've agreed to live in town, and she went ahead and made the decision, anyway."

"But, Dad, it was a brilliant idea." The enterprise had been a money-maker from the first. The house was in decent condition, but had enough quirks to keep his father occupied with a variety of repair projects. The bed-and-breakfast employed the best of both his parents' skills. Phil was a natural organizer and his mother was personable and warm, good at making people feel welcome.

His father's eyes clouded. "It *was* brilliant, but at the time I didn't see it that way. I don't mind telling you I was mad enough to consider ending our marriage."

Cal frowned. "You didn't mean it, Dad."

"The hell I didn't. I would've done it, too, if I hadn't been tied down to that hospital bed. It gave me time to think about what I'd do without Mary in my life, and after a few days I decided to give your mother a second chance."

Cal laughed outright.

"You think I'm joking, but I was serious and your

mother knew it. When she left the hospital, she asked me to have my attorney contact hers. The way I felt right then, I swear I was determined to do it, Cal. I figured there are some things a man won't let a woman interfere with in life, and as far as I was concerned at that moment, Mary had crossed the line."

Ah, so this was what Cal was meant to hear. In her lack of trust, Jane had crossed the line with him, too. Only, *he* hadn't been the one who'd chosen to break up the family. That decision had rested entirely with Jane.

"I notice you haven't pried into my situation yet," Cal murmured.

"No, I haven't," Phil said. "That's your business and Jane's. If you want out of the marriage, then that's up to you."

"Out of the marriage!" Cal shot back. "Jane's the one who wants out. She decided not to return to Promise. The day of her father's funeral, she told me she was staying with her mother...indefinitely."

"You agreed to this?"

"The hell I did!"

"But you left."

Cal had replayed that fateful night a hundred times, asking himself these same questions. Should he have stayed and talked it out with her? Should he have taken a stand and insisted she listen to reason? Three weeks later, he still didn't have the answer.

"Don't you think Jane might have been distraught over her father's death?" Phil wanted to know.

"Yeah." Cal nodded. "But it's been nearly a month and she hasn't had a change of heart yet."

"No, she hasn't," Phil said, and sighed. "It's a shame, too, a real shame."

"I love her, Dad." Cal was willing to admit it. "I miss her and the kids." He thought of the day he'd found Paul's blankey. After all the distress that stupid blanket had caused him, Cal was so glad to see it he'd brought it to his face, breathing in the familiar scent of his son. Afterward, the knot in his stomach was so tight he hadn't eaten for the rest of the day.

"I remember when Jennifer left you," Phil said, growing melancholy, "just a couple of days before the wedding. You looked like someone had stabbed a knife straight through your gut. I knew you loved her, but you didn't go after her."

"No way." Jennifer had made her decision.

"Pride wouldn't let you," Phil added. "In that case, I think it was probably for the best. I'm not convinced of it this time." His father shook his head. "I loved your mother, don't misunderstand me—it damn near killed me when she died—but as strong as my love for her was, we didn't have the perfect marriage. We argued, but we managed to work out our problems. I'm sure you'll resolve things with Jane, too."

Cal hoped that was true, but he wasn't nearly as confident as his father.

"The key is communication," Phil said.

Cal held his father's look. "That's a little difficult when Jane's holed up halfway across the country.

Besides, as I understand it, communication is a two-way street. Jane has to be willing to talk to me and she isn't."

"Have you made an effort to get in touch with her?"

He shook his head.

"That's what I thought."

"Go ahead and say it," Cal muttered. "You think I should go after her."

"Are you asking my opinion?" Phil asked.

"No, but you're going to give it to me, anyway."

"If Jane was my wife," Phil said, his eyes intent on Cal, "I'd go back for her and settle this once and for all. I wouldn't return to Promise without her. Are you willing to do that, son?"

Cal needed to think about it, and about all the things that had been said. "I don't know," he answered, being as honest as he could. "I just don't know."

Nicole Nelson arrived for work at Tumbleweed Books bright and early on the Friday morning after Thanksgiving. With the official start of the Christmas season upon them, the day was destined to be a busy one. She let herself in the back door, prepared to open the bookstore for Annie, who was leaving more and more of the responsibility to her, which proved—to Nicole's immense satisfaction—that Annie liked and trusted her.

Nicole had taken a calculated risk over Thanksgiving and lost. In the end she'd spent the holiday alone, even though she'd received two dinner invitations. Her plan had been to spend the day with Cal. She would've made sure he didn't feel threatened, would have couched her suggestion in compassionate terms—just two lonely people making it through the holiday. Unfortunately it hadn't turned out that way. She'd phoned the ranch house twice and there'd been no answer, which made her wonder where he'd gone and who he'd been with. Needless to say, she hadn't left a message.

At any rate, the wife was apparently out of the picture. That had been surprisingly easy. Jane Patterson didn't deserve her husband if she wasn't willing to fight for him. Most women did fight. Usually their attempts were just short of pathetic, but for reasons Nicole had yet to understand, men generally chose to stay with their wives.

Those who didn't...well, the truth was, Nicole quickly grew bored with them. It was different with Cal, had always been different. Never before had she shown her hand more blatantly than she had with Dr. Jane. Nicole felt almost sorry for her. Really, all she'd done was enlighten Jane about a few home truths. The woman didn't value what she had if she was willing to let Cal go with barely a protest.

The phone rang. It wasn't even nine, the store didn't officially open for another hour, and already they were receiving calls.

"Tumbleweed Books," Nicole answered.

"Annie Porter, please." The voice sounded vaguely familiar.

"I'm sorry, Annie won't be in until ten."

"But I just phoned the house and Lucas told me she was at work."

"Then she should be here any minute." Playing a hunch, Nicole asked, "Is this Jane Patterson?"

The hesitation at the other end confirmed her suspicion. "Is this Nicole Nelson?"

"It is," Nicole said, then added with a hint of regret, "I'm sorry to hear about you and Cal."

There was a soft disbelieving laugh. "I doubt that. I'd appreciate it if you'd tell Annie I phoned."

"Of course. I understand your father recently passed away. I am sorry, Jane."

Jane paused, but thanked her.

"Annie was really upset about it. She seems fond of your family."

Another pause. "Please have her call when it's convenient."

"I will." Nicole felt the need to keep Jane on the line. *Know your enemy,* she thought. "My friend Jennifer Healy was the one who broke off her engagement with Cal. Did you know that?"

The responding sigh told Nicole that Jane was growing impatient with her. "I remember hearing something along those lines."

"Cal didn't go after Jennifer, either."

"Either?" Jane repeated.

"Cal never said who wanted the separation—you or him. It's not something we talk about. But the fact that he hasn't sent for you says a great deal, don't you think?"

"What's happening between my husband and me is none of your business. Goodbye, Nicole." Her words were followed by a click and then a dial tone.

So Dr. Jane had hung up on her. That didn't come as a shock. If anything, it stimulated Nicole. She'd moved to Promise, determined to have Cal Patterson. Through the years, he'd never strayed far from her mind. She'd lost her fair share of married men to their wives, but that wasn't going to happen *this* time.

So far she'd been smart, played her cards right, and her patience had been rewarded. In three weeks, she'd only contacted Cal once and that was about a book order. Shortly after he'd returned from California alone, the town had been filled with speculation. The news excited Nicole. She'd planted the seeds, let gossip water Jane's doubts, trusting that time would eventually bring her hopes to fruition. With Jane still in California, Nicole couldn't help being curious about the status of the relationship, so she'd phoned to let him know the book Jane had ordered was in. Only Jane hadn't ordered any book...

Playing dumb, Nicole had offered to drop it off at the ranch, since she was headed in that direction anyway— or so she'd claimed. Cal declined, then suggested Annie mail it to Jane at her mother's address in California. Despite her efforts to keep Cal talking, it hadn't worked. But he'd been in a hurry; he must've had things to do. And he probably felt a bit depressed about the deterioration of his marriage. After all, no man enjoyed failure. Well, she'd just have to comfort him, wouldn't she? She sensed that her opportunity was coming soon.

It was always more difficult when there were children involved. In all honesty, Nicole didn't feel good about destroying a family. However, seeing how easy it'd been to break up this marriage made her suspect that the relationship hadn't been very secure in the first place.

She'd bide her time. It wouldn't be long before Cal needed someone to turn to. And Nicole had every intention of being that someone.

After speaking to that horrible woman, Jane felt wretched. Nicole had implied—no, more than implied—that she and Cal were continuing to see each other. Sick to her stomach, Jane hurried to her bedroom.

"Jane." Her mother stepped into the room. "Are you all right? Was that Cal on the phone? What happened? I saw you talking and all of a sudden the color drained from your face and you practically ran in here."

"I'm fine, Mom," Jane assured her. "No, it wasn't Cal. It wasn't anyone important."

"I finished writing all the thank-you notes and decided I need a break. How about if I take you and the children to lunch?"

The thought of food repelled her. "I don't feel up to going out, Mom. Sorry."

"You won't mind if I take the kids? Santa's arriving at the mall this afternoon and I know Paul and Mary Ann will be thrilled."

An afternoon alone sounded wonderful to Jane. "Are you sure it won't be too much for you?"

"Time with these little ones is *exactly* what I need."

"Is there anything you want me to do while you're out?" Jane asked, although she longed for nothing so much as a two-hour nap.

"As a matter of fact, there is," Stephanie said. "I want you to rest. You don't look well. You're tired and out of sorts."

That was putting it mildly. Jane felt devastated and full of despair, and given the chance, she'd delight in tearing Nicole Nelson's hair out! What a lovely Christian thought, she chastised herself. For that matter, what a cliché.

"Mom." Paul stood in the doorway to her bedroom.

"Aren't you going with Grandma?" Jane asked.

Paul nodded, then came into the room and handed her his blankey. "This is for you." Jane smiled as he placed the tattered much-loved blanket on her bed.

"Thank you, sweetheart," she said and kissed his brow.

Jane heard the front door close as the children left with her mother. Taking them to a mall the day after Thanksgiving was the act of an insane woman, in Jane's opinion. She wouldn't be caught anywhere near crowds like that. As soon as the thought formed in her mind, Jane realized she hadn't always felt that way. A few years ago she'd been just as eager as all those other shoppers. Even in medical school she'd found time to hunt down the best buys. It'd been a competition with her friends; the cheaper an item, the greater the bragging rights.

Not so these days. None of that seemed important anymore. The closest mall was a hundred miles from the ranch, and almost everything she owned was bought in town, ordered through a catalog or purchased over the

Internet. The life she lived now was based in small-town America. And she loved it.

She missed Promise. She missed her husband even more.

Her friends, too. Jane could hardly imagine what they must think. The only person she'd talked to after the funeral had been Annie, and then just briefly. When Annie had asked about Cal, Jane had refused to discuss him, other than to say they'd separated. It would do no good to talk about her situation with Annie, especially since Nicole worked for her now.

With her son's blanket wrapped around her shoulders, Jane did sleep for an hour. When she woke, she knew instantly who she needed to talk to—Dovie Hennessey.

The older woman had been her first friend in Promise, and Jane valued her opinion. Maybe Dovie could help her muddle her way through the events of the past few months. She was sorry she hadn't talked to her before. She supposed it was because her father's death had shaken her so badly; she'd found it too difficult to reach out. Dealing with the children depleted what energy she had. Anything beyond the most mundane everyday functions seemed beyond her. As a physician, Jane should have recognized the signs of depression earlier, but then, it was much harder to be objective about one's own situation.

To her disappointment Dovie didn't answer. She could have left a message but decided not to. She considered calling her husband, but she didn't have the courage yet. What would she say? What would *he* say?

If Nicole answered, it would destroy her, and just now Jane felt too fragile to deal with such a profound betrayal.

Her mother was an excellent housekeeper, but Jane went around picking up toys and straightening magazines, anything to keep herself occupied. The mail was on the counter and Jane saw that it included a number of sympathy cards. She read each one, which renewed her overwhelming sense of loss and left her in tears.

Inside one of the sympathy cards was a letter addressed to her mother. Jane didn't read it, although when she returned it to the envelope, she saw the signature. Laurie Jo. Her mother's best friend from high school. Laurie Jo Spencer was the kind of friend to her mother that Annie had always been to Jane. Lately, though, Annie had been so busy dealing with the changes in her own life that they hadn't talked nearly as often as they used to.

Laurie Jo had added a postscript asking Stephanie to join her in Mexico over the Christmas holidays. They were both recent widows, as well as old friends; they'd be perfect companions for each other.

Jane wondered if her mother would seriously consider the trip and hoped she would. It sounded ideal. Her father's health problems had started months ago, and he'd required constant attention and care. Stephanie was physically and emotionally worn out.

If her mother did take the trip, it'd be a good time for Jane to find her own apartment. That way, her moving out would cause less of a strain in their relationship. So far, Stephanie had insisted Jane stay with her.

In another four weeks it'd be Christmas. Jane would

have to make some decisions before then. Painful decisions that would force her to confront realities she'd rather not face. This lack of energy and ambition, living one day to the next, was beginning to feel like the norm. Beginning to feel almost comfortable. But for her own sake and the sake of her children, it couldn't continue.

Jane glanced at the phone again. She dialed Dovie's number, but there was still no answer.

It occurred to her that Dovie's absence was really rather symbolic. There didn't seem to be anyone—or anything—left for her in Promise, Texas.

Eight

Cal had never been much of a drinking man. An occasional beer, wine with dinner, but he rarely broke into the hard stuff. Nor did he often drink alone. But after six weeks without his family, Cal was considering doing both. The walls felt like they were closing in on him. Needing to escape and not interested in company, Cal drove to town and headed straight for Billy D's, the local watering hole.

The Christmas lights were up, Cal noticed when he hit Main Street. Decorations were everywhere. Store windows featured Christmas displays, come of them quite elaborate. Huge red-and-white-striped candy canes and large wreaths dangled from each lamppost. Everything around town looked disgustingly cheerful, which only depressed him further. He'd never been all that fond of Christmas, but Jane was as bad as his mother. A year ago Jane had decided to make ornaments for everyone in the family. She'd spent hours pinning brightly colored beads to red satin balls, each

design different, each ornament unique. Even Cal had
to admit they were works of art. His wife's talent had
impressed him, but she'd shrugged off his praise,
claiming it was something she'd always planned to do.

Last Christmas, Paul hadn't quite understood what
Christmas was about, but he'd gotten into the spirit of it
soon enough. Seeing the festivities through his son's
eyes had made the holidays Cal's best ever. This year
would be even better now that both children—the
thought pulled him up short. Without Jane and his family,
this Christmas was going to be the worst of his life.

Cal parked his truck outside the tavern and sat there
for several minutes before venturing inside. The noise
level momentarily lessened when he walked in as people
noted his arrival, then quickly resumed. Wanting to be
alone, Cal chose a table at the back of the room, and as
soon as the waitress appeared, he ordered a beer. Then,
after thirty minutes or so, he had another. Even this
place was decorated for Christmas, he saw, with inflated
Santas and reindeer scattered about.

He must have been there an hour, perhaps longer,
when an attractive woman made her way toward him
and stood, hands on her shapely hips, directly in front
of his table.

"Hello, Cal."

It was Nicole Nelson. Cal stiffened with dread, since
it was this very woman who'd been responsible for most
of his problems.

"Aren't you going to say it's nice to see me?"

"No."

She wore skin-tight jeans, a cropped beaded top and a white Stetson. At another time he might have thought her attractive, but not in his present frame of mind.

"Mind if I join you?"

He was about to explain that he'd rather be alone, but apparently she didn't need an invitation to pull out a chair and sit down. He seemed to remember she'd done much the same thing the night she'd found him at the Mexican Lindo. The woman did what *she* wanted, regardless of other people's preferences and desires. He'd never liked that kind of behavior and didn't understand why he tolerated it now.

"I'm sorry to hear about you and Jane."

His marriage was the last subject he intended to discuss with Nicole. He didn't respond.

"You must be lonely," she went on.

He shrugged and reached for his beer, taking a healthy swallow.

"I think it's a good idea for you to get out, mingle with friends, let the world know you're your own man."

She wasn't making any sense. Cal figured she'd leave as soon as she realized he wasn't going to be manipulated into a conversation.

"The holidays are a terrible time to be alone," she said, leaning forward with her elbows on the table. She propped her chin in her hands. "It's hard. I know."

Cal took another swallow of beer. She'd get the message eventually. At least he hoped she would.

"I always thought you and I had a lot in common," she continued.

Unable to suppress his reaction, he arched his eyebrows. She leaped on that as if he'd talked nonstop for the past ten minutes.

"It's true, Cal. Look at us. We're both killing a Saturday night in a tavern because neither of us has anyplace better to go. We're struggling to hold in our troubles for fear anyone else will know the real us."

The woman was so full of malarkey it was all Cal could do not to laugh in her face.

"I can help you through this," she said earnestly.

"Help me?" He shouldn't have spoken, but he couldn't even guess what Nicole had to offer that could possibly interest him.

"I made a terrible mistake before, when Jennifer broke off the engagement. You needed me then, but I was too young to know that. I'm mature enough to have figured it out now."

"Really?" This entire conversation was laughable.

Her smile was coy. "You want me, Cal," she said boldly, her unwavering gaze holding him captive. "That's good, because I want you, too. I've always wanted you."

"I'm married, Nicole." That was a little matter she'd conveniently forgotten.

"Separated," she corrected.

This woman had played no small part in that separation, and Cal was seeing her with fresh eyes.

"I think you should leave," he said, not bothering to mince words. Until now, Cal had assumed Jane was being paranoid about Nicole Nelson. Yes, they'd bumped into each other at the Mexican Lindo. Yes, she'd baked him a casserole and delivered it to the house. Both occasions meant nothing to him. Until today, he'd believed that Jane had overreacted, that she'd been unreasonable. But at this moment, everything Jane had said added up in his mind.

"Leave?" She pouted prettily. "You don't mean that."

"Nicole, I'm married and I happen to love my wife and children very much. I'm not interested in an affair with you or anyone else."

"I...I hope you don't think that's what I was saying." She revealed the perfect amount of confusion.

"I know exactly what you were saying. What else is this 'I want you' business? You're right about one thing though—I know what I want and, frankly, it isn't you."

"Cal," she whispered, shaking her head. "I'm sure you misunderstood me."

He snickered softly.

"You're looking for company," she said, "otherwise you would've done your drinking at home. I understand that, because I know what it's like to be alone, to want to connect with someone. You want someone with a willing ear."

Cal had any number of family and friends with whom he could discuss his woes, and he doubted Nicole had any viable solutions to offer. He groaned. Sure as hell, Jane would get wind of this encounter and consider it grounds for divorce.

"All right," Nicole said, and pushed back her chair. "I know this is a difficult time. Separation's hard on a man, but when you want to talk about it, I'll be there for you, okay? Call me. I'll wait to hear from you."

As far as Cal was concerned, Nicole would have a very long wait. He paid his tab, and then, because he didn't want to drive, he walked over to the café in the bowling alley.

"You want some food to go with that coffee?" Denise asked pointedly.

"I guess," he muttered, realizing he hadn't eaten much of anything in days. "Bring me whatever you want. I don't care."

Ten minutes later she returned with a plate of corned-beef hash, three fried eggs, plus hash browns and a stack of sourdough toast. "That's breakfast," he said, looking down at the plate.

"I figured it was your first meal of the day. Your first decent one, anyhow."

"Well, yeah." It was.

Denise set the glass coffeepot on the table. "You okay?" He nodded.

"You don't look it. You and I went all the way through school together, Cal, and I feel I can be honest with you. But don't worry—I'm not going to give you advice."

"Good." He'd had a confrontation with his brother earlier in the day about his marriage. Then he'd heard from Nicole. Now Denise. Everyone seemed to want to tell him what to do.

"I happen to think the world of Dr. Jane. So work it out before I lose faith in you."

"Yes, Denise." He picked up his fork.

Cal was half finished his meal when Wade McMillen slipped into the booth across from him. "Hi, Cal. How're you doing?"

Cal scowled. This was the very reason he'd avoided coming into town until tonight. People naturally assumed he was looking for company, so they had no compunction about offering him that—and plenty of unsolicited advice.

"Heard from Jane lately?" Wade asked.

Talk about getting straight to the point.

"No." Cal glared at the man who was both pastor and friend. At times it was hard to see the boundary between the two roles. "I don't remember inviting you to join me," he muttered and reached for the ketchup, smearing a glob on the remains of his corned-beef hash.

"You didn't."

"What is it with people?" Cal snapped. "Can't they leave me the hell alone?"

Wade chuckled. "That was an interesting choice of words. Leave you *the hell alone.* I imagine that's what it must feel like for you about now. Like you're in hell and all alone."

"What gives you that impression?" Cal dunked a slice of toast into the egg yolk, doing his best to appear unaffected.

"Why else would you come into town? You're going stir-crazy on that ranch without Jane and the kids."

"Listen, Wade," Cal said forcefully, "I wasn't the one who wanted a separation. Jane made that decision. I didn't want this or deserve it. In fact, I didn't do a damn thing."

His words were followed by silence. Then Wade said mildly, "I'm sure that's true. You didn't do a damn thing."

Cal met his gaze. "What do you mean by that?"

"That, my friend, is for you to figure out." Wade stood up and left the booth.

For the tenth time that day, Dovie Hennessey found herself staring at the phone, willing it to ring, willing Jane Patterson to call from California.

"You're going to do it, aren't you?" Frank said, his voice muted by the morning paper. "Never mind everything you said earlier—you're going to call Jane."

"I don't know what I'm going to do," Dovie murmured, although she could feel her resolve weakening more each day. When she learned that Cal and Jane had separated, Dovie's first impulse had been to call Jane. For weeks now, she'd resisted. After all, Jane was with her mother and certainly didn't need advice from Dovie. If and when she did, Jane would phone her.

Everything was complicated by Harry Dickinson's death. Jane was grieving, and Dovie didn't want to intrude on this private family time. First her father and then her marriage. Her friend was suffering, but she'd hoped that Jane would make the effort to get in touch with her. She hadn't, and Dovie was growing impatient.

Few people had seen Cal, and those who did claimed he walked around in a state of perpetual anger. That sounded exactly like Cal, who wouldn't take kindly to others involving themselves in his affairs.

Dovie remembered what he'd been like after his broken engagement. He'd hardly ever come into town, and when he did, he settled his business quickly and was gone. He'd been unsociable, unresponsive, impossible to talk to. Falling in love with Jane had changed him. Marrying Dr. Texas was the best thing that had ever happened to him, and Dovie recalled nostalgically how pleased Mary had been when her oldest son announced his engagement.

"Go ahead," Frank said after a moment. "Call her."

"Do you really think I should?" Even now Dovie was uncertain.

"We had two hang-ups recently. Those might've been from Jane."

"Frank, be reasonable," Dovie said, laughing lightly. "Not everyone likes leaving messages."

"You could always ask her," he said, giving Dovie a perfectly reasonable excuse to call.

"I could, couldn't I?" Then, needing no more incentive, she reached for the phone and the pad next to it and dialed the long-distance number Annie Porter had given her.

On the third ring Jane answered.

"Jane, it's Dovie—Dovie Hennessey," she added in case the dear girl was so distraught she'd forgotten her.

"Hello, Dovie," Jane said, sounding calm and confident.

"How are you?" Dovie cried, unnerved by the lack of emotion in her friend. "And the children?"

"We're all doing fine."

"Your mother?"

Jane sighed, showing the first sign of emotion. "She's adjusting, but it's difficult."

"I know, dear. I remember how excruciating everything was those first few months after Marvin died. Give your mother my best, won't you?"

"Of course." Jane hesitated, then asked, "How's everyone in Promise?"

Dovie smiled; it wasn't as hopeless as she'd feared. "By everyone, do you mean Cal?"

The hesitation was longer this time. "Yes, I suppose I do."

"Oh, Jane, he misses you so much. Every time I see that boy, it's all I can do not to hug him…."

"So he's been in town quite a bit recently." Jane's voice hardened ever so slightly. The implication was there without her having to say it.

"If that's your way of asking whether he's seeing Nicole Nelson, I can't really answer. However, my guess is he's not."

"You don't know that, though, do you? I…I spoke with Nicole myself and, according to her, they've been keeping each other company."

"Hogwash! What do you expect her to say? You and I both know she's after Cal."

"You think so, too?" Jane's voice was more emotional now.

"I didn't see it at first, but Frank did. He took one look at Nicole and said that woman was going to be trouble."

"Frank said that? Oh, Dovie, Cal thinks…" Jane

inhaled a shaky breath. Then she went quiet again. "It doesn't matter anymore."

"What do you mean? Of course it matters!"

"I made an appointment with a divorce attorney this morning."

Stunned, Dovie gasped. "Oh, Jane, no!" This news was the last thing she'd wanted to hear.

"Cal made his choice."

"I don't believe that. You seem to be implying that he's chosen Nicole over you and the children, and Jane, that simply isn't so."

"Dovie—"

"You said Nicole claimed she was seeing Cal. Just how trustworthy do you think this woman is?"

"Annie trusts her."

"Oh, my dear, Annie hasn't got a clue what's happening. Do you seriously believe she'd stand by and let Nicole ruin your life if she knew what was going on? Right now all she's thinking about is this pregnancy and the changes it'll bring to *her* life. I love Annie, you know that. She's a darling girl, but she tends to see the best in everyone. Weren't you the one who told me about her first husband? You said everyone knew what kind of man he was—except Annie. She just couldn't see it."

"I…I haven't discussed this with her."

"I can understand why. That's probably a good idea, the situation being what it is," Dovie said. "Now, let's get back to this business about the lawyer. Making an appointment—was that something you really *wanted* to do?"

"Actually, my uncle Ken suggested I get some

advice. He's right, you know. I should find out where I stand legally before I proceed."

"Proceed with what?"

"Getting my own apartment, joining my uncle's medical practice and…" She didn't complete the thought.

"Filing for divorce," Dovie concluded for her.

"Yes." Jane's voice was almost inaudible.

"Is a divorce what you want?"

"I don't know anymore, Dovie. I just don't know. Cal and I have had plenty of disagreements over the years, but nothing like this."

"All marriages have ups and downs."

"I've been gone nearly six weeks and I haven't even heard from Cal. It's almost as…as if he's blotted me out of his life."

Dovie suspected that was precisely what he'd been trying to do, but all the evidence suggested he hadn't been very successful. "What about you?" she asked. "Have you tried to reach him?"

Jane didn't want to answer; Dovie could tell from the length of time it took her to speak. "No."

"I see." Indeed she did. Two stubborn, hurting people, both intent on proving how strong and independent they were. "What about the children? Do they miss their father?"

"Paul does the most. He asks about Cal nearly every day. He…he's taken to sucking his thumb again."

"And Mary Ann?"

"She's doing well. I don't think she realizes her father's out of the picture."

"You don't seriously believe that, do you?"

Jane breathed in deeply and Dovie could tell she was holding back tears. "I'm not sure anymore, Dovie." There was a pause. "She's growing like a weed, and she looks so much like Cal."

"She deserves to know her father."

"And I deserve a husband."

"Exactly," Dovie said emphatically. "Then what are you doing seeing an attorney?"

"Cal will never do it. He'll be content to leave things as they are. He seems to think if he ignores me long enough, I'll come to my senses, as he puts it, and return home. But if I did that, I'm afraid everything would go back the way it was before. My feelings wouldn't matter. He'd see himself as the long-suffering husband and me as a jealous shrew. No, Dovie, I'm not going to be the one to give in. Not this time."

"So this is a battle of wills?"

"It's much more than that."

Dovie heard the tears in her voice, and her heart ached for Jane, Cal and those precious children. "This is all because of Nicole Nelson," she said.

"Partially. But there's more."

"There's always more," Dovie agreed.

"I guess Nicole crystallized certain…problems or made them evident, anyway." Jane paused. "She as good as told me she wants him."

That Dovie could believe. "So, being the nice accommodating woman you are, you're just stepping aside and opening the door for her?"

This, too, seemed to unsettle Jane. After taking a moment to consider her answer, she said, "Yes, I guess I am. You and everyone else seem to think I should fight for Cal, that I have too much grit to simply step aside. At one time I did, but just now…I don't. If she wants him and he wants her, then far be it from me to stand between them."

"Oh, Jane, you don't mean that!"

"I do. I swear to you, Dovie, I mean every word." She stopped and Dovie heard her blowing her nose then, a murmured "I'm fine, sweetheart, go watch Mary Ann for me, all right?"

"That was Paul?" Dovie asked. The thought of this little boy, separated from his father for reasons he didn't understand, brought tears to her eyes.

"Yes. He gave me a tissue." She took a deep breath. "Dovie, I have to go now."

"Sounds like you've made up your mind. You're keeping that appointment with the divorce attorney, then?"

"Yes. I'll be getting an apartment right after Christmas, and I'll move in the first of the year."

"You aren't willing to fight for Cal," she said flatly.

"We've been over this, Dovie. No, as far as I'm concerned, he's free to have Nicole if he wants, because he's made it quite plain he isn't interested in me."

"Now, you listen, Jane Patterson. You're in too much pain to deal with this right now. You've just lost your father. That's trauma enough without making a decision about your marriage. And isn't it time you thought about your children?"

"My children?"

"Ask yourself if they need their father and if he needs them. You won't have to dig very deep to know the answers to those questions. Let them be your guide."

To Dovie's surprise, Jane started to laugh. Not the bright humorous laughter she remembered but the soft knowing laughter of a woman who's conceding a point. "You always could do that to me, Dovie."

"Do what?"

Jane sniffled. "Make me cry until I laugh!"

Cal knew something was wrong the minute Grady Weston pulled into the yard. The two men had been neighbors and best friends their whole lives. As kids, they'd discovered a ghost town called Bitter End, which had since become a major focus for the community. Along with Nell Bishop and the man she'd married, writer Travis Grant, they'd uncovered the secrets of the long-forgotten town. It was the original settlement— founded by Pattersons and Westons, among others—and later re-established as Promise.

Grady jumped out of his pickup, and Cal saw that he had a bottle of whiskey in his hand.

"What's that for?" Cal asked, pointing at the bottle.

"I figured you were going to need it," Grady said. "Remember when I was thirteen and I broke my arm?"

Cal nodded. They'd been out horseback riding, and Grady had taken a bad fall. Both boys had realized the bone was broken. Not knowing what to do and fearful of what would happen if he left his friend, Cal had ridden like a madman to get help.

"When you brought my dad back with you, he had a bottle of whiskey. Remember?"

Cal nodded again. Grady's dad had given him a couple of slugs to numb the pain. It was at this point that Cal made the connection. "You've got something to tell me I'm not going to want to hear."

Grady moved onto the porch, and although it was chilly and the wind was up, the two of them sat there.

"I'm not getting involved in this business between you and Jane," Grady began. "That's your affair. I have my own opinion, we all do, but what happens between the two of you…well, you know what I mean."

"Yeah."

"Savannah was in town the other day and she ran into Dovie."

Cal was well aware that Dovie and Jane were good friends, had been for years. "Jane's talked to Dovie?"

"Apparently so."

"And whatever Jane told Dovie, she told Savannah and Savannah told Caroline and Caroline told you. So, what is it?"

Grady hesitated, as though he'd give anything not to be the one telling him this. "Jane's filing for divorce."

"The hell she is." Cal bolted upright, straight off the wicker chair. "That does it." He removed his hat and slapped it against his thigh. "Enough is enough. I've tried to be patient, wait this out, but I'm finished with that."

"Finished?"

"We start getting lawyers involved, and we'll end up hating each other, sure as anything."

Grady chuckled. "What are you going to do?"

"What else can I do? I'm going after her." He barreled into the house, ready to pack his bags.

"You're bringing her home?" his friend asked, following him inside. The screen door slammed shut behind Grady.

"You bet I'm bringing her home. Divorce? That's just crazy!" So far, Cal had played it cool, let Jane have the distance she seemed to need. Obviously that wasn't working. He hadn't thought out his response to the situation, had merely reacted on an emotional level. In the beginning he was too angry to think clearly; then his anger had turned to bitterness, but that hadn't lasted long. Lately, all he'd been was miserable, and he'd had about as much misery as a man could take.

Grady gave him a grin and a thumbs-up. "Good. I wasn't keen on handing over my best bottle of bourbon, so if you have no objection, I'll take this back with me."

"You do that," Cal said.

"Actually this is perfect."

"How do you mean?"

Grady laughed. "A Christmas reunion. Just the kind of thing that makes people feel all warm and fuzzy." The laughter died as Grady looked around the kitchen.

"What?" Cal asked, his mood greatly improved now that he'd made his decision. He loved his wife, loved his children, and nothing was going to keep them apart any longer.

"Well…" Grady scratched his head. "You've got a bit of a mess here."

Cal saw the place with fresh eyes and realized he'd become careless again with Jane away. Their previous reunion had been tainted by a messy house. "I'd better do some cleaning before she gets home. She was none too happy about it the last time."

"You're on your own with this," Grady said. He headed out the door, taking his whiskey with him.

"Grady," Cal said, following him outside. His friend turned around. Cal was unsure how to say this other than straight out. "Thank you."

Grady nodded, touched the brim of his hat and climbed into his truck.

Almost light-headed with relief, Cal went back to the kitchen and tackled the cleaning with enthusiasm. He started a load of dishes, put away leftover food, took out the garbage, mopped the floor. He was scrubbing away at the counter when it occurred to him that after three weeks of caring for her parents, Jane must have been completely worn out. Upon her return to Promise, she'd faced a gigantic mess. *His* mess.

Cal hadn't understood why she'd been so upset over a few dishes and some dirty laundry. He recalled the comments she'd made and finally grasped what she'd really been saying. She'd wanted to be welcomed home for herself and not what she could do to make his life more comfortable. He'd left her with the wrong impression, hadn't communicated his love and respect.

He had to do more than just straighten up the place, Cal decided now. Glancing around, he could see plenty of areas that needed attention. Then it hit him—what

Grady had said about a Christmas reunion. God willing, his family would be with him for the holidays, and when Jane and the children walked in that door, he wanted them to know they'd been in his thoughts every minute of every day.

Christmas. Jane was crazy about Christmas. She spent weeks decorating the house, and while he didn't have time for that, he could put up the tree. Jane and the kids would love that.

Hauling the necessary boxes down from the attic was no small task. He assembled the tree and set it in the very spot Jane had the year before. The lights were his least-favorite task, but he kept thinking of Jane as he wove the strands of tiny colored bulbs through the bright green limbs.

Several shoe boxes were carefully packed with the special beaded ornaments she'd made. He recalled the time and effort she'd put into each one and marveled anew at her skill and the caring they expressed. In that moment, his love for her nearly overwhelmed him.

When he'd finished with the tree, he hung a wreath on the front door. All this activity had made him hungry, so he threw together a ham sandwich and ate it quickly. As he was putting everything back in the fridge—no point in undoing the work of the past few hours—he remembered his conversation with Wade McMillen a week earlier. Cal had stated vehemently that he hadn't "done a damn thing," and Wade had said that was the problem. How right his friend had been.

This separation was of his own making. All his wife had

needed was the reassurance of his love and his commitment to her and their marriage. Until now, he'd been quick to blame Jane—and of course the manipulative Nicole—but he'd played an unsavory role in this farce, too.

Because of the holidays, he had to pay an exorbitant price for a plane ticket to California the next day, December twenty-second. The only seat available was in business class; and considering that he was plunking down as much for this trip as he would for a decent horse, he deserved to sit up front.

The next phone call wasn't as easy to make. He dialed his mother-in-law's number and waited through four interminable rings.

Voice mail came on. He listened to the message, taken aback when Harry Dickinson's voice greeted him. Poor Harry. Poor Stephanie.

He took a deep breath. "Jane, it's Cal. I love you and I love my children. I don't want to lose you. I'll be there tomorrow. I just bought a ticket and when I arrive, we can talk this out. I'm willing to do whatever it takes to save our marriage and I mean that, Jane, with all my heart."

Nine

"Dovie! Have you heard anything?" Ellie asked, making her way along the crowded street to get closer to Dovie and Frank Hennessey. She had Johnny by the hand and Robin in her stroller. Both children were bundled up to ward off the December cold.

The carolers stood on the opposite corner. Glen was with the tenors, and Amy McMillen, the pastor's wife, served as choral director. Carol-singing on the Saturday night before Christmas had become a tradition for Promise Christian Church since the year Wade married Amy. The event was free of charge, but several large cardboard boxes were positioned in front of the choir to collect food and other donations for charity.

"I did talk to Jane," Dovie murmured for Ellie's ears only.

"Again?" Ellie asked, unable to hide her excitement.

Dovie nodded. "She's feeling very torn. I gather her mother's relying on her emotionally."

"But…"

"Don't worry, Ellie," Dovie whispered. "She's halfway home already. I can just feel it!"

"How do you mean?" Ellie was anxious to learn what she could. This episode between Cal and Jane had taken a toll on her own marriage. Glen was upset, so was she, and they'd recently had a heated argument over it, each of them taking sides.

It'd all started when Ellie and Glen decorated their Christmas tree, and Ellie had found the beautiful beaded ornament Jane had made for her the previous year. She'd felt a rush of deep sadness and regret and had said something critical of Cal. Glen had instantly defended his brother.

She was baffled by how quickly their argument had escalated. Within minutes, what had begun as a mere difference of opinion had become a shouting match. Not until later did Ellie realize that this was because they were so emotionally connected to Cal and Jane. She wasn't sure she could ever put that special ornament on the tree again and not feel a sense of loss, especially if the situation continued as it was.

"Did she keep the appointment with the attorney?" Ellie asked. The fact that Cal and Jane had allowed their disagreement to escalate this far horrified her; at the same time it frightened her. Ellie had always viewed Cal and Jane's marriage as stable—like her own. If two people who loved each other could reach this tragic point so quickly, she had to wonder if the same sad future was in store for her and Glen.

The intensity of their own quarrel had shocked her,

and only after their tempers had cooled were Ellie and Glen able to talk sensibly. Her husband insisted they had nothing to worry about, but Ellie still wondered.

Dovie shrugged. "I don't know what happened with the attorney. Doesn't Cal discuss these things with Glen?"

Ellie shook her head. "Cal won't, and every time Glen brings up the subject, they argue. When I told Glen about Jane seeing an attorney, he was furious."

"With Jane?"

"No, with Cal, but if Glen said anything to him, he didn't tell me."

"Oh, dear." Dovie wrapped her scarf around her neck.

The singing began and Ellie lifted Robin out of the stroller and held her up so the child could see her father. Johnny clapped with delight at the lively rendition of "Hark Go the Bells," and Robin imitated her brother.

Ellie's eyes met her husband's. Even though he stood across the street, she could feel his love and it warmed her. This ordeal of Cal's had been difficult for him. They both felt terrible about it. She wished now that she'd done something earlier, *said* something.

A warning about Nicole Nelson, maybe. A reassurance that this problem would pass. Anything.

"I have a good feeling," Dovie said, squeezing Ellie's arm. "In my heart of hearts, I don't think Cal or Jane will ever let this reach the divorce courts."

"I hope you're right," Ellie murmured and shifted Robin from one side to the other.

The Christmas carols continued, joyful and festive,

accompanied by a small group of musicians. The donation boxes were already filled to overflowing.

"You're bringing the children over for cookies and hot chocolate, aren't you?" Dovie asked.

Ellie sent her a look that suggested she wouldn't dream of missing it. So many babies had been born in Promise recently, and several years ago, Dovie and Frank started holding their own Christmas party for all their friends' children. Dovie wore a Mrs. Claus outfit and Frank Hennessey made an appearance as Santa. Even Buttons, their poodle, got into the act, sporting a pair of stuffed reindeer antlers. For a couple who'd never had children of their own, Dovie and Frank did a marvelous job of entertaining the little ones.

"Johnny and Robin wouldn't miss it for the world," Ellie assured her. "I wish…"

Ellie didn't need to finish that thought; Dovie knew what she was thinking. It was a shame that Paul and Mary Ann wouldn't be in Promise for the Hennesseys' get-together.

"I'm just as hopeful as you are that this will be resolved soon," Ellie said, forcing optimism in her words. She wanted so badly to believe it.

"Me, too," Nell Grant said, standing on the other side of Dovie. "The entire community is pulling for them." She blushed. "I hope you don't mind me jumping into the middle of your conversation."

"Everyone's hoping for the best," Dovie said with finality. Then, looking over at the small band of musicians, she turned back to Nell. "Don't tell me that's Jeremy playing the trumpet? It can't be!"

Nell nodded proudly. "He's quite talented, isn't he?"

"Yes, and my goodness, he's so tall."

"Emma, too," Nell said, pointing at the flute player.

"That's Emma?" Ellie asked, unable to hide her shock. Heavens, it hadn't been more than a couple of months since she'd seen Nell's oldest daughter, and the girl looked as though she'd grown several inches.

With this realization came another. It'd been nearly six weeks since Cal had seen his children. At their ages, both were growing rapidly, changing all the time. She could only guess how much he'd missed—and felt sad that he'd let it happen.

Despite her disagreement with Glen, Ellie still blamed Cal. Eventually he'd come to his senses. She hoped that when he did, it wouldn't be too late.

Her mother's mournful expression tugged at Jane's heart as she finished packing her suitcase.

"You're sure this is what you want?" Stephanie Dickinson asked. Tears glistening in her eyes, she stood in the doorway of Jane's old bedroom.

"Yes, Mom. I love my husband. Things would never have gone this far if—"

"It's my fault, isn't it, honey?"

"Oh, Mom, don't even think that." Jane moved away from the bed, where the suitcases lay open, and hugged her mother. "No one's to blame. Or if anyone is, I guess I am. I let everything get out of control. I should've fought for my husband from the first. Cal was angry that I doubted him."

"But he—" Her mother stopped abruptly and bit her lip.

"You heard his message. He loves me and the children, and Mom…until just a little while ago I didn't realize how *much* I love him. It's taken all this time for us both to see what we were doing. I love you and Derek and Uncle Ken, but Los Angeles isn't my home anymore. I love Promise. My friends are there, my home and my husband."

Jane could tell that it was difficult for her mother to accept her decision. Stephanie gnawed on her lower lip and made an obvious effort not to weep.

"You talked to Cal? He knows you're coming?"

"I left him a message."

"But he hasn't returned your call?"

"No." There was such wonderful irony in the situation. Her mother had taken the children on an outing while Jane was scheduled to meet with the attorney. But as she'd sat in the waiting room, she'd tried to picture her life without Cal, without her family and friends in Promise, and the picture was bleak. She could barely keep from dissolving in tears right then and there.

Everything Dovie had said came back to her, and she'd known beyond a doubt that seeing this attorney was wrong. Paul and Mary Ann needed their father, and she needed her husband. For the first time since her father's illness, Jane had felt a surge of hope, the desire to win back her husband. If Nicole thought Jane would simply walk away, she was wrong. At that moment, she'd resolved to fight for her marriage.

Without a word of explanation, Jane left the attorney's office and rushed home. The message light alerted her to a call, and when she listened to it, Cal's deep voice greeted her. His beautiful loving voice, telling her the very things she'd longed to hear.

In her eagerness to return his call, her hand had shaken as she punched out the number. To her consternation she'd had to leave a message. She'd tried his cell phone, too, but Cal was notorious for never remembering to turn it on. Later phone calls went unanswered, as well. Her biggest fear was that he'd already boarded a plane, but she still hoped to stop him, and fly home with the children and meet him in San Antonio. With that in mind, she'd booked her flight.

"I'll try to call him again."

"You could all spend Christmas here," her mother suggested hopefully.

"Mom, you're going with Laurie Jo to Mexico and that's the end of it."

"Yes, I know, but—"

"No buts, you're going. It's exactly what you need."

"But your father hasn't even been gone two months."

Jane shook her head sternly. "Staying here moping is the last thing Dad would want you to do."

Her mother nodded. "You're right…but I'm worried about you and the children."

"Mom, you don't have to be. We'll be fine."

"But you can't go flying off without knowing if Cal will be at the airport when you arrive!"

"I'll give Glen and Ellie a call. They'll see he gets the

message. And if they can't reach him, don't worry—
someone will be at the airport to pick us up." Jane sincerely hoped it would be Cal. And this time she'd make
sure their reunion was everything the previous one wasn't.

Her mother frowned and glanced at her watch. "You
don't have much time. I really wish you weren't in
such a rush."

"Mother, I've been here nearly two months. Anyone
would think you'd be glad to get rid of me." This wasn't
the most sensitive of comments, Jane realized when her
mother's eyes filled with tears and she turned away, not
wanting Jane to see.

"I shouldn't have depended on you and the children
so much," Stephanie confessed. "I'm sorry, Jane."

"Mom, we've already been through this." She closed
the largest of the suitcases, then hugged her mother again.
"I'll call Ellie right now and that should settle everything.
She'll let Cal know which flight I'm on, or die trying."

She wished her husband would phone. Jane desperately
wanted to speak to him, and every effort in the past three
hours had met with failure. Funny, after all these weeks
of no communication, she couldn't wait to speak with him.

"Mommy, Mommy!" Paul dashed into the bedroom
and stuffed his blankey in the open suitcase. Then,
looking very proud of himself, he smiled up at his
mother. "We going home?"

"Home," she echoed and knelt to hug her son. She
felt such joyful anticipation, it was all she could do to
hold it inside.

Luckily, reaching Ellie wasn't difficult. Her sister-in-law was at the feed store and picked up on the second ring. "Frasier Feed," Ellie said in her no-nonsense businesswoman's tone of voice.

"Ellie, it's Jane."

"Jane!" Her sister-in-law nearly exploded with excitement.

"I'm coming home."

"It's about time!"

"Listen," Jane said, "I haven't been able to get hold of Cal. He left a message that he's flying to California, but he didn't say when. Just that he's coming today."

"Cal phoned you?"

"I wasn't here. This is so crazy and wonderful. Ellie, I was sitting in the attorney's office and all of a sudden I knew I could't go through with it. I belong with Cal in Promise."

"Whatever you need, I'll find a way to do it," Ellie said. "You have no idea how much we've all missed you. None of us had any idea what to think when we didn't hear from you."

"I know. I'm so sorry. It's just that…" Jane wasn't sure how to explain why she hadn't called anyone in Promise for all those weeks. Well, she'd tried to reach Dovie, but—

"Don't apologize. I remember what it was like after my father died. One night I sat and watched some old westerns he used to love and I just cried and cried. Even now I can't watch a John Wayne movie and not think of my dad."

"You'll make sure Cal doesn't leave Promise?" That

was Jane's biggest concern. She hated the thought of getting home and learning he was on his way to California. If that did happen, he'd find an empty house, because her mother would be in Mexico.

"You can count on it."

"And here, write down my flight information and give it to Cal—if you catch him in time."

"I'll find him for you, don't you worry."

Jane knew her sister-in-law would come through.

Cal spent the morning completing what chores he could, getting ready to leave. Glen was attending a cattlemen's conference in Dallas and would be home that evening, but by then Cal would be gone.

Now that his decision was made, he wondered what had taken him so long to own up to the truth. His love for Jane and their children mattered more than anything—more than pride and more than righteousness. His friends and family had tried to show him that, but Cal hadn't truly grasped it until he learned how close he was to losing everything that gave his life meaning.

His father had urged him to listen to reason with that conversation during Thanksgiving dinner, and Phil's advice hadn't come cheap. Not when Cal was paying the bill at the Rocky Creek Inn.

Glen had put in his two cents' worth, and his comments had created a strain in their relationship. Cal hadn't been able to listen to his younger brother, couldn't accept his judgment or advice—although he wished he was more like Glen, easygoing and quick to forgive.

Even Wade McMillen had felt obliged to confront Cal. Every single thing his friends and family said had eventually hit home, but the full impact hadn't been made until the night Cal had gone to Billy D's.

Only when Nicole Nelson had approached his table had he seen the situation clearly. He'd been such a fool, and he'd nearly fallen in with her schemes. His wife was right: Nicole *did* want him. Damned if he knew why. It still bothered Cal that Jane hadn't trusted him. He hadn't even been tempted by Nicole, he could say that in all honesty, but he'd allowed her to flatter him.

Cal had made his share of mistakes and was more than willing to admit it. He regretted the things he'd said and done at a time when Jane had been weakest and most vulnerable. Thinking over the past few months, Cal viewed them as wasted. He wanted to kick himself for waiting so long to go after his family.

As he headed toward the house, he saw Grady's truck come barreling down the driveway. His neighbor eased to a stop near Cal, rolled down his window and shouted, "Call Ellie!"

"Ellie? What about?"

"No idea. Caroline called from town with the message."

"All right," he said, hurrying into the house.

Grady left, shouting "Merry Christmas" as his truck rumbled back down the drive.

When Cal reached his front door, he saw a large piece of paper taped there. "CALL ELLIE IMMEDI-ATELY," it read. "Good Luck, Nell and Travis."

What the hell? Cal walked into his house and grabbed the phone. He noticed the blinking message light, but not wanting to be distracted, he ignored it.

"Is that you, Cal?" Ellie asked, answering the phone herself.

"Who else were you expecting?"

"No one."

She sounded mighty cheerful.

"You doing anything just now?" his sister-in-law asked.

"Yeah, as a matter of act, I am. I've got a plane to catch. It seems I have some unfinished business in California."

He'd thought Ellie would shriek with delight or otherwise convey her approval, since she'd made her opinion of his actions quite clear.

But all she said was "You're going after Jane?"

He'd be on the road this very minute if he wasn't being detained. He said as much, although he tried to be polite about it. "What's with the urgency? Why is it so important that I call you?"

"Don't go!"

"What?" For a moment Cal was sure he'd misunderstood.

"You heard me. Don't go," Ellie repeated, "because Jane and the kids are on their way home."

"If this is a joke, Ellie, I swear to you—"

She laughed and didn't let him finish. "When was the last time you listened to your messages?"

The flashing light condemned him for a fool. He should have realized Jane would try to reach him. In his eagerness he'd overlooked the obvious.

"What flight? When does she land?" He'd be there

to meet her and the children with flowers and chocolates and whatever else Dovie could recommend. Ah yes, Dovie. Someone else who'd been on his case. He smiled, remembering her less-than-subtle approach.

Ellie rattled off the flight number and the approximate time Jane and the children would land, and Cal scribbled down the information. "How did she manage to get a flight so quickly?" With holiday travel, most flights were booked solid.

"I don't know. You'll need to ask Jane."

Cal didn't care what she'd had to pay; he wanted her home. And now that the time was so close, he could barely contain himself.

As soon as he finished his conversation with Ellie, Cal listened to his messages. When he heard Jane's voice, his heart swelled with love. He could hear her relief, her joy and her love—the same emotions he was experiencing.

With his steps ten times lighter than they'd been a mere twenty-four hours ago, Cal jumped into the car and drove to town. Before he left, though, he carefully surveyed the house, making sure everything was perfect for Jane and the children. The Christmas tree looked lovely, and he'd even bought and wrapped a few gifts to put underneath. Not a single dirty dish could be seen. The laundry was done, and the sheets on the bed were fresh. This was about as good as it got.

Cal dropped in at Dovie's, and then—because he couldn't resist—he walked over to Tumbleweed Books.

Sure enough, Nicole was behind the counter. Her face brightened when he entered the store.

"Cal, hello," she said with an eagerness she didn't bother to disguise.

"Merry Christmas."

"You, too." People were busy wandering the aisles, but Nicole headed directly toward him. "It's wonderful to see you."

He forced a smile. "About our conversation the other night…"

Nicole placed her hand on his arm. "I was more blunt than I intended, but that's only because I know what it's like to be lonely, especially at Christmastime."

"I'm here to thank you," Cal said, enjoying this.

Nicole flashed her baby blues at him with such adoration it was hard to maintain a straight face.

"You're right, I have been terribly lonely."

"Not anymore, Cal, I'm here for you."

"Actually," he said, removing her fingers from his forearm, "it was after our conversation that I realized how much I miss my wife."

"Your…wife?" Nicole's face fell.

"I phoned her and we've reconciled. You helped open my eyes to what's important."

Nicole's mouth sagged. "I…I wish you and Jane the very best," she said, obviously struggling to hide her disappointment. "So you decided to go back to her." She shrugged. "Too bad. It could have been great with us, Cal."

Her audacity came as a shock. She'd actually believed he'd give up his wife and family for her. If he hadn't already figured out exactly the kind of woman she was and what she'd set out to do, he would have known in that instant. He should have listened to Jane— and just about everyone else.

"Stay out of my life, Nicole. Don't *just happen* to run into me again. Don't seek me out. Ever."

"I'm sorry you feel this way," she mumbled, not meeting his eyes.

During the course of his life, Cal had taken a lot of flack for being too direct and confrontational. Today he felt downright pleased at having imparted a few un-adorned facts to a woman who badly needed to hear them. He walked out of the bookstore, and with a determination that couldn't be shaken, marched toward his parked car. He was going to collect his wife and children.

Jane's flight landed in San Antonio after midnight. Both children were asleep, and she didn't know if anyone would be at the airport to meet her. During the long hours on the plane, she'd fantasized about the reunion with her husband, but she'd begun to feel afraid that she'd been too optimistic.

All the passengers had disembarked by the time she gathered everything from the overhead bins and awakened Paul. The three-year-old rubbed his eyes, and Jane suspected he was still too dazed to understand that they were nearly home. Dragging his small backpack behind him, he started down the aisle. Mary Ann was asleep against her shoulder.

Their baggage was already on the carousel, and with

a porter's assistance, she got it all piled on a cart. Then she moved slowly into the main area of the airport. Her fear—that Cal might not be there—was realized when she didn't see him anywhere. Her disappointment was so intense she stopped, clutching her son's hand as she tried to figure out what to do next.

"Jane…Jane!" Cal's voice caught her and she whirled around.

He stood at the information counter, wearing the biggest smile she'd ever seen. "I didn't know what to think when you weren't here. I thought you—"

"This is your family?" the woman at the counter interrupted.

"Yes," he said happily.

Paul seemed to come fully awake then and let out a yell. Dropping his backpack, the boy hurled himself into Cal's waiting arms.

Cal wrapped his son in his embrace. Jane watched as his eyes drifted shut and he savored this hug. Then Paul began to chatter until his words became indistinguishable.

"Just a minute, Paul," Cal said as he walked toward Jane.

With their children between them—Paul on his hip, Mary Ann asleep on her shoulder—Cal threw one arm around Jane and kissed her. It was the kind of deep open kiss the movies would once have banned. A kiss that illustrated everything his phone message had already explained. A real kiss, intense and passionate and knee-shaking.

The tears, which had been so near the surface

moments earlier, began to flow down her cheeks. But they were no longer tears of disappointment; they were tears of joy. She found she wasn't the least bit troubled about such an emotional display in the middle of a busy airport with strangers looking on.

"It's all right, honey," Cal whispered. He kissed her again, and she thought she saw tears in his eyes, too.

"I love you so much," she wept.

"Oh, honey, I love you, too. I'm sorry."

"Me, too— I made so many mistakes."

"I've learned my lesson," he said solemnly.

"So have I. You're my home, where I live and breathe. Nothing's right without you."

"Oh, Jane," he whispered and leaned his forehead against hers. "Let's go home."

They talked well into the night, almost nonstop, discussing one subject after another. Cal held her and begged her forgiveness while she sobbed in his arms. They talked about their mistakes and what they'd learned, and vowed never again to allow anyone—man, woman, child or beast—to come between them.

Afterward, exhausted though she was from the flight and the strain of the past months, Jane was too keyed up to sleep. Too happy and excited. Even after they'd answered all the questions, resolved their doubts and their differences, Jane had something else on her mind. When her husband reached for her, she went into his arms eagerly. Their kisses grew urgent, their need for each other explosive.

"Cal, Cal," she whispered, reluctantly breaking off the kiss.

"Yes?" He kissed her shoulder and her ear.

"I think you should know I stopped taking my birth control pills."

Cal froze. "You what?"

She sighed and added, "I really couldn't see the point."

It was then that her husband chuckled. "In other words, there's a chance I might get you pregnant again?"

She kissed his stubborn wonderful jaw. "There's always a chance."

"How would you feel about a third child?"

"I think three's a good number, don't you?"

"Oh, yes—and if it's a boy we'll name him after your father."

"Harry Patterson?" she asked, already picturing a little boy so like his father and older brother. "Dad would be pleased."

Two nights later Cal, Jane and the children drove into town to attend Christmas Eve services. Their appearance generated considerable interest from the community, Jane noted. Every head seemed to turn when they strolled into the church, and plenty of smiles were sent in their direction. People slipped out of their seats to hug Jane and slap Cal on the back or shake his hand.

When Wade stepped up to the pulpit, he glanced straight at Cal, grinned knowingly and acknowledged him with a brief nod. Jane saw Cal return the gesture and nearly laughed out loud when Wade gave Cal a discreet thumbs-up.

"You talked to Wade?" she asked, whispering in his ear.

Her husband squeezed her hand and nodded.

"What did he say?"

"I'll tell you later."

"Tell me now," Jane insisted.

Cal sighed. "Let's just say the good pastor's words hit their mark."

"Oh?" She raised her eyebrows and couldn't keep from smiling. Being here with her husband on Christmas Eve, sharing the music, the joy, love and celebration with her community, nearly overwhelmed her.

Not long after Jane and Cal had settled into the pew, Glen, Ellie and their two youngsters arrived, followed by her father-in-law. Phil's eyes met Jane's and he winked. Jane pressed her head to her husband's shoulder.

Cal slid his arm around her and reached for a hymnal, and they each held one side of the book. Organ music swirled around them, and together they raised their voices in song. "O, Come All Ye Faithful." "Silent Night." "Angels We Have Heard on High." Songs celebrating a birth more than two thousand years ago. Songs celebrating a rebirth, a reunion, a renewal of their own love.

The service ended with a blast of exultation from the trumpet players, and finally the "Hallelujah" chorus from the choir. More than once, Jane felt Cal's gaze on her. She smiled up at him, and as they gathered their children and started out of the church, she was sure she could feel her father's presence, as well.

Phil was waiting for them outside. Paul ran to his grandfather and Phil lifted the boy in his arms, hugging him.

"We have a lot to celebrate," he said quietly.

"Yes, Dad, we do," Cal agreed. He placed one arm around his father and the other around Jane, and they all headed for home.

* * * * *

MAIL-ORDER BRIDE

In memory of Ron Cowden
and for his son, Max,
beloved New Zealand friends

Prologue

"I'm so worried about dear Caroline," Ethel Myers murmured thoughtfully, sipping tea from a dainty porcelain cup. Her fingers clutched a delicate lace-trimmed handkerchief and when a droplet of moisture formed in the corner of her eye, she dabbed it gently. "Sister, I do believe the brew is stronger today."

"Yes," Mabel admitted. "But remember what Father said about the brew enhancing one's ability to solve problems."

"And we must do something to help Caroline."

Mabel shook her head sadly. "Perhaps if you and I had married suitable gentlemen all those years ago..."

"Oh, yes, then maybe we'd know how to help that sweet, sweet child." Ethel's faded blue eyes brightened momentarily. "You do remember that George Guettermann once asked for my hand."

"As I recall, Mother was quite impressed with him."

Ethel's shoulders sagged. "But Father was suspicious from the first."

Mabel sighed heavily. "Mr. Guettermann did cut such a dashing figure."

A wistful expression marked Ethel's fragile features. "If only he hadn't already been married."

"The scoundrel!"

"We must learn to forgive him, Sister."

Mabel nodded and lifted the steaming pot of brew. "I was thinking of Caroline's young man. Another cup, Sister?"

"Oh dear, should we?" Ethel's hand flew to her mouth to smother a loud hiccup, and she had the good grace to look embarrassed.

"We *must* find a way to help her."

"Yes," Ethel agreed as Mabel filled her cup to the bright gold rim. "Poor, poor Caroline."

"There was something in his eyes."

"George?"

"No, Sister. Caroline's young man."

"Indeed, there was something about his eyes." Ethel took another sip and lightly patted her chest at the strength of their father's special recipe. "Sister, the brew…"

"We must think!"

"Oh, yes. Think. What can we do for dear Caroline?"

"If only her mother were alive."

"Or grandmother."

"Grandmother?"

"Her great-great-grandmother, perhaps. *She* would know what to do." Ethel smiled. "Do you recall how she frowned on courting? Said it simply wasn't necessary."

"Grandmother would. Asa Myers brought her to

Seattle with the other mail-order brides. She and Grandfather knew each other less than twenty-four hours before they were married."

"A courtship wasn't necessary and they were so happy."

"Very happy and very compatible."

"With seven children, they must have agreed quite nicely," Ethel said and giggled delightedly.

"It's such a shame marriages aren't arranged these days," Mabel said, taking another long sip of tea.

"If only we could find Caroline a husband."

"But, Sister…" Mabel was doubtful. For over fifty years they'd been unable to find husbands of their own. So how could they expect to come up with one for their beloved niece?

Ethel's hand shook as she lowered the cup to its saucer. "Sister, Sister! I do believe I have the solution." Her voice quavered with excitement as she reached for the morning paper.

"Yes?"

"Our own Caroline will be a mail-order bride."

Mabel frowned. "But things like that aren't done in this day and age."

Ethel fumbled with the paper until she located the classified section. She folded back the unwieldy page and pointed to the personal column. "Here, read this."

Mabel read the ad aloud, her voice trembling. "Wanted—Wife for thirty-two-year-old Alaskan male. Send picture. Transportation provided." The advertisement included the name Paul Trevor and a box number.

"But Sister, do we dare?"

"We must. Caroline is desperately unhappy."

"And she did have the opportunity to select a husband of her own."

"She chose poorly. The beast left her standing at the altar."

"The scoundrel!"

"We mustn't tell her, of course."

"Oh, no, we can't let her know. Our Caroline would object strenuously."

"Sister, I do believe the brew has helped."

"Indeed! Some more?"

Ethel raised her cup and her older sister automatically refilled it. A smile of satisfaction lifted the edges of her mouth. "Father's recipe was most beneficial."

"It always is, Sister."

"Oh, yes. Yes, indeed."

One

Caroline Myers waited at a Starbucks in the Seattle-Tacoma airport, accompanied by her great-aunts. She could hardly believe she would soon depart the state of Washington for unknown adventures in Alaska.

"Do you have everything, dear?" Mabel asked her for the third time.

"Aunt Ethel, Aunt Mabel, please—I can't allow you to do this."

"Nonsense," Ethel said briskly. "This vacation is our gift to you."

"But Alaska in October?"

"It's lovely, dear heart. I promise."

"Yes, lovely," Ethel agreed, trying to hide a smile. "And we have the nicest surprise waiting for you."

Caroline stared suspiciously at her great-aunts. Something that could only be mischief danced in their sparkling blue eyes. At seventy-nine and eighty, they were her only living relatives in Seattle, and she loved them dearly. Despite their age, she'd always called them simply *aunt*.

"But this trip is too much," she said.

"Nonsense."

"Hurry, dear. Go and check in or you'll miss your plane."

"One question."

Ethel and Mabel exchanged fleeting glances. "Yes?"

"Why the blood tests? I didn't know anything like that was necessary for travel within the United States."

Mabel paused to clear her throat, casting her eyes wildly about the terminal. "It's a new law."

"A gubernatorial decision, I…I believe," Ethel stammered.

"It's such a pity," Mabel said, changing the subject. "We wanted to give you a thermos with Father's special tea to sustain you during the flight, but all these rules…" She shook her head.

"It's probably just as well," Caroline said, doing her utmost to swallow a chuckle. She'd been eighteen when she'd first discovered the potency of her great-grandfather's special recipe.

"We put some sandwiches in that bag, though." Ethel pointed at the duffel the aunts had packed for her. "Plus tea for when you land. And a little something extra."

Caroline smiled her thanks, feeling a bit foolish about dragging food, not to mention the "tea," all the way to Alaska. She wondered if the duffel with its special wares would survive the baggage handlers.

"Do write. And call," Mabel said anxiously.

"Of course. I'll send postcards." Caroline kissed both aunts on the cheek and hugged them gently. Ethel sniffled, and Mabel cast her a look of sisterly displeasure. Caroline grinned. Her two great-aunts had been a constant delight all her life. They were charming, loving and thoroughly enchanting. They'd done everything they could to cheer her after Larry's defection. The sudden memory of the man she'd loved with such intensity produced a fresh wave of pain that threatened to wash away the pleasure of this moment.

Ethel sniffled again. "We shall miss you dreadfully," she announced, glaring at her sister.

Caroline threw back her head and laughed aloud. "I'm only going to be gone a week." Ethel's and Mabel's eyes avoided hers and Caroline wondered what little game they were playing.

"But a week seems so long."

"You have your ticket?" Mabel asked hurriedly.

"Right here." Caroline patted the side of her purse.

"Remember, a nice young man will be meeting you in Fairbanks."

Caroline nodded. Her aunts had gone over the details of this vacation a minimum of fifty times. "And he's taking me to—"

"Gold River," the great-aunts chimed in, bobbing their heads in unison.

"There I'll be met by—"

"Paul Trevor." Ethel and Mabel shared a silly grin.

"Right, Paul Trevor." Caroline studied her aunts surreptitiously. If she didn't know better, she'd think they had something up their sleeves. For days, the two of them had been acting like giddy teenagers, whispering and giggling. Caroline had objected to this vacation from the first; Alaska in early October wasn't exactly her first choice. She wouldn't have argued nearly as much had they suggested Hawaii, but her aunts had been so insistent on Alaska that Caroline had finally agreed. This was their gift to her in an effort to heal a broken heart, and she wasn't about to ruin it by being stubborn. She couldn't bear to inform them that it would take a whole lot more than a trip north for her heart to mend.

Caroline hugged her aunts and secured her purse strap over her shoulder, then got up to join the line at the airline counter.

"Do be happy, dear," Ethel said tearfully, pressing her frilly lace handkerchief under her nose.

Mabel's voice seemed strained as she echoed her sister's words and clasped Caroline's free hand. "Happiness, child. Much, much happiness."

Shaking her head at their strange behavior, Caroline checked in, went through Security and dropped off her bags. She got to the departure lounge without much time to spare. Ten minutes later, she entered the long, narrow jetway that led to the Boeing 767. The flight attendant directed her to the business section and, again, Caroline had to wonder how her aunts could possibly afford this trip.

Ethel and Mabel left the airport pleased with themselves yet already missing their beloved niece.

"It's fate, Sister," Mabel said softly.

"Oh, indeed. Paul Trevor chose her over all those other women."

"He sounds like such a good man."

"And so handsome."

"Only he wrote that he has a beard now. Does Caroline like men with beards?"

Ethel shrugged. "I really couldn't say."

"She'll grow to love him."

"Oh, yes. Given time, she'll be very happy with Paul."

"Perhaps she'll be as compatible with him as Grandmother was with Grandfather."

"Seven children. Oh, Sister!" Ethel brought her gloved hands to her rosy cheeks.

Doubts vanished and the two exchanged a brilliant smile.

"We did our best for her," Mabel said happily. "Her mother would've been proud."

"Her great-great-grandmother, too," Ethel said, and as they giggled with pure delight, several onlookers cast curious glances in their direction.

Caroline slept for most of the night flight to Fairbanks. She was exhausted from a hectic week at work. As a nurse for Dr. Kenneth James, an internist, she often put in long days. Dr. James gave her the week off without complaint and then, on Friday afternoon, shook her hand and wished her much happiness. Now that she thought about it, Caroline found his words puzzling. Vacations were about fun. Happiness came from having a satisfactory relationship. Like hers and Larry's... His name drifted into her mind with such ease that Caroline shook her head in an effort to dismiss it.

Straightening in her seat, she opened her eyes. The cabin lights were dimmed, and the only other passenger in business class was asleep. The two attendants were drinking coffee, but when one of them noticed that Caroline was awake, she immediately approached her.

"You missed the meal. Would you care for something to eat now?"

Caroline shook her head. "No, thanks."

The tall brunette responded with a smile and a slight nod and returned to her coffee. Caroline watched as she walked away. Maybe this flight attendant was the type of woman her ex-fiancé should marry, she mused. She'd known from the beginning how completely dissimilar Larry's and her tastes were. Larry liked late, late nights and breakfast in bed, while she was a morning person, eager to begin each new day. Caroline enjoyed the outdoor life— hiking, camping, boating. Larry's idea of roughing it was doing without valet service. She liked cornflakes with chocolate syrup poured over the top and spaghetti for breakfast. Larry preferred formal dinners with nothing more exotic than meat and potatoes. And those were just the superficial differences between them. But they'd loved each other enough to believe they could compromise. *She* had loved *him*, Caroline corrected herself. At the last minute, Larry had buckled under his doubts and had sent his witless brother to contact her an hour before the wedding ceremony. Once again, humiliation engulfed her.

For the first week, Caroline had hidden from the

world. Her two beloved aunts had hovered over her constantly, insisting that she eat and sleep, taking her temperature in case she developed what they called the ague. Caroline assumed it must be some kind of fever and allowed them to fret over her. At the time, it would've taken more energy to assure them she was fine than to submit to their tender ministrations.

A month passed and Caroline gradually worked her way out of the heavy depression that had hung over her like a thundercloud. She smiled and laughed, but suspected that her aunts were unconvinced. Every time she was with them, they stuck a thermometer under her tongue and shook their gray heads with worried frowns.

Larry called her only once to stammer his regrets and to apologize repeatedly. If she hadn't been so much in love with him, she might've been able to accept that he'd probably done them both a favor. Now there were whole hours when she didn't think about him, or hunger for information about him, or long to be held in his arms. Still, the thought of him with another woman was almost more than Caroline could tolerate. In time, however, she would learn to accept that as well.

The disaster with Larry had taught her that she possessed a far stronger constitution than she'd ever believed. She'd been able to hold her head high and return to work a week after the aborted wedding. It hadn't been easy, but she'd done it with a calm maturity that impressed even her. She was going to come out of this a much wiser, more discerning woman. Someday there'd be a man who would love her enough to appreciate her sometimes unconventional ways. When they fell in love, she'd think about marriage again. But not for a long time, Caroline decided—not for a very long time.

As the plane descended into Fairbanks, Caroline gathered her jacket and her purse, preparing to disembark. It was still dark, but dawn was starting to streak the sky. Just as her aunts had promised, there was someone waiting for her at the airport. She had no sooner walked off the plane than a middle-aged man with bushy eyebrows and a walrus mustache held up a piece of cardboard with her name printed across it in bold letters.

"Hello, I'm Caroline Myers," she told him, shifting her purse from one hand to the other.

"Welcome to Alaska," he said with a wide grin and offered his hand. "Name's John Morrison."

Caroline shook it. She liked him immediately. "Thank you, John."

The man continued to stare at her and rubbed the side of his square jaw. Slowly, he shook his head and a sly grin raised the edges of his mouth. "Paul did all right for himself," he mumbled.

"Pardon?"

"Ah, nothing," John responded, shaking his head again. "I'm just surprised is all. I didn't expect him to come up with anyone half as attractive as you. I don't suppose you have a friend?"

Caroline hadn't the faintest idea what this burly bush pilot was getting at, or why he'd be curious about her friends. Surely he'd flown more than one woman into the Alaskan interior. She was like any other tourist visiting Alaska for a one-week stay. She planned to get plenty of rest and relaxation on the direct orders of her aunts. In addition, she hoped to take invigorating walks and explore the magic of the tundra. Her aunts had mentioned Paul Trevor's name on several occasions and Caroline assumed they'd hired him as her guide. She wouldn't mind having someone show her the countryside. There was so much to see and do, and Caroline was ready for it all.

Once John had collected her suitcase, plus the duffel bag her aunts had so determinedly packed, he escorted Caroline to the single-engine Cessna and helped her climb aboard.

"Won't be long now," he said, placing the earphones over his head and flipping several switches. As he zipped up his fur-lined coat, he glanced in her direction with a frown. Then the control tower issued instructions and John turned his attention to the radio. Once on the runway, the plane accelerated and was soon aiming for the dawn sky in a burst of power that had Caroline clenching her hands. She was accustomed to flying, but not in anything quite this small. In comparison to the wide-bodied jet, this Cessna seemed tiny and fragile.

"You might want to look in some of those boxes back there." He jerked his head toward the large pile of sacks and cardboard boxes resting next to her suitcase at the rear of the plane.

"Uh, what should I be looking for?"

"A coat. It's going to get damn cold up here. That little jacket's never gonna be warm enough."

"Okay." Caroline unfastened the seat belt and turned around to bend over the back of her seat. She sorted through the sacks and found a variety of long underwear and flannel shirts.

"Paul's right about you needing this. I hope the boots fit. I got the best available."

"Boots?"

"Lady, trust me. You're going to need them."

"I imagine they were expensive." She had her credit cards with her, but if Paul Trevor expected her to pick up the tab on a complete winter wardrobe, then he had another think coming.

Caroline pulled out a thick coat, but it was so bulky that she placed it over her knees. She took off her jacket and slipped her arms into a cozy flannel shirt. She'd put on the coat when they landed.

"What did you bring with you?" John asked, eyeing the duffel bag at Caroline's feet.

She rolled her eyes. "My aunts sent along some food."

John chuckled.

Now that she'd mentioned it, Caroline discovered she was hungry. It'd been hours since she'd last eaten, and her stomach growled as she opened the bag to find half a dozen thick sandwiches and—the promised thermos. There was also a brightly wrapped gift.

Somewhat surprised, Caroline removed the package and tore off the bright paper and ribbon. The sheer negligee with the neckline and sleeves trimmed in faux fur baffled her even more.

John saw her blink and laughed loudly. "I see they included something to keep your neck warm."

Caroline found his humor less than amusing and stuffed the gown back inside the bag. She'd never thought of her aunts as senile, but their recent behavior gave her cause to wonder.

She shared a turkey sandwich with John and listened as he spoke at length about Alaska. His love for this last frontier was apparent in every sentence. His comments included a vivid description of the tundra and its varied wildlife.

"I have a feeling you're going to like it here."

"Well, I like what little I've seen," Caroline said. She'd expected the land to be barren and harsh. It was, but there was a majestic beauty about it that made Caroline catch her breath.

"That's Denali over there," John told her. "She's the highest peak in North America."

"I thought McKinley was."

"Folks around here prefer to call her Denali."

"What's that?" Caroline pointed to the thin silver ribbon that stretched across the rugged countryside below.

"The Yukon River. She flows over two thousand miles from northwest Canada to the Bering Sea."

"Wow."

"Anything you'd like to know about Paul?"

"Paul Trevor? Not really. Is there anything I *should* know?" Like her aunts, John seemed to bring up the other man's name at every opportunity.

He gave another merry chuckle. "Guess you'll be finding out about him soon enough."

"Right." She eyed him curiously. She was anxious to get a look at this man who insisted she have all this costly gear.

"He's a quiet guy. Hope you don't mind that."

"I usually chatter enough for two. I think we'll get along fine. Besides, I don't plan on being here that long."

John frowned. "I doubt you'll ever get Paul to leave Alaska."

Caroline was offended by the brusque tone. "I don't have any intention of trying."

The amusement faded from John's rugged face as he checked the instruments on the front panel. "You aren't afraid of flying, are you?"

She hadn't thought about it much until now. "Afraid? Why should I be afraid?"

"Looks like we may be headed into a storm. Nothing to worry about, but this could be a real roller-coaster for a while."

"I'll be fine." The sudden chill in the cabin caused Caroline to reach for the thermos. "My aunts make a mean cup of tea. Interested?"

"No, thanks." He focused on the gauges. Caroline re-fastened her seat belt, fingers trembling.

The first cup of spiked tea brought a rush of warmth to her chilled arms, and when the plane pitched and heaved, she carefully refilled the plastic cup and gulped down a second. "Hey, this is fun," she said with a tiny laugh twenty minutes later. If the truth be known, she was frightened out of her wits, but she put on a brave front and held on to her drink with both hands. Her aunts' tea was courage in a cup.

By the time John announced that they were within a half hour of Gold River, Caroline felt as warm as toast. As they made their descent, she peeked out the window at the uneven row of houses. A blanket of snow covered the ground and curling rings of smoke rose from a dozen chimneys.

"It's not much of a town, is it?" she murmured.

"Around three hundred. Mostly Athabascans— they're Indians who were once nomadic, following caribou and other game. When the white settlers arrived, they established permanent villages. Nowadays, they mostly hunt and fish. Once we get a bit closer you'll see a string of caribou hides drying in the sun."

"How...interesting." Caroline had no idea how else to respond.

"What does Paul do?" she asked a few minutes later.

John gave her a curious stare. "Don't you know? He works for the oil company. Keeps tabs on the pump station for the pipeline."

She brushed aside the blond curl that fell over her face. "I thought he was a guide of some sort."

As the Cessna circled the village, Caroline saw people

scurrying out of the houses. Several raised their arms high above their heads and waved. "They see us," she said.

"They've probably spent days preparing for your arrival."

"How thoughtful." The village must only entertain a handful of tourists a year, she figured, and residents obviously went to a great deal of trouble to make sure that those who did come felt welcome. Caroline rubbed her eyes. The whole world seemed to be whirling. The people and houses blurred together and she shook her head, hoping to regain her bearings. The thermos was empty; Caroline realized she was more than a little intoxicated.

A glance at the darkening clouds produced a loud grumble from John. "Doesn't look like I'm going to be able to stick around for the reception."

"I'm sorry." John was probably a local hero. This welcoming party was likely as much in his honor as hers. It appeared that the entire village was outside now, with everyone pointing toward the sky and waving enthusiastically. "I don't see a runway."

"There isn't one."

"But…"

"There's enough of a clearing to make a decent landing. I've come down in a lot worse conditions."

Caroline's nails cut into her palm. She didn't find his words all that reassuring. Why her aunts would choose such a remote village for her vacation was beyond her. This whole trip was turning into much more of an adventure than she'd ever dreamed—or wanted.

As the plane descended, she closed her eyes until she felt the wheels bounce on the uneven ground. She was jostled, jolted and jarred, but otherwise unscathed. Once they came to a complete stop, Caroline could breathe again.

The single engine continued to purr as John unhooked his seat belt. "Go ahead and climb out. I'll hand you the gear."

Using her shoulder to push open the airplane door, Caroline nearly fell to the snow, despite her effort to climb down gracefully. A gust of wind sobered her instantly. "It's cold!"

"Yeah, but Paul will warm you," John shouted over the engine's noise. He tossed out her suitcase and a large variety of boxes and sacks. "Good luck to you. I have a feeling you're the best thing to happen to Paul in a long time."

"Thanks." She stood in the middle of the supplies and blinked twice. "Aren't you coming with me?"

"Can't. I've got to get out of here before this storm hits." He shut the door and a minute later was taxiing away.

With a sense of disbelief, Caroline watched him leave. Already she could see several snowmobiles and a team of dogs pulling a large sled racing toward her. She waved on the off-chance they couldn't see her. Again the earth seemed to shift beneath her feet, and she rubbed her eyes in an effort to maintain her balance. Good grief, just how much of that tea had she drunk?

By the time the first dogsled arrived, she'd mustered

a smile. "Hello," she greeted, raising her hand, praying no one would guess she was more than a little tipsy.

"Welcome."

The man, who must be Paul Trevor, walked toward her and handed her a small bouquet of flowers. He was tall and dark, and from what she could see of his bearded face, reasonably attractive. Untamed curls fell with rakish disregard across a wide, intelligent brow. His eyes, as blue as her own, gazed at her critically. She'd taken to John Morrison immediately, but Caroline wasn't sure she'd like this man. John had spoken of him with respect, and it was obvious that he was considered a leader among the villagers. But his intensity unnerved her. Caroline wasn't about to let him intimidate her; however, now wasn't the time to say much of anything. Not when her tongue refused to cooperate with her brain.

"Thank you." Caroline closed her eyes as she smelled the flowers, expecting the sweet scent of spring, only to have her nose tickled by the prickly needles. She gave a startled gasp and her eyes flew open.

"They've been dried."

"Oh." She felt like a fool. There weren't any flowers in Alaska this time of year. "Of course—they must be."

"Everything's ready if you are."

"Sure." Caroline assumed he was speaking of the welcoming reception.

The large group of people quickly loaded her suitcase and the other boxes onto several sleds. Caroline took a step toward Paul and nearly stumbled. Again the ground pitched under her feet. She recognized it as the potency of the tea and not an earthquake, but for a moment she was confused. "I'm sorry," she murmured. "I seem to be a bit unsteady."

Paul guided her to the dogsled. "It might be better if you sat." He pulled back a heavy blanket and helped her into the sled. A huge husky, clearly the lead dog, turned his head to examine her and Caroline grinned sheepishly. "I don't weigh much," she told him and giggled. Then she groaned. She was beginning to sound like her aunts.

The trip into Gold River took only minutes. Paul helped her out of the sled and led her into the long narrow building in the center of the village. Candles flickered all around the room. Tables filled with a variety of dishes lined the walls. A priest, Russian Orthodox, Caroline guessed, wore a long gold robe. He smiled at her warmly and stepped forward to greet her, taking her hand in his.

"Welcome to Gold River. I'm Father Nabokov."

"I'm pleased to meet you, Father." Caroline prayed that he didn't smell her aunts' brew on her breath.

"Are you hungry?" Paul had shed his thick coat and she removed hers, passing it to him. The force of his personality was revealed in his stance. On meeting him, Caroline understood why both John and her two aunts had found occasion to mention Paul. His personality was strong, but there was a gentleness as well, a tenderness he preferred to disguise with the sense of remoteness she'd noticed earlier.

"Hungry? No…not really," she replied tentatively, realizing that she was staring at him. Paul didn't seem to mind. For that matter, he appeared to be sizing her up as well, and judging by the lazy, sensual smile that moved from his mouth to his eyes, he seemed to like what he saw.

If only Caroline could have cleared her mind, she felt she might've been able to strike up a witty conversation, but her thoughts were preoccupied with the murmuring around her. It looked as though the entire village was crammed inside the meeting hall. Someone was playing music, but it wasn't on an instrument Caroline recognized. A fiddle player joined the first man and the festive mood spread until everyone was laughing and singing. Several helped themselves to plates and heaped food on them from the serving dishes.

"Perhaps it would be best if we started things now," Father Nabokov suggested. "It doesn't look like we'll be able to hold things up much longer."

"Do you mind?" Paul glanced at Caroline.

"Not in the least. Why wait?" Nearly everyone was eating and drinking as it was, and she could see no reason to delay the party. Someone brought her a glass of champagne and Caroline drank it down in one big swallow. The room was warm and she was so thirsty. The hardest part was keeping her eyes open; her lids felt exceptionally heavy and, without much effort, she could have crawled into bed and slept for a month.

Paul raised his hand and the music stopped, followed by instant silence. The townspeople shuffled forward, forming a large circle around Paul, Caroline and the priest.

Caroline smiled and closed her eyes, awaiting the announcement that was obviously forthcoming. She felt so relaxed. These wonderful, wonderful people were holding some kind of ceremony to welcome her. If only she could stay awake...

Father Nabokov began speaking in a soft, reverent voice. The smell of incense filled the air. She made an honest effort to listen, but the priest's words were low and monotonous. The others in the room seemed to give heed to his message, whatever it was, and Caroline glanced around, smiling now and then.

"Caroline?" Paul's voice cut into her musings.

"Hmm." She realized the meeting hall was quiet, each face regarding her expectantly as though waiting for a response. Paul slipped an arm around her waist, pulling her closer to his side.

"Would you like him to repeat the question?" Paul asked, studying her with a thoughtful frown.

"Yes, please," Caroline said quietly. If she knew what these people expected of her, then maybe she could reply. "What did he say?"

"He's asking if you'll honor and cherish me."

Two

"Honor and cherish?" Caroline repeated, stunned. This reception was more than she could grasp. How she wished she hadn't had quite so much of her aunts' brew. Obviously this little get-together in her honor was some kind of elaborate charade—one in which Caroline had no intention of participating.

The circle of faces stared anxiously, growing more and more distressed at the length of time it took her to respond to the question.

"Caroline?" Even Paul's gruff voice revealed his uneasiness.

Caroline opened her mouth to tell them that if they were going to play silly tricks on her, she didn't want anything to do with this party. She looked at Paul and blinked. "I thought you were supposed to be my guide." Apparently folks took the guiding business seriously in these parts.

Father Nabokov smiled gently. "He will guide you throughout your life, my child."

A clatter rose from the crowd as several people started arguing loudly. Father Nabokov raised his arms above his head and waved. "Miss Myers." He paused to wipe his brow with a clean kerchief that magically appeared from inside his huge sleeve. "This is an important decision. Would you like me to ask the question again?"

Paul's intense blue eyes cleared as his gaze pinned hers, demanding that she answer the priest.

An older man, an Athabascan who was apparently a good friend of Paul's, interceded. "You can't back down now—you already agreed."

"I did?" What had her aunts gotten her into? The other guests continued to glare at her and Caroline felt unsettled by the resentment she saw in their eyes. "Could I have something cold to drink?"

"It's a bit unusual," Father Nabokov said, frowning. For the second time, he reached for the kerchief and rubbed it over his forehead.

"Walter," Paul called to the older man, who immediately stepped forward.

A minute later, he approached them with a glass of champagne, which Paul handed to Caroline. She hurriedly emptied it and sighed audibly as the bubbles tickled the back of her throat. She returned her glass to the man Paul had called Walter and smiled. "This is excellent champagne."

Walter nodded abruptly and glanced in Paul's direction. "Paul wanted the best for you."

Feeling uneasy, Caroline noted the censure in the old man's voice. "What was it you wanted me to say again?"

Paul's posture stiffened as he expelled an impatient sigh. "*Yes* would suffice."

"All right then," she agreed in an attempt to be as amicable as possible. Everyone had gone to so much trouble on her behalf, cooking and planning this reception for her arrival. She hated to disappoint them, although she wondered if all tourists were graced with this kind of party—the priest, the champagne, not to mention the presence of the entire village. Her adorable aunts had sent her to the one place in the world where she'd be welcomed with an ardor befitting royalty.

"You do?" Father Nabokov looked greatly relieved.

"Sure," she concurred brightly, shrugging her shoulders. "Why not?"

"Indeed." The priest grinned, then turned to Paul. His eyes glowed as he gazed upon them both. Caroline felt Paul slide his arm around her once again, but she didn't object. She attempted to give the priest her full attention, but the room was so warm.... She fanned her face and with some difficulty kept a stiff smile on her lips.

Paul took her hand and slipped a simple gold band on her ring finger. It looked like a friendship ring and Caroline thought it a lovely gesture.

"I now pronounce you husband and wife," Father Nabokov proclaimed solemnly. He raised his right hand, blessing them both. "You may kiss the bride."

Wife! Kiss the bride! Caroline was completely shocked. She tried to smile, but couldn't. "What's he talking about?" she muttered.

Paul didn't answer. Instead, he turned her in his arms

and his eyes narrowed longingly on her mouth. Before she could voice her questions and uncertainties, he lowered his head. Caroline's heart thundered nervously and she placed her hands on his chest, gazing up at his bearded face. Surely he could tell how confused she was. A wedding ceremony! She must be dreaming. That was it—this was all a dream. Paul's blue eyes softened. Gradually, as though in slow motion, his mouth settled warmly over hers. His touch was firm and experienced, moist and gentle—ever so gentle. *Nice dream,* Caroline mused, *very nice, very real.* She hadn't expected a man of his size to be so tender.

Enjoy it, girl, she thought, kissing him back. Dreams ended far too quickly. The world began to spin, so she slipped her arms around Paul's neck to help maintain her balance. Bringing her body closer to his was all the encouragement he needed. His hands slid over her hips, pressing her body invitingly against his own. Caroline surrendered willingly to the sensual upheaval. Ever since Larry had left her at the altar, she'd been dying to be held in a man's arms, dying to be kissed as if there was no moment but this one.

Father Nabokov cleared his throat, but Caroline paid no heed to the priest's disapproval. She might have had her doubts about Paul, but she had to admit he was one great kisser. Breathless, they broke apart, still staring at each other, lost in the wonder of their overwhelming response.

Paul draped his wrists over Caroline's shoulder. A slightly cynical smile touched his mouth. "For a minute there, I didn't think you were going through with it."

"Is this a dream?" Caroline asked.

Paul gave her a funny look. "No."

She laughed. "Of course you'd say that."

His eyes were as blue as anything Caroline had ever seen and she felt as though she was drowning in their depths. She managed a tremulous smile, her mouth still on fire from his kiss. Involuntarily, she moistened her lips and watched as his eyes darkened.

"Let's get out of here," he growled. Without another word, he hauled Caroline into his arms and stalked toward the door.

Caroline gasped at the unexpectedness of the action, but the villagers went crazy, resuming their dancing and singing. "Where…where are we going?"

"The cabin."

"Oh."

By now his lengthy strides had carried him halfway across the floor. The guests cleared a path and Walter stood ready, grinning boyishly as he opened the large wooden doors. Walter chuckled as Paul moved past him. "Don't be so impatient. You've waited this long."

Paul said something under his breath that Caroline couldn't understand and continued walking.

"How far is the cabin?" she asked.

"Too far," Paul said with a throaty chuckle. Her response to his kiss had jolted him. He'd thought he should progress to their lovemaking with less urgency— court her, let her become acquainted with him first. Yet the moment her mouth had opened to his, he'd realized there wasn't any reason to wait.

Leaning back in his arms, Caroline sighed wistfully. "Why is it dark?"

"It's October, love."

"Love?" she repeated, and sudden tears sprang to her eyes. She hadn't expected to be anyone's love—not after Larry—not for a very long time.

Paul went still. He could deal with anything but tears. "What's wrong?"

"Nothing," she murmured, sniffling. She should know not to drink champagne—especially after her aunts' special tea. Champagne always led to tears.

"Tell me." He smoothed the hair from her temple and softly kissed her there.

If he hadn't been so gentle, Caroline could have fought the unwelcome emotion. As she felt hot tears sear a path down her flushed face, she bit the corner of her bottom lip. "He left me," she whispered.

"Who?"

"Larry." She turned abruptly, wrapping her arms around Paul's neck, and sobbed into his shoulder. She wouldn't have believed she had any more tears, but her aunts' tea and the champagne had weakened her resolve to put Larry from her mind.

"You loved him?"

She nodded. "Sometimes I wonder if I'll ever stop."

The words stabbed his heart with the brutality of an ice pick. He'd known, or at least he should have known, that a woman like Caroline Myers wouldn't have agreed to marry him and live in the Alaskan wilderness without a good reason. Her letter had been so brief, so polite, unlike the others who'd tried to impress him with their wit and entice him with the promise of sexual fulfillment.

To his utter amazement, the response to his brief advertisement had been overwhelming. Dozens of letters had poured in that first week, but he hadn't bothered to read any once he'd opened Caroline's. Her picture had stopped him cold. The wheat-blond hair, the blue eyes that had spoken to him as clearly as the words of her letter. She was honest and forthright, sensual and provocative, mature and trusting. Her picture told him that, and it was confirmed by her letter. The next day he'd sent her the airplane ticket and for the past two weeks had waited in eager anticipation.

"In time, you'll learn not to love Larry," he said, kissing her temple again.

With her arms around his neck, Caroline nestled her head against his chest. "I don't know why I told you about Larry. I don't want to think about him anymore. I really don't, but he's there in my thoughts every minute."

"I'll chase him away," Paul teased.

"But how?"

"I'll find a way."

Silently they approached a log cabin and Caroline smiled at how quaint it looked with a huge set of moose antlers above the wooden door. A stepladder leaned to the right of the only window and there was a woodpile that reached up to the eaves beside it. An oblong, galvanized steel tub hung to the left of the door, along with a pair of snowshoes.

"It's so homey. You must love it here," Caroline said as she saw the soft light in the lone window.

"I do."

"I'm sure I'll like it." She sighed deeply. She wasn't dreaming, after all—or at least not anymore.

Paul bent awkwardly to turn the door handle. The warmth that greeted them immediately made Caroline feel that this tiny cabin was the perfect place for her vacation. "It's adorable," she said, looking around.

Without question, the cabin was small—so compact that the living area and kitchen were one room. Bookcases stood beside a large potbelly stove, and a kitchen counter lined the opposite wall. A doorway led to another room that Caroline assumed would be her bedroom. Everything was spotlessly clean.

Reluctantly, Paul released her from his arms. Her feet touched the floor and she stepped back. She barely knew the man, yet she'd spilled her deepest secrets to him as though he was a lifelong friend. "Are…are you staying?"

"Would it embarrass you?"

She blinked twice. Once again they were having a conversation she didn't quite comprehend. It had to be the alcohol. Caroline shook her head to clear her muddled thoughts. "If you don't mind, I'd like to go to bed."

One side of Paul's mouth edged upward. "I was hoping you'd suggest that. Would you feel more comfortable if I left?"

"Perhaps that would be best. I have lots of questions for you, but I'm too sleepy now. We'll talk in the morning, okay?" She took a step toward the doorway and her peripheral vision picked up the sight of the silky nightgown that had been a gift from her aunts. It was spread out across the large brass bed.

"I'll give you some time alone then," Paul said, heading for the door.

It closed after him and Caroline stood in the middle of the cabin, puzzled by the events of the day. She'd traveled thousands of miles and participated in some strange Alaskan ceremony. For a while she'd thought she was dreaming, but now realized she definitely wasn't. That meant she'd actually kissed a man whose name she hardly knew and then wept in his arms.

Moving into the single bedroom, undressing as she went, Caroline paused to admire the thick, brightly colored handmade quilt. The small lamp on the table illuminated the room and Caroline recognized her clothes hanging in an open closet beside those belonging to a man. She assumed they were Paul's. He was a gentleman, letting her use his cabin for the week and going somewhere else to sleep without complaint.

Caroline had a hazy memory of the word *wife* and wondered what *that* craziness was all about; she'd figure it out in the morning. She might even be married. A giggle escaped her as she sat on the edge of the bed. Married! Wouldn't Larry love that. Well, if she was, Paul would understand that there'd been a mistake. Her initial impression of him had been wrong. He'd intimidated her at first, but he was gentle and considerate. She'd witnessed that quality in him more than once in the past hour.

{

Her clothes fell to the floor as she stripped. With complete disregard, she kicked them under the bed. She'd pick them up in the morning, since she was too tired to do it now.

The sheer gown slid over her outstretched arms and down her body. The faux fur tickled her calves and Caroline smiled, recalling John's comment about how it would keep her warm. Alaskan men obviously had a sense of humor, although she hadn't been too amused at the time.

The gown *did* look like part of a wedding trousseau. Wedding? Married? She couldn't be… When she woke, they'd straighten everything out.

The bed looked soft and warm, and Caroline crawled between the sheets. Her head was cushioned by a feather pillow and her last thought before she flipped off the lamp was of the mountain she'd seen from the plane—Denali. Somehow its magnificence comforted her and lured her into sleep.

Outside, Paul paced in front of the cabin, glancing at his watch every twenty seconds. He was cold and impatient. With the music from the reception echoing around him, he refused to return to the meeting hall. Caroline had wanted some time to prepare herself and he'd reluctantly granted her that, but he wasn't pleased. Eventually she'd learn to be less shy; there wouldn't be room for modesty when winter arrived.

Once he was sure she'd had as much time as any woman would possibly require, Paul went back into the cabin. The bedroom light was off and he could see the outline of her figure in the bed. His bed. Waiting for him. He recalled the way her body had felt against his. With vivid clarity he remembered how she'd looked at him, her blue eyes huge, when she'd suggested going to bed. Then she'd asked him if she was dreaming. The woman was drunk—drunk on her wedding night. From the day he'd received her letter, Paul had decided to wait for the rewards of marriage. Yes, he'd wait until she was ready. But, oh boy—that kiss. For a moment he'd thought she was as eager as he. He wanted their lovemaking to be slow and easy, but hadn't anticipated her effect on him. The restraint he needed not to rush to her side made him feel weak. The taste of her lips lingered on his own and left him craving more. He took a deep breath and leaned against the counter.

Hoping to gain some perspective, Paul took down the bottle of Jack Daniel's from the cupboard and poured a stiff drink. He had to think things through. He suspected she didn't believe their marriage was real, yet she had to know he'd brought her all this way for exactly that purpose. During the wedding she'd looked so confused and unsure. As her husband, he expected to claim his marital rights—only he preferred to wait until she was sober. He wanted a wife and had made that evident in his letter. This was to be a real marriage in every way, and she'd come to him on his terms. Yet he couldn't help feeling nervous.

He sat at the table and gulped down the drink, hoping to feel its numbing effect—fast. But if anything, imagining Caroline in his bed, dressed in that see-through silk gown, had the *opposite* effect on him. He'd hoped to cool his passion with sound reasoning and good whiskey, but had ended up fanning the flames.

Standing, Paul took his empty glass to the sink and saw that his hands were trembling. He felt like a coiled spring, tense, ready. Oh, yes, he was ready.

He moved into the bedroom and undressed in the dark, taking time to fold each piece of clothing and set it on the dresser. For a moment he toyed with the idea of sleeping at Walter Thundercloud's place, but quickly rejected the thought. He'd be the laughingstock of the entire community if he spent the night anywhere but with Caroline.

She was asleep, he realized from the evenness of her breathing. He was grateful for that. Much as he wanted her, he felt certain *she* wasn't ready and he needed to respect that.

The mattress dipped as he carefully slid in beside her. She sighed once and automatically rolled into his arms, nestling her head against his chest. Paul's eyes widened with the force of his resolve.

She stroked her fingertips over his lean ribs. He swallowed convulsively against the sweet torture of her touch and strengthened his self-possession by gently removing her hands. He wished she could appreciate what he was giving up....

"Love," he whispered in her ear. "Roll onto your side, okay?"

"Hmm?" Caroline was having the sweetest dream. And this time, she felt sure it really *was* a dream.

"I know you'd prefer to wait." Paul found it ironic that he was telling her this; she'd come so willingly into his arms.

"Wait?"

"Never mind," he whispered. "Just go back to sleep." Unable to resist, he kissed her forehead and shifted away from her.

Unexpectedly, the comforting, irresistible warmth beside her moved and Caroline edged closer to it. With a sigh of longing, she buried her face in the hollow of his neck.

"Caroline, please, this is difficult enough," he whispered, inhaling harshly. She flattened her hand against his abdomen and slowly brushed her lips over his.

With every muscle, Paul struggled for control. Seconds later, he was lost—irrevocably and completely lost. Their kiss was unlike any he'd ever experienced.... But Paul was the one to break contact, twisting so that he lay on his back. His control, such as it was, seemed to be slipping fast; another minute and he wouldn't have been able to stop.

Caroline felt unbearably hot, as if she was sitting directly in front of a fireplace. The thought was so illogical—she was in bed, wasn't she?—that she bolted upright, giggling, and tossed the blankets aside. She fell back onto the pillow and raised her hands above her head, intertwining her fingers. The ceiling was spinning around and around. In an effort to block out the dizzying sight, she closed her eyes and sought anew the security of the dream.

Again Paul tried to move away from her but Caroline

wanted him close. She couldn't understand why he kept leaving her. If he was part of her dream, the least he could do was stick around! She reached for him, locking her arms around his neck, kissing him.

"Caroline, stop it!"

"Why?"

"Because you're drunk," he hissed.

She giggled. "I know." Her fingers roamed over his shoulders. "Please kiss me again. Has anyone ever told you that you're a great kisser?"

"I can't kiss you." *And remain sane,* he added silently.

"But I *want* you to." She sounded like a whiny child and that shocked her. "Oh, never mind, I wouldn't kiss me either." With that she let out a noisy yawn and rested her cheek against his chest. "You have nice skin," she murmured before closing her eyes.

"You do, too," he whispered, and slid his hand down the length of her spine. "Very nice."

"Are you sure you don't want to kiss me?"

Paul groaned. His nobility had limitations, and he wasn't going to be able to hold off much longer if she asked him to kiss her every ten seconds.

"Good night, love," he whispered, hoping his voice had the ring of finality. He kissed the crown of her head and continued to hold her close, almost savoring the sweet torture.

Caroline smiled, content. Just before she gave in to the irrepressible urge to sleep, she felt his kiss, and prayed that all her dreams would be this real and this exciting.

* * *

Snuggling closer to the warm body at her side, Caroline woke slowly. Her first conscious thought was that her head ached. It more than ached; it throbbed with each pulse and every sluggish heartbeat as her memory returned, muddled and confused. She rolled onto her back, holding the sides of her head, and groaned aloud. She was in bed with a man she barely knew. Unfortunately, he appeared to be well acquainted with her. Extremely well acquainted. Her first inclination was to kick him out of the bed. He'd taken advantage of her inebriated state, and she bit back bitter words as a flush of embarrassment burned her cheeks.

Opening her eyes was an impossible task. She couldn't face the man.

"Good morning," the deep male voice purred.

"It…wasn't a dream, was it?" she asked in a tone that was faint and apprehensive.

Paul chuckled. "You mean you honestly don't remember anything?"

"Some." She kept her eyes pinched shut, too mortified to look at him.

"Do you remember the part about us getting married?"

Caroline blinked. "I'm not sure."

"In case you don't, I suppose I should introduce myself. I'm Paul Trevor, your husband."

Three

"Then it *was* real!" Still holding her head, Caroline struggled to a sitting position. Gradually her eyes opened and she glared down at the bearded man beside her.

Paul was lying on his side, watching her with an amused grin. He rose up on his elbow and shook his head. "I can't believe you didn't expect to be married."

She felt as though the heat in her face was enough to keep the cabin warm all winter. "I knew at the time you…you weren't completely a dream." She had to be honest, even at the expense of her stubborn pride.

"We're married, love."

"Stop calling me your love! I am not your love, or any other man's. And we've certainly got to do something about annulling this…this marriage." She winced at the flash of pain that shot through her head.

"If you'd rather I didn't call you love, I won't."

"Call me Caroline or Ms. Myers, anything but your love."

"I *am* your husband."

"Will you stop saying that?"

"I have the paperwork to prove it."

Caroline tucked the blankets under her arms and scowled at him with all the fury she could muster. "Then I challenge you to produce them."

"As you wish." He threw aside the blankets and climbed out of bed, standing only partially clothed before her.

Caroline looked away. "I would really appreciate it if you'd put something on."

"Why?" He sent a questioning glance over his shoulder.

The red flush seeped down to her neck and she swallowed convulsively. "Just do it.... Please."

Chuckling again, Paul withdrew a slip of paper from his shirt pocket. "Here," he said, handing it to her.

Caroline grabbed it and quickly unfolded it, then scanned the contents. The document looked official and her name was signed at the bottom, although she barely recognized the signature as her own. Vaguely she remembered Paul having her sign some papers when they'd entered the meeting hall. She'd been so bemused she'd thought it had to do with registering a guest.

"I signed first," Paul explained, "and gave you the pen."

"Yes...but at the time I assumed it was something all tourists did." It sounded so ridiculous now that she wanted to weep at her own stupidity. "The party yesterday was our wedding reception, wasn't it?"

"Yes."

Caroline shook her head. "I...I thought Gold River got so few tourists that they greeted everyone like that."

"Caroline, you're not making any sense."

"*I'm* not?" she shouted, then winced. "You should look at it from my point of view."

"But you agreed to marry me weeks ago."

"I most certainly did not!"

"I have the letter."

"Now that I'd like to see. I may not have been in full control of my wits yesterday, but I know for a fact I'd never heard of you until…" The words died on her lips. "My aunts—my romantic, idealistic, scheming aunts… they couldn't have. They wouldn't…"

Paul regarded her suspiciously. "What aunts?"

"Mine. Just get the letter and p-please…" she stammered, "please put something on. This is all extremely embarrassing."

Grumbling under his breath, Paul reached for his pants and pulled them on, snapping them at the waist. Next he unfolded his shirt and slipped his arms inside the long sleeves, but he left it unbuttoned. "There. Are you satisfied?"

"Somewhat." Speaking of clothes reminded Caroline of her own skimpy state of dress. When Paul's back was turned, she scurried to the very edge of the mattress in a frantic search for her cords and sweater. She remembered undressing, but she couldn't recall where she'd put her things.

Stretching down as far as possible, Caroline made a wide sweep under the bed and managed to retrieve her sweater. Fearing Paul would be back at any minute, she slid her arms into the bulky sleeves and yanked it over her head. As she shook her hair free of the confining collar, Caroline came eye to eye with Paul.

He stood over her, his grin slightly off center. "Just give me that letter," Caroline demanded.

"Would you like me to read it to you?"

"No." She grabbed for it, but he held it just out of her reach. "I don't appreciate these sophomoric games, Paul Trevor."

"Go ahead and read it for yourself while I fix us something to eat."

"I'm not hungry," she announced sharply, jerking the envelope from his hand. Food was the last thing on her mind.

Humming as though he didn't have a care in the world, Paul left the bedroom while Caroline's eyes narrowed on his back. How dare he act so...so unruffled by this unexpected turn of events.

The instant Paul was out of sight, Caroline tore into the letter. The creases were well worn and with a mild attack of guilt she realized he must have read the neatly typed page repeatedly.

Dear Paul,
My name is Caroline Myers and I'm responding to your advertisement in the *Seattle Post-Intelligencer.* I am seeking a husband to love. My picture is enclosed, but I'm actually more attractive in person. That isn't to say, however, that I'm the least bit vain. I enjoy fishing and hiking and Scrabble and other games of skill. Since I am the

last of the Ezra Myers family left in the North-west, I am interested in having children. I'm a nurse currently employed by Dr. Kenneth James, but can leave my employment on two weeks' no-tice. I look forward to hearing from you.
Most sincerely,

The evenly shaped letters of her name were penned at the bottom of the page in what Caroline recognized as her Aunt Mabel's handwriting.

With sober thoughts, Caroline dressed, then joined Paul in the kitchen. He pulled out a chair and handed her a cup of coffee.

She laid the letter on the table. "I didn't write this."

"I figured that might've been the case."

Her face flushed, she wondered just what had happened after the ceremony. Surely she'd remember something as important as that. "I have these two elderly aunts…." Caroline hedged, not knowing where exactly to start her explanation.

"So I gathered." He pulled out the chair across from her and placed his elbows on the table. "They answered my advertisement?"

"Apparently so."

"How'd they convince you to marry me?"

"That's just it…. They didn't." Caroline dumped a tablespoon of sugar into the coffee and stirred it several times.

"Then why did you go through with it?"

"I…wasn't myself yesterday. I…I didn't fully realize

what was happening." She knew how ridiculous that sounded and hurried to explain. "You see, Aunt Mabel and Aunt Ethel—they're really my great-aunts, but I've always called them Aunt—anyway, they told me they were giving me a trip to Alaska."

"Why?"

She wasn't sure how much she wanted to reveal. She understood the reason her two scheming aunts had answered Paul's ad. They'd been worried about her after the breakup with Larry. The question was: How was she going to untangle herself from this unfortunate set of circumstances? "The purpose for my agreeing to come to Alaska isn't important," she told him stiffly.

"Not too many people visit Alaska on the brink of winter," he said.

She wished he'd stop arguing with her. Keeping her composure under these conditions was difficult enough.

"Was it because of Larry?"

Caroline felt her blood run cold. "They told you about Larry?"

"No, you did."

"I did!" She opened her eyes wide, then quickly lowered them. "Is there anything I didn't tell you?"

"I imagine there's quite a bit." He paused to drink his coffee. "Please go on. I'm curious to hear how you got yourself into this predicament."

"Well, Aunt Mabel and Aunt Ethel insisted I take this trip. I'd never been to Alaska and they kept telling me how beautiful it is. I didn't know how they could afford it, but—"

"They didn't."

"What do you mean?" She held the mug with both hands. This was getting more complicated by the minute.

"I paid for it."

"Terrific," she groaned. She'd need to repay him for that and God only knew what else.

She paused for a sip of coffee and continued her explanation. "Then John Morrison met me in Fairbanks and the ride to Gold River got a bit rugged, so I drank the thermos of tea my aunts sent along."

"Tea?"

"Not regular tea," Caroline corrected. "My aunts have a special brew—their father passed the recipe to them."

"I see." One corner of his lip curved upward as he made an obvious—but futile—effort to contain his smile.

Caroline wasn't fooled. "Would you stop looking amused? We're in one heck of a mess here."

"We are?" He cocked an eyebrow expressively. "We're married, Caroline, and the ceremony is as legal as it gets. We stood before God, with the whole village as witness."

"But you don't honestly expect me to honor those vows…. You can't be that unreasonable."

"We're married."

"It was a mistake!"

"Not as far as I'm concerned."

"I'll have it annulled," she threatened.

His grin was wide and cynical. "After last night?"

Her cheeks flamed even hotter. So something *had* happened. "All right," she said tightly, "we'll get a divorce."

"There will be no divorce."

Caroline placed her mug on the table. "You can't be serious! I have no intention of staying married to you. Good heavens, I don't even *know* you."

"You'll have plenty of time for that later."

"Later? Are you nuts? I'm not staying here a second longer than necessary. There's been a terrible mistake and I want out before something else happens."

"And I say we make the best of the situation."

"Just how do you propose we do that?"

"Stay married."

"You're crazy." She stood up so abruptly that the chair went crashing to the floor. "Let's talk about this in a logical fashion."

"The deed is done." In Paul's opinion, there was nothing to discuss; she was here in his home and they were legally married.

"Deed," Caroline echoed, feeling slightly sick to her stomach. "Then we...I mean, last night, you and I...we...?" Her eyes implored him to tell her what they'd done.

Paul yearned to assure her they'd shared only a few kisses, but the instant he told her that nothing—well, almost nothing—had happened, she'd bolt. "Caroline, listen to me. It's too late for argument."

"Not from my point of view." Her arms were wrapped around her stomach as she paced the floor. "I want out of here and I want out now."

Paul shrugged. "That's unfortunate because you're staying."

"You can't force me!"

His frustration was quickly mounting. "Would you give us a chance? I'll admit we're getting off to a shaky start, but things will work out."

"Work out!" she cried. "I'm married to a man whose face I can't even see."

Paul ran his hand over the neatly trimmed beard. "It's winter and my beard's there to protect my face from the cold. I won't shave until spring."

"I…I don't know you," she said again.

"I wouldn't say that."

"Will you stop bringing up the subject of last night?"

Caroline was surprised by Paul's low chuckle. "*Now* what's so funny?" she asked.

"You're a passionate woman, Mrs. Trevor. If it's this good between us at the beginning, can you imagine how fantastic it'll be when we know each other better?"

"Stop it!" Furious, she stalked across the room and stood in front of the window. A thin layer of snow covered the ground and in the distance Caroline could see the form of a small plane against the blue sky. Her heart rate soared as she contemplated her means of escape. If the plane landed in Gold River, maybe she could sneak out before Paul discovered she was missing.

"Caroline?"

She turned back to him. "Were you so desperate for a wife that you had to advertise? That doesn't say a whole lot about your sterling character."

"There are very few opportunities in Alaska, love. I don't often get into Fairbanks."

"I already asked you not to call me that."

"I apologize."

He didn't look the least bit contrite and his attitude infuriated her further. "Why did you choose *me?* You must've received more than one response."

"I received…several." *Hundreds, if the truth be known.* "I chose you because I liked your eyes."

"Wonderful!" She threw her hands in the air.

"But your aunts were right—you are more attractive in person."

Caroline couldn't believe what she was hearing. Paul Trevor apparently expected her to honor her vows and live here on this chunk of ice. She was growing increasingly frantic. "I…have disgusting habits. Within a week you'll be ready to toss me to the wolves."

"There isn't anything we won't be able to work out."

"Paul, please, look at it from my perspective." Her eyes pleaded with him.

Paul struggled with the effect they had on him. It was difficult to refuse her anything, but the matter of their marriage was something on which he couldn't compromise. "We'll discuss it later," he told her stiffly and turned away. "I've got to get to the station."

"What station?"

"The pump station by the pipeline."

"Oh. John mentioned it." Already her mind was scheming. She'd let him go and pray that the plane circling overhead would land. If it did, she could convince the pilot to get her out of Gold River before Paul even knew she was gone.

"I won't be more than an hour or two."

"All right." She slowly rubbed the palms of her hands together. "And when you get back, I'm sure we'll be able to reach some agreement. I might even be willing to stay."

Paul eyed her suspiciously, not trusting this sudden change of heart. While he shrugged into his coat, he said, "I want your word, Caroline, that you'll remain in the cabin."

"Here? In this cabin?"

"Your word of honor."

Caroline swallowed uncomfortably; she hated lying. Normally she spoke the truth even to her own detriment. "All right," she muttered, childishly crossing her fingers behind her back. "I'll stay here."

"I have your word?"

"Yes." Without flinching, her eyes met his.

"I won't be long." His hand was on the doorknob.

"Take your time." The plane was landing; she could hear it in the distance. "While you're gone, I'll find my way around the kitchen," she said brightly. "By the time you return, I'll have lunch ready."

Again Paul eyed her doubtfully. She sounded much too eager for him to leave, but he didn't have time to worry now. Giving her a few hours alone was probably for the best. She'd promised to stay and he had no choice but to trust her. He was already an hour late. Walter had said he'd stand in for him, but Paul had refused. The station was his responsibility.

The second the door closed after Paul, Caroline dashed into the bedroom and jerked her clothes off the hangers, stuffing them back inside her suitcase. With a sense of guilt, she left the winter gear that Paul had purchased on her behalf. He'd gone to a great deal of trouble and expense for her, but she couldn't be blamed for that.

A quick check at the door revealed that Paul was nowhere in sight. She breathed a bit easier and walked cautiously outside. Although the day was clear, the cold cut straight through her thin jacket.

A couple of Athabascan women passed Caroline and smiled shyly, their eyes curious. She returned their silent greeting and experienced a twinge of remorse at this regrettable subterfuge. If he'd been more reasonable, she wouldn't have had to do something so drastic.

The plane was taxiing to a stop at the airstrip where she'd been dropped off less than twenty-four hours earlier.

Caroline watched from the center of town as the pilot handed down several plywood crates. A few minutes later, the dogsleds and snowmobiles arrived.

"Hi." She stepped forward, her calm smile concealing her anxiety.

The tall burly man seemed surprised to see her. "Hello."

"I'm Caroline Myers." She extended her hand for him to shake and prayed he wouldn't detect her nervousness.

"Burt Manners. What can I do for you?"

"I need a ride to Fairbanks," she said quickly. "Is there any way you could fly me there?"

"Sorry, lady, I'm headed in the opposite direction."

"Where?" She'd go anyplace as long as it was away from Gold River and Paul.

"Near Circle Hot Springs."

"That's fine. I'll go there first, just so it's understood that you can fly me to Fairbanks afterward."

"Lady, I've already got a full load. Besides, you don't want to travel to Circle Hot Springs. It's no place for a lady this time of year."

"I don't care. Honest."

"There isn't any room." He started to turn away from her.

"There must be *some* space available. You just unloaded those crates. Please." Caroline hated the whiny sound of her voice, but she was desperate. The sooner she escaped, the better.

"Is that the warmest coat you've got?"

He was looking for excuses and Caroline knew it. "No. I've got another coat. Can I come?"

"I don't know…." Still, he hesitated.

"I'll pay you double your normal fee," Caroline said, placing her hand on his forearm. "I *have* to get to Fairbanks."

"Okay, okay." Burt rubbed his neck. "Why do I feel I'm going to regret this?"

Caroline hardly heard him as she made a sharp turn and scurried across the snow toward the cabin. "I'll be right back. Don't leave without me."

She got to the cabin breathless with excitement and relief, and hurried into the bedroom. Taking the coat Paul had purchased for her went against all her instincts, but she'd repay him later, she rationalized, once she was safely back in Seattle. To ease her conscience, she quickly scribbled an IOU and left it on the kitchen table, where he was sure to find it, along with a note apologizing for the lie. Her suitcase stood just inside the doorway. She reached for it with one hand and her purse with the other.

The pilot was waiting for her when she returned and she climbed aboard, feeling jubilant. Getting away from Paul had been much easier than she'd expected. Of course he could follow her, but that was doubtful unless he had a plane, and she didn't see a hangar anywhere.

As Burt had explained, the seating was cramped.

He talked little on the short trip, which suited Caroline just fine. She didn't have a whole lot to say herself.

The landing strip at Circle Hot Springs looked even more unreliable than the one at Gold River. Caroline felt her stomach pitch wildly when the Cessna's wheels slammed against the frozen ground, but she managed to conceal her alarm.

They were met by a group of four hunters who unloaded the plane, delivering the gear to a huge hunting lodge. When they'd finished, one of the men brought out a bottle of whiskey and passed it around. The largest hunter, a man called Sam, offered the bottle to Caroline.

"No, thanks," she said shaking her head. "I prefer to drink mine from a glass." Burt had said that Circle Hot Springs wasn't any place for a lady, but she'd assumed he'd been concerned about the climate.

"Hey, guys, we've got a classy dame with us." Sam

laughed gruffly and handed her the bottle. "Take a drink," he ordered.

Fear sent chills racing up and down her spine as Caroline looked frantically at Burt. "I said no, thank you."

"Lay off, you guys," Burt called. "She doesn't have to drink if she doesn't want to."

An hour later, Caroline was convinced she'd made a horrible mistake. The men sat around drinking and telling dirty jokes that were followed by smutty songs and laughter. Their conversation, or at least what she could hear of it, was filled with innuendo. The more she ignored them, the more they seemed to focus on her.

While the men were engaged in a discussion about the next day's plans, Caroline crept close to Burt's side, doing everything possible to remove attention from herself.

"You okay?" Burt muttered.

"Fine," she lied. "When do we leave for Fairbanks?"

He gave her an odd look. "Not until tomorrow morning."

"Tomorrow morning? That long?" She gulped. What had she gotten herself into now?

"Hey, lady, you asked for this."

"Right." She'd left the frying pan and landed directly in the hot coals of the fire. "I'll be ready first thing in the morning." Although it was the middle of the afternoon, the skies were already beginning to darken.

The hunting lodge had a large living room with a mammoth fireplace. The proprietor/guide appeared and introduced himself, then brought out another bottle of whiskey to welcome his latest guests. Caroline refused a drink and inquired politely about renting a room for the night.

"Sorry, honey, we're full up."

His eyes were twinkling and Caroline didn't believe him.

"You can stay with me," Sam offered.

"No, thanks."

"Polite little thing, ain't you?" Sam slipped his arm around her shoulders and squeezed hard. The smell of alcohol on his breath nearly bowled her over. "The boys and me came here for some fun and we're real glad you decided to join us."

"I'm just passing through on my way to Fairbanks," she explained lamely. She cast a pleading glance at Burt, but he was talking to another of the men and didn't notice her. She groaned inwardly when she saw the glass of amber liquid in his hand.

"Like I said, we came into Circle Hot Springs for a little fun," Sam told her, slurring his words. "You knew that when you insisted on flying here, I'll bet." Again he gave her shoulders a rough squeeze.

Caroline felt as if her vocal cords had frozen with fear. As the evening progressed, things went from bad to worse. After the men had eaten, they grew louder and even more boisterous. Burt had started drinking and from the looks he was giving her, Caroline wondered just how much protection he'd be if worse came to worst. Judging by the way he was staring at her, Caroline realized he wouldn't be much help against the burly men.

Sam polished off his glass of whiskey and rubbed the back of his hand across his mouth. "I don't know about the rest of you yahoos," he shouted, "but I'm game for some entertainment."

"What do you have in mind?"

"Burt brought it for us. Ain't that right, little lady?"

Once again Caroline's eyes pleaded with Burt, but he ignored her silent petition. "I…I didn't say anything like that, but…but I think you should know, I'm not much of a singer."

The men broke into loud guffaws.

"I can dance a little," she offered, hoping to delay any arguments and discover a means of escape. Her heart felt as though it were refusing to cooperate with her lungs. She'd never been so scared in her life.

"Let her dance."

The whiskey bottle was passed from one member of the party to the next as Caroline stood and edged to the front door. If she could break free, she might be able to locate another cabin to spend the night. Someplace warm and safe.

"I'll…need some music." She recognized her mistake when two of the men broke into a melody associated with strippers.

"Dance," Sam called, clapping his hands.

"Sure." Caroline was close to tears of anger and frustration. Swinging her hands at her sides, she did a shuffle she'd learned in tap dance class in the fifth grade.

The men booed.

She sent them a feeble smile and stopped. "I guess I'm not much of a dancer, either."

"Try harder," someone shouted, and they all laughed again.

The log door swung open and a cold north wind caused the roaring fire to flicker. A man entered, his head covered with a hood. He flipped it back and stared at Caroline.

"Paul!" She'd never been so glad to see anyone in her life. She wanted to weep with relief.

"What's going on here?" he said gruffly.

"We're just havin' a little fun," Burt said, lurching to his feet. "Do you know the lady?"

Paul looked directly at Caroline and slowly shook his head. "Nope. Never seen her before in my life."

Four

Caroline stared with utter astonishment as Paul took a seat with the other men, removing his parka and setting it aside. Someone passed him a drink, which he quickly downed. Not once did he glance in her direction.

"Well," he said after a moment, "what's stopping you? Dance."

"Dance?" Caroline repeated.

"Dance!" all the men shouted simultaneously.

"And no more little-girl stuff, either."

Caroline's anger simmered just below the surface. Couldn't Paul see that she was up to her neck in trouble? The least he could do was rescue her. All morning he'd kept saying he was her husband and nothing she could do would change that. Well, good grief, if she'd ever needed a husband it was now. Instead, he appeared to find her predicament humorous. Well, she'd show him!

Heaving a deep sigh, she resumed her soft-shoe shuffle, swinging her arms at her sides. She really did need music and if the men weren't going to provide it, she'd make her own. Perhaps because of the snow outside, all she could think of was Christmas songs. "Jingle bell, jingle bell, jingle bell rock..." she bellowed out.

The only one she seemed to amuse was Paul, but his laugh could be better described as a snicker. Although Caroline made a point of not looking at him, she could feel the heat of his anger. All right, so she'd lied. And she'd taken the coat. She did intend to pay him for it, plus what he'd spent on her airplane fare.

The men were booing her efforts again.

"I told you, none of that kid stuff," Sam shouted, his voice even more slurred. "You're supposed to *entertain* us."

As much as she hated to reveal her fright, Caroline stopped and she silently begged Paul for help. Again he ignored her.

"Take your clothes off," Sam called out. "That's what we want."

"Paul?" she whispered, and her voice trembled. "Please." When she saw him clench his fists, she knew she'd won.

"All right, guys," he said, agilely rising to his feet. "The game's over. I'd like you to meet my wife."

"Your wife!" In a rush, Burt Manners jumped from his sitting position. "Hey, buddy, I swear I had no idea."

"Wait a minute!" Sam burst out. "You said you didn't know her and—"

"Don't worry about it," Paul cut in.

"She came to me begging to leave Gold River. I

told her Circle Hot Springs was no place for a lady, but she insisted."

Paul's mouth thinned. "I know."

"You need me to fly you back to Gold River?" Burt asked eagerly.

"No, thanks, I've got someone waiting."

"You do?" Caroline was so relieved, she felt faint. Another minute of this horrible tension would have been unbearable. The men were looking at her as though she was some cheat who'd swindled them out of an evening's fun and games. And from the way Paul kept avoiding eye contact, she wondered what he'd say once they were alone. She'd gone from the frying pan into the fire and then back to the frying pan.

Burt stepped out of the hunting lodge with them to unload Caroline's suitcase from his plane. With every step, he continued to apologize until Caroline wanted to scream. Paul knew she'd practically begged the other man to take her away from Gold River. He didn't need to hear it over and over again.

"Fact is," Burt said, standing beside his Cessna, his expression uneasy, "I didn't hear you were married. If I'd known she was your wife, I never would've taken her."

Paul offered no excuse for her behavior. He was so silent and so furious that Caroline thought he might explode any minute. Without a word, he escorted her to the waiting plane and helped her inside, every movement that of a perfect gentleman. But she had no doubt whatsoever that he was enraged.

Once aboard the plane, Caroline smiled faintly at the

pilot and slipped into her seat. No sooner had she buckled her safety belt than the engines roared to life and the Cessna taxied away.

Paul was quiet for the entire flight. By the time they circled Gold River, Caroline was weak with dread—and guilt. She'd lied to Paul, stolen from him and embarrassed him in front of his friends. Maybe he'd be so glad to get rid of her that he'd give her the divorce. Maybe this whole fiasco could be annulled. Oh heavens, why wouldn't he tell her what had happened last night? She rubbed her temples, trying to recall the events following her arrival. She remembered him kissing her and how good it felt, but beyond that her memory was a blur.

When the plane approached the runway, Caroline closed her eyes. The sensation of the frozen tundra rising to meet the small aircraft made her dizzy. The Cessna jerked hard once, then again, and for a moment Caroline was sure they were going to crash. A fitting end to her day, she thought gloomily—death. She swallowed a cry of alarm and looked frantically at Paul, who was seated beside her. His face was void of expression, as though such a bumpy landing was nothing out of the ordinary. They eased to a stop, and Caroline sagged against the back of the seat, breathless with relief.

Walter was standing with a team of huskies to meet them. His ageless eyes hardened when he caught a glimpse of Caroline, and his angry glare could have split a rock.

"Could you see that Bill has a hot meal and place to spend the night?" Paul asked his friend, apparently referring to the pilot.

"Sure thing."

Once inside the cabin, Caroline turned her back to the woodstove and waited. Paul walked past her, carrying her suitcase into the bedroom.

Caroline removed her parka and hung it beside Paul's. The cabin was warm and cozy, some kind of stew was simmering on top of the stove and the enticing smell was enough to make Caroline feel limp. She hadn't eaten all day.

Still, Paul didn't speak and she waited another minute before she broached a conversation.

"Okay, I'm ready," she said when she couldn't stand it any longer.

"Ready for what?"

"For whatever you're going to say or do to me."

"I'm not going to say or do anything."

"Nothing?" Caroline uttered in stunned disbelief.

Paul crossed the tiny kitchen and took two bowls from the cupboard.

"But I lied to you."

His eyes narrowed. "I know."

"And I stole the coat."

He nodded.

"And…" Her voice trembled. "I made a fool out of us both."

Paul lifted the lid of the cast iron kettle, filled each bowl to the top with stew and brought them to the table.

Caroline gripped the back of the kitchen chair. "You must be furious with me."

"I am."

"Then don't you think you should divorce me? I mean—it's obvious I'm not the woman you want. If I were you, I'd be willing to admit I made a bad choice and go from there." She eyed him hopefully.

He sat down, unfolded his napkin and laid it across his lap. "There will be no divorce."

"But I don't *want* to be married! I—"

"The deed is done."

"What deed?" she screamed. If she'd had a wedding night, a *real* wedding night, surely she'd remember it.

"We're legally married," he said calmly, reaching for his spoon. "Now sit down and eat."

"No." Stubbornly, she crossed her arms over her chest.

"Fine. Then don't eat."

Caroline glanced at the steaming bowl of stew. Her mouth began to water and she angrily pulled out the chair. "All right, I'll eat," she murmured, "but I'm doing it under protest." She dipped her spoon into the thick mixture.

"I can tell," Paul said.

When they'd finished, it was Paul who cleared the table and washed the dishes. Wordlessly, Caroline found a dish towel and dried them, replacing the bowls in the overhead cupboard. Her mind was spinning with possible topics of conversation, all of which led to one central issue: their marriage. She prayed she'd find a way of getting him to listen to reason.

An hour after dinner, Paul turned off the lights in the living room and moved into the bedroom. Caroline could either follow him or be left standing alone in the dark. She didn't even consider turning on the lights again.

The instant her gaze fell on the bed, Caroline knew she could delay no longer. "Paul, listen to me—there's been a terrible mistake."

"There was no mistake," he countered, starting to unbutton his shirt.

Briefly, Caroline recalled running her fingers down his chest. She felt the blood drain from her face and turned away in an effort not to look at him. If there was anything else to remember, she didn't want to do it now. "The mistake wasn't yours, I'll admit that. But you must understand that I didn't know anything about the wedding."

"We've already been through this and no amount of talk is going to change what happened. We're married, and as far as I'm concerned that's how we're going to stay."

"But I don't want to be married," she wailed.

Paul heaved a disgusted sigh. "Would it make any difference if I was your beloved Larry?"

"Yes," she cried, then quickly changed her mind. "No, it wouldn't. Oh hell, I don't know."

"The subject is closed," Paul said forcefully. "We won't discuss it again."

"But we have to."

From behind her, Caroline heard Paul throw back the covers and climb into bed. Slowly, she turned, feeling more unhappy and depressed than at any other time in her life.

"Surely you don't believe I'm going to sleep with you?"

"You're my wife, Caroline."

"But…"

"Why do you insist on arguing? We're married. You're my wife and I want you to sleep in my bed."

"I won't."

"Fine," he grumbled. "Sleep on the floor. When you get cold enough you'll come to bed." With that, he rolled onto his side and flipped off the light, once again leaving Caroline in the dark. She remained where she was for a long moment, indecisive, exhausted, bewildered.

"Paul?"

"Hmm?"

"If I... If I come to bed, will you promise not to touch me?"

Silence. Finally he said, "After the stunt you pulled today, I doubt that I could."

Caroline supposed she should've been relieved, but she wasn't. Slowly, she undressed and climbed under the blankets. She shivered once and curled up tightly. As weary as she was, she'd expected to fall directly into a deep sleep, but she didn't. In fact, a half hour later, she lay wide awake, surprisingly warm and cozy.

"Paul?" she whispered.

"What?"

She bit her bottom lip to hold back the tears. "I'm sorry about today."

"I know."

"Under normal conditions, I would never have done anything so stupid."

"I know that, too."

"Do you know everything?" she snapped.

"No."

"I'm glad to hear it."

Another five minutes passed. "Paul?"

"What is it now?"

"Good night."

"Good night, love." She could hear the relief in his voice and her eyes drifted shut.

The next thing Caroline knew, Paul was leaning over her, gently shaking her awake.

"Caroline, it's morning."

Her eyes flew open in alarm and she brushed the hair from her face. "What time is it?"

"Five o'clock. You'll need to get up and dressed. There's coffee on the dresser for you."

Maybe he'd relented and had accepted the impossibility of their circumstances. She struggled into a sitting position, her eyes finding his. "Up and dressed? Why?" she asked, hoping he'd decided to send her back to Seattle.

"You're coming with me."

"Where?"

"To the pump station."

Her spirits sagged. "But why? I don't know anything about—"

"I can't trust you. So I don't have any choice but to bring you with me."

"I'm not going to run away again. I promise."

"You promised before. Now get up."

"But, Paul, I won't—"

"I don't have time to argue with you. Either you do as I say or I'll take you with me dressed as you are."

Caroline didn't doubt him for a second. "Aye, aye, commander," she said and gave him a mocking salute. Furious, she threw back the sheets and reached for her clothes.

Caroline had never spent a more boring morning in her life. Paul sat her down in a chair and left her to twiddle her thumbs for what seemed like hours. After the first thirty minutes, she toyed with the idea of walking back to the cabin, which she found preferable to sitting in a chair, a punishment more befitting a badly behaved child. However, she quickly discarded that idea. All she needed was to have Paul return to find her gone. If he was furious with her after yesterday, it would be nothing compared to his anger if she pulled the same trick twice. So, although she was bored senseless, Caroline stayed exactly where she was.

Paul returned and she brightened, pleased to have some human contact. But to her dismay, he walked directly past her to another desk and took out a huge ledger, proceeding to record data.

"Paul?"

"Shh."

She pressed her lips together so hard they hurt.

He lifted his head when he'd finished and looked at her expectantly. "You wanted something?"

"I want to go back to the cabin."

"No."

"After what happened yesterday, you can't believe I'll try to get away again." He returned to his work and refused to look at her, ostensibly studying his ledger. Caroline's blood was close to the boiling point. "What are you going to do? Keep me with you twenty-four hours a day?"

"You gave me no option."

"You *can't* be serious. I'm not going to run away." She pointed to the front door. "There are crazy people out there."

He didn't respond.

"Paul, please, I'll go out of my mind with nothing to do."

"Get a book and read." His response was as uncaring as the arctic wind that howled outside the door.

"Oh, I see," she said in a high-pitched, emotional voice. "This is to be my punishment. Not only are you going to keep me as your prisoner, but I have to suffer your company as well. How long?"

"How long what?" With deliberate care, he set his pen aside.

"How long before you learn to trust me? A week? Ten days? A month?"

"I can't answer that. It depends on you."

She flew to her feet, her fists clenched. "Well then, you'd be wise never to leave me alone, because the minute I get a chance, I'm high-tailing it out of here. Somehow or other, I'll find a way to escape. You can't keep a person against his or her will. This is the United States of America and kidnapping is against the law."

"I didn't kidnap you, I married you."

"Well, then, you're the worst possible husband a

woman could have. I refuse to be your wife, no matter what some piece of paper says." She waited for him to argue with her and when he didn't, she continued her tirade. "Not only that... You've got to be the most stubborn man I've ever met. Stubborn and unreasonable and...and...chauvinistic to boot!"

Paul nodded. "I know. But given time, you'll learn to love me."

"Never," Caroline vowed. "Not while I live and breathe."

"We'll see."

He sounded so sure of himself, so confident, that she wanted to throttle him. Drained, she sank back into her chair. To her horror, tears filled her eyes and fell hot against her cheeks. She wiped them aside and sniffled loudly to hold back the flood. "Paul," she cried softly. "I just want to go home. Please."

His mouth grew hard and inflexible. "You are home. The sooner you accept that, the better for both of us."

With that, Caroline buried her face in her hands and wept until there were no tears left. Her eyes burned and her throat ached.

Paul felt the weight of Denali pressing against his back, and prayed he was doing the right thing. He could deal with her harangues, even her feisty anger, but her tears were another matter. They brought all his doubts to the surface. A month—he'd promised himself a month. If things hadn't improved by the end of October, he'd send her back to Seattle. Looking at her now, bent over, weeping as though she hadn't a friend in the world, he felt guilt—and an overwhelming compassion. It would be so easy to love her. She had spunk and character and was more woman than he'd ever dreamed he'd find. He knew in his heart that this really could work, that this marriage could be genuine and happy. He knew because—except for one occasion—his instincts hadn't steered him wrong yet and where there was such intense attraction between a man and a woman, there was a chance for lasting love.

By midafternoon, Caroline had read one adventure novel, written her two maiden aunts a scathing letter, destroyed that, and had drawn several pictures of a distorted Paul with a knife through his heart. She couldn't help it; after eight hours of complete monotony, she felt murderous.

Toward evening, Paul handed Caroline her parka. "Are you ready to go back to the cabin?"

Was she ever! But she had no intention of letting him know that. With a regal tilt of her chin, she reached for her jacket and slipped her arms inside the thick sleeves. She hadn't spoken a word to Paul in hours and he hadn't had the decency to reveal the least bit of concern. Well, she could hold out longer than he could. By the time she returned to Seattle, he'd be so glad to be rid of her, he'd give her the divorce without even arguing.

More snow had fallen during the day, and although the cabin was only a short distance from the pumping station, they needed snowshoes to trek their way back. It was the first time that Caroline had ever worn them, and she was forced to squelch her natural delight.

Again, dinner had been left on the stove. Tonight it was a roast with onions, potatoes and carrots simmered in the gravy. Caroline wondered who did the cooking, but she refused to ask Paul a thing. And she was hungry; lunch had consisted of a peanut butter sandwich many hours before.

As he had the previous night, Paul placed the silverware on the table and brought their meal from the stove. More than once Caroline felt his gaze on her, but she was determined not to utter a word.

"I must admit," Paul said halfway through their dinner, "that I prefer the silence to your constant badgering."

"Badgering!" Caroline shrieked. "I do not badger. All I want is an end to this despicable marriage."

Paul grinned boyishly. "Has anyone told you how beautiful your eyes are?"

Caroline pressed her lips together and stabbed her meat with unnecessary force. "I wish that was your heart. Oops, my mistake. You don't have one."

Paul laughed outright at that. "But I do, love," he said a few minutes later. "And it belongs to you."

"I don't want it." She struggled to hold back tears of frustration. "Didn't you say you'd received lots of letters in response to your ad? Those women all *wanted* to be your wife. Let me go, Paul. Please let me go. I'll repay you the money you've already spent. I swear I will."

He shook his head. "I refuse to discuss the matter again." Until the end of the month, he added to himself, hoping that by then there'd be nothing to discuss.

"Yes, your Majesty," Caroline returned, just barely managing to regain her composure.

Neither one of them ate much after that. Caroline toyed with the food on her plate, but her appetite had vanished, and with it her will to fight.

Standing, she carried her plate to the sink and scraped it clean. Paul brought over his dishes and they worked silently together, cleaning away the dinner mess.

"Paul," she said, after he'd wiped the last dish dry, "do you play Scrabble?" She knew he must; she'd seen the game on his shelf.

"A bit. Why?"

"Could you and I play? To help pass the evening?"

"I suppose."

For the first time in two days, Caroline's smile was natural and real. Her aunts loved Scrabble and had taught it to her as a child. With such expert tutoring, she was practically unbeatable. Her whole world became brighter. "It would be far more interesting, though," she said with a feigned thoughtful look, "if we played for something, don't you think?"

"How do you mean?"

She brought the game down from the shelf and unfolded the board. "Simple. If I win you'd grant me one request, and vice versa."

"And of course you'd ask for a divorce. No way."

"No, not a divorce." She'd work up to that.

"If not a divorce, what would you request?"

"Privacy."

"Privacy?"

"Yes, I want to sleep alone."

Skeptical, he eyed the recliner. "For how long?"

She'd go easy on him. "One night."

"Agreed." He pulled up a chair, twisted it around and straddled it. "And on the off chance I win?" He could see the mischief in her brilliant blue eyes. She clearly expected to beat him.

"Yes?" She regarded him expectantly. "What would you want?"

"A kiss."

"A kiss?"

"And not a peck on the cheek either. I want you to kiss me so well it'll turn me inside out." Not that it would take much, he mused.

Caroline hesitated. "But no more than a kiss, right?"

"No more. Agreed?"

With a saucy grin, she stuck out her hand. "Agreed." They shook on it and Caroline laughed. It felt so good to laugh again; she hated the constant bickering. Besides, this was going to be like taking candy from a baby.

"Let the games begin," Paul said, grinning back at her.

For a moment, it was hard to take her gaze off him. His eyes were smiling and although she couldn't see the rest of his face through the beard, she felt he must be a handsome man. His eyes certainly were appealing. Playfully, she held up her hand and flexed all her fingers.

"You draw first." In gentlemanly fashion, Paul handed her the small velvet bag with the letters of the alphabet.

Caroline inserted her hand and drew out an A. She gave him a triumphant look and set it on her letter holder. "I go first."

"Right."

It wasn't until they were a couple of plays into the game that Caroline recognized Paul's skill. He was going to provide some stiff competition. In fact, their scores remained close throughout the match. Caroline was down to her last five letters when Paul gained a triple word slot, added up his score and beamed her a proud look.

"Paul!" Caroline glanced at the board and gasped, unable to hold back her shock. "That's a four-letter word! A dirty four-letter word!"

"I'm well aware of that, love."

"You can't use that. It…it's indecent."

"It's also in the dictionary. Would you care to challenge me?"

She knew if she did, she'd immediately forfeit the game. "No," she grumbled. "But I consider that word in poor taste."

Paul's response was a soft chuckle. "You can challenge me if you wish."

"What's the score?" Five letters left… If she could use them all, she might be able to pull into the lead.

"Three hundred and twenty to two eighty-eight," Paul informed her gleefully. "Do you concede?"

"Never!"

"I'm afraid you have to. I'm out of letters."

"You won," Caroline said, almost in a daze. She'd lost only one game of Scrabble since her junior year in high school. She'd played brilliantly, yet Paul had outdone her.

"Yes, love, I won."

For a minute all she could do was stare at the board in shocked disbelief.

"Love? I believe you owe me a kiss."

She should object to his calling her "love," but she was too bemused. "You beat me at Scrabble," she said. "And I'm a good player. Very good."

"I'm fairly well versed in the game myself," Paul said. "There's not much else for Walter and me to do on those long winter nights."

Caroline's eyes narrowed. He'd known all along that he had an excellent chance of winning.

"I believe you owe me a kiss," he said again.

"You cheated," Caroline cried. "You used a four-letter word and—"

"Don't tell me you're a poor sport, too."

As fast as she could, Caroline removed the wooden pieces from the playing board. "You mean in addition to being a liar and a thief."

"I didn't say that," Paul told her soberly.

"Well, you needn't worry, I'll give you what I promised, but I still think it's unfair of you to use that word."

"You'd use it, too, if you had to," Paul said, folding up the game and placing it back on the bookcase.

"I wouldn't!"

"If you were down to four letters and that word placed you on a triple word score and would guarantee you a win, then I don't doubt you'd use it!"

"Well," Caroline hedged, a smile lifting the edges of her mouth. "I'd be tempted, but I don't think I'd stoop that low."

"Yes, you would. Now pay up, love."

Reluctantly, Caroline stood and rounded the table to his side.

"A kiss that'll turn me inside out," he reminded her.

"I remember," she said ruefully. She stood in front of him and Paul's arm circled her waist, pulling her onto his lap. She offered him a weak smile and set her hands on his shoulders. His palms slid around her back, directing her actions.

She twisted her head to the right, then changed her mind and moved it to the left. Slowly, she bent forward and placed her parted mouth on his. Paul's lips were moist and warm and brushed hers in a slow, sensuous way. Then his kiss grew wilder, and she responded with equal intensity.

They broke apart, panting and drained.

"Oh, Caroline," he breathed against her neck. Their mouths fused again. Although she'd initially had no intention of giving him more than the one kiss, she felt as eager for the second as he was.

Again his mouth nuzzled her neck. "Another game, Caroline, love? Only this time the stakes will be slightly higher."

Five

"Another game of Scrabble?" Caroline repeated, feeling content.

Dream or not, her memory served her well; Paul Trevor was one fantastic kisser. Suddenly her eyes flew open and she jerked herself free from Paul's arms. Mere hours before she'd vowed to freeze him out and here she was, sitting on his lap with her arms around his neck, kissing him with all the fervor in her heart.

"Our Scrabble days are over, Paul Trevor," she said coldly, placing her hand on the table to help maintain her balance. She felt a heated flush in her cheeks.

"You mean you're quitting because I'm a better player than you?" Paul returned with a laugh.

"Better player, my foot!"

The whole situation appeared to amuse him, which only angered Caroline more. She stormed into the bedroom and sat on the end of the bed, sulking. Until she'd met Paul, she'd considered herself an easygoing, fun-loving person. In two days' time he'd managed to change all that. With her arms crossed, she fumed, contemplating a hundred means of making him suffer.

It wasn't until they were in bed, Paul asleep at her side, that Caroline acknowledged the truth—she was more furious with herself than Paul. He'd played an honorable Scrabble game, except for that four-letter word, and had won their wager fair and square. What infuriated her most was her overwhelming response to his kiss. She didn't *want* to feel this way; it was far too difficult to hate him when he was so loving, so gentle, so…exciting.

In the morning, Paul woke her. "Time to get up, sleepyhead," he whispered in her ear.

Caroline's eyes fluttered open. Paul sat on the edge of the bed, smiling down at her. "Coffee's ready," he said.

"Paul," she pleaded, trying to appeal to his better nature. "Do I have to go to the pumping station with you again? It's so boring. I hate it."

"I'm sorry, love."

"I promise I won't pull any tricks."

He stood, shaking his head. "No, Caroline, you're coming with me."

Arguing would do no good, she realized with a frown, and tossed aside the heavy quilts to climb out of bed, grumbling as she did. Paul left her to dress in privacy, for which she was grateful.

Caroline prepared herself for the long, tedious hours. She took a deck of cards, some reading material and a pen and paper.

As he had the day before, Paul joined her at the desk

beside hers a couple of hours into the morning. He smiled as he pulled out the ledger.

She waited to be sure she wasn't disturbing him before speaking. "Paul, who does the cooking for you?"

He didn't look up from the ledger as he spoke. "Tanana Eagleclaw. You met her the day you got here."

"There were so many people," she explained feebly.

He grinned, but didn't tease her about her memory lapse.

"Paul." She tried again. "I'm a good cook." That might have been a bit of an exaggeration, she added silently, but anything was better than sitting around this infernal pumping station ten hours a day.

"Hmm." He barely acknowledged her, apparently finding his ledgers more compelling.

"Really, I'm an excellent cook." She was getting desperate now. "I could prepare our meals. In fact, I'd like to do it."

"Tanana does an admirable job."

"Yes, but I want to do it!"

"You can't."

"Why not?"

"Because you're here with me, that's why not."

"Do you mean to tell me you're going to drag me here for the rest of my life?"

Paul sighed expressively. "We're going over the same territory as yesterday. You'll stay with me until I feel I can trust you again."

"Wonderful," she said in a sour voice. She couldn't begin to guess when that might be.

* * *

A week passed and each morning a sleepy Caroline traipsed behind Paul to the pumping station and each night she followed him home. No amount of pleading could get him to change his mind. He wanted her where he could see her every minute of every day. But, despite herself, she took comfort from his presence—even if she'd never admit as much.

The mail was delivered twice a week and a letter was sitting on the table addressed to Mr. and Mrs. Paul Trevor when they arrived back from the station during Caroline's second week in Gold River.

"A letter!" Caroline cried, as excited as a child on Christmas morning. Contact with the outside world. A tie with the past. She hurriedly read the return address. "It's from my aunts."

Paul smiled. "The two schemers?"

Eagerly, Caroline tore open the envelope. "The very ones." She hadn't forgiven them for their underhanded method of getting her to Alaska, but she missed them dreadfully.

"What do they have to say?" Paul coaxed.

"They're asking how I like my surprise. In case you don't know, that's you."

"And?" he prodded with a soft chuckle.

"And what?"

"How do you like me?"

It was Caroline's turn to laugh. "I find you…surprising."

"Typical."

"Aunt Mabel, she's the romantic one, says she feels that we're going to be happy and have…oh my goodness."

"What?"

Color seeped up from Caroline's neck and flushed her cheeks. "She predicts seven children, which is how many my great-great-grandmother had as a mail-order bride."

"I'm willing," Paul informed her with a grin.

"Be quiet, I'm reading. And Aunt Ethel…" She hesitated, her eyes scanning the rest of the page. "It was nothing." With her heart pounding frantically, and hoping to appear nonchalant, she refolded the letter and placed it back inside the envelope.

Paul joined her at the kitchen table. "What did she say?"

Caroline dropped her gaze. "It wasn't important."

"Shall I read the letter myself?"

"No…" she said and hid it behind her back. He could have insisted she hand it over, but didn't, although his cutting gaze reminded her that the letter had been addressed to both of them and he had every right to read it. "She told me that Larry Atkins dropped by when…when he couldn't get hold of me. Aunt Ethel said she took great delight in telling him I'm a married woman now."

"I see," Paul said thoughtfully.

"I'm sure you don't." Caroline braced her hands against the kitchen counter as she fought a bout of self-pity. Her relationship with Larry had been over weeks before she'd come to Alaska. It shouldn't hurt this much now, but it did. Her heart yearned to know why he'd contacted her and how he'd reacted to the news that she was married to Paul. She wanted to inform Larry that it wasn't a real marriage—not the way theirs would have been.

Paul placed his hands on her shoulders. "Caroline, here." He turned her into his arms and held her quietly. It wasn't the embrace of a lover, but that of a caring, loyal friend.

She laid her face against his chest and drew in a wobbly breath. His hand was in her hair, stroking the back of her head in a soothing, comforting motion.

"Do you still love him?" he asked after a moment.

Caroline had to analyze her feelings. She'd been crazy in love with Larry for months. She missed him, thought about him often, wished him the best. But did she love him?

As she pondered his question, Paul decided that holding Caroline was the closest thing to heaven he'd ever experienced. He'd barely touched her in a week, wanting to give her time to know him. Their relationship was in an awkward stage; he wasn't convinced he could trust her yet. She'd outright told him that the first time he left her alone, she'd run away. Winter was coming on, and for her own safety he couldn't leave her until he was sure she wouldn't try to escape. He ached to hold her and kiss her until he felt he'd go mad. His successful restraint should make him a candidate for sainthood, he thought wryly. He regretted that he hadn't made love to her on their wedding night, and yet he'd never coerce Caroline or any woman, never force himself on her.

From her ramblings that night, Paul knew about Larry. The situation was less than ideal and he'd played the role of patient husband, difficult though that was. She'd been with him nine days, and yet it had aged him a hundred lifetimes to be with her—at meals, at the station, especially in bed—knowing her mind was on another man. A man who'd rejected her, for that matter.

"Caroline," he pressed, needing to know. "Do you still love him?"

"I…yes," she answered truthfully, her voice strained and low. This was difficult. Paul was her husband, in fact if not in deed, and she couldn't deny either her attraction to him or his kindness to her. She had no desire to be cruel to him. "You don't stop loving people because they've hurt you," she told him softly, relishing the comfort of his arms. "I'm trying not to love him…. Does that help?"

Tenderly, Paul kissed the side of her face. "It makes it easier to accept. I appreciate what it cost you to be honest."

A polite knock at the door drew them reluctantly apart. A very pregnant young woman walked in. Her smile was almost bashful, as though she felt she'd intruded on their lovemaking. "Did you need me, Paul?"

"Yes." Paul slipped his arm around Caroline's waist. "Caroline, this is Tanana Eagleclaw. Tanana, my wife, Caroline."

"How do you do, Mrs. Trevor?" the girl said formally.

"Fine, thank you, Tanana. And please call me Caroline. When is your baby due?" From the way she looked, it could've been any day.

"Six weeks." Again the young woman smiled shyly, obviously pleased about the pregnancy.

Caroline guessed she was in her early twenties. "You're a very good cook."

"Thank you."

Paul said something to her in her native tongue and Tanana nodded eagerly, her gaze moving briefly to Caroline. She left soon afterward.

"What was that all about?" Caroline asked.

"You said you wanted to meet Tanana, so I had her come over."

"But that wasn't the only reason. What did you say to her?"

"When?"

"Just now." Caroline gave him a bewildered look until she realized he was purposely playing dumb. "Never mind. You obviously don't want me to know, so forget it." She did understand one thing; Tanana's feelings would be hurt if Caroline were to take over the cooking. Perhaps when her baby was born, Caroline could assume the task without causing any loss of pride. If she was still here, of course...

That night, sitting in front of the fireplace, Caroline wrote her aunts a long reply. She told them that in the beginning she was furious with what they'd done, but gradually she'd changed her mind. Paul was a good man, a decent man, she wrote, and in that regard, she told the truth. But she couldn't tell them that she hoped and prayed that, given time, Paul would let her return to Seattle. That kind of information would only upset them, and there was no need to disillusion those two romantics. Nor did she say that if she was going to be a bride, she wanted the opportunity to choose her *own* husband. When Paul sent her back, and Caroline believed he would, there'd be time enough to explain everything. For now, she'd play their game and let them think they'd outsmarted her and that she was a happy, blushing bride. It could do no harm.

That night, Caroline fell into bed, exhausted. Paul joined her a little later, and as she did every night, she pretended to be asleep when he slipped in beside her.

"'Night, love," he whispered.

She didn't respond and a few minutes later drifted into a natural, contented sleep.

A noise woke her. She stirred—discovering that she'd been sleeping with her head on Paul's chest. His arm secured her to him.

"Is it morning yet?" she murmured, closing her eyes again, reluctant to leave the warmth pressing against her.

"In a few minutes."

Paul rose before her every morning to stoke the fire and put on the coffee. Caroline had no idea whether she touched him in her sleep and feared that she'd wake in his arms one morning and embarrass them both.

"Do I do this often?" she asked, a little flustered.

"Not nearly enough," he returned. His hand ran down the length of her spine, stopping at the small of her back. He paused and inhaled sharply.

Caroline realized it was that soft rumble from his throat that had awakened her. Still she didn't move. He felt incredibly good—warm, strong…male.

Five minutes passed, then ten. Caroline knew she had to pull herself away; each minute was more pleasant than the one before.

"I'll make the coffee this morning," she murmured, easing away from him.

Paul stopped her. "There's no rush. Go back to sleep if you'd like."

"To sleep?" She lifted her head enough to search his face. "Aren't you going to the station?"

"I'll be there, but you won't."

Caroline was sure she'd misunderstood him.

"I asked Tanana to spend the day with you," he explained. "She's going to introduce you to the other women in the village."

For a moment, Caroline was too stunned to grasp what he was saying. "Paul, do you mean it? I don't have to go to the station?" Without thought, she wrapped her arms around his neck and covered his cheeks and forehead with a series of tiny, eager kisses.

Paul's hands found her head and guided her mouth to his for a kiss that was long and hard. Leisurely, her lips moved against his. Without her being certain how it happened, Paul reversed their positions with such ease that she lay on her back, staring up at him. Slowly, as though he couldn't resist her a second longer, he lowered his mouth to hers in a kiss that stirred her, heart and soul. Caroline couldn't possibly have denied herself that kiss. Her hands sought his face, luxuriating in the feel of his beard.

Paul broke off the kiss and, with a sigh that seemed

to come from deep inside, buried his face in the hollow of her throat.

Caroline entwined her arms around his neck and released her own sigh of contentment. She was shocked at how right it felt to have Paul hold and kiss her. Her heart raged to a primitive beat and her body throbbed with a simmering passion. She didn't want to feel these things. When she left him, she didn't want to be weighed down with regrets.

He raised his head then, and compelled her gaze to meet his own, but she turned her head. "You're going to be late."

He nodded.

No time clock waited for him, and they both knew it. He eased away from her and sat on the edge of the bed for a moment to regain his strength. Caroline made him weak in ways he didn't understand. She wanted him; he could almost taste her eagerness. And yet, she had to say *yes* to him with complete certainty. With commitment as well as desire.

Exasperated, he plowed his fingers through his hair. He'd be patient a little longer, but he wasn't going to be able to withstand many more of her kisses. She fascinated him. She'd captured his heart and held it in the palm of her hand with as much concern as she would an unwanted sweet.

Although it was midmorning, Caroline was barely up and dressed when Tanana arrived. Again the young woman knocked politely at the door before stepping inside.

"Morning, Mrs. Trevor," she said shyly. "Caroline…"

"Morning, Tanana. I was just fixing myself some breakfast. Would you like some?"

She shook her head. "You come now, please?"

"Now?"

Tanana nodded.

"There isn't time for breakfast?"

"No time."

Muttering disparaging words under her breath, Caroline removed the skillet from the stove and put the eggs back in the refrigerator while Tanana grabbed Caroline's boots and parka.

"Where are we going?"

"The meeting hall."

"The other women are already there?"

"Yes. Many of them."

Caroline had no idea what they were waiting for, but she was so pleased to be able to talk to another human being that she wouldn't have cared if they were only going to sit around and drink weak coffee.

As Tanana had promised, there were seven or eight women gathered inside the large hall that served as the heart of the small community. Smiling faces greeted her when they walked in and Tanana led an astonished Caroline to an empty chair that stood in the center of the room—obviously the seat of honor.

She soon recognized that the women were giving a party in her honor, something like a bridal shower. One by one, each woman stepped forward and offered her a gift. Not all the women spoke English, but Tanana acted as their interpreter. The gifts were mostly homemade, displaying such talent and skill that Caroline's breath caught in her throat at their beauty. She received a stunning hand-knit sweater, slippers made from sealskin, several pieces of intricate scrimshaw with scenes that depicted Indian life in the frozen North, as well as smoked salmon and venison. Caroline watched in wide-eyed wonder as they approached her. When it came to material things, they had so little and she had so much, yet they were lovingly sharing a precious part of their lives. Tears gathered in her eyes and she swallowed down a thickness forming in her throat, not wanting to embarrass these friendly, generous women.

When they'd finished, Caroline stood and went to each one to personally thank her. Later, after they'd served lunch, the women gathered their yarn and started to knit.

"What are they making?" Caroline asked Tanana.

"Sweaters for the tourists."

"Gold River gets that many tourists?"

"Some, but they're mostly for the stores in Fairbanks, Juneau and Anchorage."

"Oh."

"All the women of the village work on the sweaters in wintertime," Tanana continued. "Each day we meet here."

"I knit, too," Caroline said, broaching the subject carefully. She wanted to be part of this community—at least, for as long as she lived here. Although her skill might not have been at the level of these women, she could learn. They'd been so kind to her that she wanted to return their kindness.

"Would you like to join us?" Tanana asked politely.

"Please." A moment later, Caroline was handed a pair of needles, several skeins of thick yarn and, with Tanana to guide her, was set to work.

That night, Caroline was bursting with excitement, so much that she could hardly contain it. When Paul walked in the cabin door, she practically flew across the room.

"Hi," she greeted him. "Did you know about the…party?"

His smiling eyes delved into hers. "Tanana told me about it last week. She said it was time I let you out of bed long enough to meet the village women."

Caroline decided to ignore that comment. "They're wonderful people."

"I know, love." Once he'd removed his parka and hung it in the closet, Caroline grabbed his hand and led him into the bedroom. She'd placed the nonfood items on the quilt for him to examine. He picked up each piece and nodded his pleasure at the village's generosity, praising the skill and beauty of their art. When he came to the oddly shaped piece of knitting, he regarded it skeptically. "And what's this?"

"Oh, yes, I nearly forgot. The women knit, but I guess I already know that. Anyway, they let me sit and work with them this afternoon. Of course I'm not nearly as good as they are and my poor sweater wouldn't be anywhere near good enough to sell to the tourists." She laughed. "It's funny to think that some tourist might buy a sweater assuming it was knit by a local Athabascan only to discover it was made by a Seattle nurse." She giggled again. "At the end of the afternoon, I think Tanana was afraid of hurting my feelings so I asked if I could do something else with my first effort."

"And what was that?"

"I told them I wanted to knit this sweater for you."

"What did they say to that?"

"Oh, they were pleased, but then they would be, since they probably couldn't sell it." She waltzed out of the bedroom and into the kitchen. "And I made dinner. Tanana looked so tired that I offered. Naturally, she argued with me, but not too strenuously."

"So you had a good day."

"I had a marvelous day!" She turned her back to him to stir the simmering gravy. All afternoon she'd been trying to come up with a way of persuading Paul that she should join the other women on a daily basis. He'd been so unyielding in other matters that she dreaded a confrontation now.

"I suppose you want to go back?"

Caroline whirled around, her heart in her eyes. "Yes. Are you okay with that?"

"I think it's more your decision than mine."

She understood what he was saying, but bit back a ready reply while she took slices of meat from the oven and forked them onto a platter, which she set on the table.

"Unless you trust me again," she said, her eyes

holding his, "I know I won't ever be able to prove I'm trustworthy in your eyes."

"Then do as you wish."

Caroline was so pleased that she was hard-pressed not to throw her arms around his neck and kiss him the way she had that morning. It wasn't until after they'd eaten that she realized how much she actually wanted to kiss him, but quickly pushed the thought from her mind.

Later, she found herself humming while washing the dinner dishes, and paused, surprised at herself. She was happy—truly content. She turned to find Paul watching her as he dried their plates and they shared a smile.

Once again they played a heated game of Scrabble, but without any wagers. This time Caroline won.

"You'll note that I didn't use a single dirty word," she told him with a proud snicker.

Paul chuckled and reset the board for a second game.

That next afternoon and for several more that followed, Caroline joined the village women for their daily knitting session. The first few days, the women were shy and didn't say much to her. Gradually they opened up and she became privy to the village gossip. More than one of the women seemed to find something about Caroline amusing. Every time they looked in her direction, they leaned over to the woman next to them and whispered something that made the other smile. Finally, when Caroline's curiosity got the better of her, she asked Tanana about it.

The young woman blushed. "They say you are a fortunate woman."

"Fortunate? I don't understand."

"Yes, you have Paul for your lover. They are envious that at night he sleeps at your side and holds you in his arms. They say you will have many healthy babies with Paul. He is…I don't know the English word."

"Never mind," Caroline returned, her fingers tightening around the knitting needles. "I know what you mean." Did she ever! So Paul was a virile male who had sampled the delights of the village women before her arrival.

By the time she got back to the cabin, Caroline was so furious that she paced the small enclosure, ready to give her husband a piece of her mind the instant he returned home. She'd never dreamed, hadn't thought he'd ever do anything that low. No wonder he wanted a wife. From the looks the women had been sending her way, they'd probably started fighting over him. Well, they could have him. She was finished with him. Nothing could keep her in Gold River now. She didn't care what it took, she was leaving Paul just as soon as she could.

When the wooden door opened and the howling wind whirled through the cabin, it was only a spring breeze compared to the ice around Caroline's heart.

"Hi," Paul said with a grin, but one look at her contorted, angry features and his smile quickly faded. "What's wrong?"

She didn't wait for him to remove his coat. Her index finger found its mark in the middle of his chest. "You are despicable. You are lower than a snake. You are…" Words failed her as hot tears blurred her vision. "I can't find the words to tell you how much I despise you!"

Paul didn't look particularly concerned. "Was it something I said, or are you still mad about that four-letter word I used in the Scrabble game?"

Six

"You think you're so clever, don't you?" Caroline flared. Her outrage got the better of her and she picked up a book from the end table and hurled it at him.

With a dexterity few could manage, Paul caught the book and the saltshaker that immediately followed. The amusement fled his eyes. "Caroline, what's gotten into you?"

"You…animal!"

"Tell me what I did."

"You…*beast!*" The pepper shaker whizzed past his ear.

"Caroline!"

"You…you…adulterer!" That might not make complete sense, since he hadn't been married, but it conveyed her disgust.

Stunned, Paul watched as she stormed into the bedroom and viciously slammed the door. For a minute he did nothing but stand with a book and saltshaker in his hand, too bemused to move. Beyond her explosive fury, what shocked Paul most was the hurt he saw in her eyes.

"Adulterer?" he repeated in an astonished whisper.

Inside the room, Caroline sat on the edge of the bed. Stinging tears threatened to run down her face and she rubbed the heels of her hands against her eyes in a futile effort to restrain them. Damn it all, she was falling in love with him—head over heels in love with a man who had neither morals nor conscience. If she didn't love him, then knowing what he'd done wouldn't hurt this much. Caroline cried harder. She didn't *want* to love him. A hiccupping sob ripped through her throat and she buried her face in her hands.

Her crying devastated Paul. He'd planned to wait until her anger had dissipated before trying to reason with her, but he couldn't. Every sob felt like a punch to his abdomen.

"Caroline," he called from the other side of the door. "Can we talk about this?"

Silence.

"Caroline, believe me, I haven't the foggiest idea what you're talking about."

"I'll just bet you don't!"

"I don't." He tried the knob, but she'd locked the door. "As your husband, I demand that you open this door immediately." He felt foolish saying it, but couldn't think of anything else.

She snickered.

"Caroline... Please." When she didn't respond, he rammed his hands in his pants pockets. "Are you angry about our wedding night? Is that it?" Standing directly in front of the door, he muttered, "I can see it isn't going to do any good to try talking to you now. You're in no mood to be reasonable."

With that, the bedroom door opened so unexpectedly that he almost fell through.

Caroline glared at him with renewed animosity. "Do you mean to tell me that…that on the night we were married you…you took advantage of me?"

"Caroline, if you'd listen…"

"O-o-h." Her clenched fists pummeled his chest until her hands felt numb with pain.

"That's enough." Paul caught her wrists and pinned her against the wall. Her shoulders heaved with exertion, and tears streaked her face and brimmed in her wide, blue eyes.

Trembling, she collected herself and drew in a ragged breath. Briefly, she struggled, but Paul's hold tightened. His fierce look held her as effectively as his hands. Caroline met his eyes with open defiance.

"Love." His voice was a hoarse whisper of bewilderment and confusion, his face mere inches from her own. "What is it?"

He spoke with such gentleness that it would be easy to forget what he was and what he'd done. "Let me go," she said, her rage gone now, replaced by a far deeper, more crippling emotion—sorrow.

Paul saw the pain in her eyes and was filled with such perplexity that he reacted instinctively. In an effort to comfort, his mouth sought hers.

His kiss was insistent, demanding, relentless. Almost against her will Caroline parted her lips to meet his. Her eagerness for him grew, an eagerness that rocked her soul. Gradually both she and Paul relaxed, the crucial need abated. He loosened his grip, but continued to hold her wrists. Caroline became aware of the heavy thud of his heart while her own pulsed with a frantic rhythm.

They breathed in unison. Paul's eyes searched her face as he looked for any clue that would help him understand her irrational behavior. Hot color stained her cheeks, but he didn't know if it was from her anger or her excitement during their kiss. Her lips were moist, and he bent his head to taste their sweetness again. When he finally drew back, he and Caroline were both trembling.

He released her hands and Caroline dropped them to her sides. "I was with the women today," she began, in a voice so fraught with pain that Paul wrapped her securely in his arms. "And they told me…"

"Told you what, Caroline?"

"That…you're a fantastic lover."

He frowned. "Ah," he whispered slowly, then cupped her face with his hands, kissing her briefly. "And you assumed they meant it literally?"

"How else was I supposed to take it?"

"I've been living here for several years now," he began. "I've become friends with many of them and their families.They're, uh, kind enough to favor me with certain attributes they *believe* I possess."

Caroline's gaze met his. "They sounded so…so knowledgeable."

He grinned widely. "Hey, I'm only one man. I couldn't possibly have had that many lovers."

"Have you had…even one?" Her intense gaze locked with his.

"By everything I hold dear, I swear to you that I've never had a single lover in Gold River." Paul had assumed she'd welcome his assurance, but his words produced the most uncanny response; tears flooded her eyes and streamed down her face. Caroline hugged him fiercely, burying her face in his sweater. Half laughing, half crying, she lifted her head and spread eager kisses mingled with salty tears on his face. Gently Paul held her, wondering if he'd been outside civilization so long he'd lost his ability to understand women. He sighed; perhaps he had.

Their relationship altered after that night. The changes were subtle ones and came about so naturally that Paul could only guess their meaning. The first thing he noticed was that Caroline had placed her suitcase under the bed, as though she'd finally accepted her position in his life and planned to remain. He yearned for her to forget her hope of returning to Seattle.

He knew she spent a lot of time with Tanana and apparently they'd worked out an agreement concerning dinner, since Caroline started cooking all their meals. She'd once told him she was an excellent cook and he learned that she hadn't exaggerated. She was clever, inventive and resourceful. It wasn't every woman who could make dried eggs edible.

Everyone was her friend; even Walter had become her ally. Paul had been in the village six months before the old man had fully accepted him. Walter's acceptance of Caroline was typical of the love she received from all the people of Gold River. The children adored her; Caroline couldn't walk out the door without two or three of them running to her side. One day Paul discovered Caroline in the meeting hall, skipping rope with the sixth-grade girls. Another day he found her involved in a heated soccer game with the junior-high boys.

When an old woman had a toothache, she came to Caroline. A feverish baby was brought to her as well. A little boy with a stomach ache showed up unexpectedly one afternoon. The medical clinic was open once a week when a team from the Public Health Department flew in for appointments, but it was Caroline the villagers came to. At first she used her own personal quantity of painkillers and bandages; then, as a qualified nurse she received access to the clinic's supply. Paul felt absolutely delighted that she could use her training this way.

But now he was so much in love he thought he'd die from wanting her. But to rush into lovemaking now would be foolish. She was so close to recognizing she loved him, and when that day came it would be right and beautiful, although he often wondered how much longer he could hold out. He endured the sweetest torture every morning when he woke to find her in his arms. At night, the agony was far greater; he dreaded her touch and at the same time craved it.

That evening after dinner, Caroline brought out a large package and placed it on the ottoman in front of him.

Paul lowered the two-day-old newspaper and raised questioning eyes to his wife. "What's this?"

"Open it and see." She'd worked so hard on this sweater that if it didn't fit, she'd burst into tears. "I probably should've saved it for Christmas, but…" It was silly to be this nervous. She wanted to please him and the holidays were still six weeks away. Besides, she couldn't think of a better way to tell Paul she loved him.

"But what, love?"

"But I thought you deserved it now." For calming her angry tirades, for being so patient with her, for his gentleness and a hundred other admirable qualities. And because she longed to be his wife in the truest sense of the word.

Carefully, Paul removed the paper and held up the Irish cable-knit sweater. "Caroline, I'm…stunned. It's a fine piece of work."

"If it doesn't fit, I can redo it." She couldn't believe she'd made that offer; the pattern was difficult and complicated. If it hadn't been for Tanana's and the other women's help, she would've given up and unraveled the sweater weeks before.

"I'm sure it'll fit perfectly." To prove his point, he stood and pulled it over his head. "Where did you get the yarn?" he asked, running his hand over the sleeves. The sweater was a lovely shade of winter wheat and far lighter than the material the village women typically used.

"I sent away for it. Mary Finefeather had a catalog."

"How did you pay for it?" She'd never come to him for money, although he would've been more than pleased to give it to her. They had little need for cash in

Gold River. The supply store and grocery sent him monthly accounts and his paychecks were automatically deposited in the Fairbanks Savings and Loan.

"I used my credit card."

He nodded and kissed her lightly. "Thank you, love. I'll always treasure it."

Caroline's returning smile was weak, as though she was disappointed by his response. Paul watched her leave and wondered if he'd said something to offend her. He began to doubt that he'd ever understand her.

Hours later, Paul lay at her side. His even breathing convinced Caroline he was sound asleep as she lay on her back wide-eyed, staring at the ceiling. She was now convinced that she was a failure. For two weeks, she'd been trying to tell Paul that she was ready to be his wife in *every* way. How a man could be so completely blind was beyond her. If it hadn't been for a few secret looks of longing she'd intercepted, she would have abandoned her cause. She made excuses to be close to him, to touch him. All the signals she'd been sending him would have stopped a freight train! The sweater had been her ace in the hole and even that had failed. In return, he'd kissed her like an affectionate older brother.

Ah well, there was always tomorrow. Maybe if she wore the nightgown her aunts had given her... She smiled and her eyes drifted shut. She couldn't get any more obvious than that.

The next day was a busy one. The small town was holding an early Thanksgiving feast, and it seemed half of Alaska had been invited. People had been arriving from the outlying areas all morning. Caroline and Tanana were responsible for decorating the meeting hall and the two of them made a comical sight. Caroline wouldn't allow Tanana, who was in an advanced stage of pregnancy, to climb the ladder to hang the crepe paper streamers, so Caroline wrapped them around her neck and hauled them up herself.

"This isn't fair," Tanana complained. "All I'm doing is holding the ladder for you."

"I'm not going to let you stand on this rickety old thing," Caroline muttered, stretching as far as her limbs would allow to stick a thumbtack into the beam.

"If Paul ever saw this, he'd be mad."

"He isn't going to know, and you're not going to tell him—right?"

"What will you bribe me with?"

Caroline laughed. "Hush, now, and hand me another streamer." She climbed down a couple of steps and Tanana gave her the next set of bright orange and yellow crepe paper strips.

When they'd finished, the two women surveyed the hall, proud of their accomplishment. It was astonishing how much a little color added to the festive spirit.

Mary Finefeather, a foster grandmother to many of the village kids, delivered sandwiches to Caroline and Tanana. Typical of the old woman's personality, Mary spoke in choppy one-word sentences.

"Eat," she said with a grin.

"I think that's an order," Caroline commented, and

looked at Tanana, who smiled in reply. The younger woman had lost much of her shyness now and Caroline considered her a valued friend.

"What are you getting Paul for Christmas?" Tanana asked, studying Caroline.

"I...don't know. I gave him the sweater last night." She wished she hadn't; with the holidays fast approaching, she had wasted her best gift—seemingly for naught.

"I know what he wants."

"You do?"

Tanana placed her hand on her swollen abdomen and stared at her stomach. "He wants a son."

Caroline nearly swallowed her sandwich whole. "Oh?"

"You'll give him fine sons? And daughters?"

Embarrassed, Caroline looked away. "Someday."

"Soon?"

"I...I don't know." Caroline couldn't very well announce that she and Paul had never made love, at least not that she could remember.

Caroline worked for part of the afternoon, then returned to the cabin, frustrated and tired. She'd slept poorly, and tonight would be another late night. Before she could talk herself out of the idea, she climbed onto the bed and closed her eyes, intending to rest for only a few minutes.

Paul found her there an hour later, barely visible in the soft light of dusk. He paused in the doorway of their bedroom and experienced such a wave of desire that he sucked in a tight breath. Her blouse had ridden up to expose the creamy smooth skin of her midriff. Blood pounded in his head and his feet seemed to move of their own accord, taking him to her side.

His gaze lingered on the smooth slant of her brow and a smile briefly touched his face. She could make a clearer statement with an arch of her eyebrow than some women said in twenty years. Her nose was perfect and her sweet, firm lips were enough to drive a man insane. He thought about the last time they'd kissed and how, for hours afterward, he'd been in a foul mood, barking at Walter and the others until Walter had suggested that Paul do something to cure whatever was ailing him.

Caroline was ailing him. He wanted to touch her, to— Caroline yawned and rolled over.

Paul jumped away from her as though he'd been caught doing something wrong. His knees felt like slush in a spring thaw. On unsteady feet, he walked over to the dresser.

"Caroline, it's time to get up." He hardly recognized the strained, harsh voice as his own.

Slowly she opened her eyes. She'd been having the most wonderful dream about giving Paul the child Tanana claimed he wanted so badly. One look at her husband, who stood stiffly on the other side of the room, was enough to return her to the cold world of reality. His back was to her.

"Hi," she said, stretching her hands high above her head and yawning loudly.

"Hi," he said gruffly. He didn't dare turn around. If her midriff had been showing before, he could only imagine what he'd glimpse now. He felt himself go weak all over again.

Caroline frowned at his abruptness. "Did you have a good day?"

"Sure." He pulled open the top drawer and took out a clean T-shirt. "You'd better get dressed or we'll be late for the party."

"What time is it?"

"Five."

Caroline's frown deepened. No one was expected before seven. "We've got plenty of time."

No, we don't, Paul wanted to shout. He, for one, was at the end of his rope.

"Paul, what's wrong?"

"Nothing." He slammed the drawer shut with unnecessary force. "I just happen to think it's time you got out of bed."

"Are you angry because I took a nap?"

"No," he snapped.

She rose to a sitting position and released a long sigh. "Sometimes I don't understand you."

"That makes two of us."

"Will you please turn around? I don't like talking to your back." She made the request softly, confused by his mood. She'd never known Paul to be so short-tempered and illogical.

"If you don't mind, I'm busy."

Caroline blinked. She replayed the conversation with Tanana, and a heaviness settled on her shoulders. She loved Paul and yearned to have his child, but instead of growing together they seemed to be drifting apart. Sudden tears misted her eyes. She'd thought that once she acknowledged she was in love with him everything would be perfect. Instead, it had gotten worse—much worse.

Paul tossed his sweater on the bed. "Good grief, don't tell me you're crying! One day you're hurling saltshakers at me and the next you're weeping because I tell you to hurry and get ready for a party you've been working on all day."

Her eyes widened with determination to hold back the tears. "I'm not crying. That's ridiculous. Why should I be crying?"

He threw up his hands. "Who knows? I've given up trying to understand you."

The party was a grand success. The meeting hall was filled to the rafters with friends and loved ones from nearby communities. The dinner proved to be delicious and Caroline received rave reviews for her apple pies and decorating efforts. Although she smiled and made all the appropriate responses, she couldn't seem to get into the party mood.

When the tables were cleared and the dancing began, Caroline saw how Paul seemed to dance with every woman in the room but her. Not that Caroline was given much time to notice. One partner after another claimed her hand for a turn around the floor. After an hour, she pleaded exhaustion and sat down, fanning her flushed face with one hand.

To her surprise, Paul joined her, sitting in the chair

beside hers. His lips were pinched, his face grim. "I imagine you're pleased to have every man for a hundred miles panting after you."

Caroline's mouth fell open at the unjust accusation. Quickly she composed herself, stiffening her back. "I'm going to forgive you for that remark, Paul Trevor, because you owe me one. But from here on we're even." She stood up and purposely walked away from him. Her eyes clouded by confusion, she nearly stumbled into Walter, and glancing up at him, hurriedly stammered an apology.

"Didn't you promise me this dance?" Walter said.

Still unable to find her tongue, Caroline nodded.

Studying her, the older man guided her onto the dance floor. A waltz was playing and Caroline slipped one arm around his neck and placed her hand in his.

"All right, girl, tell me—what's made you so unhappy?"

Caroline's mouth formed a poor excuse for a smile. "Paul. I don't know how any man can be so stupid."

"He's blinded by his love for you."

"I sincerely doubt that's it." Caroline looked directly into Walter's face. "I have the feeling he's ready to ship me back to Seattle." There'd been a time when she'd prayed for exactly that, but now her heart ached at the mere thought of leaving him.

Standing by the punch bowl, Paul watched her. Caroline could feel his dark gaze on her back. With every passing minute, his eyes grew darker and more angry.

Walter chuckled. "Paul would rather cut off his arm than send you away. Have you told him you love him?"

Caroline's shocked gaze clashed with the man's wise old eyes. "No."

"Then do it, and soon, before he makes an even bigger fool of himself."

When the dance ended, Walter delivered her to Paul's side and quietly left them. Caroline and Paul stood glaring at each other until the music started.

"Shall we?" Caroline asked, glancing toward the crowded floor.

"Why not? You've seen fit to dance with every other male here tonight."

"Paul," she whispered. "Are you jealous?"

He didn't answer her, but she saw that his face was as grim as she'd ever seen it. His hold on her was loose, as if he couldn't bear to touch her.

Caroline swallowed her pride. "There isn't anyone here I'd rather dance with than you."

Still he said nothing. His eyes were focused straight ahead and she didn't see so much as a flicker in his rock-hard features to indicate that he'd heard her or that her words had any effect.

"When I first came to Gold River, I hated it."

If possible, his mouth grew harder, more inflexible.

"But…things changed and I realized I was happy here. There's a wildness to this land. A challenge that makes people strong and wise. I've seen that in you and admired your patience and gentleness."

Momentarily, Paul dropped his eyes and studied her as though he didn't quite trust what she was saying.

Caroline thought her heart would burst with pain when he quickly glanced away.

"You idiot," she said and brought her shoe down hard on the top of his foot.

Paul let out a small yelp of pain.

"I'm trying to tell you I love you, but you can forget it! And while you're at it, you can forget about our son, too!" She broke away and left him holding one leg like a flamingo while he nursed his injured foot.

At the door, Caroline grabbed her boots and parka and stormed out of the meeting hall, too angry for tears, too frustrated to consider what she was doing. She knew only that she had to escape.

"Caroline!"

His frantic call came to her before she reached the cabin door. With heightened resolve, she pretended she hadn't heard him.

"Caroline! Would you wait?"

She ignored his pleading as well. By the time he arrived, she was sitting by the fireplace with a book in front of her face.

"Caroline…what did you just say?" He was breathless, his voice rushed and uneven.

"It was nothing."

"It was everything," he whispered in awe. "*Do* you love me? Caroline, would you please look at me?"

"No."

Paul felt he was going to explode with happiness. "And what was that crazy remark about a son?"

She turned the page of her book and glanced with

keen interest at the beginning of the next chapter, although she had no idea what was going on in the story.

Paul fell to his knees at her side and pried the book from her stiff fingers. She refused to meet his eyes.

"Caroline…" He breathed her name with a heart overflowing with expectancy and hope. "Are you telling me you're ready to be my wife?"

"I couldn't have made it any plainer. I've flaunted myself in front of you all week. I gave you the sweater… hoping… Paul Trevor, you're an idiot! For days, I've been throwing myself at you and you…you've been so blind and so stupid."

"You have?" Paul was flabbergasted. "When? Days?"

"Weeks!"

"Weeks?" He *had* been blind, but no longer.

His hands framed her face as he guided her lips to his, kissing her with such hungry intensity it robbed her of breath. Somehow he lifted her from the chair, cradled her in his arms and carried her into their bedroom. He placed her on the mattress and knelt over her, studying her to be sure this wasn't a dream.

Caroline stared into his eyes and twined her arms around his neck, bringing his mouth back to her own. "You idiot," she whispered again.

"Not anymore, love."

Their lips met over and over, as though each kiss was sweeter and more potent than the one before. Holding back nothing, Caroline surrendered to him with joyful abandon. He explored her face, her neck, her shoulders, charting undiscovered territory with his lips as he helped her undress. Finally they were both free of restricting clothes and Paul kissed her until she responded with a wantonness she didn't know she possessed. They broke apart, winded and panting.

"Caroline," he murmured, his face keen and ardent in the moonlight. "Are you sure?"

"I've never been more sure of anything in my life."

Deeply content, Caroline lay with her cheek against her husband's chest. Her leg stroked his and she sighed her happiness. There was no turning back for them now; they were truly husband and wife, their commitment to each other complete.

Paul's hand smoothed the tumbled hair from her face. "Are you happy, love?"

"Very." Her nails scraped playfully at his chest. "Why didn't you tell me it was this good? If I'd known, I would've demanded my wifely rights." She raised her head to kiss the strong, proud line of his chin. "Tanana and the other women guessed correctly—you *are* a fantastic lover."

Paul opened his mouth to answer her when there was a loud knock on the front door. Caroline gave him a look of dismay; no one would come unless there was trouble.

Paul rolled to his feet, his body alert. He reached for his clothes and threw them on, then hurried to the door.

Caroline dressed in a rush, anxious now. When she entered the living room, she found Paul speaking to Thomas Eagleclaw, Tanana's husband.

"Tanana's gone into labor," Paul explained. "Her mother's with her, but she wants you."

Caroline nodded. "I'll be there in a minute."

Seven

By the time Caroline arrived at Tanana's cabin, her heart was pounding, not with exertion from the long walk, but with excitement and, she admitted, anxiety. Her experience was limited to a sterile hospital delivery room with a doctor, other nurses and all the necessary emergency equipment. None of that existed in Gold River, and Caroline had never felt more inadequate.

Thomas, Tanana's husband, and Paul led the way to their cabin. Tanana lay in the center of a double bed, her face glistening with perspiration, her eyes wide with pain. The young woman held out her hand to Caroline. "Thank you for coming."

"When did the contractions start?" Caroline asked, sitting on the edge of the bed.

Tanana lowered her gaze. "This afternoon."

"Why didn't you tell me?"

"I wasn't sure they meant I was in labor."

Caroline understood. Tanana had mentioned twice that week that she'd been experiencing "twinges" and

Caroline had told her those were normal and she needn't worry.

The older woman in the bedroom rose to greet her. Tanana's mother smiled her welcome and returned to her rocking chair, content to let Caroline assume the role of midwife. Caroline went to the kitchen to wash her hands, praying silently that this would be an easy birth, routine in every way.

It wasn't. Hours later, both Caroline and Tanana were drenched in sweat. The girl was terrified. Caroline, although outwardly calm, was equally frightened. Tanana's mother continued to rock, offering an encouraging smile now and then.

"It shouldn't be long now," Caroline said, smoothing the hair from Tanana's brow and wiping her face with a cool washcloth.

Tanana tried to smile, but the effort was too great. "Rest as much as you can between pains," Caroline instructed.

Tanana nodded. She closed her eyes and rolled her head to the side, ruthlessly biting the corner of her lip as another contraction took hold of her body.

"Don't fight it," Caroline said. "Try to breathe through the pain."

Tanana's death grip on Caroline's fingers slackened and Caroline relaxed, too. "You're doing great, Tanana. I'll check you with the next contraction and we'll see how far things have progressed."

Caroline's worst fears were confirmed; the baby was breech. A knot of fear clogged her throat. Didn't this baby realize she didn't have a lot of experience in this area? The least it could do was cooperate! "I'm going to get some fresh water," she told Tanana, and stood to leave the bedside. Tanana's eyes revealed her fear. "Don't worry," Caroline said with a reassuring smile, "I'll be right back."

In the next room, Paul was playing cards with Thomas, although it was easy to see that neither man's attention was on the game. One look at Caroline's distraught eyes, and Paul moved to her side at the kitchen sink. "What's wrong?"

"The baby is breech. Paul, I'm frightened. This is far more complicated than anything I've ever handled. My training was all in a hospital setting, and I've worked in a doctor's office for two years. You don't get much experience delivering breech babies in an office building."

"Tanana needs you."

"I know." Paul was referring to strength and confidence, but she couldn't offer the poor girl something she didn't have herself.

"If you think it's more than you can cope with, we'll call in a plane and fly her to Fairbanks."

"Yes. Please call." But that would take hours and they both knew it. "In the meantime I'll…do my best."

"I know you will, love." His hands cradled her face and he kissed her, his lips fitting tenderly over hers, lending her his own strength. A whimper from Tanana broke them apart and Caroline hurried back to her friend's side.

The hours sped by, but Caroline was barely aware of their passing. She was busy every minute, talking softly, encouraging Tanana, calling on not only her experience but her instincts. Her friend's fortitude and inner strength impressed her. When the squalling infant was finally released from the young woman's body, unrestrained tears of happiness filled Caroline's eyes.

"You have a son," she said, gently placing the baby on his mother's stomach.

"A son." Tanana's wide smile revealed her overwhelming delight and with a cry of joy, she fell back against the pillow.

A few minutes later, Caroline entered the kitchen, carrying the crying infant in her arms. Her eyes met Paul's as the two men rose slowly to their feet.

"A boy," she said softly.

Thomas let out a hoot of exhilarated happiness and paused to briefly inspect his son before he rushed past Caroline to join his wife.

Paul looked down at the small bundle in her arms. His eyes softened at the wrinkled face and tiny fingers protruding from the blanket. "You must be exhausted," he said, studying Caroline.

Lightly, she shook her head. She'd never experienced such a feeling of bliss in her life. It was as though she'd labored to deliver this child herself and he'd been born of her own body. "He's so beautiful." Unabashed tears rained from her eyes and she kissed the baby's sweet brow.

"Yes, but not as beautiful as you, love," Paul said tenderly, his heart constricting at the sight of a baby in his wife's arms. The day would come when they'd have a child of their own and the thought filled him with happy anticipation.

An hour later, the emergency medical team had been and gone, pronouncing both mother and son in good health. Paul took Caroline back to their cabin. Now that the surge of high spirits had faded, Caroline realized how weary she was. "What time is it?"

"Noon."

"*Noon?* Really?"

Paul led her directly into their bedroom and sat her on the bed, where she fell back on the rumpled sheets and heaved a sigh, closing her eyes. Smiling down at her, Paul removed her shoes.

"Paul?"

"Hmm?" He unzipped her jeans next and slid them down her long legs. A surge of desire shot through him and he forced himself to look at her face and remember how exhausted she was. Given the least amount of encouragement, he would've fallen into bed beside her.

"Tanana told me you wanted a son." Her eyes still closed, she felt lethargic, yet oddly contented.

"A daughter would do as well."

"Soon?"

"Sooner than you think if you don't get under these blankets," he grumbled, covering her with the quilts.

Caroline smiled, feeling warm and secure. "I love you," she murmured dreamily.

Paul stood by the edge of the bed, unsteady. "You love me?" She didn't answer him and he knew she was already asleep. His heart swelled with such joy that he felt like shouting and dancing around the small room. Instead, he bent down and kissed her temple. To stay with her now would be torture and although it was a different kind of agony, Paul left the room and curled up on the recliner, meaning only to rest his eyes.

Caroline found him there several hours later. "Paul," she whispered, shaking his shoulder.

With reluctance, he opened his eyes. When he saw it was Caroline, he grinned tiredly. "Did you sleep?"

"Like a baby. Why are you out here?"

"Because you needed your rest, love." His arm circled her waist and he brought her into his lap, where he nuzzled her neck. She felt so good in his arms, soft, feminine, his—all his. Larry was in the past now and gone forever.

Paul thought of his life before she'd come to him and wondered how he'd managed all those years without her. She was as much a part of him as his own heart. She was his world, his sun, his stars. All these weeks she'd led him down a rock-strewn trail, but every minute had been worth the wait. She was more than he'd ever dreamed.

Caroline smiled. Her hands directed his mouth to hers and she kissed him hungrily. He didn't need to tell her why he'd slept on the recliner; she knew and she loved him for it.

"Oh, Caroline," he groaned. "Do you realize what you're doing?"

She answered him by unfastening the buttons of his shirt and slipping her fingers inside to stroke his chest.

The wild sensations he aroused in her were so exquisite, she wanted to weep.

The sounds of their lovemaking filled the cabin. Whispered phrases of awe followed as Paul removed her blouse.

"Caroline," he moaned. "If we don't stop right now, we're going to end up making love in this chair."

"I don't want to stop…."

In the days afterward, Caroline could hardly believe that they'd waited so long to become lovers when everything was so extraordinarily right between them. Now they seemed to be making up for lost time. His desire for her both delighted and astonished her. They made love every night and often Paul couldn't seem to wait until their usual bedtime. One evening, in the middle of a Scrabble game, she found him looking at her with a wild gleam in his eye.

"Paul?"

He glanced toward the bedroom and raised his brows in question.

"It's only seven o'clock," she said, laughing.

His expression was almost boyish. "I can wait…I think."

Caroline smiled, stood and walked around the table to take him by the hand. "Well, I can't."

They never finished playing Scrabble that night. Instead they invented new games.

Some days, Paul was barcly in the door when he wanted her.

"What's for dinner?" he'd ask.

She'd tell him and catch that look in his eye and automatically turn down the stove. "Don't worry, it can simmer for an hour."

Their dinner simmered and they sizzled. This was the honeymoon they'd never had and Caroline prayed it would last a lifetime.

She yearned to get pregnant, but the first week of December, she discovered sadly that she wasn't.

"If the truth be known," Paul said comfortingly, "I'd rather have you to myself for a while."

Caroline nestled close to his side, her head in the crook of his arm. "It may not be so easy for me. My mother had difficulty getting pregnant."

"Then we'll just have to work at it, love."

Caroline laughed; if they worked any harder, they'd drop from sheer exhaustion. Paul kissed her and held her close. "I never thought I'd find such happiness," he told her.

"Me neither." He wasn't a man of many words or flowery speeches. Nor did he shower her with expensive gifts. But his actions were far more effective than mere words. He loved her, and every day he did something to let her know how much he cared.

One morning after Paul had gone to work, Caroline realized she'd nearly let all this happiness slip through her fingers. The pain of Larry's rejection had nearly blinded her to Paul's love—and her own feelings. When Larry had left, Caroline had almost died inside. Now she realized how mismatched they were. They'd been friends, and had erroneously assumed their friendship meant they'd also be good lovers. Not until she'd slept with Paul could Caroline acknowledge that marriage to Larry would have been a mistake. Larry had recognized the truth long before she did.

Undoubtedly, he was torturing himself with guilt. Her aunts had mentioned his visit in their first letter and although his name was brought up briefly in subsequent letters, Caroline knew he'd been back to visit her aunts, eager for word of her.

In an effort to ease her friend's mind, Caroline decided to write him a letter. It was the least she could do. He'd feel better and she could tell him herself how happy she was. She wished him the best and was eternally grateful that he'd had the wisdom and courage to keep them both from making a colossal mistake.

Caroline had originally intended her letter to be short, but by the time she was done, she'd written five pages. She told him about Paul and how much she loved her husband and thanked Larry for being her friend. She added bits and pieces about her life in Alaska and how beautiful the land was. Come summer, Paul had promised to take her hiking and fishing, and she joked with Larry because he got queasy at the sight of a worm. When she'd finished, Caroline read the letter and realized her happiness shone through every word. Larry would have no more doubts.

After stuffing the five pages into an envelope, Caroline carried the letter to the supply store, which also served as the local post office.

"Good afternoon, Harry." She greeted the proprietor with a ready smile.

"Mrs. Trevor," he returned formally. "Nice day, isn't it?"

"It's a beautiful day." She handed him the letter. "It already looks like Christmas." The snow was drifting slowly down, sparkling and pristine.

He nodded. "This all I can do for you?"

Caroline shrugged. "It is unless you can sell me a pizza. I've had the craving for a thick, cheesy pizza all week."

He chuckled and rubbed the side of his jaw. "Sorry. Can't help you there."

"That's what I figured. Oh, well." With a cheery wave, she was gone.

Paul rounded the corner of the supply store just as Caroline disappeared. "Afternoon, Harry. Was that my wife?"

"Yup, you just missed her. She came to mail a letter."

He glanced over at Caroline, but she was too far away for him to shout.

"Thick letter, too, now that I look at it. She might be needing an extra stamp. I'd best weigh it."

Paul nodded, hardly hearing the man. "She's fond of those aunts of hers."

"Her aunt has a funny name then. Larry Atkins."

The name sliced through Paul as effectively as a knife. He attempted to hide his shock and anger from Harry, but wasn't sure he'd succeeded. Without bothering to buy what he'd come for, Paul left and went back to the pumping station. He tried reasoning with himself that it was only a letter, then he recalled all the times Caroline had walked letters over to Harry, preferring to deliver them herself, claiming she needed the exercise.

His anger increased when he remembered how she'd sat at the desk across from his own at the station and vowed to find a means of escaping him. Her voice had been filled with conviction and vengeance. In his foolishness, Paul had believed her feelings had changed. He certainly hadn't expected her to be so deceitful.

"That's ridiculous," Paul said aloud. "No woman is that good an actress."

All the talk of a child. He groaned. She knew his greatest weakness. He sat at his desk and slumped forward, burying his face in his hands. He couldn't condemn her on such flimsy evidence, but he couldn't trust her either. She'd taught him that once—when she'd walked out on him with Burt Manners—but it seemed he was a slow learner.

By the time Paul arrived home that evening, he was, to all appearances, outwardly calm.

Caroline whirled around when he entered the cabin. "Guess what I'm making for dinner." Her smile was brighter than the sun had been all day.

"What's that, love?"

"Pizza."

"Pizza?"

"Well, a close facsimile. I didn't have a round pan so I'm using a square one. And I didn't want to make bread dough, so I'm making do with biscuit batter. And last but not least, we didn't have any sausage so I'm using ground caribou."

"A caribou pizza?"

"How does that sound?"

"Like we'll be eating scrambled eggs later."

"Oh, ye of little faith."

Paul laughed shortly; she didn't know the half of it.

Dinner was only partially successful. To her credit, the caribou pizza wasn't bad. He managed to eat a piece and praised her ingenuity.

"What's for dinner tomorrow night? Moose Tacos?"

She laughed and promised him fried chicken.

While Caroline did the dishes, she watched Paul. He sat in the recliner with the paper resting on his lap as he stared into space. His face was so intent that she wondered what could be troubling him.

"Paul."

He shook himself from his reverie.

"Is something wrong?" she asked.

"No. I was just thinking."

"About what? You looked so pensive."

"Life." His grin was wry.

"Life?"

"It's taken an unexpected turn for us, hasn't it?" He eyed her carefully, hoping to read her heart and recognize the truth. He saw the love and devotion shining from her eyes—and didn't know what to believe.

"Tanana let me watch Carl for her this afternoon," she announced, smiling. "He's growing so fast."

"You love that baby, don't you?"

"As much as if he were our own."

Tenderness wrapped its way around his heart, suffocating his doubts. He loved Caroline more than life itself. If she was playing him for a fool, then he was the happiest idiot alive. He planned to hold on to that contentment, hug it close and treasure every minute she was with him for as long as it lasted. She might dream of her precious Larry, she might even write the bastard, but it was in the curve of his arm that she slept. It was his body that filled hers and gave her pleasure. It was his name she now had and later, God willing, it would be his children she bore.

When they made love that night, it was as if a storm of passion had overtaken them. As if electricity arced between them, the current more powerful than lightning. Each caress became a fire fueled by their love.

Afterward, Caroline lay limp and drowsy in her husband's arms. Her cheeks were bright with the blush of pleasure, her breath uneven. Paul closed his eyes, wondering how he could ever have doubted her. He buried his face in her hair, savoring the fragrance, and held her against him until her breathing grew even and regular.

Caroline wasn't sure what woke her. One minute she was asleep and the next awake. It took her a moment to realize Paul wasn't asleep, either.

"Paul, what's wrong?"

"Not a thing, love."

She slipped her hand over his ribs and kissed his throat. He'd been so quiet this evening and their lovemaking had been a desperate act of passion. Paul wasn't himself and Caroline wondered what had happened. "I've failed you in some way, haven't I?"

He hesitated. "No, love, I fear I may have failed you."

"Paul, no. I'm happy, truly happy."

"Do you miss Seattle?"

"I miss my aunts," she admitted. "I wish you could meet them. And now and then I think about my friends, but there's nothing for me in Seattle now that I'm with you."

"I love you, Caroline."

She smiled and kissed the side of his mouth. He'd shown her his love in a hundred ways, but he'd never said the words. "I know."

"You're laughing at me, aren't you?" His grip on her tightened, and Caroline jerked away from him with a gasp.

"Paul, what's gotten into you?"

He held himself rigid and didn't speak for an interminable moment. "I told you I loved you and I know you were smiling."

"I…was happy." She lay on her stomach, her hands beneath her.

Another long minute passed. "I'm sorry, love. I didn't mean to frighten you."

She nodded and rolled away from him. Their happiness was shattering right before her eyes and she was powerless to stop it.

"Caroline," he said at last, reaching for her. "I talked to Harry after you were in the store today. I saw the letter you'd written to Larry Atkins."

"It's obvious you didn't read it."

"Why?"

"If you had, your reaction would be altogether different."

"Have you written him in the past?" Paul hated his jealousy. All day he'd been brooding, furious with himself and unreasonable with Caroline. If love did this to a man, he wanted no part of it, and yet he wouldn't, couldn't, give her up.

"This is my first letter to him."

"Why did you feel it was necessary to contact him now?"

"To thank him."

"What?"

"It's true. You mean, *this* is what's been bothering you?"

He didn't answer, ashamed of his behavior.

"Why didn't you ask me earlier? I would've told you all about it. I wrote Larry to let him know he'd done me a gigantic favor by standing me up at the altar."

"You told him that?"

"Not exactly in those words, but basically that's what I said."

"Why didn't you tell me you were writing him?"

Caroline expelled her breath on a nervous sigh. "To be truthful, I didn't think about it. My mistake. Are you always going to be this irrational?"

"When it comes to my wife contacting another guy, I guess I am."

"It isn't the way you're making it sound."

"I have only your word for that."

Caroline fumed, feeling insulted and angry, but rather than argue, she turned her back on him. "Good night, Paul," she grumbled. It wouldn't help matters to talk to him now. In the morning things would be better.

For two days they put the incident behind them. Their happiness was too complete to be destroyed over a silly letter and they each seemed to realize it. On the third day, Paul got home two hours before his usual time.

"You're home early." She looked up from writing Christmas cards, delighted to see her husband.

He sat at the table across from her. "I've got to fly into Fairbanks for a few days."

"Oh, Paul, Fairbanks? I can hardly wait! The first thing I'm going to do is order a real sausage pizza with extra cheese and then I'm going to shop for twelve hours nonstop. You have no idea how much I want to buy Tanana and the baby something special for Christmas. Why didn't you tell me earlier?"

"Because—"

"And you know what else I'm going to do?" She answered her own question before he had the chance, her voice animated and high-pitched. "I'm going to soak in a hot bubble bath and watch television and then I'm—"

"Caroline," he broke in gruffly, his gaze avoiding hers. "This is a business trip. I hadn't planned to bring you along."

Eight

It took a minute for the words to sink in. "You're not taking me with you?" With deliberate patience, Caroline set down the pen and pushed the Christmas cards aside. "Why?"

Paul refused to meet her probing gaze. "I've already explained that it's a business trip."

"That's not the reason and you know it." She'd thought they'd come so far, but the only one who'd moved had been her. She'd walked into his arms and been so blinded by her love she hadn't even seen the chains that bound her.

"I don't know what you're talking about."

"Like hell!"

"I go to Fairbanks every other month or so...."

"Every other month?"

"You can come with me another time."

"I want to go now."

"No!"

"Why not?" She was growing more furious by the moment.

"Because—"

"Because you saw that stupid letter to Larry and you're convinced I've made arrangements to escape. To catch a plane out of Fairbanks."

"Don't be ridiculous." But her accusation was so close to the truth that Paul's heart pounded hard against his ribs.

Caroline's smile was sarcastic. "Since I'm your prisoner, after all, you might as well lock me in a cell."

"You're my wife!"

"I'm the woman who was forced to stay married to you. What we have isn't a marriage!" She saw him open his mouth to contradict her, then close it again. "It takes more than a piece of paper."

"Caroline, you're making too much of this."

"Yes, master," she said, gazing straight ahead, refusing to look at him. "Whatever you say, master." She bent low in a mocking bow, folding her hands in front of her.

"Caroline, stop that."

"Anything you say, master." He wanted a slave? Fine! She'd give him one. She'd speak only when spoken to, accede to his every wish, smother him with servitude.

Her unflagging calmness shocked her. It was as though the sun had come out, revealing all the glaring imperfections of their relationship. She stared at the flaws, saddened and appalled. She'd come to love Paul and Alaska. She'd found happiness with him— only to discover it was badly marred. She was no better off now than she'd been that first week, when he'd turned her into his shadow. The only difference was that she'd grown more comfortable in her cell.

Another thought came to her and she forgot her resolve not to speak. "How…how do I know you don't have a lover in Fairbanks?"

Paul stood, pushing back the kitchen chair so suddenly it threatened to topple. "That's crazy! I can't believe you'd even think such a thing!"

"Why? I've lived with you for these past two months, so I'm well aware of your appetite for—"

"The only lover I have is you!" He shouted the words and shoved his hands inside his pants pockets.

"If you can't trust me, there's nothing that says I have to trust you." She didn't think for a minute that Paul did have another woman, but she wanted him to sample a taste of her own frustration. "The fact that you don't want me along speaks for itself. It's obvious you're hiding something from me." She arched her brows speculatively. "Another woman, no doubt."

Paul's mouth was tight. "That thought is unworthy of you."

"What else am I supposed to believe?"

His expression darkened. "I'm leaving for Fairbanks and you're staying here and that's the way it's going to be."

"Yes, master." She bowed in a sweeping, exaggerated manner.

He sighed loudly. "Are we back to that?"

She didn't answer. Instead she walked across the cabin and reached for her parka and boots. "I'm going to see Tanana unless my master demands that I remain here."

"Caroline." He stopped her just before she opened the door, but she didn't turn around and Paul knew she was fighting back tears. He felt himself go weak; he loved her and wished he could take away the pain, but it was too late to change his plans. "Never mind," he said gruffly.

Caroline left, closing the door behind her.

Paul paced the room, his emotions in conflict. Caroline was right; she'd given him everything—her love, her heart, her trust... And yet, he wasn't satisfied. He wanted more.

The cold wind cut through Caroline's jacket as she trudged the frozen pathway that led to the Eagleclaws' cabin. She needed to get away and think. Paul had hurt her; he'd never guess the extent to which his doubts and his exclusion had pained her sensitive heart.

Tanana answered the knock at her door, looking relieved to discover it was Caroline. The baby cried pitifully in the background.

"Carl cried all night. I'm afraid he's sick."

Caroline didn't bother to take off her parka, but walked directly to the baby's side. Gently, she lifted him from the crib. His little face was red and his legs were drawn up against his stomach.

"He might have colic."

"Colic?"

"Does he cry after each feeding?"

"And before. All he does is cry."

From the young woman's obvious exhaustion, Caroline could believe it. "Then I think you should make an appointment with the medical team for next week."

Tanana agreed with a brief nod.

"Lie down for a while and rest," Caroline said. "I'll hold Carl."

"You spoil him."

Caroline grinned and kissed the top of his small head. "I know, but let me do it, okay?"

"You'll make a good mother for Paul Trevor's sons."

Caroline quickly averted her face so her friend couldn't read her distress. She spent most of the afternoon with Tanana and the baby, leaving only when she was sure Carl would sleep and that his mother had received a few hours' rest.

"Send Thomas if you need me," she said on her way out the door.

Paul met Caroline halfway back to the cabin. His eyes held hers in a long, steady look. "I'll be leaving in a few minutes."

"Does my master wish me to carry his bags to the airstrip?"

"Caroline...don't, please."

Keeping up this charade was hard enough when her heart was breaking. "Carl has colic and poor Tanana's been up with him for two nights." She tried to cover the uncomfortable silence.

Paul's eyes caressed her. "Don't go to the airstrip. There's no need."

She lowered her gaze, already feeling herself weaken.

Walter met them and loaded Paul's suitcase onto the back of his sled. He seemed to realize that Paul and Caroline needed time alone.

"Caroline," Paul began. "You're not a prisoner." He took her in his arms and held her close, shutting his eyes to savor the feel of her against him. Their coats were so thick, holding each other was awkward and he reluctantly dropped his arms.

Caroline swallowed her anger. "When will you be back?"

"In four days, possibly five."

It seemed a lifetime, but she said nothing. His hands caressed her face with such tenderness that Caroline closed her eyes and swayed toward him. When he covered her mouth with his, her lips parted in eager welcome. The kiss was long and thorough, making her all the more aware of the seductive power he held over her senses. Of their own volition, her arms slid upward and around his neck. One kiss and he'd destroyed her resolve. Caroline didn't know whether she was more furious with Paul or with herself.

"Oh, love," he breathed against her lips. "Next time maybe you'll come with me."

Purposefully, she stepped away from him. She was frustrated with herself for being so weak and even more so with Paul for not trusting her. "I'll be happy to go with you if I'm still here."

The shock that contorted Paul's features and narrowed his eyes caused Caroline to suck in her breath. Abruptly he turned away, marching to the airstrip without a word of farewell.

Caroline wondered what had made her say something so stupid. She regretted her sharp tongue, but Paul had hurt her and she wanted him to realize that.

"Damn!" She stamped her foot in the dry snow. If she'd hoped to build a foundation of trust, she'd just crumbled its cornerstone.

Caroline stood where she was until Paul's plane had taxied away and ascended into the gray sky. Only then did she return to the cabin, disillusioned and miserable. She was astonished by how empty the place felt. She remained standing in the middle of the living room for several minutes, hardly able to believe that in the span of a few hours, her entire world could have been jolted so badly.

That night, Caroline slept fitfully. She was too cold, then too hot. Her pillow was too flat and the mattress sagged on one side. After midnight, she admitted it wasn't the bed or the blankets. The problem was that the space beside her was empty. With a sigh, she turned and stared up at the ceiling, trying to think of ways to repair her marriage.

Paul set his suitcase on the carpeted floor of the Hotel Fairbanks. His room was adequate—a double bed, dresser, television and chair. He stared at the TV set and experienced a twinge of regret. The sensation multiplied when his gaze fell on the bathtub.

Regret hounded him. Not once in all the weeks that Caroline had been in Gold River had she complained about the less-than-ideal living conditions. Yet she'd been denied the simplest of pleasures.

Slowly, Paul removed his parka and tossed it carelessly on the bed, then rubbed his eyes. He was determined to rush this trip so he could get back to Caroline and rebuild what his jealous doubts had destroyed.

After he'd undressed and climbed into the soft bed, Paul lay on his back, arms folded behind his head. It didn't feel right to be here without Caroline. He smiled as he recalled how quickly she'd dropped her self-imposed role of servant; she had too much fire in her to play the part with any conviction.

He thought about her being alone in the cabin, curled up and sleeping in his bed, and experienced such an overwhelming surge of desire that his body tightened and tension knotted his stomach. She often slept in that thin piece of silk her aunts had given her. Usually it rode up her slim body so that if he reached for her, his hand met warm, soft skin.

Paul inhaled sharply at the memory. Her eagerness for his lovemaking had been a surprise and a delight. She hadn't refused him once, welcoming his ardor with an enthusiasm he hadn't dared expect. He wouldn't leave her again, wouldn't take another trip unless she could join him. He planned on telling her so the minute he returned to Gold River.

Caroline woke early the next morning. As usual it was dark. The hours of daylight were becoming shorter and shorter as they approached the winter solstice. More and more of each day was spent in complete darkness. She contemplated the summer and what it would be like to have the sun shine late at night. Then she wondered if she'd be in Gold River to see it. The thought stunned her. Of course, she'd be in Gold River. This was her home now.

No sooner had she dressed and made breakfast than there was a knock at her door. Walter Thundercloud stood on the other side.

"Good morning, Walter."

He nodded politely, and stepped inside, looking a bit uneasy.

Without asking, she poured him a cup of coffee and set it on the table.

"You okay?" he asked gruffly.

"Of course I am."

"Paul asked me to check on you."

Caroline pulled out a chair and sat across from the old man. Naturally Paul would want to be sure his prisoner was in her cell, she told herself wryly. Her hands tightened on the thick mug. "I'm fine. You needn't worry about me."

Walter hesitated. "Paul's been in Gold River for several years now."

Her husband's friend seemed to be leading up to something. She nodded, hoping that was encouragement enough for him to continue.

"When he first came, he had the cabin built for privacy. The oil company had supplied his quarters, but he wanted a larger place—more homey—so he could bring his wife to live with him."

"His wife!" Caroline nearly choked on her coffee.

"Oh, the woman wasn't his wife yet. She'd only promised to be."

"I…see." Paul had been engaged! "What happened?"

"He never told me, but one day he got a letter and after he read it, Paul left the station and got sick drunk. He never mentioned her name again."

Nor had he mentioned the woman to Caroline. The

heat of jealous anger blossomed in her cheeks. The night of her arrival, she'd spilled her guts about Larry. Apparently, Paul had gone through a similar experience and hadn't bothered to tell her. Talk about trust!

"For many months, Paul was angry. He worked too hard, not sleeping some nights. He scowled and snapped and drank more than he should."

"He didn't leave Gold River and try to work things out with this woman?"

"No."

Caroline took another sip of her coffee, somehow not surprised. He had an overabundance of pride, often to his own detriment. "Why are you telling me this?"

"For the first time since Paul moved to Gold River, he smiles every day. He laughs. Before my eyes I've seen him change. He's happy now. These changes began when you came here."

So Walter wanted to reassure her. She smiled softly and stared at her coffee. His words only proved how little she knew of the man who was her husband.

"What made Paul decide to get married now?"

Walter shrugged. "He wants a family."

She nodded. Tanana had told her that, too.

"He loves you," Walter continued. "I don't believe Paul ever thought he'd be fortunate enough to find a woman as good as you. He put the ad in the paper because he was lonely."

"But why did he advertise for a wife? Surely there were women who'd want to marry him. Someone in Fairbanks, maybe?"

Walter added sugar to his coffee, stirring it a long time. "You'll have to ask him that."

Alarm turned her blood cold. "He has a woman in Fairbanks?"

Walter chuckled and shook his head. "He advertised for a bride because he didn't have time to properly date someone and build a relationship by the usual means. I also think he was afraid the same thing would happen to him a second time and she'd change her mind."

No wonder he'd been so insistent that they stay married. "Why is a child so important to Paul?"

"I suppose because he didn't have a family when he was growing up."

This was another shock to Caroline. Paul had spoken only briefly about his background. He'd been raised somewhere in Texas. As far as she knew, he hadn't contacted his parents about their marriage and now that she considered it, Paul seemed to change the subject whenever she asked about his childhood.

The faded eyes brightened. "I'm not telling you these things to stir up trouble." The old man paused. "I can see that most of what I've said has been a shock. Paul might not appreciate my loose tongue, but I felt you should know that he's gone through some hard times. You've been good for him."

"Our relationship is still on rocky ground."

"I can see that. I was surprised he didn't take you to Fairbanks and when I mentioned it, he nearly bit my head off."

"You were right when you guessed that I love him."

"He feels the same way. He'd move heaven and earth to see that you were happy. He—"

An abrupt knock sounded, drawing their attention to the front door. Thomas Eagleclaw stepped in without waiting for an invitation. His eyes were frightened. "Mrs. Paul, please come."

"What is it?"

"Tanana and the baby are sick."

As Walter and Thomas spoke in low voices, Caroline stood and reached for her coat. Momentarily, her gaze collided with Walter's. The older man pulled on his parka, as well, and followed her to the Eagleclaws' cabin. Even before they arrived at the small log structure, Caroline had a premonition of disaster.

The baby lay in his crib, hardly moving. He stared at her with wide eyes and when Caroline felt his skin, he was burning up with fever. "How long has he been like this?"

"Apparently Tanana's been ill, too." Walter answered for the young man.

"Why didn't you let me know?" Caroline asked Thomas.

"Tanana probably told him not to. She didn't want to trouble you," Walter whispered, standing at Caroline's side.

"But Carl's very sick."

"Mary Finefeather has a fever," Thomas announced.

"Mary, too?"

Caroline turned to Walter. "I'll do what I can here and meet you at Mary's. We may need to get help."

Walter nodded and left.

Tanana's face felt hot, and the girl whimpered softly when Caroline tried to talk to her.

The young husband stood stiffly by the bedside. "She's much worse this morning."

"Oh, Thomas, I wish you'd come for me," Caroline said, more sharply than she intended.

The young man looked guiltily at the floor.

"How are you feeling?"

He shrugged, still not looking at her.

Caroline pressed the back of her hand to his forehead and shook her head. "Get into bed and I'll be back when I can."

Although she tried to stay calm, her heart was racing. She hurried from the Eagleclaws' to Mary's. Once there, Caroline discovered that the older woman's symptoms were similar to Tanana's and the baby's.

"Walter, contact the Public Health Department and see if they can fly in some help. I don't know what we've got here, but I don't like the looks of it."

Walter's eyes met hers. "In the winter of 1979 we lost twelve to the fever."

"We're not going to lose anyone this time. Now hurry!"

After his meeting with the oil company engineers, Paul paused on the sidewalk outside the jewelry store to study the diamond rings on display. It'd never occurred to him to ask Caroline if she wanted a diamond. She wore the simple gold band he'd given her and hadn't asked for anything more. Now he wondered if she was disappointed with the simplicity of the ring.

He thought about the gifts he'd already purchased and realized he'd probably need to buy another suitcase to haul them all back to Gold River. He smiled at the thought. He'd bought her everything she'd ever mentioned wanting and, in addition, purchased gifts for Tanana and the baby, knowing Caroline had wanted to get them something special. Paul was trying to make up to her for excluding her from this trip. Never again would he leave her behind. He decided he'd buy her a ring and save it for Christmas. Everything else he'd give her when he got home.

Never had he been more anxious to return to Gold River.

The Public Health Department flew in a doctor and two nurses that same afternoon. The community meeting hall served as a makeshift hospital and the sickest were brought there. Tanana, the baby and Mary Finefeather had been the first to become seriously ill. Others soon followed. Within two days, Caroline and the medical staff were tending twenty-five patients. The following day it was thirty, then thirty-five.

"How long has it been since you slept?" Dr. Mather asked Caroline on the third day.

Her smile was weak. "I forget."

"That's what I thought. Go get some rest, and that's an order."

She shook her head. She couldn't leave when so many were sick and more arrived every hour. The other staff members had rested intermittently. "I'm fine."

"If you don't do as I say, you'll be sick next."

"I'm not leaving."

"Stubborn woman." But his eyes spoke of admiration.

Later that day, Walter brought her something to eat and forced her to sit down. "I think I should contact Paul."

"Don't." She placed her hand on his forearm and silently pleaded with him. "He'd only worry."

"He should worry. You're working yourself into an early grave."

"I'm totally healthy."

"You won't be if you go on like this."

Walter gave her one of his looks and Caroline sighed. "All right, we'll compromise. I'll go lie down in a few minutes, but I'll have someone wake me after an hour."

Mary Finefeather died early the next morning. Caroline stood at Dr. Mather's side as he pulled the sheet over the woman's face, relaxed now in death. Tears burned Caroline's eyes, but she dared not let them flow. So many needed her; she had to be strong.

"Are you doing okay?" the doctor asked.

"I think so," Caroline answered in a strangled voice. "What about the baby?" She'd held Carl for most of the night. He was so weak, too weak even to cry. He'd lain limp in her arms, barely moving.

The doctor hesitated. "It doesn't look good. If he lasts through the day, then his chances will improve."

The floor pitched beneath her feet. She'd known it herself, but had been afraid to admit it. "And his mother?"

"She's young and strong. She should make it."

"Anyone else?"

"Two others look serious."

Caroline bit the inside of her cheek and followed him to the next bed.

At the end of the fourth day, his meetings finished and his shopping done, Paul returned to the hotel, packed his bags and checked out. He felt as anxious as a kid awaiting the end of school. He was going home to Gold River, home to Caroline. After a short trip to a pizza parlor, the taxi delivered him to the airport. If Burt Manners was late, Paul swore he'd have his hide.

The pilot was waiting for Paul at the designated area inside the terminal. Burt rose to his feet as Paul approached.

"I've got bad news for you," he said, frowning as he eyed the pizza box.

"What's that?"

"We aren't going to be able to fly into Gold River."

"Why not?" Frustration made Paul tighten his grip around the handle of his bag.

"A white-out."

"Damn!" Paul expelled the word viciously. A white-out was dangerous enough to put the finest, most experienced pilot on edge. Visibility plummeted to zero, and flying was impossible. The condition could last for days.

"There's nothing more you can do." Dr. Mather spoke gently to Caroline and attempted to remove the lifeless four-year-old child from her arms.

"No, please," she whispered, bringing the still body

closer to her own. "Let me hold her for a few more minutes. I...I just want to say goodbye."

The doctor stepped aside and waited.

Caroline brushed the hair from the sweet face and kissed the smooth brow, rocking her to and fro, singing the little girl a lullaby she'd never hear. Anna was dead and Caroline was sure Carl was next. Tears rained unchecked down her cheeks. She took a moment to compose herself, then handed the child to the doctor. "I'll tell her mother."

A week after Paul had left Gold River, he returned. Walter was at the airstrip waiting for him when the plane taxied to a standstill. One look at the other man's troubled frown and sad eyes, and Paul knew something was terribly wrong.

"What is it?"

"The fever came. Five are dead."

Fear closed Paul's throat. "Caroline?"

"She's been working for days without sleep. Thank God you're back."

"Take me to her."

By the time Paul reached the meeting hall, his heart was pounding. Rarely had he moved more quickly. If anything happened to Caroline, he'd blame himself. He'd left her, abandoned her to some unspeakable fate. He stopped in the doorway, appalled at the scene. Stretchers littered the floor, children crying, staff moving from one patient to another.

It took him a moment to find Caroline. She was bent

over an old woman, lifting the weary head and helping her sip liquid through a straw. Caroline looked frail, and when she straightened, she staggered and nearly fell backward.

Paul was at her side instantly. She turned and looked at him as though he were a stranger.

"I'm getting you out of here," Paul said, furious that she'd worked herself into this condition and no one had stopped her.

"No, please," she said in a voice so weak it quavered. "I'm fine." With that, she promptly fainted.

Paul caught her before she hit the floor.

Nine

Caroline struggled to open her eyes. The lids felt incredibly heavy. She discovered Paul sleeping awkwardly in a kitchen chair by her bed. She realized he must have brought her home. He was slouched so that his head rested against the back. One arm hugged his ribs and the other hung loosely at his side. Caroline blinked. Paul looked terrible; his clothes were wrinkled, his shirt pulled out from the waistband and half-unbuttoned.

"Paul?" she whispered, having difficulty finding her voice. She forced herself to swallow. When Paul didn't respond, Caroline raised her hand and tugged at his shirttail.

His eyes flew open and he bolted upright. "Caroline? You're awake!" He rose to his feet and shook the unkempt hair from his face, staring down at her. "How do you feel?"

The past week suddenly returned to haunt her. She thought of Mary Finefeather and Anna, the bubbly four-year-old. An overwhelming sadness at the loss of her friends brought stinging tears to her eyes.

"Carl?" She managed to squeeze the name of the baby from her throat.

"He's improving and so is Tanana."

"Good." Caroline closed her eyes because sleep was preferable to the memories.

When she awakened again, Paul was sitting in the chair beside their bed. Only this time his elbows were resting on his knees, his face buried in his hands. She must have made a sound because he slowly lifted his head.

"How long have I been asleep?" she asked.

"Almost twenty-four hours."

She arched her eyebrows in surprise. "Did I catch the fever?"

"The doctor said it was exhaustion." Paul stood and poured a glass of water and supported her so she could sip from it. When she'd finished, he lowered her back to the bed.

Caroline turned her face away so she wouldn't have to watch his expression. "I want to go home."

"Caroline, love, you are home."

Her eyes drifted shut. She hadn't thought it would be easy.

"Caroline, I know you're upset, but you'll feel different later. I promise you will."

Despite her resolve not to cry, tears coursed down her cheeks. "I hate Alaska. I want to go where death doesn't…doesn't come with the dark, where I can hear children laugh and smell flowers again." People had died here—people she'd loved, people she'd come to care about. Friends. Children. Babies. The marriage she'd worked so hard to build wasn't a real one. The only thing that held it together was Paul's indomitable pride—he wasn't going to let her go after he'd already lost one woman.

"You don't know what you're saying," he told her, discounting her words as he reached for her hand.

"I want to go home. To Seattle."

He released her hand and she heard him stalk to the other side of the room. "I'll fix you something to eat."

Alone now, Caroline pushed back the covers, then carefully sat up. The room spun and teetered, but she gripped the headboard and gradually everything righted itself.

Suddenly she felt terribly hungry. When Paul returned, carrying a tray of tea, toast and scrambled eggs, she didn't even consider refusing it.

He piled her pillows against the headboard and set the tray on her lap. When it looked as though he meant to feed her, Caroline stopped him with a gesture

"I can do it."

He nodded and sat back in the chair. "Walter said you nearly killed yourself. You wouldn't leave or rest or eat. Why did you push yourself like that, love?" He paused and watched her lift the fork to her mouth in a deliberate movement. "He told me about little Anna dying in your arms."

Caroline chewed slowly, but not by choice; even eating required energy. She didn't want to talk about Anna, the fever or anything else. She didn't answer Paul's questions because she couldn't explain to him something she didn't fully understand herself. In some incomprehensible way, she felt responsible for the people in Gold River. They were her friends, her family, and she'd let them down.

"I can't tell you how bad I feel I left you here to deal with—"

"Why didn't you mention her?"

Paul gave her an odd look. "Mention who?"

She glared at him. "You *know* who."

"Don't tell me we're going through this again. Should I duck to avoid the salt and pepper shakers?" Mockingly he held up his hands, his eyes twinkling.

For a moment, Caroline was furious enough to hurl something at him, but that required more energy than she had.

"Caroline, love…"

"I'm not your love," she said heatedly.

Paul chuckled. "You can't honestly mean that after the last few weeks."

"Correction," she said bitterly. "I'm not your *first* love."

Paul went still and his eyes narrowed. "All right, what did you find?"

"Find?" Caroline discovered she was shaking. "Find? Do you mean to tell me you've got…memorabilia stored in this cabin from that…that other woman?"

"Caroline, settle down.…"

"Oh-h-h." It took all her restraint not to fling a leftover piece of toast at him. He must have noticed the temptation because he quickly took the tray from her lap and returned it to the kitchen.

While he was gone, Caroline lay back down and tried

to compose her thoughts. He'd loved another woman so much that it had taken him years to commit himself to a new relationship. Caroline was simply filling some other woman's place in his life. What bothered her most was that he'd never told her about this previous lover. The more she learned, the more imperative it became to leave.

He entered the bedroom again, his steps hesitant. He'd slipped the tips of his fingers in the back pockets of his jeans. "This isn't the time to talk about Diane. When you're feeling better, I'll tell you everything you want to know."

"Diane," Caroline repeated, vowing to hate every woman with that name. An eerie calm came over her as she raised her eyes to meet Paul's. "This…Diane didn't happen to be blond, blue-eyed and about five-five, did she?"

Paul looked stunned. "You knew her?"

"You idiot, that's me!" She grabbed a pillow and heaved it at him with all her strength. She was so weak it didn't even make it to the end of the bed.

Paul shook his head. "Love, listen, I know what this sounds like."

"Get out!"

"Caroline…"

"I'm sure the doctor told you I should remain calm. The very sight of you boils my blood, so kindly leave before there's cardiovascular damage!"

He advanced toward her and Caroline scrambled to her knees and reached for the glass of water. "You take one more step and you'll be wearing this!"

Exasperated, Paul swore under his breath. "How you could be so utterly unreasonable is beyond me."

"Unreasonable!" She lifted the tumbler and brought back her arm, making the threat more real. That persuaded him to exit the room. Once he'd gone, Caroline curled up in a tight ball, shaking with fury. Not only hadn't he told her about Diane, but he'd chosen *her* because she obviously resembled the other woman. He'd told her often enough that as soon as he'd seen her picture, he'd known. Sure he'd known! She was a duplicate of the woman he'd once loved…. And probably still did.

Caroline escaped into a deep, blissful slumber. When she awakened, she felt stronger and, although she was a bit shaky on her feet, she managed to dress and pull the suitcase from beneath the bed. Her hands trembled as she neatly folded and packed each garment.

"What are you doing?" Paul asked from behind her.

Caroline stiffened. "What I should've done weeks ago. Leaving Gold River. Leaving Alaska. Leaving you."

He didn't say anything for a long, tense moment. "I realize things are a bit unsettled between us," he finally muttered, "but we'll work it out."

"Unsettled. You call this *unsettled*? Well, I've got news for you, Paul Trevor. Things are more than just unsettled. I want out. O-U-T. Out!"

"I won't agree to a divorce."

"Fine, we'll stay married if that's what you want. We'll have the ideal marriage—I'll be in Seattle and you can live here. No more arguing. No more disagreements. No more Scrabble." Frantically, she stacked her sweaters in the open suitcase. "Believe me, after this experience I have no desire to involve myself with another man ever again."

"Caroline—"

"I'll tell you one thing I'm grateful for, though," she said, interrupting him. "You taught me a lot about myself. Here I was, playing Clara Barton to an entire town as if I were some heroine, dispensing medical knowledge and good will. But...but people *died*."

"Caroline—"

"I even fooled myself into thinking you and I could make a go of this marriage. I thought, 'Paul Trevor's a good man. Better than most. Fair. Kind. Tender.' I'll admit the events leading up to our marriage were bizarre to say the least, but I was ready to stick it out and make the best of the situation. Things could've been worse—I could've married Larry." She laughed without amusement.

His hands settled on her shoulders and he attempted to turn her around, but Caroline wouldn't let him. "Please don't touch me." His touch was warm and gentle, and she couldn't resist him. Her eyes filled with tears and Paul swam in and out of her vision as she backed away from him.

"I can't let you go, love," he said softly.

"You don't have any choice."

"Caroline, give it a week. You're distraught now, but in a few days, I promise you'll feel differently."

"No," she sobbed, jerking her head back and forth. "I can't stay another day. Please, I need to get out of here."

"Let me hold you for just a minute."

"No." But she didn't fight him when he reached for her and brought her into the circle of his arms.

"I know, love," he whispered. "I know." He felt his heart catch at the anguish in her tormented expression. She hid her face in his shirt and wept, her shoulders shaking with such force that Paul braced his feet to hold her securely.

"Anna—she died in my arms," she wailed.

"I know, love, I know." His hand smoothed her hair in long, even strokes. Regret cut though him. He'd abandoned her to face the crisis alone, never dreaming anything like this would happen, thinking only of himself. He'd been so selfish. And despite the way she'd disparaged her own efforts, she *had* been a heroine.

When her tears were spent, Caroline raised her head and wiped her face. Paul's shirt bore evidence of her crying and she guiltily tried to rub away the tear stains.

His hand stopped hers and he tenderly brought her palm to his mouth. He kissed it while his eyes held hers. She didn't want him to be so gentle; she wanted to hate him so she could leave and never look back.

"Please don't," she pleaded weakly.

Paul released her hand.

"Caroline," he said seriously. "You can't go."

"Why not? Nothing binds us except a piece of paper." He flinched at her words and she regretted hurting him.

"I love you," he whispered.

Knotting her hands into fists, she raised her chin a fraction. "Did you love Diane, too?"

Paul's face seemed to lose its color.

"Did you?" she cried.

"Yes."

Caroline pressed her advantage. "You let *her* go. You didn't go after her and force her to marry you and live on this frozen chunk of ice. All I'm asking for is the same consideration."

"You don't know—"

"I do. I know everything I need to know about Alaska and Gold River. I know I can't live here anymore. I know I can't look you in the face and feel I'm your wife and you're my husband. I know I can't bear any more pain. Please, Paul, let me go home." She was weeping again, almost uncontrollably.

Paul advanced a step toward her. "You'll feel better tomorrow," he said again, then turned and left the room.

Caroline slumped on the bed and wept until her eyes burned and there were no more tears. Spent, she fell asleep, only to wake in a dark, shadowless room. Paul had placed a blanket over her shoulders. She sat up and brushed the unruly mass of hair from her face.

Instantly, Paul stood in the doorway. "You're awake."

"Yes, master."

He sighed, but said nothing more.

"I've fixed you something to eat. Would you like to come out here or would you rather I brought it in to you?"

"Whatever my master wishes."

He clenched his fists. "It'll be on the table when you're ready."

"Thank you, master." Her words were spoken in a sarcastic monotone.

Patience, Paul told himself. That was the key. Caroline had been through a traumatic experience that had mentally and physically exhausted her. She needed to know she was loved and that he'd be there to protect her. For the hundredth time, he cursed himself for having left her while he'd gone off to Fairbanks.

He ladled out a bowl of vegetable soup and set it on the table, along with thick slices of sourdough bread. Next he poured her a tall glass of milk.

While he was in the kitchen, Caroline changed clothes and brushed her teeth and hair. She looked a sight; it was a wonder Paul hadn't leapt at the chance to be rid of her.

Paul glanced up expectantly when she entered the room and pulled out a kitchen chair for her. Caroline sat down, staring at the meal. Although it smelled delicious, she had no appetite.

Her lack of interest must have been obvious because Paul spoke sharply. "Eat, Caroline."

"I…I can't."

"Try."

"I want to go home."

Paul's fists were so tight his fingers ached. *Patience,* he reminded himself—and she'd only been awake a few hours.

He took the chair across from her and watched her as she methodically lifted the spoon to her mouth. "I brought you some things from Fairbanks. Would you like to see them?" he coaxed.

She tried to smile, but all she could think about was

Seattle and her two aunts and the life she'd inadvertently left behind. A life of comfort and security she suddenly, desperately, missed. There was too much pain in Gold River. "Will you let me go home if I do?"

He felt a muscle leap in his temple, but didn't respond. He stood, opened the closet door and brought her an armful of packages.

"Go ahead and open them," he said, then changed his mind. "No. You eat, I'll open them for you." From the first package, he produced a bottle of expensive perfume, a brand she'd once mentioned. He smiled at her, anticipating her delight.

Caroline swallowed down her surprise. He could be so loving and she didn't want him to be. Not now, when all she could think about was leaving him.

"Well?"

"It's very nice. Thank you, master."

Paul had had it. He shot to his feet. "Don't ever call me your master again!"

"Yes."

"I wish you'd stop this silly game."

"Will you let me go home if I do?" Caroline asked and took another spoonful of soup.

Paul ignored the question. From the second package he withdrew a huge teddy bear and was pleased when she paused, the spoon halfway to her mouth.

"For Carl," he explained. "You said you wanted something special for him. I thought we'd save it for Christmas."

She nodded and recalled how close they'd come to losing the baby. Tears filled her eyes.

Paul turned the bear over. "You push this button in the back and Mr. Bear actually talks."

Caroline's nod was nearly imperceptible.

"Would you like to see what I got Tanana?"

"Not now...please." She looked straight ahead, feeling dizzy and weak. Setting the spoon back on the table she closed her eyes. "Would it be all right if I lay down for a minute?"

"Of course." He moved to her side and slipped an arm around her waist as he guided her back to the bedroom. The suitcase was open on the bed. Paul moved it and put it on the floor.

Caroline felt sluggish and tired. "Do I really look like her?"

"Her? You mean Diane?"

Caroline nodded.

"I suppose there's a certain resemblance, but it's superficial."

"Why didn't you tell me about her?"

"It's a long story. Too long and complicated for right now."

"And you think my involvement with Larry *wasn't* long and complicated?"

Paul sighed and closed the lid of her suitcase. "The two aren't comparable."

"Then there's your family..."

Paul went tense. "Who told you about my family?"

"We're married," she said sadly, "and yet you hide your life from me."

"I have no family, Caroline. I was raised in a series of foster homes."

"So you're willing to tell me about your childhood, but not Diane. I think I know why."

Irritated, Paul shook his head, his mouth pinched and white. "I love you."

"Then let me go back to Seattle," she said.

"Please don't ask me that again. Give this—us—a chance."

"Yes, master," she said dully.

Paul groaned and slammed the door.

If Paul thought Caroline would forget her quest to return to Seattle, he was wrong. For two days, she sat in the cabin, listless and lethargic, gazing into space. She never spoke unless spoken to and answered his questions with as few words as possible. She wore her unhappiness like a cloak that smothered her natural exuberance.

He tried to draw her out, tried reasoning with her. Nothing helped. By the time they climbed into bed at night, he was so frustrated with her that any desire for lovemaking was destroyed. He longed to hold her, yearned to feel her body close to his, but each time he reached for her, she froze.

She didn't talk about Seattle again. But her suitcase remained packed and ready, a constant reminder of how eager she was to leave him. He placed it back under the bed once, but she immediately pulled it out and set it by the front door. He didn't move it after that.

Every morning Paul promised himself that Caroline

would be better, but nothing seemed to change. He had to find a way to reach her and was quickly running out of ideas.

But today, he vowed, would be different. He had a plan.

After dinner that evening, Paul sat in his recliner, reading the Fairbanks paper. His mind whirled with thoughts of seduction; he missed Caroline; he missed having his warm, loving wife in his arms. It had been nearly two weeks since they'd made love and if anything could shatter the barriers she'd built against him, it was their lovemaking. He smiled, content for the first time in days.

"Caroline."

She turned to him, her eyes blank. "Yes?"

"Dinner was very good tonight."

"Thank you."

"Would you come here a minute, please?"

She walked toward him with small, measured steps, refusing to meet his eyes, and paused directly in front of his chair.

"Sit on my lap."

Caroline hesitated, but did as he requested.

His hand massaged the tense muscles of her back. "Relax," he whispered.

Caroline found it impossible to do so, but said nothing.

"Okay, put your hands on my shoulders."

She did that, too, with a fair amount of reluctance.

"Now kiss me."

Her eyes narrowed as she recognized his game.

"You're so fond of calling me 'master,' I thought you might need a little direction."

She didn't move.

"Just one kiss, love?"

Lightly, she rested her hands on his shoulders and leaned forward.

"Now kiss me...."

Caroline stared at him blankly, then touched her mouth to his.

"No, a *real* kiss."

She brushed her closed mouth over his in the briefest of contacts.

"Come on, Caroline. It'll be Christmas soon, and even a grinch could do better than that."

With the tip of her tongue, she moistened her lips and slanted her head to press her mouth over his. She felt as if this was all a dream, as if it wasn't really happening.

The kiss was routine. Paul wove her hair around his fingers, placing his hand against the back of her head, holding her to him. His warmth seemed to reach her heart and Caroline felt herself soften.

"I've missed your kisses, my love." His eyes held hers. "I've missed everything about you."

Caroline couldn't seem to tear her gaze from his.

"Kiss me again—oh, Caroline, you taste so good."

He tasted wonderful, too. She settled her mouth over his, and with a sigh, she surrendered.

He continued to kiss her with an urgency that quickly became an all-consuming passion. She felt weak, spent. Her arms clung to Paul and when he ran his hand along the inside of her thigh, she squirmed, craving more and more of him. Her fingers shook almost uncontrollably as she pulled the shirttail from his waistband and rubbed her palms over his chest.

"I want you," he whispered.

Somehow those words permeated the fog of desire when the others hadn't. With a soft moan, she lifted her head to stare at him with tear-filled eyes.

"Love?" He reached for her and she moved away as though he held a gun in his hand.

"Paul, I can't live here anymore. It hurts too much. Please don't make me stay."

His face lost all color. He could see it was pointless to reason with her and shook his head in defeat. "Alaska is my home."

"But it isn't mine."

"You'll get over this," he told her.

"I *can't*...I won't. I tried, Paul, I honestly tried."

He was silent for so long that she wondered if he was going to speak again. "I won't come after you, Caroline. I didn't with Diane and I won't with you."

She nodded numbly. "I understand."

He clenched his fists at his side. "I give up. I won't keep you against your will."

Tears streaked her face and when she spoke, her voice was low and hoarse. "Thank you."

"Shall I arrange for the divorce or would you rather do it yourself?"

Ten

"Oh, Sister," Ethel Myers said with a worried frown, "I don't think the brew will help dear Caroline this time."

"We must deliberate on this, and you know as well as I do that we do it so much better with Father's brew." Mabel Myers carefully poured two steaming cups of the spiked tea and handed one to her younger sister. Soft Christmas music was punctuated by the clinking of china.

"Poor Caroline."

Mabel placed the dainty cup to her lips, paused and sighed. "She sounded so happy in her letters."

"And she tries so hard to hide her unhappiness now."

"Paul Trevor must be a terrible beast to have treated her so—"

"He isn't, Aunt Mabel," Caroline said from the archway of her aunts' parlor. "He's a wonderful man. Good, kind, generous."

Ethel reached for another porcelain cup. "Tea, dear?"

"Not me," Caroline said with a grin, recalling the last time she'd sampled her great-grandfather's brew. Before she'd known it, she'd ended up married to Paul Trevor—and in his bed.

"If he wasn't a beast, dear, why did you leave him?"

Caroline took a seat on the thick brocade sofa and shrugged. "For the wrong reasons, I suppose."

"The wrong reasons?" Ethel echoed, and the two older women exchanged meaningful glances.

"Then, dear, perhaps you should go back."

Caroline dropped her gaze to her lap. "I can't."

"Can't?" Mabel repeated. "Whyever not?"

"There was another woman...."

"With him?" Ethel sounded shocked. "Why, that's indecent. He *is* a beast."

"He loved a woman named Diane a long time ago," Caroline corrected hurriedly. "He never actually told me about her, but when he gave me the ticket home, he said he didn't go after Diane and he wasn't coming after me."

Mabel put her hand on Caroline's in a comforting gesture. "Do you love him, dear?"

Caroline nodded again. "Very much."

"Then you must go to him."

Her two aunts made it sound so easy. Every day since she got home, Caroline had thought of Paul. He'd been right. Time had healed her, and she'd reconciled herself to the shock of losing her friends to the fever. She'd been distraught; the people who'd died were more than patients. They'd been friends—part of her Alaskan family. Each one had touched her in a special way.

"Go to him?" Caroline repeated. "No, I can't."

"*No?*" both sisters exclaimed.

"If he loved me enough, he'd come to me. I need that, although I don't expect anyone else to understand the reasons."

The doorbell chimed and Caroline stood. "That must be Larry. We're going to a movie."

"Have a good time, dear."

"Oh yes, dear, have a good time."

No sooner had the front door closed than Ethel glanced at her sister, her eyes twinkling with mischief. "Shall I get the stationery or will you?"

"Hi." Larry kissed Caroline lightly on the forehead. "At least you've got some color in your face tonight."

"Thank you," she said, and laughed. Leave it to Larry to remind her that she'd been pale and sickly for weeks. "And you're looking handsome, as usual." It frightened her now to think that they'd almost married. Larry would make some woman a wonderful husband, but Caroline wasn't that woman.

"Is there any movie you'd like to see?" he asked.

"You choose." Their tastes were so different that anything she suggested would only be grounds for a lively discussion.

"There's a new musical comedy at the Fifth Avenue. Some kind of Christmas story."

His choice surprised Caroline. He wasn't really interested in musicals, preferring action movies, the more violent the better.

"Is that okay?"

Caroline looked up at him and had to blink back

tears. She hadn't cried since she'd returned to Seattle. Tears were useless now. She was home and everything was supposed to be good. Only it wasn't, because Paul wasn't there to share it with her. They might have begun their marriage at a disadvantage but she'd grown to love him. And she loved his small Alaskan town, more than she would ever have believed. She'd been a fool to leave him and even more of one not to acknowledge her mistake and go back.

"I've said something to upset you?" Larry asked anxiously. "I'm sorry." His kindness only made her weep louder.

"Caroline?"

"Paul liked musicals," she explained, sniffling. "He can't sing, but that didn't stop him from belting out songs at top volume."

"You really liked this guy, didn't you?"

"He was the only man I ever met who could beat me at Scrabble."

"He beat you at Scrabble?" Even Larry sounded impressed. "As far as I can see, you two were meant for each other. Now, when are you going to admit it?"

"Never," she said and an incredible sadness came over her.

Ethel Myers sat in front of the ancient typewriter—no computers for them!—and glanced at her sibling. "Pour me another cup of tea, will you, Sister?"

"Certainly, Sister."

They looked at each other and giggled like schoolgirls.

"Caroline must never know."

"Oh, no. Caroline would definitely not approve."

"Read the letter again, Sister."

Ethel picked up the single sheet of paper and sighed. "My darling Paul," she said in a breathless whisper, as though she were an actress practicing her lines. "I feel you should know that I find myself with child. Your loving wife, Caroline."

"Excellent. Excellent."

"We'll put it in the mail first thing tomorrow."

"More tea, Sister?"

Ethel giggled and held out her cup. "Indeed."

A few days later, Caroline lay on her bed and finally admitted there was no hope. Paul wasn't coming for her. He'd told her he wouldn't, so it shouldn't be any great shock, but despite that, she'd hoped he would. If he loved her, he would have forsaken his pride and come to Seattle. So much for dreams.

She turned onto her side. Surely he realized she was waiting for him. She needed proof of his love—proof that she was more important to him than Diane had ever been. More important than his pride. She was his wife, his love. He'd told her so countless times.

Caroline sighed and closed her eyes. She missed baby Carl and Tanana and their long talks. She missed the women of the village, missed knitting the "authentic" sweaters for tourists. She missed the dusk at noon and the nonstop snow and even the unrelenting cold.

Most of all she missed Paul. He might have been

able to live without her, but she was wilting away for lack of him.

With the realization that Paul's pride would keep him in Alaska came an unpleasant insight; it was up to her to swallow her own pride and go to him.

Within twenty minutes, her luggage was packed. She'd waited long enough; another day was intolerable. She'd go to him. She hated the thought of not being here to share Christmas with her aunts, but her love for Paul was too strong to give her peace.

"Are you going someplace, dear?" Aunt Mabel asked as Caroline descended the stairs, a suitcase in each hand.

"Alaska."

"Alaska?" Mabel cried, as though Caroline had said outer space.

Immediately Ethel appeared and Mabel cast a stricken gaze toward her sister. "Caroline says she's going to Alaska!"

"But she can't!"

"I can't?" Perplexed, Caroline glanced from one addled face to the other. Only last week they'd suggested she return.

"Oh, dear, this is a problem."

Ethel looked uncomfortable. "Perhaps we should tell her, Sister."

"Perhaps we should."

Caroline knew her lovable and eccentric aunts well enough to figure out that they'd been plotting again. "I think you'd better start at the beginning," she said in a resigned voice.

Ten minutes later, after hearing all the details, Caroline accepted a cup of the special tea. She needed it. "Paul will come," she murmured. If he believed she was pregnant he'd certainly show up.

"He'll come here and then you'll be happy. Isn't that right, dear?"

Her aunts gave her a look of such innocence, she couldn't disillusion them. "Right," Caroline said weakly.

"You were going back to him," Ethel pointed out.

"Yes." But this was different. At least if she returned to Gold River, Paul would have his pride intact. But now, he'd realize he'd been tricked again.

"You're not unhappy, are you, dear?" Mabel asked softly.

"I'm happy," she replied. "Very happy."

Nodding with satisfaction, her aunts brought the teapot back to the kitchen while Caroline remained in the room off the entry that her aunts insisted on calling the parlor. The doorbell gave a musical chime and, still bemused from the tea and her aunts' schemes, Caroline rose to answer it.

The man who stood outside was tall and well-built. Attractive. Caroline glanced up at him expectantly and blinked, finding him vaguely familiar.

"Caroline, I know…"

"Paul?" She widened her eyes and felt her mouth drop open. It was Paul, but without a beard. Good grief, he was handsome! Instinctively, she lifted her hand to his clean-shaven face and ran the tips of her fingers over the lean, square jaw.

"May I come in?"

For a moment, Caroline was too shocked to react. "Oh, of course. I'm sorry." Hurriedly, she stepped aside so he could enter the Victorian house, then led him into the parlor with its beautifully decorated Christmas tree. "Please sit down."

He wore gray slacks, the Irish cable knit sweater she'd made for him and a thin jacket. Everyone else in Seattle was wearing wool coats and mufflers and claiming it was the coldest winter in fifty years.

"How are you, Caroline?"

She was starving for the sight of him and couldn't take her eyes off his smooth jaw. "Fine," she said absently. Then she remembered what her aunts had told him and frowned. She'd have to tell him the truth, which would no doubt disappoint him. "How are you?" she asked, stalling for time.

"Fine."

Having forgotten her manners once, Caroline quickly tried to reverse her earlier lack of welcome. "Would you like some tea?"

"Coffee, if you have it." He paused to look at the portraits of her aunts on the mantel and added, "Just plain coffee."

"But you drank your coffee with cream before."

"I meant with cream. It's the other, uh, additions I'm hoping to avoid."

Her bewilderment must have shown in her eyes. "I don't want any of your aunts' brew."

"Oh, of course."

Caroline rushed into the kitchen and brought back a cup of coffee for Paul and a glass of milk for herself. Her aunts joined her and when the three of them entered the room, Paul stood.

"You must be Ethel and Mabel," he said politely.

They nodded in unison.

"He's even more handsome in person, don't you think, Sister?" Mabel trilled.

"Oh, very definitely."

"Caroline," Paul murmured when the two older women showed no signs of leaving the parlor. "Could we go someplace and talk?"

"Oh, do go, dear," Ethel encouraged with a broad grin.

"Someplace *private*," Mabel whispered, and the way she said it suggested a hotel room. Even Caroline blushed.

Paul escorted her to the car, a rental, and opened the passenger door for her. She couldn't stop staring at him. He looked so different—compelling, forthright, determined.

Once she was seated, he ran his hand over the side of his face. "I feel naked without it."

"Why...why did you shave?"

He gave her an odd look. "For you."

"Me?"

"You once said you refused to stay married to a man whose face you couldn't see."

Caroline remembered his response, too. He'd told her to get used to his beard because it was nature's protection from the Alaskan winter. He'd adamantly refused to shave then, but he'd done it now because this pretend pregnancy was so important to him. She should be the happiest woman alive, but unexpectedly Caroline felt like crying.

"I said a number of things," she told him, her gaze lowered to her clenched hands in her lap. "Not all of them were true." She dreaded telling him there wasn't any baby. False pretenses and disappointment—this was no way to negotiate a reconciliation. "How's Tanana?" she asked, changing the topic.

"Much better. She misses you and so do the others. Carl's growing every day."

"I…miss them too."

"Do…did you miss me?" he asked starkly.

He sounded so unsure of himself, so confused, that finding the words to tell him what was on her mind was impossible. Instead she nodded vigorously.

"I know I've made some mistakes…. I know I haven't got any business asking you to reconsider the divorce, but I love you, Caroline, and I'll do whatever you want to make things right between us."

"I know," she said miserably.

"If you know that, then why are you acting like my being here is all wrong? It's that Larry guy, isn't it? You've started seeing him again, haven't you?"

"Yes…no. We went to one movie and I cried through the whole thing because I was so miserable without you. Finally Larry told me I should go back to you where I belong."

"He told you that?"

She nodded again.

"Is Alaska the problem, love? Would you rather we lived somewhere else?"

"No," she said quickly. "I love Alaska. It was the fever and the exhaustion and everything else that scared me off. You were right—a week after I got here, I knew Seattle would never be my home again. My home is with you."

"Oh, love, I've been going crazy without you. Nothing's good anymore unless you're there to share it with me." Although it was awkward in the front seat of the car, Paul gathered her in his arms and kissed her with the hunger of long absence. His mouth moved over hers slowly, sensuously, as though he couldn't believe she was in his arms and he was half afraid she'd disappear.

Caroline wrapped her arms around his neck and kissed him back with all the passion of the lonely weeks. Tears dampened her face and she buried her nose in his throat, heaving a sigh. "There's something you should know."

"What's that, love?"

"I…I didn't write the letter."

He went still. "What letter?"

"The one that told you I was pregnant."

Caroline could feel the air crack with electricity. The calm before the storm; the peace before the fury; the stillness before the outrage. She squeezed her eyes shut, waiting.

"You're not pregnant?"

"I swear I didn't know my aunts had written to you. I can only apologize. If you want, I—"

"Love." His index finger under her chin raised her eyes to his. "I didn't receive any letter."

"You... What? No letter?"

"None."

"You mean... Oh, Paul, Paul." She spread kisses over his face. She kissed his eyes, his nose, his forehead, his chin and his mouth.... Again and again, until they were both winded and exhilarated.

"I didn't ever think I'd be thanking the postal service for their bi-weekly delivery," Paul said and chuckled.

"You love me more than Diane." She said it with wonder, as though even now she wasn't sure it could possibly be true.

"Of course. You're my wife."

"But..."

"Diane was a long time ago."

"But you saved things to remember her by."

"Only her letter. She decided she wasn't the type to live in the wilds of Alaska. She said if I loved her, I'd be willing to give up this craziness and come to her."

"But why keep the letter?"

"To remind me that it takes a special kind of person to appreciate the challenge of Alaska. It's not right for every woman, but it's right for you, Caroline."

"Because *you're* right for me." Her face shone with her love. She was so happy. So very happy...

"I can't promise you there won't be fevers or accidents or that things won't go wrong, but I vow I'll never leave you to face them alone and I'll never doubt you again."

"I promise you the same thing." She felt like singing and dancing and loving this man for the rest of her days. She placed her head on his shoulder and sighed. "Can we go home soon? I miss Gold River. I want to spend Christmas there! With you."

"Yes, love. When would you like to go?"

"Is today too soon? Oh, Paul, I had the most marvelous idea about getting some additional medical training so we could open a permanent clinic."

He chuckled. "I sent for a mail-order bride, not a doctor."

"But I could've done so much more when the fever broke out if I'd had the proper supplies."

Paul's hand slipped under her sweater to caress her skin. "I have a feeling you're going to be too preoccupied for a while to be doing much studying."

"But it's a good idea, isn't it?"

"Yes, love. It is."

"Oh, Paul, thank you for loving me, thank you for coming for me and thank you for playing Scrabble with me."

"No, love," he said seriously. "Thank *you*."

With a happy, excited laugh, she hungrily brought her mouth to his.

"Merry Christmas, Caroline," he whispered a long moment later.

"Merry Christmas, Paul. This is the best Christmas gift I ever got."

"Me, too, love. Me, too."

* * * * *

*If you loved THE MANNING SISTERS and
THE MANNING BRIDES, you'll adore
THE MANNING GROOMS!*

Jason, the fifth Manning, always thought marriage
wasn't for him—but then he falls for Charlotte Weston,
his "Bride on the Loose."

And James Wilkens was *almost* a Manning groom, until
he was jilted by Jason's sister, Christy. But on New
Year's Eve in Las Vegas, he meets Summer
Lawton…and when he arranges to see her again "Same
Time, Next Year," he discovers that marriage is in the
cards.

*Enjoy the latest in the Manning family series with this
two-in-one book. Catch up with the characters you've
already met and find out what happens to Jason and
James!*

*THE MANNING GROOMS is available in
December 2008, wherever books are sold.*

#1 *New York Times* Bestselling Author

DEBBIE MACOMBER

Dear Reader,

I have something to confide in you. I think my husband, Dave, might be having an affair. I found an earring in his pocket, and it's not mine.

You see, he's a pastor. And a good man. I can't believe he's guilty of anything, but why won't he tell me where he's been when he comes home so late?

Reader, I'd love to hear what you think. So come on in and join me for a cup of tea.

Emily Flemming

8 Sandpiper Way

"Those who enjoy good-spirited, gossipy writing will be hooked."
—*Publishers Weekly* on *6 Rainier Drive*

On sale August 26, 2008!

MDM2578

A COMPELLING STORY BY

ROBYN CARR

Last Christmas, Marcie Sullivan said a final goodbye
to her husband, Bobby. This Christmas she's come to
Virgin River to find the man who saved his life.

Fellow marine Ian Buchanan dragged Bobby's shattered
body onto a medical transport in Fallujah four years ago—
and then disappeared. Marcie tracks Ian to the tiny mountain
town of Virgin River and finds a man wounded emotionally.
Yet Marcie manages to discover a sweet but damaged soul
beneath his rough exterior.

Ian doesn't know what to make of the young widow. But it is,
after all, a season of miracles and maybe, just maybe, it's time to
banish the ghosts and open his heart.

A VIRGIN RIVER
CHRISTMAS

"The Virgin River books are so compelling—
I connected instantly with the characters."
—#1 *New York Times* Bestselling Author Debbie Macomber

REQUEST YOUR
FREE BOOKS!

2 FREE NOVELS
FROM THE ROMANCE/SUSPENSE
COLLECTION PLUS 2 FREE GIFTS!

YES! Please send me 2 FREE novels from the Romance/Suspense Collection and my 2 FREE gifts (gifts are worth about $10). After receiving them, if I don't wish to receive any more books, I can return the shipping statement marked "cancel." If I don't cancel, I will receive 4 brand-new novels every month and be billed just $5.49 per book in the U.S. or $5.99 per book in Canada, plus 25¢ shipping and handling per book plus applicable taxes, if any*. That's a savings of at least 20% off the cover price! I understand that accepting the 2 free books and gifts places me under no obligation to buy anything. I can always return a shipment and cancel at any time. Even if I never buy another book from the Reader Service, the two free books and gifts are mine to keep forever.

185 MDN EF5Y 385 MDN EF6C

Name _____ (PLEASE PRINT)

Address _____ Apt. #

City _____ State/Prov. _____ Zip/Postal Code

Signature (if under 18, a parent or guardian must sign)

Mail to **The Reader Service:**
IN U.S.A.: P.O. Box 1867, Buffalo, NY 14240-1867
IN CANADA: P.O. Box 609, Fort Erie, Ontario L2A 5X3

Not valid to current subscribers to the Romance Collection,
the Suspense Collection or the Romance/Suspense Collection.

**Want to try two free books from another line?
Call 1-800-873-8635 or visit www.morefreebooks.com.**

* Terms and prices subject to change without notice. N.Y. residents add applicable sales tax. Canadian residents will be charged applicable provincial taxes and GST. Offer not valid in Quebec. This offer is limited to one order per household. All orders subject to approval. Credit or debit balances in a customer's account(s) may be offset by any other outstanding balance owed by or to the customer. Please allow 4 to 6 weeks for delivery. Offer available while quantities last.

Your Privacy: Harlequin is committed to protecting your privacy. Our Privacy Policy is available online at www.eHarlequin.com or upon request from the Reader Service. From time to time we make our lists of customers available to reputable third parties who may have a product or service of interest to you. If you would prefer we not share your name and address, please check here. ☐

BOB08R